T0366094

ENTANGLED

George Parrent

Order this book online at **www.trafford.com**
or email orders@trafford.com

Most Trafford titles are also available at major online book retailers.

Printed in the United States of America.

ISBN: 978-1-4669-0526-9 (sc)
ISBN: 978-1-4669-0528-3 (hc)
ISBN: 978-1-4669-0527-6 (e)

Library of Congress Control Number: 2011961632

Trafford rev. 12/22/2011

 www.trafford.com

North America & International
toll-free: 1 888 232 4444 (USA & Canada)
phone: 250 383 6864 ♦ fax: 812 355 4082

AUTHOR'S NOTE

"Entangled" is fiction. The characters and events that comprise this story are all completely fictional and in no way related to any real persons, past or present. "Entangled" presents an extrapolation of some contemporary sociological, scientific, political and moral trends to a plausible and possible outcome, the 'Outrage', a direct threat to the President of the United States, and. Indeed, a threat to the entire world as we know it. While a work of fiction, "Entangled" does have some roots in reality. For instance, the allegorical butterfly effect was used by a prominent MIT meteorologist to illustrate chaos theory as applied to meteorology. There was indeed a mysterious Russian outbreak of anthrax that was never satisfactorily explained. Furthermore, micro-biologists have indeed been working with "the molecules of life," RNA and DNA, but nothing like the developments presented in "Entangled" exist, or has been openly discussed in the scientific literature.

This tale is narrated by a Chronicler writing as though at the request of the President of the United States. The story is presented as a series of scenes, vignettes of seemingly independent events or actions, by persons unknown to each other, often widely separated in both space and time. Furthermore, the vignettes are presented in the order in which a historian might have discovered them in preparing his report, rather than in the chronological order in which they actually occurred. A sampling of the events ultimately related to the Outrage includes the following events: a Killer Bee attack at a 4H fair; an epidemic of dying babies, the emergence of the sleeping cow disease, a small boy chasing chickens and killing ants, a new generation of computers, a CIA agent's study, an out of state abortion, a very unusual young man, a 'hit and run' raid in a South American War, a seemingly pointless vandalism of a glass factory and a college professor's marginal comment on a student's term paper. The reader who is familiar with chaos theory or meteorology may recognize the fluttering of Butterfly Wings in these vignettes.

As the story unfolds, various government agencies and facilities, replete with acronyms, emerge. Like the characters themselves these agencies and the related acronyms are purely fictional with a few well known exceptions, e.g., NASA and the CIA, which are included here simply as part of the environment of the times. The CIA Special Agent and his studies are purely imaginary. It is true that some of the items mentioned in his report were in fact gleaned from reports in the press but in a totally unrelated context: they are included in this story simply as a exemplar of the global political environment at the time of our story. Since our tale stresses the interactions and the entanglements of apparently unrelated persons and actions, rather than following the exploits of a few people, it involves a relatively large cast of characters some of whom enter the story in several different vignettes while others appear only once. The enjoyment of the story does not require that you follow each character; if fact in the broadest sense it is more thought provoking to simply let the characters and the details of the event flow through.

INTRODUCTION

The Chronicler's Note

Since I was in no way associated with the event that President Prescott Winters refers to as The Outrage, I feel it is necessary to explain how I came to be its Narrator or, as I prefer, Chronicler. At the time it occurred, the actual crisis and events associated with it, were of course widely reported and discussed at length and in some depth; furthermore, many of the background events, indeed in some cases the enabling events, which preceded The Outrage were previously reported as isolated events at the times of their occurrence; but they have never before been explicitly related to The Outrage itself. Rather, many of the characters and incidents were interesting in their own right, and since in most cases their relationships to The Outrage were obscured by space and time, it was the events themselves that were examined and reported. In many cases the truly pertinent events preceded The Outrage by years and were geographically separated by thousands of miles; hence, their possible connection to The Outrage could not have been foreseen or reported at the time they occurred.

It was certainly not the President's wish, nor is it my intention to expand the coverage of those events or to provide further in depth analyses of them. In fact, since I was largely out of the country for most of the twenty years preceding The Outrage, it may seem unusual that I am writing about the crisis at all. Indeed, were it not for an incidental meeting of two mid-western college sophomores some thirty years ago, I would not be involved in telling of this story in any capacity. Those two students, Preston Winters and I, were to become, respectively President of the United States and an obscure mathematician. However, we did in fact meet and share a coffee break and a table in a crowded and noisy student union. From that chance meeting a lasting friendship emerged. Despite our choosing diametrically opposed professional careers, his of course in politics and mine in esoteric mathematical research, we maintained both contact and friendship. None-the-less, I was surprised to receive his call a few weeks after The Outrage had finally receded to the back pages of most newspapers and magazines and was only rarely merited mention by the television news media.

After the expected "catch up" conversation, Prescott moved directly to his purpose for inviting me to the White House. "Burl, the shocking events of the recent past were of course widely studied and reported. A seemingly endless number of "experts" have pontificated on the political, psychological, social and religious significance of the actions and the perpetrators thereof. Surely, even you were able to drag yourself away from your equations long enough to at least skim the coverage of the events. In any case, it seems to me that the truly amazing thing is not the event itself, as Outrageous as it was, nor the individuals involved in planning and executing it, but, rather, the tenuous or apparently non-extence interrelationships between the people involved and the random occurrence of seemingly totally independent events; rather the interesting question is what brought them all together. How did they merge into a single coherent stream of events that exploded into "The Outrage"? It appeared to me that the entire process leading to The Outrage was a collection of completely unrelated events." Here he paused as though waiting for me to catch up, i.e. make the same logical quantum jump that he had made. When I failed to do so, he continued.

"No sooner had I had that thought than a phrase you once used, but that I have never truly understood, flashed through my mind. Remember, we were sharing a pitcher of beer and you had just begun studying 'a terrific new branch of mathematics, chaos theory'. As I remember, we met for lunch in Chicago where you were speaking at some obscure mathematics conference. You told me you had just presented a paper on 'chaos theory.' I nodded sagely; but of course you were not fooled; you knew full well that I had no idea what the hell that meant; but you were kind enough to an old friend not to pontificate about it. I remember your attempting to explain the key concepts by mentioning something you called the 'butterfly effect.' Of course I did not follow a word of what you said; in those days I rarely did; but the overall idea seemed to be that a series of apparently unrelated events were often woven together to produce unexpected results. Now, I feel that I have an inkling of what the term might mean and I have a favor to ask of you. Do you have the time and interest to chronicle the events surrounding and leading to this Outrage? I do not need or wish to have a deep analysis of the events themselves; but, rather, I would like to see if any sensible connection between the events and persons can be found." Refusing Preston was never a strong point of mine and consequently, my reluctance to undertake such a project was quickly overcome by the President's charisma and persuasiveness.

Before beginning the tale, I should remind you that I am a mathematician, not a reporter. I will use factual references when and where I can; however, many of the events involved in this tale were not witnessed by participants in the Outrage; nor were they reported upon in any depth at the time they occurred. Thus, some of the descriptions, comments, thoughts and actions reported here are simply the results of deduction based upon the actions which had been reported by others.

Indeed, as with many story tellers, there are times when I report that which I presume to have been in some character's mind, e.g. his or her intentions, motivations or feelings at some particular point in the narrative. Since it is obvious that I could not actually know people's inner thoughts, I will not explicitly draw attention to the fact that such insights are in fact simply inferences entered as though by an omniscient author. However, there are other cases in which, I, acting as the Chronicler, wish to provide some "after the fact insight" into the significance of some particular comment or activity as it relates specifically to the Outrage. When from time to time I exercise this particular author's prerogative, I will emphasize that they are my personal opinions by writing them in italics.

While this project was initiated by the President, I am the author of the study and any errors that creep into the tale should be laid clearly at my doorstep, not the President's. One other difference before we get started, the President refers to the culminating event of this tale as The Outrage. But the story as he requested it is not really about The Outrage itself, but rather about the intermingling of the characters and circumstances from which it grew. I have, therefore, as my first exercise of the prerogative of authorship; I named this Chronicle "Entangled." I have selected that title because I feel that the importance of the work if indeed there is any lies in the interweaving of unrelated or at best remotely and tangentially related events and persons.

Entangled deals with important scientific achievements and tells the story of a devious and complex series of crimes. However, it is neither a science fiction nor a mystery tale. Nor is it a story about a particular person, hero or villain. It is a story about unrelated minutiae that combine in unexpected ways. **Entangled** illustrates Chaos Theory in societal terms. The individual elements of the story, including the characters, are to be viewed and considered not as important individual events or characters, but rather as autonomous and seemingly unrelated parts of the whole, The Outrage. As usual, President Winters was intuitively correct. **Entangled** is a perfect example of chaos theory in society.

Since having at least a cursory notion of the 'Butterfly Effect" in the back of one's mind is a significant help in understanding how the various elements of the story are Entangled to produce The Outrage I will digress briefly to provide at least a peek at the Effect. If you choose to skip over this paragraph on Chaos Theory and the Butterfly effect, you will still be able to follow the story; you will simply miss some of the nuance. If you do wish to skip this background you may go directly to the first scene, or vignette, '**A Motorcycle Strikes A *Pedestrian*'** in the following page.

The earliest known use of the term 'Butterfly Effect' is widely attributed to Edward Lorenz, a renowned MIT meteorologist of the 1960s, who used it to illustrate the concept that very small changes in initial conditions may yield large variations in long term behavior. The concept was metaphorically illustrated by the suggestion that when a butterfly flapped its wings in Brazil the course of a Texas tornado was altered. The idea is not that the butterfly wing provided the energy for the tornado but, rather, that it was one of many, innumerable, global events occurring at the time which when taken all together resulted in the tornado. That is, the idea is not that there is a direct causal relationship between the butterfly and the storm but rather that the butterfly wing was one of a multitude of factors which taken together resulted in the storm. The term was picked up and popularized by fiction writers in the nineteen seventies and eighties. However, those works tended to dwell on the impact of the "butterfly wing," more or less ignoring the myriad of other initial conditions without which the butter fly would have been totally ineffective. While the term "Butterfly Effect" never appears in **Entangled**, the story is precisely about a collection of such effects. For example the allegorical butterflies contributing to The Outrage include a professor's notation on a term paper, which while contributing in its own small way to a key event in the final Outrage, that notation itself is not a direct cause but rather a minute part of the human environment in which the tale evolves and its various events and characters are Entangled. Numerous other factors contributed to the situation. They include a new generation of computers, a major breakthrough in understanding the chemistry of living things, a South American war and the establishment of the world's most secure research facility. Other contributing events that we will explore will appear equally disconnected to the roots of The Outrage. For instance social taboos of the time, a spider bite, a meaningless vandalism raid, a motorcycle accident, dying cows, politics, fear, mistrust, international intrigue, suspicion, secrecy all which are among the "butterflies" involved in the storm the President refers to as The Outrage. The roots of The Outrage include numerous other, seemingly incidental factors, a jilted co-ed, a female martial artist, an unusual child, a disillusioned student's binge, a barroom brawl and the untimely death of a crusader, all of these also played significant roles in the evolution of the tale.

My assignment from Prescott was to chronicle The Outrage concentrating on the way these fragile threads are enwined to produce the final event.

One last explanation is required. Most of these threads are revealed here by introducing an array of unrelated characters. As the lives of these disparate characters intertwine, are **Entangled,** the symbolic butterfly evolves into the enabling factor of a national crisis that forces the President of the US to make concessions to a blackmailer to avert a threat to the very peace and health of the entire earth. In researching this tale I did not discover all of the important elements in a well ordered chronological sequences nor will I present them in that way. I will present the information more or less in the order in which I learned it. I believe that such a presentation retains and reinforces the chaos concept while a chronological ordering of the presentation might erroneously suggest a stronger causal relationship between characters and events. This approach of reporting in the order discovered by me naturally involves numerous jumps from one vignette, a time or place, to another. I will, therefore, not attempt to break this chronicle into chapters. Rather, at each 'scene jump' I will indicate a new epusode by using bold face type to name the scene. Usually, an author's aside will accompany each such sudden scene shift.

To provide some semblance of order, the time spanned by the tale, roughly thirty years, will be broadly divided into three eras; The Rootlets Era in which the earliest events occur. The events in this era seemingly have no connection to each other. The Evolution Era in which the rootlets grow, multiply and begin to take on form. The characters and events in this era will begin to exhibit at least faint connections with each other. The Tangled Era in which all of the disparate factors merge to produce The Outrage.

ERA 1

Rootlets

The events and characters of this Era include some of the earliest and most tenuously connected but none the less important elements of The Outrage. Because they have, here to fore, not been related to The Outrage, there will more of my 'asides' in the elements of this Era than in the later two Eras.

I begin this tale not with the earliest event involved in The Outrage but rather with an event, the attack of the Killer Bees, that illustrates the roots of the concerns of the general population aroused by the technologies to be discussed in this chronicle. Incidental to the attack is its observation by a town drunk in a small Texas town. He can in no way be considered responsible for The Outrage, but his name appears in connection with two of the very important events of the tale. Such loose connections that may or may not be related are characteristic of chaotic events.

At the time of this episode, the technologies associated with bio-engineering applications had already produced some startling and significant results as well as serious concerns and fears. I will introduce and discuss but a few of those developments as the story unfolds. The effects of this particular event were discussed at length by the major news media, but were never before explicitly related to The Outrage.

A particularly violent and virulent mutation of the famous Killer Bee had evolved naturally somewhere in South America; and for years its ponderous migration north had been tracked. Even though its arrival in the US was widely anticipated, the seemly random meandering of the marauding insects made prediction of its actual arrival date difficult; and the majority opinion was that their arrival would be at least several years in the future.

The Killer Bee Arrives

"Jesus H Christ!" Pete Mallick stared in slack-jawed disbelief at the larger-than-life television screen above the bar. "What the hell're they sellin'? Must be one of them special effects I heard about, tricks with cameras and computers and such. Nah! All them people are running like crazy. They look real. Dam, they are real; they really are!" His hand dropped to the bar, spilling drops of the amber liquid from his tightly gripped shot glass.

Only moments ago, Pete's world had seemed a perfect place . . . .

Smelling of yesterday's Madeira combined with several weeks of sweat and grime. Pete had shuffled into Friendly Joe's Horseshoe Bar, one of the few local bars in South Texas that would tolerate him. As a panhandler and part of the town scenery for as long as anyone could recall; Pete rarely had had the cash to go there. Instead, sucking up sweet fortified wine from a bottle poorly concealed in a crumpled brown paper bag had become his style. But today, he was flush! A passing motorcyclist had brushed a pedestrian, rolling him roughly over the curb onto the cracked sidewalk and dislodging his wallet. While the other bystanders were concerned with the injured pedestrian, Pete had grabbed the wallet that had been jarred loose and landed just in front of him. It held three hundred dollars, a fortune to Pete who had never seen that amount of money before.

To Pete, the multicolored credit cards represented opportunities that were simply too significant to be soberly contemplated; that's why he had hastened to Friendly Joe's. After ordering a shot of scotch, he had seated himself squarely in front of the large television screen to drink in a rare visual treat to accompany his libation. For someone like Pete living on the streets, a large screen television was a special treat since he rarely saw any television at all, except perhaps through the windows of a furniture store; it fascinated him. He was entranced by the display of flashing colors as he watched the newsman explore the cheerful, noisy crowds at the annual 4-H Club Fair being held in the next county. But, the festive scene was suddenly shattered by a piercing scream of agony and fear. A young blond girl burst into the picture at top speed with a bright blue show ribbon was bouncing above her breast and her yellow skirt was flying. A swirling brownish cloud shaped like a miniature tornado followed her. As she fell screaming to the ground, her tormented cries were drowned out by the deafening buzz of hundreds of thousands of tiny wings. The frightened crowd panicked and fled in all directions; separate whirling brown clouds pursuing each of them. Although the camera tumbled from the photographer's shoulder to the ground, it still filmed the whirling brown clouds. This film was all the proof that the Killer Bee had arrived in South Texas.

Though he was only a television observer, the effect on Pete was immense; he vowed to stay sober and get out of Texas and thanks to the motorcyclist, he had the money with which to do so. The next day he began the long hitch hiking trip to Chicago in search of a job. He was not highly qualified but managed to find work as a night watchman. While the memory of that scene never left him, he never suspected that it or the singularly strange events he experienced as a night watchman many years later were in any way related to The Outrage. In the later event he was only slightly more involved than he had been in this episode. In his later experience he was not only a very close observer but also the only reporter of the scene that had developed on his watch.

The Killer Bee Is Defeated

Fortunately, the invasion of the Killer Bee had not been unexpected. For years their unrestrained progress had been tracked northward from Central America through Mexico toward the Texas border. Throughout the South West, chemists, biologists, environmentalists, and all relevant government agencies had been preparing to defend our country against the marauding insects. But it was only after the state fair catastrophe, that all stops were pulled out producing a fully coordinated attack on the invading insects. Regardless of their state of development and testing, all available weapons were simultaneously thrown at the buzzing hordes.

The next day, the morning papers and talk shows reported that thirty five exhibitors and visitors had died in the unprecedented attack of the Killer Bee. Hundreds more had been hospitalized in the worst insect attack in living memory and the only one ever recorded by color television!

In a few short months they had been defeated by a newly maturing technology, bio-engineering, which had produced a microbe labeled MB-Twelve. Three months after MB-Twelve was introduced to the Texas ecosystem, the Killer Bee was history and a collective sigh could be heard across the entire country. There was widespread relief and various government agencies and other organizations clamored to claim credit for the defeat of the 'Bee.'

However, it would be some time before the complete consequences of MB-Twelve were understood. Two important elements of the looming Outrage had just appeared and their significance of course went unnoticed.

A New Computer is Born

The development of MB-Twelve had evolved from two separate but parallel paths, a gigantic advance in the speed and capacity of computers and a ground breaking new bio chemical theory. Some years before and half a continent away those two technological advances began to coalesce when a professor had looked up from reading a technical paper and forecast the possible effects of a new computer design concept. However, his remarks went largely unnoticed.

"Wow!!! John this is the stuff Nobel prizes are made of! If your figures are correct, that damned process of yours is a breakthrough!" Buzz Cochran, exclaimed as he tugged at his already loosened tie. "Why, at these rates and with this level of miniaturization, you could achieve two orders of magnitude. No even more! Over three, perhaps four, orders of magnitude higher computation rates than with any other system in the world. Do you realize that if you're correct you have just revolutionized whole areas of scientific endeavor? Tremendous! And look at the size! With this level of miniaturization you have developed the basis for the robot brain dreamed of by science fiction writers the world over!"

Buzz, Professor Benton Cochran, was a mathematician internationally known for the wide range of scientific fields to which his insight had been successfully applied. In addition to holding an appointment as a full professor at nearby Randolph University, Buzz consulted for the nation's largest computer company. While he spent little time there, his retainer was rumored to be the largest ever paid to a university scientist. Normally a calm individual who maintained his relaxed attitude by regular exercise, weight lifting, and the conscientious practice of transcendental meditation, he was now excitedly pacing back and forth before the long white board covered with logic diagrams, Greek symbols and scribbled calculations of operational rates.

Removing his rumpled tweed jacket and tossing it carelessly over a nearby chair, Buzz scribbled more numbers on the already crowded board. To make space to complete his latest calculation, he grabbed a cloth and removed a large segment of the schematic he had drawn only moments before. After a few more hasty scribbles, essentially unintelligible to anyone but himself, he dropped the marker onto a nearby table and turned back to his companion.

"Yes! You've done it. You could pack the computing power of the largest existing computers into a space the size of a man's head! Damn, John! Do you realize the significance of these findings of yours? Of course you do. How soon can you build prototype? Where do I fit into the program? Smack in the middle, I hope. I can get a sabbatical; I haven't had one in years. Classes have just ended. I can start in the morning. Well?"

"Whoa, hold on Professor! Of course we want you 'smack in the middle'; I was counting on your being available. We're very excited about the development. Though I must say none of us at the Research Center are quite as optimistic as you are. There are still quite a few problems to overcome."

"Never mind the problems. You'll solve them. Look at the significance! There are countless opportunities in microbiology alone; it will be completely revolutionized. Did you know that a paper published by the world's most famous theoretical micro-biologist, Dr. Millard Morris, contains a mathematical model of chemical interactions so sophisticated that even the interactions of living molecules can be accurately predicted by simply evaluating some equations? However, the use of his model requires immense computing power, which of course he didn't have. So his work was mothballed the very day it was published. But now! John, you may have just made laboratory chemistry a thing of the past. Bio-engineering will become a computer application; good-bye to trial and error concocting witch's brews from which a useful organism might or might not emerge."

"I'll say this Professor, you surely do have vision; I've never known anyone else who could jump from one scientific field to another as quickly and easy as you do. But I still say it's too soon to tell where this will go. There's still an enormous amount of work to do."

"John will solve the hardware development; but I am starting the software development tomorrow," Buzz planned as he left the lab.

Somewhere In DC A Study Is Completed

At a different time and a different place another rootlet emerged. Not all of the bio-engineering applications were taking place in the United States. And some of the real or imagined foreign applications of the theory were to play a totally unintended but significant role in the unfolding events that enabled the development of The Outrage. Indeed, the world political scene was an essential element of the environment that enabled the development of that near catastrophic event. I present here a snap shot of how one such set of circumstances proved to be of fundamental importance in the development of The Outrage.

While thousands of tourists flocked through the streets of the nation's capital, defying the heat and humidity to scurry from one monument to other, Special Agent David Bradley contemplated his latest assignment. Briefly glancing out the window at the cloudless, smog-filled sky, he thought, "It'll be another scorcher", and turned his attention to the reports on his desk.

Though a top CIA research agent, David's surroundings were typical of 'government issue' civil service furnishings. He sat at a metal desk in his small and crowded office. Vinyl tiles filled the space between walls of simple battleship gray metal partitions that defined his space. Overhead, above the ceiling tiles an invisible infrared beam silently scanned the open space for signs of intrusions or listening devices. Dangling by its hasp above the open top drawer of a five-drawer file cabinet, a combination lock silently shouted, "Open Safe" the signal was reinforced by a heavy locking bar leaned against the wall beside the file. As if the dangling lock and missing locking bar could be overlooked, a bright red sign stuck into the handle of the protruding drawer proclaimed it to be "OPEN".

David's desk was cleared of anything not directly related to his current assignment. To his left lay the pile of folders he had already examined this morning. On his right was a legal-sized yellow pad. Its top page was covered with notes and doodles and, like every other page in the pad, its top and bottom margins bore the bright red label "SECRET WORKING PAPERS". Directly in front of him rested another legal-sized yellow pad similarly imprinted. The words 'Peters's Report' were neatly hand printed across the top of its first sheet.

"Who the hell is this Dr. Nathan Peters?" the special agent asked himself for the hundredth time. True, he had been cleared at the highest level and personally introduced to David by the Chief; but "Who the hell is he and where did he get such clout?"

David recalled their first meeting. "David, I'd like you to meet Dr. Nathan Peters," the Chief had begun as he introduced the young scientist. "He's a biochemist, and he's here as part of a special Presidential Study". Wincing with displeasure at the admission he was about to make, he continued, "We are, not cleared for his mission. However, we have been directed to cooperate fully with Dr. Peters in any way we can. Specifically, he requires some information on certain Soviet bloc research which he will detail for you."

Sitting there in the only extra chair in David's office, the intense young PhD had carefully and explicitly outlined his areas of interest. Despite his top-secret clearance and a CERTIFICICATE OF COMPELLING NEED To Know for all weapons systems, chemical, biological or otherwise, Special Agent David Bradley had not been told the purpose of the study. Other than carefully, almost pedantically, detailing his requirements, his visitor had said nothing, not even a comment on the torturously hot and humid weather of that particular afternoon. The uncommunicative Dr. Peters had been cleared by State Department Intelligence for UNLIMITED ACCESS, and David had been assigned to help him prepare a presentation for a White House briefing, period!

As an experienced and highly regarded agent, David resented being treated like gofer, a non-entity, and was pleased that the assignment was essentially finished. It had not been a difficult task. There was an extensive classified file on Soviet biological and chemical weapons, and David had prepared a synopsis of the areas of particular interest to the biochemist, Dr. Nathan Peters. As David slammed the file drawer shut with one hand, his other hand was emptied by Dr. Peters who snatched the report and left the office without comment.

Of course David could not have known it at the time, and perhaps he never would know it, but he had just supplied Dr. Peters with the tools vital to the development of one of the most highly classified facilities ever envisioned by man and an absolutely essential element for the emergence of The Outrage.

A Battle is Joined

Not all of the factors influencing the culmination of our story are science or computer related. Some principle elements depend entirely on individual personal traits and skills that while not remotely related to technical factors of The Outrage, do in fact prove crucial to several aspects of this chronicle. An example is to be found in this Rootlet Era challenge faced by a young woman.

Laurie Bass felt the tension mounting as she circled slowly, warily, her eyes fixed on an equally watchful figure crouching before her. She felt exposed and very much alone; she could feel her pulse quicken. She acknowledged a wisp of fear but her attention was completely focused on the dark-skinned man before her. His eyes seemed never to waver or blink. They were riveted on her. His breathing was heavy but carefully controlled. They'd been facing each other for seconds only, and already she could feel the sweat run under her arms and down the small of her back. Cautiously, she changed her direction and circled slowly to her left and paused occasionally, as though tensing her muscles to flee from the struggle she knew was imminent. She was well aware that she was too uptight to handle this situation. She tried to relax and let her body get into the flow. "Let your training and reflexes take over, girl, or you'll have no chance at all", she admonished herself. To relieve the tension, she stared across at him, focusing her attention on his pale hazel eyes, which gleamed with confidence and anticipation. He sensed success. "He's done this before, many times", she thought. "That's his main advantage; he knows exactly what to expect and he expects to handle me as easily as he did all the others".

She flinched at the thought of his "handling her" at all. "Come on, Laurie, it's just a figure of speech. Pay attention", she scolded herself, "If you want to get out of this without being disgraced. Yes, he has every reason to be sure of himself. But, wait". She had noticed something else, not evident in his eyes but in the way he moved. "His steps are too short, overly cautious", she thought. "He's wary too"! "He's got a lot at stake here," she suddenly realized. "Of course he has! I'm a twenty-year-old female, and all his macho pride is on the line. If I should emerge from this encounter un-humbled, he'll have a lot of explaining to do". That thought comforted her. It helped to know that he had something to lose also.

She could feel her tension easing, just a bit. Her arms were held slightly in front of her, raised and bent so that her hands, while open, were held like a boxer's. Her feet were spread just enough to keep her weight centered comfortably between them; her knees were slightly bent and she moved with a fluid, gliding grace, an almost flatfooted motion that maintained her balance continuously. With her breathing finally under control, she shook her long fingers lightly, a nervous reflex. "Testing the looseness of my muscles," she would probably have explained, had she been asked.

Crouched before her and similarly balanced, the dark-skinned man she knew as Chico mistakenly interpreted her shaking fingers as an insult, daring him to attack., Momentarily forgetting where he was or why, he yelled "Aie ah ya!" and leapt forward, his arms outstretched. That short lapse in concentration was all it took.

Just before his hands reached her lapels, there was another yell, "Kaa-taa!" As she expelled air from her lungs, she bent her knees, deepening her crouch. Spinning, she drove the ball of her foot into his midsection. Continuing the spin, she delivered a sharp karate chop to his back, which had been exposed as he bent over in pain. It's all over, she exulted silently. Chico lay beaten on the mat, and Laurie Bass had earned her coveted black belt.

Her striking good looks, as well as patience, quick reactions and the skills she had just displayed were all to prove crucial in the unfolding of the catastrophic effects of "The Outrage".

The Cows Are Dying.

In the period of time following the defeat of the Killer Bees another apparently unrelated event added to the angst of the nation's general mood of fear and distrust of the concepts of bio-engineering. Without this general feeling of dread the conditions leading to The Outrage could not have occurred. Of course I never witnessed the meeting described in this vignette but it and many similar ones took place after the defeat of the raging insects. Scenes like this were a in fact major factor in creating the environment for The Outrage.

Burt was the fourth Texas dairyman to visit Dr. Hanes this morning. He shifted uncomfortably from one foot to another like a nervous schoolboy, "I tell ya, I aint never seen nothin' like it Doc. Them damned cows won't eat a bite or drink a drop lessen ya cram it right under their damned faces. Them that used to feed on the north patch are gettin' so they won't eat even if you hand-feed 'em." The large-boned Texan had been watching his milk production fall off for several weeks. Last week he had watched two cows die of "just plain damned laziness." Now he had begun to fear for his entire herd.

Dr. Howard Hanes dropped heavily into the worn leather chair behind his desk. For several weeks he had watched in helpless frustration as prize herds all over the county withered, and worried dairymen edged closer to panic.

The story was always the same. The first symptom of the disease was a slow motion laziness. The herd became listless, unwilling to go out to pasture. The animals simply seemed to have no interest in moving. They would eat and drink normally if the food and water were sufficiently easy to obtain, but they showed no interest in seeking nourishment. Within a few weeks of the first symptoms, the effort of eating and drinking became too burdensome. The cattle eventually died of thirst or, more rarely, of starvation. Dr. Haynes thought Burt's herd was suffering from the same disease, whatever the hell it is.

Burt had not seen the number of cases that the veterinarian had; but it was obvious from his defeated expression that he had seen enough. Hanes had known Burt for years now and was well aware that he would want: "No bullshit or big words, Doc. Just tell me what to do." In this case Hanes had no idea what to do.

Trying unsuccessfully to hide his frustration, Dr. Hanes explained. "There's an epidemic wreaking havoc with the dairy herds around here. I'm sure you already know that. No one in all of American veterinary medicine has the slightest idea what's causing it. Every vet lab in the county's working on it, but I can't promise you a cure any time real soon."

"I knew you'd tell it straight, Doc, and I guess I knew in my gut that you'd say you got no cure. But for chrissake, what's a man to do? I can't just stand by and watch everything I ever owned or worked for in my whole life just 'be pissed away' by cows that are too goddamned lazy to eat."

"Burt, it's happening throughout the region. I know that's no consolation, but, strangely, it _is_ a source of some hope. This malady is totally unknown outside of Texas, and within Texas it's mostly limited to this area, within a hundred miles of this office. That degree of localization should help in isolating the cause. But for now, I can only treat the symptoms and maybe help you keep as much of the herd alive as possible while we wait for a cure to be discovered. There is a cure, dammit! Some of these cows simply get better by themselves. Meantime, add this stuff to their water and food the way it says on the label." He slid a prescription form across the desk. "It's a strong stimulant. Won't cure a thing, but it will keep them eating and drinking for a while longer, maybe until we find out what to do.

"Oh, and most importantly, don't sell the milk from cows taking that stimulant. A good portion of it passes through their system in the milk and could produce near fatal results in humans."

Depressed by what he had been told, Burt thanked the veterinarian, picked up the prescription, and dragged himself out of the office.

Sighing heavily, Hanes sank back into the familiar comfort of his desk chair and closed his eyes. "The good Lord does seem to be singling out this region of Texas for special curses lately. First those damned bees and now this terrible lazy-cow disease.

Dr. Hanes was well aware that the treatment he had prescribed was little more than a placebo, and was more for Burt's benefit than for his cows. The disease, Bovine Lassitude Syndrome, BLS, the medical journals were calling it, had been around barely long enough to be named, but its development was well documented. BLS was usually a fatal malady. The number of spontaneous recoveries could be counted on the fingers of one hand. And treating the symptoms with the medication he prescribed did very little to save the herds. He was not, however, aware of the fact that his very "placebo prescription" for the treatment of BLS was to become yet another factor in creating the environment of the tangled web that was to become The Outrage.

Babies Are Dying

The general feeling of distrust of the bio-technology was even more heavily influenced by yet another seemingly unrelated biological event which at first had seemed to be a spontaneous event. This catastrophic event was not only an important factor in its own right but it also had a direct and lasting influence on the personality of one of the players in the upcoming crisis.

Kim Newcombe, an attractive if slightly plump first-year intern recently assigned to the pediatric ward of South Texas City Hospital, paced anxiously back and forth in her cramped and cluttered office. Wringing her hands, she turned and kicked at the wall in frustration.

Dr. Newcombe was a neat and orderly person with a strong belief in the simple morality of her Midwestern upbringing. Her belief that hard work could accomplish essentially anything had never before failed her. But now! It seemed the harder she worked the worse the situation became. Not only did her hard work not save her small, twisted patients, but their numbers were growing. "Why? Why?" she asked aloud in the empty room. "What in the world is going on?" She kicked out again, as if to punish the wall for not helping her. Just then the door abruptly swung open, and Russell Rainer, the chief pediatrician, cautiously entered the small office.

"Hello. What's going on in here?" he asked, although he suspected that he knew the answer. His new intern was as competent as any he had ever seen. Technically, she was undoubtedly the best qualified. "But she does have a tendency to become too attached to the patients," he had explained to the Director just yesterday, when he turned in his monthly review of her performance. "On balance, I'm not sure she belongs in pediatrics. Too bad. She really is a compassionate and qualified young lady. However, it's early yet and I've been wrong before. I would sure like to see her talent devoted to this field."

"Are you okay, Kim?" he said.

"Yes," she answered; "but," she continued as she stripped off her surgical gloves and tossed them into the waste basket, "I feel so helpless."

Dr. Rainer looked up from the chart he had just completed before coming to comfort her. The effect the epidemic was having on Kim was clear from the most cursory glance around her office which was now in total disarray. He recalled the first day they had been introduced. "Incredibly fastidious," the director had described her. Strange the way we tend to label people with totally irrelevant labels, he thought to himself. What matters in her chosen profession is that she be competent and compassionate. She's all of that. Now that very compassion is tearing her apart.

"Easy Kim," he said. "Please try to relax if only as a favor to me. I know it is torture to stand by helplessly and watch as we just did. But someone has to watch if we're ever to find the cause and locate a cure. Someone has to provide what treatment there is to be had. I'm afraid we're going to be involved with more of these cases before we get to the bottom of this cursed epidemic."

"I don't want to sound like an overreacting student, but that's the eighth death in a week. One day they're healthy and the next they're turning blue, their little bodies twisted like pretzels. They writhe, for minutes, sometimes for a couple of hours, sometimes a day or more and then they die. All of that agony occurred without a sound. It's . . . I don't know, it's just terrible."

Throughout the city there had been forty-eight deaths from this contorting disease in the last two weeks. No one had come anywhere near an explanation, let alone a cure. The impact of the situation forced Kim to eventually abandon pediatrics for a career in medical research. That career change planted her firmly in the center of The Outrage. Like Laurie, her involvement was not related to technology but rather to her character as influenced by the events just reported.

A Politician Speaks

The unfolding events surrounding and resulting from the Killer Bee attack and its defeat of course attracted significant political attention as illustrated by the campaign of a talented Texan. Once the connection between the several events just reported became clear, politicians of all stripes sought to exploit the atmosphere of fear and near panic that spread across the continent. One of the politicians to most directly benefit from addressing those fears was Prescott Winters.

Prescott Winters, one of the youngest Texans ever to present himself as a candidate for the U.S. Senate, paced nervously around the confined backstage space. He was awaiting the applause that would signal the end of a long-winded introduction and call him to the podium. The central theme of his campaign was the strict need for control of the emerging new field of microbiological engineering. He was comfortable with this theme and very well informed on the topic.

At last, there was a loud applause and cheers. After a very brief greeting, Prescott moved directly to the speech he was confident would eventually carry him to Washington.

"Yes, it's true that the contributions of bio-engineering have been nearly miraculous; but at what price? We developed a microbe, MB-twelve, to destroy the Killer Bee, but it went berserk, destroying half the cattle in Texas and threatening to render the entire state uninhabitable. Weeks passed before the connection was made between MB-twelve, the lazy-cow disease, and the dying babies. More weeks passed and more cows slept themselves to death and more babies died in the horrible contortions resulting from effects of the severe stimulant in the in the milk were analyzed and a suitable means for eliminating the manmade microbiological terror was developed. We are told that the artificial microbe mutated when exposed to sunlight and high temperatures, so it acted upon chlorophyll to yield a compound, Bovine-t, which proved to be highly toxic to cattle. This toxin found its way into a cow's milk where an even more horrifying modification occurred: the Bovine-t molecule was converted to an extremely toxic lactose derivative that killed over four hundred babies!

"These modifications should have been discovered before the MB-twelve was released. The discovery should have been made in a laboratory, not in the pastures and nurseries of Texas!! The bees should have been eliminated from Texas in other safer ways, with no side effects and no deaths. This was a genuine disaster of epic proportions. Today, new products and new methods of producing old reliable ones, or the apparent equivalents of old reliable ones, are emerging at an increasing rate and the world is demanding the immediate use of these new wonder products. Where is it all going to lead? How many more of our children must die as a result of using untested micro-biological treatments that cure one problem only to create an even larger one? I say that the cribs of Texas will never again be used as substitutes for test tubes!"

As a pragmatic politician, Prescott Winters knew that the concept of Bio-engineering accidents would provide an emotional issue upon which to build a winning campaign. However, he also knew that the population craved the benefits of bio-engineering; no one wanted forego the miracles of bio-engineering

His campaign and that of his entire party was based not upon the elimination of bio-engineering but rather on better governmental control and testing of its products. The central plank of the party's platform was the creation of a National Agency for Micro-Biological Engineering, NAMBE. The plan had gained considerable popular support, and the acronym for the new agency was already a part of the American vocabulary. He was sincerely committed to the formation of NAMBE; and he was justifiably satisfied that his eloquence on this topic and his general charisma would carry him to DC as the next senator from Texas.

A Weapons Research Proposal

Some time later, but still within the Rootlet Era, the studies of David Bradley were put to the use for which they had originally been intended by the wily and talented Dr. Peters. Armed with those studies he single handedly convinced the President and a select of experts and advisors that the nation needed a secure, complex and secretive laboratory complex which came to be called the Facility.

His black bushy eyebrows bobbing as though they had a life of their own, a nervous young biochemist sat anxiously outside the Oval Office waiting to be called into the special Presidential Conference. The bobbing eyebrows and absentminded chewing of the top of his pen, broadcast his anxiety concerning the upcoming meeting. He had never before briefed the President of the United States. He was conscious of his nervousness and knew that he must get it under control before starting to speak.

In spite of himself his mind strayed to earlier times. It was a long way from Hollis, New Hampshire, to the Oval Office he reflected.

In 1960 Nathan Peters had been born on a modest farm in the picturesque village of Hollis, New Hampshire. Like his father, he was an intelligent fiercely independent, very conservative Republican; unlike his father, he was also extremely ambitious. The Hollis farm had supported the Peters family adequately but could not cover the cost of his education. Nathan had provided that himself.

He mused, "I must've had every kind of menial part-time job in America during my high school and early college years . . . and if I hadn't won that bio-engineering scholarship, who knows," he mused. "I was also damned lucky with the selection of my thesis topic . . . and the research fellowship. It didn't really pay much better than the part time jobs. But those esoteric seeming chromosome modeling studies were the foundation of everything I've done since—several papers, international symposia, and three patents."

Those three patents had made him independently wealthy and free to pursue his research. At first the freedom was exhilarating, but he had soon lost interest in working alone. "Too dry and too far from the applications," he had complained. However, he soon discovered that what he considered the ultimate field of research was excruciatingly expensive. Unfortunately, even his royalties were woefully inadequate to fund the program he envisioned. Only the government could afford it.

Given his reputation, he had no problem obtaining a position of influence in the government's technical hierarchy. His specialty was in great demand even though most of the programs were classified. He had easily found support for his views among his colleagues; but he also quickly learned that there was a long bureaucratic gauntlet to run before a significant new program could be launched.

"But, worse yet," he reasoned, "even if I could convince the powers that be to authorize my program, it would take a century to get it past the sign carrying protesters."

Wincing, he recalled his father's constant complaints about the knee jerk liberals just to the south of New Hampshire in MA. Those flag-carrying protesters and legal stalling tactics had delayed the opening of the much-needed Sea Brook Nuclear Power Plant by more than two decades. He recalled that they had successfully delayed and disrupted the construction of the plant, resulting in the bankruptcy of the power company building it. The facility was eventually opened, however, by the financially restructured company.

"The mobs would surely pack the streets on my project," he thought. He had nearly despaired of ever getting funded. But then, just a year ago, opportunity sprung from an unexpected source, the invasion of the Killer Bee.

After that, things moved incredibly fast. Justifying the original study was a snap; and the report written by that Agency spook, Bradley, had proven extremely useful. Even arranging this meeting through the proper channels had been simple though tedious and time-consuming. It is awe-inspiring sitting here waiting to be ushered into the Oval Office", he thought. It's tough enough to prepare for a meeting with the President—you get so damn little time; but I had to prepare for two meetings; and even the first one, the scheduled one, won't be easy. It's a tricky issue, not all black and white, especially in the present international climate. Furthermore, the small audience in the scheduled meeting will include both supporters and detractors. I must succeed in that briefing or there will be no second meeting; and that's the only one that counts."

His father's constant derision of the Clamshell Alliance had made a deep impression on Nathan Peters, and he was wary of even the members of this august panel. How could he be sure one of them was not a member of some protest group, or a silent supporter of one, or simply the Congressman for the area? He couldn't. Therefore, unlike the first briefing, the second had not been scheduled through channels. Indeed, it had not been scheduled at all. Not even the President was aware that there was to be a second meeting!

Although he had read them countless times, he turned once again to his papers and stared at the notes he had extracted from Special Agent David Bradley's report. Four points were key to his argument in the second meeting, if he could in fact have the second meeting.

1. **1972—International convention prohibiting the stockpiling significant quantities of bio-weapons**
2. **1979—Sverdlovsk, site of Soviet military facility engaged in biological warfare research, reports worst outbreak of anthrax in history.**
3. **1982—Yellow rain in Laos and Kampuchea, believed at first to be a biological warfare agent, turned out to be Bee feces, at least according to one U.S. investigator.**
4. **1988—Three leading Soviet scientists visit the U.S. for the sole purpose of "proving that the 1979 anthrax incident was the result of natural causes." They address meetings at the National Academy of Sciences and the Harvard Academy of Arts and Science.**

Nathan found this last item to be the most compelling because the meetings seemed totally out of character for the Soviets. True, there had been outbreaks of anthrax before. However, the 1979 episode was the worst ever by far: over a thousand people were hospitalized with suspicious symptoms, nearly eighty died from an intestinal form of the disease; while seventeen who had suffered from coetaneous anthrax all survived. In the United States, Soviet-watchers were convinced there had been an explosion at a biological warfare storage facility. In an effort to dispel such beliefs, visiting Russian scientists had brought evidence that the victims had died of intestinal anthrax contracted by eating infected meat. They insisted that the disease had not been spread by airborne spores. The rapid outbreak of the disease among humans in the area was attributed to their living and drinking habits rather than to an airborne release of bacteria. The scenarios provided by the Russian scientists were plausible enough, but a significant number of the better informed attendees had been unconvinced. A State Department intelligence representative, who would not elaborate on his source of information, had said of the presentation "it does not fit with the evidence and facts we have collected." The United States contended that the Soviet military was "heavily involved."

One member of the Senate Intelligence Committee stated, "The explanation provided by the Soviets contradicts data I was given at the time of the incident."

What Nathan found most disturbing was not that the explanations were incomplete or that he had a nagging feeling that they were deliberately misleading. What bothered him was one question: "Why, nine years after the incident, did the Soviets feel called upon to give any explanation at all?" It was completely uncharacteristic behavior.

No, the 1988 effort had been too extensive a cover up. Three top Soviet biochemists had been sent to the United States to deny that an event had occurred. They made presentations to two different American academies in their attempt to prove that the Soviet Union had not had such an accident eight years previously. The effort was totally out of character.

Like everyone else who thought of it at all, Nathan knew that. at least since World War I, every industrialized nation conducted research into weapons of chemical warfare; and by the end of World War II, those same nations began to consider biological warfare; furthermore, by the 1960s they all had formal programs in chemical and biological warfare underway. While these programs were rarely discussed, their existence was a very poorly kept secret. The use of Agent Orange as a defoliant in Vietnam was decried for its side effects, but the use of a chemical warfare agent was not denied. Why then should the Soviets make such a loud denial that they were engaged in such research?

These questions and the widespread support for a national Bio-engineering agency formed the core of his presentation. Peters knew that only time would tell if he was successful or not.

Those notes, derived from the work of David Bradley, provided the key to the formation of a secret facility buried in a secret facility.

A College Commencement

Though they had nothing to do with science, computers, political environment or the general mood of the country, the events reported in this section provided another element key to the emergence of The

Outrage by contributing irreversibly to the shaping of a personality trait that proved to be essential.

Commencement at last! Standing in the middle of the first row of graduates, an attractive young woman impatiently shifted her weight from one foot to the other, trying in vain to pay attention to the speaker. In spite of herself, her thoughts wandered. This could have been such a different, more wonderful day but for . . . .

Mary Ann Bovonio, born in Boston's most intensely Italian neighborhood, had been raised a Catholic, as was to be expected in that neighborhood 1980s. Contrary to modern beliefs, her parents had clung to the old tenets of the church, and their daughter's views and morals were entirely shaped by theirs. She would never have questioned the Church's teachings, had she not had that tragic illness in her late teens. The impact of that disease totally changed her life and created the psychological conditions that made her indirect impact on The Outrage possible.

Though still a virgin, she had somehow contracted a serious vaginal infection, one which was frequently, though certainly not exclusively, sexually transmitted. Eyebrows were raised; the nurses and others felt prompted to give her unsought, unwanted, and unnecessary advice on the prevention of sexually transmitted diseases. The unwarranted innuendo was bad enough; but the bombshell that was to affect her life had been exploded in her discharge interview with her physician. "Mary, the good news is I can assure you that you are fully recovered from the infection. However, I'm afraid there is one unfortunate side effect. You will never be able to conceive."

She had sat there stunned. Although she had never given any particular thought to having children, the knowledge that she could never do so was troubling. She had never discussed it with anyone; and when she thought about it which was infrequently, even before she had met Nick, the first love of her life, she had attributed her resulting depression to the outmoded view that motherhood was the ultimate goal of womanhood. She was a bright girl and had already decided to pursue a career in science. Objectively, she viewed her sterility as an asset since it obviated the distractions of child bearing and rearing.

Her studies in high school had gone well. She had begun her sophomore year at the Boston College majoring in chemistry; there, she had met Nick in an analytics laboratory class. She had had other boyfriends, but the relationships had not lasted. She found the boys she had dated to be immature and, frankly, less intelligent than she was. Nick was different. He was good-looking, though not handsome by any stretch of the imagination. He was also mature, and intelligent. He knew where he wanted to go and how to get there and was prepared work to realize his goals.

True, there had been nothing as giddy as love at first sight. She hadn't danced around the room on cloud nine, there were no bells or flashing lights. But still, almost from the first date, their relationship had the comfortable feeling of permanence. After a short time they started making plans for the future together. Then it happened. Catastrophe! Like a terrorist bomb, a totally unexpected explosion had permanently destroyed the relationship.

Thinking back on it now during her graduation ceremony, the details of that last evening were blurred and most of the conversation obscured by time. "How did it begin?" she asked herself. "Somehow my sterility came up and Nick's reaction was instantaneous. I was devastated. Of course I expected some reaction; but his language?

"You are what? You little slut! What did you catch? Sterile! For Christ's sake, how could you?"

He had rattled on in that vein, a totally irrational male chauvinist. What else did he say? Never mind, she rationalized to herself, the details don't matter now. It would not have worked anyway. Nick's future includes raising a family, and mine does not. That's all there is to it.

But, as time would tell, that was not all there was to it. She had repressed the incident, burying it beneath increased academic efforts during her remaining years at the college; however, all she now wanted from the school was to get out. The conditions affecting her very indirect role in stopping The Outrage had been firmly established.

Farmer's Son Chases Chickens and Kills Ants

The prejudices inadvertently taught to a young lad are illustrated by this scene; the role they will eventually play could not have been foreseen at this time; however, those prejudices are but one of several factors essential to our story which are revealed in the incident reported here. These events occurred rather early in Era 1; since the exact date of their occurrence is not relative to our chronicle, I did not check actual dates.

Deep in the Georgia peach country, a husky four year old boy was chasing the family chickens along the side of the house, his long blond hair bouncing in disarray. Scattering in all directions with a confusion of cackling and screeching, eight hens burst into the dusty front yard,.

"What ya up ta, Terry Parker?" a deep voice called from the front steps. "Ya leave them damn chickens be, hear? Them birds never gonna lay no eggs ya keep runnin' they asses off like that. You worse'n them "nigger" kids down ta the old Smith place. Al'ays gettin inta sump'in."

"Aw, I ain't doin' nuthin, Pa," Terry replied. "Ah was jus comin' round here ta see Uncle John, and them chickens was in the way."

"Don't be so hard on the boy, Sam Edward," John chided his younger brother in a friendly tone. "Did you ever hear of a four year old catching a full-grown chicken?" Uncle John was a teacher at the county high school. Terry was not sure what a high school was, or where it was, but Uncle John was a frequent visitor, and he always brought Terry a peppermint stick. On this occasion, Terry had settled on the steps with the older men when his uncle arrived, but he didn't understand their discussion of the new people at the Smith's place. He had never seen a "nigger" and was unsure what one was. At first he thought they must be people, but as they talked on, he was not sure. However, he was convinced that people or not 'niggers" were to be avoided; association with them could contaminate ones very soul. In any case it was boring talk and, as soon as he finished his candy, he left the porch in search of something to do.

Not quite sure that the danger of his punishment for chasing the chickens had been completed, Terry returned to the porch and sat on the porch steps near his uncle on the opposite side from his father, who was sitting on the porch floor with his back supported by the weathered railing. But Sam's anger with his son never lasted very long; it passed quickly. Terry's mother had died in childbirth and he had been center of Sam Edward's life from that day on.

Looking down at the porch floor, Terry noticed a column of ants marching across the dry decking. He grabbed a fly swatter that had been resting near his uncle and began thrashing the little red soldiers. "Die you little bastards! Die!"

Last week, Terry had received a painful sting from a shuffling spider and vowed then and there never to let a 'go'damed bug' near him again. Remembering that painful incident, he kept his wary eyes scanning for the presence of other insects even as he edged closer to the protective uncle.

"It's a good thing y'all ain't around here alla time, John. I never could teach thet boy nuthin'—y'all spoilin' him ever'day. 'Spose ya gonna give him anuther o' them peppermints now," his father retorted good-naturedly.

"That sounds like a good idea, Sam Edward. Come up here, Terry, so I can get a better look at you," Uncle John said, as he extracted another stick of candy from his pocket. "In times past, anyone as handy with chickens as you might have grown up to be a cock fighter. Not many of them left now, though. What is it you want to be when you grow up? A cowboy, I suppose. Though I don't know with those deep green eyes and that long blond hair, I'll just bet you could become quite the lady's man."

"Hesh up, John! Don't be puttin' no ideas inta the boy's head. He ain't gonna be no damned cowboy. No lady's man neither. He's goin' ta college just like you. But he gonna be more famous than y'all. He'll be a doctor 'r lawyer 'r sump'in like thet. Have his name in the papers 'n all.

While his father's vision of Terry's future was to be proved, wrong, Terry did indeed ultimately receive a lot of press coverage though infamous would prove to be a more appropriate noun than famous.

A CIA Agent's Study Paves the Way

The most secure, safest, research facility in the world, which is also the world's most open research facility, was born at a private meeting attended only by the President of the United States, a committee personally selected by the President, and an internationally known scientist. Ironically that same meeting also gave rise to the world's most highly classified research program, a Black, 'non-extant program' which was to be hidden away in a 'non-existent section' of that open facility. While Special Agent Bradley of the CIA had had no idea of the objective of the research task to which he had been assigned, the analysis he provided was enough for Dr. Nathan Peters to prevail in his first meeting with the President of the United States. That was the only meeting between the two men that was ever acknowledged before now. But, it is the second, the unacknowledged, meeting that is essential to this chronicle. Of course I did not attend either of the two meetings and even with my close relationship with President Winters I was not able to obtain a full report of the second meeting. Indeed, the existence of the meeting was never explicitly acknowledged. But that such a meeting took place is obvious and I will attempt to illustrate how the meetings may have progressed.

The topic of the first meeting was a hotly contested argument over the formation of an entirely new weapons project, simply referred to as THE PROJECT. Since the mid 1980s, when communist propaganda accused the United States of having created the AIDS virus, Biological Warfare, BW, had been the subject of many highly classified studies called "white papers". Of course such projects had been considered; but, everyone involved knew that AIDS was a purely natural mutation of some kind and not a military accident; and it was certainly not a U.S. military accident.

However, the technology to create and mass produce artificial life forms capable of inflicting widespread disease of epidemic proportions did exist in theory; and it was a matter of serious concern within both the military and the civilian sectors of the government. Of course research which involved such areas was abhorrent in the extreme. "Yet", the advocates of such research argued, "We can be sure that our enemies, and a number of our friends, are working in this area; burying our heads in the sand will not change that fact or reduce the threat. At a minimum, we need to know what is possible, and more importantly, we need to become much better at identifying, isolating, and eliminating new diseases and toxins. In short, even if we never develop a biological agent ourselves, we need to be prepared to defend against them".

Other advocates went even further. "For all we know the entire 'glasnost' movement was simply a ruse to divert attention from work on biological weapons," they said. "The willingness to reduce nuclear weapons may have been nothing more than an expression of confidence in their biological weapons. You cannot trust those Reds, and you cannot defend yourself with ignorance!"

At this point, the extensive studies of Agent Bradley had been presented with force and eloquence by Dr. Peters: he had triumphed and the PROJECT was born. A full blown BW program was to be initiated. Those opposed had then argued, "At least the PROJECT must be limited to a program of paper feasibility studies of adapting the techniques of bio-engineering to the development of weapons." But they had argued in vain.

Since the use of the A-bomb, the need to develop effective counter measures had been the umbrella of justification for all manner of weapons research; and once again those arguments carried the day.

"Furthermore," the argument went, "you can't really prepare adequate defenses without fully understanding the seriousness of the threat; and that requires knowing just how far the techniques can be developed. Then of course the clincher, 'a deterrent is certainly needed', is added to the justification. If and when the time comes that we are actually faced with a real threat, the existence of our own arsenal will be our best defense. It was the only strategy for defense against the nuclear threat, and is the only realistic defense against the biological one. There is no doubt that threats of biological warfare are at least as frightening as the possibility of nuclear war."

This argument prevailed yet again. The weapons were different, as were the speakers, but the arguments, which depended more on fear than logic, were the same. In spite of the effectiveness of such arguments on U.S. officials, these men were still politicians. As such, they were all well aware of the fact that the existence of a facility devoted to such research, and no doubt costing hundreds of millions of dollars, could not be kept secret by ordinary security measures. They further understood that should the press discover the existence of such a facility, it would spell the end of the political careers of those responsible for its creation.

The Senator from Illinois summarized the views of the select committee of elected officials present in the Oval Office. "It's all well and good to argue that we need this capability to defend ourselves. But the cost of such a program will be enormous, if I understood Dr. Peters's explanation of the facilities required for such a program. That presents us with several problems, not the least of which is successfully selling The PROJECT to the electorate. After we do that, it will no longer be a secret and not one of us will ever be re-elected to any office higher than dogcatcher."

Dr. Peters had anticipated such arguments. He quickly demonstrated that he was not only a scientist but a master of political deception as well. Violating protocol, he rose to make his next presentation, a presentation he regarded as so secret that he had personally prepared the view graphs and had made sure that there were no hard copies of them available to anyone.

"Gentlemen," he began, "we have an excellent opportunity to bury the PROJECT so deeply in the Nevada desert, both figuratively and physically, that there will be no danger of discovery, and further, the cost can be controlled to such a level that it need never show explicitly on the national budget." His standing and starting to speak without being asked had raised a few eyebrows; but after his opening comment no one wanted to miss what he had to say.

"However, we can only do so if we act quickly," he continued. "NAMBE, the National Agency for Microbiological Engineering, has just been funded amid enormous positive press coverage. The newly created agency is immensely popular and can be expected to receive both political and financial backing. It can also provide the perfect shield for the PROJECT.

"Please let me explain." He continued. "The very nature of NAMBE's research requires an expansive and highly secure facility. The agency's facility will be large, and, for safety reasons it will be seated into sections such that each laboratory can be safely and hermetically sealed from all others. Access to various portions of the facility will be through separately controlled entrances. Such fanatic attention to physical security and safety is not only essential to avoid accidental release of toxic agents but will be applauded by members of the government, the press, and the general public alike. In their hearts the public still has an irrational fear of the micro-biological research. Additionally, the staffing level of NAMBE will be number several thousand so no one can be expected to know everyone else. Under these circumstances, it will be a relatively easy task to embed a classified defense program right in the middle of the NAMBE facility, as long as it's staffed entirely by handpicked specifically cleared scientists. Essentially, we will hide a tree in a forest?" He paused and surveyed the room. "I've got them!" he thought to himself.

While everyone in the room was convinced and relieved by his arguments, certain precautions would be required if the scheme were to be workable. However, after careful analysis none of the problems were considered insurmountable.

When the general discussion died down, Dr. Peters continued. As one of the most prominent bioengineers in the country, he had served on the committee that had overseen the design of the new NAMBE facility. His next slide showed the finally agreed schematic layout.

He began with a brief review of that design. "As I am sure you all know, the NAMBE facility will be an eight story laboratory, with seven of those stories below ground."

A national contest had been held to decide on the basic design of the central laboratory facility, and just last week the selection committee had announced that it was to be octagonal in shape and was to consist of eight hermetically sealed levels seven of which will be below ground in case a seal should fail. On each level there will be eight ring corridors that form complete paths around the building and eight spoke corridors that connect the various rings. Every pie shaped sector thus formed will be capable of complete isolation from the rest and every floor will also be capable of total isolation from all others. Even without any classified work, this facility requires fanatically controlled physical security.

"The final design and construction of the facility is to be placed under the control of a Special Project Office, a SPO. This method of control provides us further opportunity to protect the security and anonymity of the BW project.

"Every minority in the country will clamor for an opportunity to participate in what will be perceived as a major construction opportunity. In order to be sure the work is fairly spread around and to assure that there is an adequate minority participation I propose that the government announce a new policy for building this facility. The SPO itself will play the role of prime contractor breaking the construction tasks down into much smaller pieces than any private industry contractor would ever dream of doing. This approach, while admittedly more costly than the conventional approach, will be seen as socially commendable. The same approach must be applied to the required living accommodations and infrastructure. We will create a Micro City. More importantly, no single contractor or subcontractor will ever realize that there will in fact be eight laboratory levels below the ground, rather than the seven that have been so widely publicized. Several additional subterranean levels are required in any case simply to house the support functions such as heating and power generation equipment, and the innumerable special bio-engineering processing systems. It will be a simple matter to hide an entire additional laboratory level."

All those in attendance agreed it was a masterful security concept. Dr. Peters paused to let his plan sink in and to observe the reactions of his audience. Pleased with what he saw, he continued, "For obvious reasons I made no copies of these View graphs except this set and I have the originals locked in my safe; Mr. President, perhaps you would like to keep this set." Rising again, he placed a manila folder containing the transparencies on the President's desk and sat down; no one except the President had noticed the small note attached to the folder! The meeting was concluded with the President agreeing to reconvene the to kick off the PROJECT which they had now dubbed PROJECT Eight because it was to be located on the nonexistent eighth level below ground.

They were led out of the White House one at a time. As he pulled up to the gate, Dr. Peters, like the others, was routinely stopped by the guard. However, he alone was directed to return to the Oval Office; and that was certainly not routine. No explanation was given, simply a directive. No explanation was needed. A broad smile of satisfaction lit up his face as he pulled back into the parking lot. The President had seen his note; there would be a second meeting.

Now, he was confident that he would succeed at that meeting as well. And, after that meeting, there would be no doubt that he would become the Director of the NAMBE SPO.

PROJECT Eight, established in that first meeting with the President, was "black," its very existence would forever be known only to a highly select group and would be strongly denied to everyone else. Even its funding would be hidden, scattered throughout other organizations. That is, apart from those explicitly cleared to work on the level eight, PROJECT Eight, only a Select Congressional Committee and a handful of civil servants were ever to know it existed. Moreover, no one, outside of the President of the United States and those with a specifically demonstrated Need to Know, would ever be aware that there even was an Eighth Level. At his second meeting, Dr. Nathan Peters had convinced the President of the need for an even more highly controversial and hence more highly classified project, PROJECT Nine, was born.

When work at the PROJECTs was initiated, 90 percent of the classified effort was concentrated on PROJECT Eight. As objectionable as it was, it was far easier to sell than PROJECT Nine. Even some of the most hawkish Directors of the newly formed and highly secret National Genetic Warfare Directorate, NAGWAD, could be expected to balk at PROJECT Nine.

The Executive Director of NAGWAD, who was responsible only to the President and who was initially the only member of NAGWAD cleared for PROJECT Nine. As he had planned, Dr. Nathan Peters was appointed Executive Director. The very existence of NAGWAD was highly classified. Within a few weeks of the

Oval Office meeting, NAGWAD was created and the President had appointed a special Presidential Oversight Committee, POC, consisting of the Secretary of Defense, the Secretary of State, the Secretary of the Interior, the President's Scientific Adviser and the President. This committee was to approve and review all programs of PROJECTs Eight and Nine. While the President would chair the meetings of the POC, he would not vote on matters requiring the approval of the Committee. This assured that at least three of his advisers approved each action. In practice, nothing passed the Committee except by unanimous approval.

Because his state had been so affected by the episode and the subsequent bio-engineering induced crisis, the junior Senator from Texas, Prescott Winters, was included on the first POC.

A new Service Is Formed

Serious security leaks at the US Embassy in Moscow may seem totally unrelated to the Outrage. However, one of the consequences of those leaks was to be the formation of a new security service; the the existence of that new service was to provide the mechanism for uniting two people who each played significant role the unraveling of a devious plot at the very center of the Outrage.

Long after the Projects had been formed a series of sexual encounters between US Embassy guards and certain Russian ladies were tied to serious security leaks. Those leaks were in no way related to bio-engineering or any other weapons systems. However, the US Governments response to those events resulted in bringing David Bradley back into the increasingly complex set of interlocking and interacting elements of this tale.

Across town from the White House in his small office with its gray walls, dropped ceiling, and regulation safe, Special Agent David Bradley carefully considered the letter on his desk. He had just read it for the fourth time. "Why not; why the hell not?" he thought.

A few years back nearly an entire detachment of Marines had been discovered to be involved with a female Russian spy ring. As a result, a movement had been instigated to form a new separate branch of the U.S. State Department one that would be dedicated to providing guard services for US installations on foreign soil. It would be staffed by persons who considered guarding the nation's secrets and facilities a career goal and not simply a steppingstone to some more generalized career.

At last, the formalities of forming the new service had been completed. Staffing of the new service was the next order of business. The decision had been made to build the new staff around experienced members of the related agencies; and accordingly recruiting letters were sent to qualified personnel.

The letter on his desk was an invitation to interview for a senior position in the Guard. He looked around the characterless office and sighed, "Why not give change a chance? At least he'd be in on the ground floor. Yes, by God, I'll do it."

The Software Is Ready

The new generation of computers powered by Professor Cochran's operating system and specialized software made it possible to fully apply the Morris Modeling techniques with results that would stun the world and incidentally make possible the chain of events that was the Outrage.

Professor Buzz Cochran leaned back in the overstuffed chair, simultaneously loosening his tie still further and stretching his long legs across the cluttered surface of his desk. His sabbatical with the research lab was nearing an end. The engineering program had been an enormous success. The new tenth generation computer, as it was now being called, had exceeded even his most optimistic estimate. Of course he had had nothing to do with the engineering program other than monitoring its progress. His work had involved the development of a software operating system that made it possible to utilize the full capabilities of the new computer.

During all the time he'd spent here on the program, he had had a single application in mind and that was to implement the Morris modeling theory. He was now convinced that the tools, both hardware and software, existed to complete that task of creating living molecules and complex cells in a test tube. He resolved to do so immediately upon returning to campus. His results were published before the building of the central facility was completed.

Abortion

Political, legal and religious conflicts surrounding abortion related activities of course had significant impact on the lives of many American women and volumes have been written on the subject. What matters to our chronicle is the impact of those conflicts on discussions between two young ladies and, more importantly, the lasting impact of those discussions on one of them. Those discussions were destined to determine a major part of her role in this tale and to be absolutely essential to the role of another important contributor.

Two young ladies discussing the genetics and the politics of abortion and birth control may seem to have no link to bio-engineering or The Outrage. However, one of two girls participating in the discussion recorded here was to have a major enabling impact on the conclusion of the tale. I was of course not present at the discussion I am reporting on below; but it seemed perfectly plausible when reported to me and I record it here because it fits and has a ring of truth about it and of course it is closely tied to The Outrage.

"I just can't believe it, Jo Ann! For God's sake, this is 1997. Of course you'll have an abortion if that is what you want; it's your body. There's no room for old fashioned religious taboos and social pressure crap," Mary Ann proclaimed.

They were just leaving the evening session of their Advanced Organic Synthesis laboratory class. Following graduation, Mary had accepted a position at a leading mid-western laboratory. Initially, her assignments had been routine, almost lab tech level. However, her work ethic and native intelligence soon won the respect of her peers and management. As her assignments became more interesting, she managed to push Nick even farther from her consciousness. After a year, the company awarded her with a fully paid scholarship at the local university. It was there she met Jo Ann, an attractive and vibrant young blonde, arguably the best chemist in the class.

From the beginning, the two young women had formed an easy, comfortable friendship.

"Hold on, Mary Ann!." Jo Ann held up her hand in mock protest. "You know I don't have any such hang ups. I'm talking about the law. In this state abortion is against the law in nearly all circumstances, certainly in mine."

"But that doesn't make sense. The government shouldn't even be involved; it's crazy. You're a mature adult with an above average intelligence; you're certainly capable of making a rational decision. If you weren't, the government's position should be to help you make a rational decision instead having some government toady forbid you to behave rationally. I . . . ."

"Hold on, girl; you'll be grabbing a sign and marching down Main Street calling for the ouster of the governor. Seriously, where have you been for the past ten years? The government has insinuated itself into the abortion question in every state, resulting in fifty different sets of rules and regulations, with a fifty first set at the federal level. This state has the most regressive laws in the country."

"But, but . . ." Mary stammered; but of course Jo Ann was right. She was well aware of the fuss created by the abortion issue in recent years. She had read the headlines and half listened to newscasts, but Mary Ann Bovonio would never be pregnant; so the question of abortion for her would never arise. "You're right, Jo Ann. My comments were naive. Of course I'm aware of all the fuss. But this isn't the only state in the union and you're not chained to it."

"You're right; I'm leaving for a very short vacation."

Some weeks later, when the whole affair was history and they were sharing a quiet evening discussing the episode, Mary Ann said, "You know, Jo Ann, the real crime of this state's idiotic abortion stance is distorting the economic structure of society."

She detected a slight grin flash across her friend's face. "No, don't laugh; it's true. Look at you for instance. You're financially able to care for a child with or without a husband; but what about the dirt poor women in the state who can neither afford your solution nor afford to rear unplanned children. They have no choice. The social structure is distorted, with an ever increasing percentage of the population being born into poor families thus making them even poorer. At the same time the wealthy and more educated people are able to control their family size regardless of the law"

"Mary Ann, I too have strong feelings on the subject. Have you thought about the genetic effects of such a policy? Those less gifted mentally simply accept the dictates of the state so this damned state is not only increasing the percentage of its poor population, it's also lowering its average mentality level, the average IQ is steadily dropping in this State. The law here moves in direct opposition to the selection process of evolution. Darwin is probably turning over in his grave."

"I never thought of it that way; but you're right. It's disgusting."

Later that evening, Mary Ann lay awake thinking about that conversation and concluded. "We were right! She thought. There _is_ a distortion of society taking place. These stupid laws run contrary to the objectives of evolution."

It occurred to her that she too could afford to raise children on her own, if necessary. While not arrogant, she knew she had above average intelligence and good health. I believe that I would be a good mother she told herself. Of course there's no chance of that. "I suppose I could adopt a child? No, it's not the same. Face it, Mary, you'll never be a mother, and you can't change the way the government manipulates society."

She considered joining one of the numerous activist groups; but she knew that that was really not her thing. Certainly marching in political protests was not her style; but as it developed her mothering instincts proved strong and germane to our purpose.

ERA 2

Early Tangles, Threads Begin To Entwine

In this Era some of the remote rootlets begin to intermingle with each other. At the times of their occurrence, no connection was made between these events and the ultimate crisis; they just seemed independent events. Even during this Era, Early Tangles, the connections between the events were still too remote to be noted in any known reports. Therefore, I will continue to report the scenes in the order in which I leaned of them with no attempt at chronological accuracy. Also, by and large, the more the events intermingle the fewer author's asides will be required to reveal or hint at their connection to each other or their relevance to the Chronicle.

Laurie Selects A Candidate

Though they arrived by totally different routes, an ex-vice squad detective and an ex-CIA were to destined to join forces to make possible a portion of their roles in the Outrage.

Her winning that black belt, years ago, had not been a consideration in Laurie's appointment; nor had her five years experience as a detective with the police vice squad been a serious factor. However, both her combative stills and the effects that years with the vice squad had on her personality, were significant factors in her various roles in this chronicle.

Laurie Bass moved slowly into her new office in the administrative section of the NAMBE central facility. Closing the door, she waltzed twice around the room, ending in a pirouette behind her desk. She was ecstatic. At age twenty six she had just been promoted to Director of Security at this national showplace. She was well aware that luck had played a role in her being appointed. The political climate in the Guards had also been to her advantage. "But," she consoled herself, "I wasn't the only female candidate. The NAMBE Guards contingent is nearly fifty percent women. Anyway, I am qualified; I wanted this job and I can certainly handle it."

Her momentary introspection did nothing to dampen her spirits as she settled into the swivel chair behind the massive oak desk. Looking down at the polished surface did, however, have a sobering effect. This desk had belonged to Fred Morton, the previous Director. Old Fred, as he had been called by his associates and staff, had died suddenly of a massive heart attack less than a month ago. This desk would always be Old Fred's desk. She had spent too many hours on the other side to ever feel comfortable behind it. "This desk has got to go," she resolved. "That's my first Executive decision!"

The only item on the desk was a manila folder marked 'CURRENT'. She opened it and found a number of memos and letters. She was not really in the mood to read a pile of correspondence, but she did flip through, noting the Subject Line of each. A letter from the Guards caught her attention; she read it more carefully.

"The short list of qualified internal applicants for the position of Senior Investigator, NAMBE, is presented with this letter. Their resumes are attached. As you know, it is our practice to select from within the organization when possible without compromising the mission. However, the mission is always the primary concern. Please review these candidates' resumes. Interviews with the candidates may be arranged with them directly; but please notify this office of your decisions." The letter continued with such needless instructions. Anyone senior enough to receive such a letter was certainly familiar with the recruiting process of the Guards. She scanned the resumes. Only one indicated extensive investigative background; David Bradley, previously of the CIA. "His experience is appropriate," she thought. "There'll certainly be no trouble clearing him on Level 8, which is the only area where we need an Investigative Officer. I wonder if I could work with an ex CIA agent. I was never very high on spooks."

Her selection might have been even easier had she been aware that David Bradley had performed the studies that had been used to justify the entire NAMBE operation, including the classified programs it housed. However, as near as I can tell neither David Bradley nor Laurie Bass were ever aware of the roll his studies had played in the evolution of the Facility or the two highly classified programs.

Mary Ann Arrives at the Facility

Twelve months later, in another section of the Facility, another dark haired young woman paced nervously up and down the corridor before Dr. Peters' locked office. His door was always locked, whether the office was occupied or not: just one of the eccentricities of the famous Dr. Peters. She knew it was pointless to knock. Dr. Peters had sent for her and he would open the door when he decided it was time.

Her road to NAMBE had not been particularly unique or noteworthy. Following her political awakening after Jo Ann's abortion, Mary Ann Bovonio's life had changed. It was not a dramatic change. She did not neglect her profession and become a political activist; but now, she never failed to find time to attend political gatherings when the abortion issue was included in the agenda. Other changes were more subtle. She had sought out Projects at the pharmaceutical laboratory that were related to women's disorders.

The fanfare associated with the foundation of NAMBE and its fantastic new facility had captured her attention. She had followed with interest the endless press reports of arguments pro and con over its formation and construction. She had even embarked on a private study of bio-engineering.

One morning, scanning the local paper at breakfast, she had noticed an article that would completely alter her life. The article was tribute to Dr. Nathan Peters. Among other things, it noted that he was a leading advocate of enforced birth control in underdeveloped countries and was also a strong supporter of a woman's right to choose to terminate a pregnancy for any reason whatever. In his view, as in hers, no other justification should be required. The more she read, the more she was impressed by this man, the man whom the press credited with almost singlehandedly creating NAMBE. She resolved to apply for a position there and in due course was appointed to the Organic Synthesis Lab. Which while not exactly what she had hoped for, it was a start.

Upon arriving, she learned that Dr. Peters was essentially retired; they referred to him as Director Emeritus. "He's probably being fired to make way for some political appointee", she had thought. Her cynicism had proven unfounded. Dr. Peters was not leaving the Facility. He was merely leaving the red tape of administration and management to a younger man, Dr. Stamford James. As it developed, it mattered very little whether Peters stayed or not since he was seen only occasionally at the monthly seminars and otherwise not at all.

At first there had been considerable speculation on the significance of this; but after a few months it was generally agreed that it was just another strange trait of Dr. Peters. Since her job had changed, she had seen a lot of Dr. Peters in spite of his rare appearances outside his own laboratory. She was on her way to see him now.

"I wonder what's on his mind this time?" she thought. They never discussed her Project, or any other Project, for that matter.

But she always had the impression that she was being interviewed for an even more restricted program than the one in which she was presently engaged; though she had no idea what such a program might be. As it developed her intuition had been correct.

"After all", she thought, "I'm currently working on a 'nonexistent program; for a 'nonexistent directorate', which is located in a 'nonexistent laboratory' on a 'nonexistent level' of the Facility; right in the heart of the most publicized, and public agency in the world. "It never ceases to amaze me. Of course, the very red tape and security measures necessitated by public fear of a microbiological disaster are what makes it possible to deliberately develop microbes capable of wreaking unspeakable havoc right here in a facility devoted to the benefit and safety of mankind." Continuing to pace before the door, she recalled her first meeting with Dr. Peters.

All in all, Mary Ann's first job at the Facility had gone well and she had been as happy as she could ever remember having been. Then, just after her second year, her work had taken on a whole new aspect. In retrospect she could see that it had all begun with her first encounter with Dr. Peters. At the time, she had thought it simply a matter of chance when they were introduced at the Sherry Hour following one of the regular seminars. She had just stepped out of the small lecture hall and, seeing no one that she recognized, had wandered over to the informal bar and selected a glass of Dry Sack. As she turned away from the bar, she noticed him walking toward her.

At about five foot five, he was short with a wide girth. His totally bald head sat atop a neck almost completely submerged in fat. His eyebrows, heavy black bushes, provided lively accent to the expressions of his eyes, which seemed to change color with his mood. He had smiled broadly as he approached her. "Ah, Miss Bovonio, I believe? I've been meaning to meet you since your presentation at last month's seminar, but my best intentions frequently go awry."

They had talked about seemingly innocuous subjects, ranging aimlessly from chemistry to politics; and she could recall some smattering of religion. At the time, she was so impressed with simply meeting him, the great Nathan Peters, and having a one on one discussion that the topic of conversation had not really registered. Thinking back on it later, after she had gotten to know him better, she realized that that casual conversation had been an interview. After that Sherry Hour meeting, she had not seen him again for four months, until after she had been invited to attend a government meeting in Washington, D.C. She had been invited ostensibly to interview for a new position elsewhere in a different government research center. She had explained that she was not interested in leaving the Facility. However, the caller had been persistent and she reasoned, "At the very least I'll have a free trip to D.C., and I haven't been there for several years." She went.

The meeting was not at all what she had expected. An entire half day was spent discussing security and politics. The interview had begun with, "What are your views on the topic of classified military research? Not necessarily weapons, but perhaps related to military missions. Do you understand the responsibilities one assumes by accepting a position that involves access to matters affecting the security of the United States?"

"No, and that's only half of it. I have not the least desire to learn." That was certainly not the sort of reply the interviewer had expected. "Dr. Peters suggested you might be interested in and highly qualified for this program. However, regardless of his recommendation, we cannot proceed without some level of security governing the discussion. The position we are discussing is extremely important, and I can assure you that it represents a significant professional opportunity. And you have come all the way from Nevada for this interview. I have a suggestion. "We can begin with your agreeing to read one document and treat that document and its contents as SECRET as defined therein. If after reading that document you wish to proceed, you will be asked to sign the document and will receive a full briefing. After that briefing you will be free to either to participate in the program being staffed or to forget the whole thing. The only restriction is that you may never discuss this with anyone not specifically cleared."

The fact that Dr. Peters had recommended her thrilled and flattered her; and the interviewer's suggestion seemed so reasonable. She was persuaded to at least read the document, though she had been confident at the time that she would not be interested in performing classified research. "That sounds reasonable," she said.

The document stated that Dr. Peters was engaged in government sponsored research on topics considered by the United States Government to be highly sensitive and SECRET WITHIN THE MEANING OF THE ACTS DESCRIBED IN THE ATTACHED BRIEFING STATEMENT.

That statement explained a lot. No wonder Dr. Peters was rarely seen, he was working most of the time on this PROJECT. It must be an important, indeed, if Dr. Peters considered it significant enough to give up the Directorship of the Facility. Of course she was interested in a chance to work more closely with Dr. Peters, wherever the damn Project was located and regardless of the security regulations. Without further discussion she had signed the documents.

She returned to the Facility expecting to be asked to resign in preparation for a transfer. Instead she was met by Dr. Peters and taken to his office. After a brief meeting during which she signed more papers detailing exactly what was classified, which was essentially everything, she was taken to a closet door that concealed Dr. Peters' private elevator. When the elevator doors finally slid open, she was introduced to level Eight and The PROJECT. For two years now she had worked on one of the genetically engineered weapons. Now, less than two minutes after the time of her appointment, the door to Dr. Peters' office swung open. Glancing at her watch, she thought, this must truly be important. Aloud she said, "Good morning, Dr. Peters."

"Good morning, young lady. Please step in. We have some important matters to discuss this morning."

Laurie and Mary Ann Discuss an Ethical Question

One of the most ethically and morally repugnant concerns surrounding the science of bio-engineering was the possibility of work on human beings directly. The fears and objections to the possible use of bio-engineering in the field of germ warfare faded into insignificance when compared to those associated with experimentation of human beings. The world was in no way ready to even consider 'designer persons.' Yet . . . .

One evening, some months earlier, Laurie Bass sat at her desk reviewing her latest staff assignments. Over the past year as Director, she had developed the habit of staying late one evening each month to keep her paperwork up to date without the necessity of spending all of each day confined to her desk. As she paused to consider an assignment change for one of her staff, she heard a soft, almost timid, knock at the office door. Looking at her watch she wondered, "Who could that be at this hour?" Aloud, she called, "Please come in."

She recognized Mary Ann Bovonio as she hesitantly walked into the office. She had met Mary Ann when she filed her clearance papers and then again when Mary Ann was briefed. Since then they had rarely spoken. Setting aside her papers, she looked up, smiling to ease the embarrassment she sensed in the other woman.

"I hope I'm not disturbing you," Mary Ann began. "I saw that your light and, well . . . I need someone to talk to, and there aren't many people cleared for what I want to talk about. If you're too busy I can come back later." Mary Ann's behavior seemed totally out of **character**. Thinking that something must really be wrong, Laurie smiled and said, "No, not at all. I'm just catching up on some boring paperwork. It would actually be a relief to take a break. How may I help you?"

"I'm not sure you can. I'm not even sure I need help." Mary Ann nervously shifted from one foot to the other. "But I do need to talk, if you could just provide a friendly ear?"

"Of course, of course, please sit down. And please relax."

Almost reluctantly, Mary Ann sat in the overstuffed chair across from Laurie's desk and gathered her thoughts. Finally, the young scientist began. "In order to make any sense at all I must review a little of the history of NAMBE. I know you have all the clearances there are and I don't want to bore you, but I'm not sure how much you know about the early days of NAMBE or the technology being employed here."

"Don't worry, you won't bore me. I know very little of the history other than what's in the handouts, and you can be sure that I know nothing at all about the technologies. You needn't worry about boring me, but you may find it difficult to describe the technical stuff on a level I can understand."

Taking a deep breath, Mary Ann began. "Before NAMBE and its secret appendage, NAGWAD, on Level Eight had even had a chance to begin, the need for still further expansion of the classified programs had been agreed upon and the objectives of Level Nine established.

"The programs of NAGWAD were not to be ordinary chemical analysis and synthesis programs. Rather, they were to deal with RNA, DNA, proteins, the very stuff of life itself. These programs actually involve designing and developing individual living molecules. That is, they could produce living tissues and organs to be used in the testing of biological weapons. In this way, the design of biological weapons could proceed at a pace never before imagined. That's how NAGWAD is usually described in the briefing papers. But there's a lot more to it than that, vastly more, as I'm sure you know." She paused. She had been speaking with her head lowered, her eyes not making contact with Laurie's. Now she looked up to see if she was being too pedantic, and insulting the Security Officer.

"Yes, I'm aware of what's in the briefing sheets, but I sense that you're about to move into territory unfamiliar to me."

Straightening her shoulders and trying not to avoid eye contact, Mary Ann continued, less hesitantly. "Once you accept that RNA and DNA can be 'designed,' the possibilities are endless. In principle, plants could be purposefully designed using these techniques. And also animals, all animals, including man." She paused again, deliberately letting the impact of her last statement sink in.

Laurie was aware that the Level Nine programs included work on RNA and DNA molecules, but she had never considered the implications of that research, certainly not the implications toward which the Mary Ann seemed to be leading her.

"But surely those are only theoretical ideas. No one would try to 'design' humans. No one would agree to that."

"Yes, they would, and indeed they did. Any ethical objections to such research were quickly squelched by the usual arguments used to justify weapons research; let me quote the arguments explicitly."

Proponents state "Can we possibly consider ourselves adequately protected if our countermeasure research does not include the genetic material of man himself? How do we understand the mechanisms available to the developer of biological and genetic weapons if we do not fully understand man as an organism? What are the weaknesses in the genetic structure of man that a genetic weapon system can exploit? What of man himself; can he be turned into a controllable weapon? What are the limits, if any, to the destructive abilities that can be bred into man? Is it possible to engineer better fighting men in some sense? Can a fearless or powerful superman like person be created? Are we sure this not what is at the core of the Russian programs that are going on at this very moment?"

She paused again; she was warming to her subject and was no longer nervous and having finished the quotation continued with her own thoughts. "These questions had been forcibly put by Dr. Peters from the very beginning." Mary Ann continued. "Dr. Peters and his supporters prevailed. A ninth level was added to the facility, and the Level Nine Project began. To this day the programs there are still referred to by number only. As you know, Level Nine houses the U.S. government's most highly classified work." From her own initial briefing into the Level Nine program, Laurie knew that Dr. Peters had played a significant role in the construction of the Facility and in the direction of its classified programs. However, she had not been aware that he played a key role in establishing the need for the programs. While this information was new to her, it was not particularly surprising; so she nodded for Mary Ann continued.

Mary Ann's next revelation was quite surprising. "Laurie, I'm convinced that from the very beginning, Dr. Peters has had no interest in biological weapons or the human weaknesses that might be exploited by such weapons. His sole interest was, and still is, in the **strengths** of man. He believes it to be not only possible but desirable, even necessary, to engineer a perfect human specimen. He has no wish to bring any such perfect people into existence. His only interest is in the feasibility studies and specimen designs. But he also has no interest in pure theory, which he considers to be sterile and vacuous. He insists on experimental proof."

Here again, she paused to let the impact of what she was saying sink in. "Dr. Peters can prove the validity of one of his designs without letting the specimen mature; it's not even necessary for it to be born. With the techniques available, all the necessary measurements are possible within eight weeks of the test tube fertilization. Well, sometimes it's necessary for some specimens to last a little longer, but never is it necessary to let the specimen mature beyond thirteen weeks. Also, the sperm and ovum used in that fertilization are sometimes entirely artificial, generated in other test tubes and flasks. That leads to some interesting questions regarding the humanity of the specimen; but Dr. Peters considers such questions to be theoretical woolgathering."

"Much of the world would disagree with him, but Dr. Peters is quite certain that such a fetus is not human, nor entitled to any human rights. He's quite happy to carry out his research into the design and engineering of human beings without ever even considering the moral issues. He's been able to conduct his research with impunity. Two things make that possible: the complex security arrangements associated with all activities below Level Seven and the high degree of automation of the laboratories.

The few assistants he needs are told that they're preparing materials and samples to be used for evaluation in one or more of the classified weapons programs of Level Eight. They're quite accustomed to the 'need to know' barriers down there and are well paid to perform their tasks efficiently and ask no questions about the applications of their work. They'd never dream of discussing their activities with anyone not specifically cleared by Dr. Peters. In fact, the technicians do prepare materials for Level Eight, as well as for Level Nine. I know; I've often used human tissue samples from Level Nine in my own work on Level Eight. Though we never discuss it, I'm sure that, just like I, all of the others just assume they came from aborted fetuses.

"The fact that some of the preparations were only used by Dr. Peters was never disclosed. Not that anyone would've been too surprised to learn he had some pet Projects under study that he didn't want to discuss before they were finished. It would just have been put down as another of his idiosyncrasies." Her knowing nod indicated that Laurie was well aware of Dr. Peters' penchant for strange behavior. Mary Ann paused in her narrative. "I see you're aware of his reputation," she added, smiling.

Returning to her topic, she continued; "He's gone on like this for the past three years; actually he's been doing it since the Facility began functioning. He's been insulated from all possible censorship. These first years of his research have moved along quietly, and he's succeeded in finding a number of ways to improve his product, mankind himself. He has quietly and secretly sequestered all of his files in his private computer. That early work dealt only with the physical characteristics of man. Rapid progress was possible in that area because the relationships between the chemical measurements and the resulting physical traits had been extensively studied and documented. The vast amount of published data regarding those relationships were so well known and documented that he was able to perform all of his own research without letting such a fetus develop beyond two months. By that time, all the measurements required to verify his theory were completed.

"But now, that's all changed! He's performed enough research to satisfy himself that he not only can create better human beings but can also tailor their physical traits to optimize them for specific tasks or lifestyles. Aldous Huxley's 'Brave New World' can now become a reality."

Mary paused for a breath before continuing. "I'm sure you know all this already and find my telling it boring, but something happened today. I had a meeting with Dr. Peters, and now I've just got to talk to someone about it; and you are the only one I can be sure is cleared."

"Oh, I'm cleared, all right, but I haven't read any of that technical stuff. I wouldn't understand it if I did. They don't teach a lot of microbiology at the police academy. I understand it when you explain it, though. At least I think I'm getting the overall picture. So please continue," Laurie replied

"Well, okay. We've now come to the topic I really want to discuss if you're sure you don't mind. Dr. Peters hasn't quite reached the 'Brave New Worlds' level, not even in his own mind, certainly not in practice. Even he admits that. Most importantly, he has not yet demonstrated that his techniques can be applied to the engineering of senses, emotional and mental traits as well as physical ones. To reach Huxley's world with its alphas, betas, gammas, and deltas you need not only purposely designed bodies but also the appropriate mental, emotional and sensual characteristics. Dr. Peters is reasonably confident that his methods are equally applicable to all of these traits. It is not yet possible to prove theories about mental traits by chemical tests. There simply has not been enough research published to establish the basic relationships between chemical measurements and mental characteristics. True, all mental disorders have long since been shown to result from specific chemical imbalances. However, chemical relationships for positive mental traits, such as memory, reflexes and intelligence, have not been nearly so exhaustively studied. Some research has been published that made significant advances in early diagnosis of mental disorders and in prenatal estimates of IQ and other positive mental traits. However, sensory skills and memory have been less studied and documented.

Using published measuring techniques currently available, Dr. Peters has convinced himself that if he could allow his artificial fetuses to live for thirteen weeks he could complete the measurements necessary to verify his theories. But to do that he'll require a staff assistant who's privy to the mechanics of the operation. Only a very specific kind of assistant will do." She paused to let Laurie consider her last statement.

Laurie looked up, wide-eyed, "You don't mean . . ."

"You got it. According to him, I'm the only one available who fills the bill.

"So this afternoon he asked me to stop by and have coffee. He was more solemn and serious than usual. There was no attempt to pretend that the meeting was anything less than a final interview, to decide whether or not I was to be asked to join some even more secret project than the one in which I am now engaged.

"He began in such a pedantic way; 'Mary Ann, as you are aware, the work of the Level Eight Project is concerned with developing weapons and counter weapons through the application of genetic engineering principles and techniques, so called bio-weapons. You're also aware that the very technology required to develop such weapons and countermeasures fortunately obviates the need to test them on living human beings. However, we do require living tissue for the final evaluation of the product. You and your associates in this Level Eight Project believe the human tissue you use has been obtained from specially preserved fetal cadavers. That is in fact not the case. The tissue samples are obtained in much the same way that the weapon is developed in the first place, through bio-engineering.' Here he paused, waiting for my reaction as the full impact of what he had just said sank in.

"When it did, I nearly dropped my coffee cup. I was so stunned that I stuttered. 'But, surely you, you don't, you can't mean . . . ; but of course you do! Goddamn it! You're creating living human tissue in one of your precious Level Eight laboratories!' At that point I was just emoting. I was sure in my mind and heart that he couldn't actually do it. I'm not an expert in the mathematics involved, but I was positive that one couldn't simply engineer and grow a section of a cornea or lung tissue out of context with the rest of the body, and I told him so.

"For some time he simply sat still and said nothing; just sat there watching me and waiting for the other shoe to drop, as his British colleagues might say. It did and I raved again.

"I don't recall exactly, but I said something like 'You can't . . . you are! You're developing total human beings behind one of those goddamned sealed doors and then dicing them up into small samples to satisfy the needs of some weapons development program! What right do you have to terminate life? For that matter, what right do you have to create life? Are you God?' At that point I was shaking and clenching my teeth until my jaw hurt.

Where do you get the ovum? Whose body is turned into a . . . a factory to satisfy your egotistic desire to play God? For Christ's sake!

"I was so upset I had to quit talking; I just sat there staring at the man I'd always placed on such a pedestal. Until that moment, I'd worshiped him." She paused and stared at Laurie who simply stared back at her saying nothing.

With a sigh Mary Ann continued. "He still hadn't moved or changed his expression. The silence was heavy, nearly tangible. Then, as I finally began to breathe normally, he spoke softly, almost condescendingly.

We have often discussed the question of abortion, voluntary abortion. You are, I believe, an advocate. I have listened to your arguments and, on the whole, I am in accord. I believe in the sanctity of the human body, male or female. The tissue with which you have been working is totally artificial in the sense that it was generated by genetic engineering and did not involve any human starting material. It could be argued that the samples are not really human at all. The cell collections, fetuses if you like, have never been allowed to mature, nor will they ever be". He paused to clear his glasses thoughtfully; then nodding his he continued before continuing.

"We need the material and we have the technology to prepare it, without waiting for the appropriate type of cadaver or getting the permission of an emotional mother who has just had a budding life eliminated from her body. This system is clean, devoid of all complex moral and emotional issues. Our living tissue is purely the product of technology, not of mating and mothering."

While still shocked by the implications of Dr. Peters' research, both women found his final argument compelling but sobering. After a moment's pause in which Mary Ann noted Laurie's concern, she concluded, "I can see that like me you have mixed emotions on this topic. So did I and in fact I still do; but in the end I did accept the logic of his position and I agreed to become Dr. Peters' assistant."

Another momentous decision in the entwining of our tale had just been made. Another important step had just been enabled by this discussion.

Smash and Run Raid

Even as our government fought to manage the challenges of a new generation of computers and major bio-engineering developments, the United States was engaged in a war, in South America. The subject of the war is of no interest to this chronicle; but the action provided training and specialized skills and created relationships that ultimately played critical roles in The Outrage.

His back braced against a tree trunk several times his own diameter, Tiny sat on the moist ground of the Central American Forest his gaping backpack propped beside him. Arrayed before him on a large sheet of camouflage GoreTex was the paraphernalia of his specialty: plastic explosive, fuses, wires, batteries, a few hand tools and other items not so easily identified by the non-specialist. As he stared into the tropical jungle surrounding the camp, his hands, seemingly of their own volition, busily selected, fondled, and carefully packed away the items he had selected for tonight's mission.

To a casual observer, Tiny's movements would have appeared random and unguided, the aimless activities of one who awaits departure on a dangerous mission he'd rather not undertake. Actually, there was nothing random about his packing; he had simply done it so often that it proceeded without his conscious guidance. When circumstances required it, as they surely would on this mission, those same hands would unerringly extract the appropriate items from the pack while his wary eyes remained free to search out the suitable spot for the placement of the charges.

Nearby, the other members of Terry Parker's squad, each lost in his private reverie, prepared himself for the coming incursion. This was the quiet time, just before the mission. Terry had told them only that they were going to move out in five minutes on a smash and run raid. He never told them much more than that before a mission. "The Army operates on a strict need to know basis," he was fond of saying; "and you bastards don't need to know anything but to damn well do as I tell you."

Tiny idly surveyed the squad; he did not really know them at all, nor did he wish to do so. Each man had his own ritual of preparation at times like these; mostly involving the checking or fondling of a particular weapon. He wondered if any of them sent forth a silent prayer. Strange! He knew the killing and tracking skills of every man in the detail; he knew their physical limits, but nothing about their backgrounds or beliefs. Oh, he had some private guesses. "Terry, the young red necked 'four stripper' in charge of the squad is from Louisiana or someplace like that. That's obvious from his talk. The bastard wouldn't last an hour spouting "nigger" and shit like that around my neighborhood, none of my god dammed neighborhoods," Tiny thought.

In this squad no one ever talked about personal matters; not girl friends or families back home. The jungle Quick Hit Squads, QHS as they were called, had the highest casualty rates of the entire campaign and Terry's guys had watched too many other QHS guys in other squads mourn the loss of close comrades. This squad had run more missions than anyone could remember, and they had always returned intact. They all knew that that record couldn't last. Their unspoken belief that the next mission would bring disaster grew with the completion of each casualty free patrol. Each success made them more wary of close relationships. They could not avoid the inevitable; but their relative anonymity might lessen the pain for the survivors.

Tiny's eyes rested finally on 'Gambler', standing just behind Terry. Gambler's long slender fingers were also busy carefully drawing the blade of a long stiletto across the face of a well worn whetstone. The stiletto was only one of numerous knives carried by Gambler. "Rat's a better name for that shifty eyed bastard with the fake English accent." Tiny thought. Even as his fingers guided the long steel blade, Gambler's eyes darted right and left, up and down, never seeming to rest anywhere. His face had the slightly pinched look, a wide forehead, receding hairline, a narrow chin, long nose and closely spaced eyes. His protruding ears accented his overall rodent like appearance. Tiny's description, however, was based not on Gambler's looks but rather on his behavior. "The son of a bitch would bet on anything. But to start betting which of us won't come back from which mission is the fuckin' limit."

Tiny's ruminations were interrupted with a shout, "Awright ya lazy bastards, off your asses and on your feet and pay attention. Seems the natives've had another drop, a big fuckin' pile o'weapons and shit. Well, we're gonna blow all that shit sky high tonight, before they got a chance to hide it all over this stinkin' bug infested jungle." Here, Terry paused before continuing, grimaced and looked nervously around his feet thinking "You can never tell where them stinking bugs might be crawling".

Terry had never recovered from his early childhood encounter with spiders and his time in the jungle only aggravated his phobia. In fact he was never to overcome his feeling of repulsion at the thought or sight of 'bugs.' Ultimately, that phobia will prove to be an important factor in this Chronicle and part of its ultimate resolution.

Aloud he added, "We know where the drop was and we know the 'insurgs' weren't ready to receive it. The stuff's just piled up waiting for the 'hidie holes' and tunnels to be dug. The bastards can dig quicker'n moles. By tomorrow evening there won't be a trace of the drop left. So we blow it tonight." Terry paused; it was the longest and most detailed explanation he had ever given to his squad. They grew restive and suspicious at this out of character behavior.

Sensing their reactions, he continued, "In this case you needed to know that. These insurgs are hard up for arms and will guard this shit like it was God's tent or somethin'. It ain't gonna be an easy strike. That's why we're the QHS that's handling it. These birds are terrific trackers and they run faster just gettin' a drink than we could do with track shoes which we ain't got. They'll run right at us once they know we're there, none of that flanking bullshit for them. It's <u>not manly enough</u>. But they don't come screamin' and hollerin' like the bloody Indians they are. They come silent, swift, and nearly invisible.

"Tiny, fix up a few bundles simple enough that even Gambler and George can plant them in the insurgs' weapons pile. You're going to be busy shielding our asses.

"We send Gambler and George on a big detour to the far side of the camp. After they're in place we stage a frontal attack on the dump. We'll attack like banshees ourselves; but we're going to give up the attack pretty quick and beat a fast retreat. You'll build a maze of traps, safe as houses when we go through and impossible to pass through right after we pass. When the fireworks start, Gambler and George will deliver the presents you make for them. Can do?"

"Course I can spring that trap. Piece a cake. But I ain't sure anyone can rig a bomb simple enough for them two assholes to operate," Tiny said good naturedly.

Tiny's creative ways of packaging explosive was crucial to the success of every raid planned by Terry. After serving his time with the military, he further honed his explosive skills in the civilian world working as a demolitions expert. Thus the way was paved for his contributions to The Outrage action plan to play a key role in The Outrage.

He didn't like either George or the Gambler, but he knew Terry was sending them in because they could each move more quietly than the natives themselves. George was a quick learner, he listened and was methodical. Gambler could kill faster with those knives than most men could with rifles and he could do it with a lot less noise. Tiny was confident that they would plant his charges if anyone could. Before he hoisted his pack his hands had extracted fuses and timers, which he stuffed into his pockets. Before they reached the destination, he would have assembled the essential parts of the bombs they needed.

"Bullshit, Tiny," Gambler hissed. "What are the odds that your God damned bombs won't go off anyway? George and I will probably have to light the bastards with a match. Never mind. Not sure I want to bet with you anyway. Anyone interested in even money that the midget doesn't return from this one?"

"Head out. We start off to the east," Terry's bellow cut off further comment. Heading out each reviewed their "after the war plans." Tiny liked blowing things up and envisioned a future in civilian demolition. Gambler had no doubts that his betting skills would lead to a vast improvement in his life style. George, on the other hand, just wanted out; he'd find something to do after that.

All four of the men of this squad would survive the war and go their separate ways and continue to hone their particular skills and ultimately reunite to play additional roles in our story.

First of Two Visitors to NAMBE

This first young man, visiting NAMBE for the very first time, would play two separate and distinct roles in evolution of The Outrage. His second role was widely acclaimed; indeed, he received the major credit for the resolution of the situation. However, his first and primary role was never officially acknowledged by anyone until this chronicle. It was in fact not even disclosed to Ames himself and had it not been for his deductive prowess he would never have known of it. As it happens, he is involved in many of the entanglements of this chronicle though in some cases one must look very closely to detect his influence.

Idly flipping the pages of the brochure he had been handed by the receptionist, Ames Fromme, a lightly tanned slender youth, stood quietly at the rear of the line entering the central auditorium of NAMBE, the National Agency for Micro Biological Engineering. Ames was intently interested in the Facility. As he scanned the handout, he was in fact memorizing its contents. Not that this required a special effort; he couldn't keep from committing it to memory any more than he could avoid remembering anything he observed with any of his senses. Remembering was simply something his mind did.

His interest was not simply the passing curiosity of a visitor who has traveled a long distance to join a tour; Ames hoped to be offered a research position at the Facility as soon as he received his master's degree this spring.

The brochure described the Facility as the most advanced microbiological research complex ever conceived. Its introduction included reference to a favored comparison.

"DEDICATED TO THE ERADICATION OF HUNGER AND THE ELIMINATION OF MAN'S DISEASES AND GENETIC DISORDERS, NAMBE IS REFERRED TO BY MANY AS THE NASA OF THE TWENTY FIRST CENTURY. SUCH REFERENCES ORIGINALLY ARE INTENDED AS CYNICAL COMMENTARY ON THE SCALE OF THE FINANCIAL COMMITMENT TO THE AGENCY. HOWEVER, THERE ARE MORE SIMILARITIES BETWEEN NASA AND NAMBE THAN COST. IN PARTICULAR:

1. LIKE NASA, NAMBE'S RESEARCH IS UNCLASSIFIED, AND THE RESULTS ARE FREELY AND OPENLY SHARED WITH THE WORLD.
2. NAMBE INVITES QUALIFIED INVESTIGATORS FROM ALL NATIONS TO PARTICIPATE, BOTH THROUGH FUNDED RESEARCH IN THEIR OWN LABORATORIES AND THROUGH TEMPORARY APPOINTMENTS AT THE FACILITY.
3. THE PUBLIC IS KEPT INFORMED OF THE PROGRAMS AND THE PROGRESS TOWARD THEIR GOALS. INDEED, THE PUBLIC IS INVITED AT REGULAR INTERVALS TO VISIT AND TOUR THE FACILITY AS YOU ARE DOING NOW."

As Ames read, *his mind* noted, detected, monitored and memorized the random sounds and movements of the rest of the tour. As they were being ushered into the main conference hall, he quietly shifted over to join them as they were led into the comfortable main auditorium with its nine hundred upholstered seats, each containing its own headset, by means of which a visitor could select any one of several languages in which to hear the presentation. The room was far too vast for the public visitors, which were limited to ninety. But the Executive Director felt that meeting here created the correct first impression for the visiting public.

It was early spring, and this tour had begun like every other tour of the NAMBE Facility, had begun with visitors receiving visitor's badges, a map, and a brochure then made their way to the main auditorium.

The entrance to the Facility had been through the Large 'Ultra Atrium' which covered several acres in front of the building. In addition to an incredibly wide variety of plants, the Ultra Atrium boasted an impressive waterfall cascading down the rugged face of a thirty-foot high butte like stone. The garden's serpentine paths were composed of glistening, tightly packed, crushed white stone and formed a meandering trail so contrived as to assure that a casual stroll would reward the pedestrian with a continually varying and sharply contrasting view of botanical wonders each of which had been produced by bio-engineering. Invisible walls of quietly moving vertical drafts separated regions of widely varying environments. After a few short steps from the near tropical area at the base of the waterfall, one passed almost without notice through the first air wall and into an arid desert. Here also a wide variety of plants bombarded the visual and olfactory senses. As one followed the winding path, other changes were less abrupt but included the entire range of botanically recognized environments. For the harried or the distracted a direct route led straight through the Ultra Atrium to the reception area bypassing these wonders of bio-engineering.

The visitors had entered through the picturesque path, ending at the reception desk. The perky receptionist had directed them to the auditorium on the ground floor, which was referred to as Level

Zero in the brochure. There, plied with coffee and doughnuts, the day's guests had finally seated themselves and awaited the arrival of their host, the eminent Dr. Quentin Quincy, Executive Director of NAMBE. It was Dr. Q's custom to enter the auditorium only after everyone was settled comfortably into their seats; he did not want less than their full attention.

Second of Two Visitors

The second visitor, a young man named Terry, also visiting NAMBE for the first time, was destined to sit at the very center of The Outrage; he and many others would describe him as the central cause of the entire chain of events. While I admit that he played a key role, it should be clear by now that there was no single isolated "cause" of The Outrage and no single central character. However, Terry's connections to the events are numerous; and to many they did appear to have been causal.

Included in the audience was another young man, this one in his late twenties, dressed in a lightweight turtleneck and a tan leather blazer. With his slightly battered briefcase lying in his lap, Terry Parker leaned back in his seat, soaking up the luxury of his surroundings. He ignored the others in the room and turned his attention to the careful study of the documents he had received at the reception desk.

His plans required that he have a reasonable feeling for the layout of this place. "Of course, the physical arrangement's easy enough to learn", he thought contemptuously. "these government jerks provide every visitor with a free scale map of the entire complex including a scaled floor plan of the Facility itself, the private airport, and the residential areas. A fool could plan the entire final phase of his operation from these documents alone."

"I'm the best," he reflected, "and this place's not the biggest challenge I've ever had. Not by a long shot. If it weren't for the money and the chance to teach 'them' a lesson, I might not do it at all. But there will be money and, man, will they ever notice! The whole damned world will know the name Terry Parker."

On the last page of the handout he found the only section of the brochure that really interested him, Facility Security.

At the time the Facility was constructed, there was considerable fear and mistrust associated with bio-engineering. Popular writers, both fictional and journalistic, had presented the public with an endless diet of horror stories and threats of monsters and runaway pestilence. The voting public wanted a central bio-engineering facility; the voting public was also afraid of such a facility. The answer lay in creating a laboratory from which even the most virulent microbe could not escape. To Terry's mind the key elements of the security system were found in its opening section which is reprinted below.

Facility Security

At the time NAMBE was formed, a law was passed requiring that any laboratory or other facility involved in the research, testing, or evaluation of bioengineered materials have a Class A Security Rating. Terry read carefully from the brochure

"THE FACILITY YOU ARE NOW VISITING IS SUCH A FACILITY: MORE PRECISELY, IT IS A COLLECTION OF SUCH FACILITIES. EVERY LABORATORY OF EVERY SECTOR OF EVERY FLOOR MAY BE SEPARATELY AND HERMETICALLY SEALED. THAT IS, ANY LAB IN ANY SECTOR CAN BE MADE AIRTIGHT. IF THE NEED SHOULD EVER ARISE, EACH SECTOR CAN BE SEALED OFF AND CAN EXIST FOR MORE THAN THIRTY DAYS ON ITS SELF-CONTAINED SUPPLY OF AIR, FOOD, AND WATER, WITH ABSOLUTELY NO CHANCE OF INFECTING ANY OTHER LABORATORY AND CERTAINLY NOT THE WORLD AT LARGE. WHILE IT IS EXTREMELY UNLIKELY THAT ANY EMERGENCY WILL OCCUR DURING YOUR VISIT, WE HAVE INCLUDED AN APPENDIX TO THIS HANDOUT ENTITLED EMERGENCY SECURITY MEASURES THAT EXPLAINS THE VARIOUS LEVELS OF ALERT WHICH ARE INVOKED TO PROTECT THE FACILITY STAFF AND THE OUTSIDE WORLD. BE ASSURED YOU HAVE NOTHING TO

FEAR FROM **NAMBE**, EITHER DURING YOUR VISIT OR
AFTER YOU RETURN HOME."

.As Terry finished reading the security section, the hall became still. The silence flowed from the front row to the rear of the auditorium, like a gentle wave washing away the buzz of whispered conversations. All attention focused on the rostrum at the center of the stage. Dr. Quincy, Executive Director of NAMBE, was acutely aware of the importance of public support to the continued existence of the Facility and it was his practice to personally welcome each of the general public tours.

Dr. Quincy was regularly referred to as Dr. Q, by those who knew him and by those who simply wished to imply that they did, began his historical review.

"Good morning, ladies and gentlemen. I am Dr. Quincy. It is my privilege to welcome you to the Facility; and it is my responsibility to provide you with an overview of our history and objectives. It is my promise to be as brief as possible. In the last decade of the twentieth century, the President was faced with a dilemma. On the one hand was the need to encourage private enterprise to continue its genetic research including the work with recombinant DNA techniques; on the other was the need for government control of these processes to prevent another episode such as followed the Killer Bee attack.

"The success of private enterprise in producing commercially viable solutions to serious health and heredity problems through genetic engineering was astounding, over taxing the government's ability to test and approve the resultant drugs. Likewise, new strains of plants, organisms and animals all had to be evaluated. The developers, as well as the public, grew impatient with the FDA's seemingly endless testing requirements, while at the same time complaining that people died needlessly because of improperly tested and evaluated treatments. They wanted results. Yet, no one dared risk another episode of sleeping cows and dying babies.

"Some of you may be too young to remember those frightening events and the panic they generated. But it would not be an exaggeration to say that one incident on a Texas fairground changed the world. Events seemed to snowball: from the horrifying Killer Bee attack which resulted in the death of the young 4H Club girl to the decimation of Texas dairy herds to the more than four hundred babies and fifty adults who died in silent contortions. The world watched in near panic. Yes, bio-engineering had eliminated the Killer Bee, but a high price was paid for that success. Like some B movie monster, the manmade microbe MB Twelve had gone berserk.

"The trail back to MB Twelve, as the source of the problems, is too circuitous to discuss here. However, for those of you interested in the history, a reasonably detailed summary of the challenges is presented in the material given to you with your brochure.

"The government's attempts to contain the crisis and avoid panic were not altogether successful. This was a genuine disaster of epic proportions. But new products and new methods of producing old reliable ones, or the apparent equivalents of old reliable ones, were emerging at an increasing rate; and even while complaining about the disaster, the public was demanding these new "wonder products."

"Extensive testing was needed to demonstrate the safety of these new developments before they were released. A major government initiative was demanded; and this agency was born. As originally conceived, NAMBE was to be simply a national testing laboratory. Events were to drastically change that view."

Nodding in one of the back rows, Terry grew impatient with the length of the speech. He mumbled, loud enough to be heard several rows away, "You better damn well change your speech, Doc, or there won't be any goddamned audience left."

But, Dr. Q droned on, "As the most important, indeed the only testing facility of its kind, NAMBE would from time to time house and handle all manner of threatening chemicals and biological deviants which could prove fatal to mankind. This fear led to the selection of this remote uninhabited location as the home of the Facility.

"Of course if there are no inhabitants there are no houses or other infrastructure. The testing facility itself would require a staff of several thousand who, with their families, would need considerable services. Micro City was carefully planned to satisfy those needs and to make this remote Nevada location not only an acceptable but actually a desirable place to live.

"The brochure shows the locations of the sports facilities, swimming pools, gymnasium, tennis courts and golf courses with biologically engineered grass of course. Micro City boasts the necessary education facilities as well as a theater and a cinema, both excellent though small. Your visit with us will include some free time to tour Micro City."

Seated well back in the audience, the attentive young Ames seemed to be listening intently to Dr. Q's presentation. In fact, Ames would later be able to repeat Dr. Q's speech verbatim should the need arise; but even as he listened to Dr. Q, he was thinking of the changes about to take place in his own life. In three short months, he a member of the genetic research staff here at the Facility. Leaving the university was often on his mind; he would be only eighteen when he finished his master's degree; and there had been numerous discussions of continuing his studies to obtain a PhD. But the university had been a total disappointment to him. He felt as estranged and alone there as he had in high school, perhaps more so.

After all these years, he still had difficulty coming to grips with the fact that he was so different. From childhood through school and college his differences always got in the way of his being accepted by his peers. Surely here, working with some of the best researcher in the world, he would not be so unusual and would easily 'fit in.' He sincerely hoped NAMBE would prove to be 'his place.'

Dr Q. dragged on, "Even before the City and the Facility were completed in the year 2000, two different, apparently unrelated scientific breakthroughs occurred that were to change the entire approach to the problem. In an almost completely ignored paper, Dr. Millard Morris had presented his theory for modeling molecular and atomic interactions by computer techniques. In theory, laboratory chemistry became totally unnecessary. However, the amount of computation required strangled the most sophisticated computers of the day. The promise of the Morris theory and the true usefulness of the model had to await another breakthrough.

"Dr. Benton Cochran's work with the tenth generation computer made Morris's modeling a reality. It would not be an exaggeration to say that these two technological breakthroughs have unalterably changed the world. Chance mutations, evolution, and time consuming crossbreeding are no longer the principal sources of new life forms or compounds. Mankind can now unerringly design even the most complicated new life form."

At this point, Dr. Q noticed the three young black women who sat up attentively apart the other visitors; from their demeanor he assumed they were students. In his experience the students who attended these tours were generally bored by the history of the Facility itself and its security measures, while they became very interested in the technical aspects of his presentations. The general public, on the other hand, reacted in just the opposite way.

"Even with the Facility's computer it often takes several days to check the required interactions for a single molecule. Such an evaluation is the equivalent of several years of testing with the actual compound or microbe. Our computers are all located on Level One, that is, on the first floor below ground level.

"The extensive laboratories on the remaining six subterranean levels of the Facility prepare, chemically and biologically, those compounds and microbes required for final testing jof a new life form.

"Of course, the highlight of your visit is the tour of the Facility itself, not a protracted and boring speech from its Executive Director. In order to encourage your questions I have arranged for some of my assistants to escort you in small groups. I do hope you will feel free to ask questions or comment on what you see. There are no secrets here at NAMBE, though there are some areas into which entry is forbidden for safety reasons. In most places you will be able to observe the activities either directly or by means of television monitors. In all cases my staff will do their best to assure that your visit is both enjoyable and informative. Thank you for your patience."

Stretching and yawning in the next to last row, Terry mumbled, "About time, you pompous old bastard."

Terry had, in fact, been scarcely aware of Dr. Q during the entire presentation. Rather, he had been recalling with relish the ease with which he had solved the problem of obtaining an army of loyal followers for his planned operation. He would not need the army for long, maybe ten minutes; but when he needed it, he would really need it. The eggheads had to be stunned into inaction for a few minutes only. After that the entire army was expendable.

He had long since realized that he was not a charismatic leader who inspired men to follow him anywhere. As he told himself, "My mind is so deep and my plans so convoluted that at best only a few could begin to understand."

He quietly reviewed his leadership style, which he perceived as 'subtle,' it involved dividing his plans into small portions, and sharing only those portions necessary with the lieutenants he recruited and controlled by one on one meetings. His three widely differing lieutenants for the present plan were not even aware of each other's existence. He grimaced at that thought. "It was a damn good thing. The only time he ever shared his entire plan with anyone his partner had totally fucked it up and landed them both in jail. No, each of those creeps served his or her purpose best if their little minds had only to cope with the minimum amount of information necessary to do their jobs. One goddamned thing the army had right was, operate on a strict 'need to know basis.' The turkeys don't need to know much.

He caught Dr. Q's final words. "You will be divided into groups of fifteen for the actual tour. On entering the conference room you were each given a colored badge to identify the group with which you will tour. Your guides are wearing similarly colored badges. Once again, thank you for your interest in our Facility."

Checking the color of his badge, Terry meandered over and joined the Red forming around a relatively plain, symmetrically featured woman whose badge identified her as Dr. Kim Newcombe. She looked crisp, neat and attractive despite her round figure and an overly practical taste in shoes.

Terry noticed that, while sexually a mixed bag, the forming around Dr. Newcombe was almost homogeneous in color, all black:

"No, not blacks, niggers. All this liberal bullshit might lead to better homes, jobs, and educations but you can't make a nigger white by calling him black instead of colored."

Still, there was one white man in the, he noted. Or was he white? Certainly, he had a white man's features. Was the color of his skin just a tan? Terry edged closer to the apparently white man. He did not particularly want to start a conversation, "But if I have to talk at least I won't talk with a nigger."

The Tour and a Visitor's Introspection Begin

Standing quietly at the back of the group and listening to Dr. Newcombe's tour outline, Ames continued to review the paths of his life that had led him here. Without interrupting his reverie or neglecting Dr. Newcombe's words, Ames noticed the slow, almost guarded approach of the man in the leather blazer and boots. His visible characteristics passed effortlessly into Ames prodigious memory: blond hair, lean, average height; small half-moon scar on the left cheek just below the eye; deep green, constantly roving eyes; short soft footsteps. All these details and considerably more, in fact every visually discernible characteristic of Terry and his clothes, were 'noticed' along with those of everyone else. For Ames, 'notice' was a generic expression he used to describe anything detected by his highly developed senses. Everything noticed by Ames could accurately and effortlessly noted and filed away. This ability along with its accompanying total recall were two of the reasons that Ames was here in the first place.

As he used it the term 'notice' also included the inferences he drew from the observation. If he observed some small facial twitch, perhaps too slight to be noticed by others, and that led him to conclude subconsciously that the person was worried or nervous, he included this inference as "noticed." There was never a conscious effort required on his part to 'notice' things. He just did.

His attempt to explain this part of his makeup had led to numerous frustrating conversations. At first, his frustration stemmed from his ignorance of the fact that he was different from others. He had naturally assumed everyone had similar sensory abilities and memories. Once over that hurdle of misunderstanding, his frustration was with his lack of ability to describe to others the workings of his mind. Out of disappointment with his failure to explain, he had developed a compromise, a canned description, for those few people who penetrated his defenses sufficiently to know there was something to explain. "My consciousness is on several levels, or parallel streams. Each or indeed all of them, as far as I know, can be explored in whatever detail I choose. The detail with which I explore has nothing to do with the amount of sensory information that is being stored in my memory, or the depth to which I am exploring one of the other streams. I don't know if there is a limit to the number of different streams of consciousness. I can use. I'm not sure I would I know how to determine the limit, if there is one. Remember, this is simply the best picture or analogy that I can think of or give; and like any analogy, it's dangerous to stretch it too far. Certainly, I can simultaneously monitor each of my senses in minute detail while at the same time pursuing another endeavor, say, playing chess. I can equally well choose not to examine the sensory streams and later recall in detail what they were. Ignoring one or more of the streams has no apparent effect on any other stream. For example, ignoring sounds does not improve my chess game."

Even this simplified picture seemed impossible for his associates and friends to understand. Those who did were invariably incredulous and insisted on a test or demonstration, after which most suspected trickery. Others were frightened by what they could not understand. Finally, end he simply chose not to attempt to explain. After a time, he developed the knack of hiding his unusual abilities. Since leaving high school, Ames had mentioned his differences to no one. Instead, he began the studies that had brought him to the Facility. After graduation, he hoped to take up a position in the Statistical Studies Section of the Genetics Department.

Even as he was recalling the paths that had led him here, another stream of his mind was comparing the young man approaching him to the images stored away in his prodigious memory. This comparing and cataloguing occurred with no conscience effort on his part. However, since entering the university he had taken pains to avoid meeting people from his past . . . at least that portion of his past of which he was aware. He knew there was a time before his continuous memory, before his father and mother, Ben and Alice, that is, who were all the parents he had ever known. He referred to that time as his "before". In his "before" there were other images, images for which there were no names and or continuity with the present, but these images were real. He kept searching for a misplaced but familiar face.

That was another bothersome thought. There could be no people, not a single person in his living past, of whom his catalogue of memories did not contain an image. He was sure of that. He was also sure there should be faces in his "before", but he had never been able to recall them.

"I never forget anything," he thought. "My memories include images, visual, auditory, olfactory, and tactical, from experiences that occurred before I even possessed a language with which to label them." I must have come from someplace. I must belong to someone like me but where and who?"

The image of the young man in the leather blazer was matched. He had appeared in a newspaper article. Terry Parker, arrested for burglary with two armed accomplices was later released on probation in exchange for giving evidence against one of his partners, a dealer in narcotics. Further details, while there for his examination, were of no particular interest to Ames at the moment and were, accordingly, ignored and filed away again. The purpose of his search had been to assure that his anonymity was not threatened. Ames quickly scanned the other members of the tour, as he had Terry, as he did everyone. They posed neither a threat to his precious anonymity nor clue to his background. The students had quite obviously traveled here together and, while not discourteous to the two Caucasians, did tend to keep to themselves much to the satisfaction of Terry. Ames, on the other hand, did not care whether or not they spoke to him. The fact of segmenting of the group along color lines passed, unremarked, into his memory. Openly snubbing him would have produced no more emotion.

Actually, he was not really capable of very deep emotional reactions or feelings. The question of his origins was perhaps the only exception. His reaction to this question could be explained as frustration at the only failure he had ever experienced in his life.

Two Quick Glimpses

Leaving the conference room, Dr. Newcombe led them directly to the desert plants of the Ultra Atrium and formally began her explanations from there.

"The Ultra Atrium is more than simply an extravagant showplace designed to consume the taxpayers' money. It is a testimonial to the power of genetic engineering in the controlled and systematic development of botanical specimens. Every plant here in every controlled zone was derived from the same seed. Characteristics of the original plant were selectively eliminated, enhanced, or otherwise modified to produce a plant suitable to each of the artificially created and controlled environments. In principle, it would not have been necessary to have even the first plant to construct the material that would eventually become this plant or that one," she explained as she pointed out two particularly vivid specimens of contrasting colors and shapes.

"Unfortunately, while we can guess a structure and then predict precisely what characteristics it will produce in its appropriate environment, our computers cannot go the other way. That is, they can't deduce the structure required to produce the characteristic. Experience, accumulated knowledge as well as occasional big intuitive jumps are required to arrive at the desired structure in an economically feasible time. Eventually, an appropriate structure is determined, usually only one of many possibilities, each with different side traits.

"In principle each of these subsidiary traits could be calculated using the Morris model. But because of the tremendous time that would be consumed with such a complete analysis, it is customary to model only those characteristics that are of particular interest to the bio-engineer. Occasionally this approach leads to some undesirable traits, and the process may have to be repeated several times to obtain a fully acceptable result. For example, color may not be a targeted characteristic in the fruit of an edible plant; however, it is not hard to imagine colors one would not like to have in table food. Should an engineered fruit contain a truly offensive color, or texture, the next run would include control of those factors."

Terry had heard enough to pass judgment on Dr. Newcombe. "What a Dumb bitch she is! She's worse than her goddamned boss."

Dr. Newcombe continued her explanations, "In producing the plants in this living museum, we took no pains to produce any particular characteristic except adaptability to the specified environment and compatibility with human life. While not necessarily tasty or nourishing, any of these plants could be ingested by the average human with no ill effects. Of course, none of these plants are allowed to reproduce or to leave this building. Where you see a group of similar plants, they are in reality all clones produced as a in the laboratory."

Terry had missed most of the description. He was uncomfortable standing near plants, especially such a vast collection of them. "Who knows what the hell kind of bugs are hidden in there, quietly waiting their chance to gorge themselves on my blood." One of the visitors brushed lightly against a large leaf causing it to brush against a smaller leaf. The resultant motion sent a small shadow across the face of the large flower at the edge of Terry's vision. He jumped back from the brightly colored plant brushing the front of his jacket. He looked around nervously, hoping no one had noticed. He concluded that no one had noticed.

However, he was wrong. The young Ames, who noticed everything within range of his senses, of course noted the entire incident, including that bug-like shadow motion that Terry had seen. With no conscience effort Ames had filed the observation was filed away.

As it happened this extraneous observation was to be later recalled and to prove extremely useful.

The tour moved on through a seemingly endless variety of simulated climates, each filled with its own botanical wonders. Terry remained totally disinterested and continually on guard for marauding insects, until at last he was relaxed enough to begin to notice that one of the students was quite shapely; "Of course, she's just a nigger, but she sure is stacked."

"Are there any questions before we proceed to the main portion of the Facility?" Dr. Newcombe asked as she concluded her latest explanation.

They had come to that portion of the Ultra Atrium designed to simulate the latter part of the Arctic growing season. To an audience dressed for a tour out west the chill was not conducive to standing around and asking a lot of questions. There was more than a little truth to the view held by the Facility staff that the Ultra Atrium tour was arranged to end here for just that reason. With only moderate success Dr. Newcombe tried to appear cheerful, as she concluded this part of the tour. "If there is nothing else at this point, we will move back into the main building. This time we will proceed beyond the auditorium to the point where the hall breaks off to the left.

But before proceeding, let me take a minute to explain the layout of the Facility. The structure is octagonal in design. Including this ground floor, the Facility has eight floors that we refer to as levels. The levels are numbered according to their position below the surface. Thus, we are on Level Zero, ground level. The inner portions of each level are all color coded, as are the radial corridors that connect them. The color codes of this level are repeated on each of the seven subterranean levels. We will enter into the Tan, or Administrative, segment. The corridor along which we are proceeding is a 'Spoke Corridor' leading to the center of the building. There are eight concentric peripheral or Ring Corridors, at fixed intervals along the spoke corridors. Each Ring Corridors passes through each of the segments. We shall precede along the Tan Spoke, to Ring 0, the one nearest to the center, and work our way clockwise around the building on the shortest route."

A Quick Glimpse

Ames looked up at the sound of footsteps coming out of the main building and hurrying toward the Arctic section of the Ultra

Atrium. The sounds were caused by the passage of a tall woman with raven black hair. Actually, she was far enough away that the sound of her gliding footsteps was unnoticed by everyone else in the room. Ames noticed that she was in a hurry long, quick strides. He was still looking in that direction when she came into view, slowing her pace perceptibly, so as not to disturb Dr. Newcombe's explanations. In his usual manner, he noted her striking good looks and her cool detachment and then turned his attention back to the tour leader "We will take a few detours through the working areas."

Suddenly, Ames' mind jerked. He pulled up short. He felt disturbed, uneasy. "What is it? Something correlated. What correlated with what? Where? How? He always knew; well, almost always. "Search slowly, stream by stream," he instructed himself. Some thought I was pursuing, an origin question perhaps? No. What was it, a smell, a sound, a touch, a taste? No. No. No. No! What then, a sighting? What?" In less time than it takes to describe, he tested every visual stimulus of the past ninety seconds against the stored images of a lifetime. "No match!"

Feeling uneasy about this apparent lapse, Ames admonished himself, "Open your memory window wider." He repeated the indescribable process, expanding the time period to include visual images of the last five minutes. No help. It, whatever it was, was gone as if it had ever existed. Only twice before in his life had he experienced such lack of a match.

"Try one more time. What was I doing? What was I thinking? Simply relaxing and letting the stimuli go unnoticed. I was half listening to the tour guide with everything else essentially on automatic. Of course I would have routinely matched every new face against my past; I've been doing that for three years now. There was only one the tall, cool, striking brunette."

Troubled and strangely anxious, he followed the tour as it moved along Tan Spoke. *Much later, during a time of crisis, he would recall those moments and those feelings and be keenly influenced by them. Their influence would be with him for the rest of his life.*

A Moment of Doubt

While trying to remain inconspicuous, Terry idled along with the tourist concentrating on memorizing the path through the maze of NAMBE corridors. In spite of his contempt for what he called "all those small minded suckers who labor over their microscopes and computer screens until blinded," he was awed by the vastness of the Facility and of the entire operation. For the first time he began to question, if only briefly, his ability to carry out the scheme he had conceived and so carefully executed up to this point.

Arrogantly, he confronted his shadow of doubt. "I totally duped those idealistic fools of the ASPGH, (what a pompous title, 'The American Society for the Preservation of God and Humanity.' They're more pompous than the famous Dr. Q. Twisting them around my little finger was simple as pie. His confidence, never very far submerged, returned with those thoughts. "The final stages of the plan will go just as smoothly in the next three months.

"Still, there are a lot of people here, and the place is gigantic. But they're all eggheads or egghead helpers; and there is no security at all. Look how easily we got in. They didn't even open my damned briefcase. It'll be child's play. Well, maybe not quite child's play; but certainly it'll be no challenge for a genius in spite the size and remoteness of the place. Those are simply two important factors in my favor; both are advantages, not difficulties. The whole world will hear of this, the biggest coup in history!" With that thought, his spirits soared and he strode along with purpose.

The Roots of a National Movement

At this point, it is no doubt clear that NAMBE and its Facility are at the center of The Outrage. Another much smaller organization considered by many to be part of the 'lunatic fringe,' also played a key role in the near catastrophe. This organization, the ASPGH, was an outgrowth of the ASPCA, which opposed the use of bio-engineering technology from two points of view: it was fundamentally both cruel to animals and counter to the will of God. A complete history of the

ASPGH would be out of place in this chronicle. However, a few of the events in the evolution of the organization had significant impacts on the developments being reported; and I will briefly report them here.

Under Clear Skies

Jane Wilde is mentioned in nearly every article that discusses The Outrage. However, such articles invariably deal solely with her relationships with the ASPCA and with the founder of the American Society for the Preservation of God and Humanity, ASPGH. However, the roots of her involvement in both of those movements and ultimately in The Outrage can be traced even further back to the ranting of a college professor. Here we get a glimpse at some of the effects of the new sciences.

In San Diego, Jane Wilde's lunch, scarcely touched, sat on the coffee table before her. Outside, gleaming sidewalks, already heated to griddle-like temperatures, continued to absorb the searing onslaught of the early afternoon sun. Not a single cloud marred the pale blue canopy of the sky. More than a hundred miles overhead, reconnaissance satellites silently and inconspicuously monitored the movement of everything larger than a mouse. The crystal clear sky provided no shield at all from the either the searing rays of the near tropical sun or the prying eyes of the satellite spies orbiting overhead.

Even those people who were old enough that smog was a part of their personal memory had difficulty reconciling their crisp vision of the surrounding mountains with the memories of burning eyes and misty-appearing views of bygone times. Southern California had changed atmospherically, but only atmospherically. The principal factor in the steadily growing population continued to be immigration. Indeed, the other kind of population growth, caused by an excessive birthrate, was no longer a problem anywhere in the United States. Few people could recall the time when San Diego and Los Angeles were separate cities, rather than merely neighborhoods of the largest megalopolis in the world. Progress? Scarcely any cocktail hour was concluded without a boisterous debate over the benefits or curses of the squeaky clean atmosphere.

The total absence of pollutants was made possible by the genetically engineered microbe, Microscopic Atmospheric Janitors, MAJ. According to the press releases, MAJ fed on sulfite ions and hydrocarbons while catalyzing the conversion of toxic carbon monoxide to harmless carbon dioxide." In deference to the fears of another episode like that following the elimination of the Killer Bee, the microbe's genetic structure had been so designed that its reproductive capacity diminished geometrically with each generation. The precise knowledge of its metabolism and its built in self destruction mechanism were both made possible by the Morris Modeling technology.

Bio-engineering made it possible to calculate precisely how many Microscopic Atmospheric Janitors, MAJ, should be released into the atmosphere each month. In this way the atmosphere was kept clean with no danger of the microbe's multiplying out of control and causing another disaster. Pollution was unknown and had been for nearly two decades now, the MAJ having been developed in the first two years of NAMBE's operation.

Of course A57 was not the only factor; pollutant controls had also helped. Indeed, one of the objections to the MAJ was that its very effectiveness made the enforcement of the antipollution laws extremely difficult; others argued that such controls were no longer necessary. The more rational complaints about the selfless cleaner of the sky stemmed from the dangers of increased exposure to ultraviolet radiation and the rejuvenated flood of immigrants who arrived after cleansing of the California skies.

Inside, Jane Wilds sat nodding absently while mouthing the words of a familiar ballad whose melancholy sound spilled forth from four corner speakers, flooding her study and blending easily with the casual disarray that surrounded her.

Picking at the remainder of her lunch, she reviewed in her mind the events of the last four years, events that had relentlessly led her from wonder to dedication, from passion to frustration and near despair, and finally to Terry and a new hope. Terry Parker was unlike anyone else she had ever known. At times his sharp mood changes frightened her. Still, without Terry, the Movement would have been finished long ago. Now, thanks to Terry's scheme, it was standing at the threshold of national no, international exposure and recognition.

"Can we actually execute the Plan? Terry has been right so far," she mused. "We all knew that it was impossible to build an effective organization without funds and it had always been difficult to raise money, even with Gregg's eloquence."

Gregg had said it best: "Few people want to hear our message, that the very technology that is repeatedly solving problem after problem for the civilized world is capable of destroying the very culture that spawned it. Yet this science is not only capable of such destruction; it is already destroying our most fundamental values, without which civilization has no meaning."

Unable to control her frustration, she had once blurted out to Terry, "Why can't they see?"

Terry had responded with characteristically vulgar sarcasm, "They are blinded by the God damned beautiful blue smog-free sky; that's why." That thought jolted her reverie back farther, to the time before Terry.

There was no disputing the fact that genetic engineering had produced many improvements in the life of mankind. She herself had been a believer. In fact it was only in researching a term paper that she began to understand the true horrors of genetic engineering in general and of the Morris Modeling process in particular. A lot had happened since the term paper; her entire outlook and understanding of the important things in life had matured since then. "Still," she wondered, "can our plan really be justified? Is there no other way?"

A Term Paper Gets Rejected

Had an unknown college professor not over-reacted to a student's term paper, the ASPGH may never have been created. The path that led from Professor Thorens to the ASPGH was clear to Jane alone, but her involvement and contributions to the Movement were a matter of pride and satisfaction for her. However, had she had the slightest inkling of how the Movement was to be hijacked and disgraced; in fact she would never know until it actually happened and it was too late.

Yes, she could and often did retrace her involvement in the Movement to that damned term paper.

During the last few months she had frequently had voiced doubts about her grand plan to elevate the ASPGH to international status. At such times, her mind could often be eased by reviewing the history of the Movement and the progress of the Morris Modeling technology. With visible effort she once again turned her mind to a review of her first visit to the local chapter of the ASPCA up to the present complex situation.

It had all begun with a term paper she had been preparing for a sociology class. Her topic, the "Effects of Bio-engineering on Modern Civilization" had been chosen by Professor Thorens. After a full day at the library her research had uncovered numerous popular articles on the Morris Modeling technology. "Living molecules can be precisely designed to perform specific functions. No longer is it necessary to run an experimental test in order to know in exquisite detail the interactions of a new life form with any other molecule."

It had seemed to Jane that if this statement were true and an overwhelming amount of evidence indicated that it was, one of the main objectives of the ASPCA had been accomplished. Animal experimentation was surely a thing of the past. This topic, not discussed in any of the articles she had read, might provide the kind of original touch that Professor Thorens appreciated.

To better document her conclusion she decided to visit the local ASPCA office. Locating the office had been a simple matter; the surprise was that it had been so quiet when she arrived. From the appearance of the small, cramped looking lobby, it was probable that the center was rarely not a quiet place. The walls were the regulation tan commonly used by developers who, with no particular tenant in mind wished to create a room that would offend no one; of course it also pleased no one; the equally bland vinyl tile floor covering did nothing to improve the ambiance. Even the wall hangings and metal furnishings, provided by the tenant, the ASPCA, did little to lend character to the room. These drab surroundings seemed to provide the perfect setting for the mousy brown haired receptionist who looked up from the paperback novel surreptitiously held in her lap beneath a partially opened desk drawer. Her startled expression was a mixture of guilt5 and surprise. It waqs clear, to her that people did not often wander into this office unexpectedly.

With noticeable effort she mustered a smile and a "Good morning; may I help you? My name is Julie." As she spoke, she examined the visitor silently noting: "Young, about my own age; average height; lovely honey colored hair, long and lightly waved; nice figure." The visitor was speaking; "My name is Jane Wilds. I'm doing a paper for school on some of the sociological effects of over two decades of Morris Modeling technology. I would like to speak to someone involved in the ASPCA to discuss the impact of all the new developments on the mission of the ASPCA. I'm looking for someone who can provide background information, Jane explained in a rush.

"That would be Mr. Gregory. He isn't in at the moment: he usually arrives around 10:00 AM. Would you like to come back in about an hour

Thinking that she had, after all, come on impulse, she pondered the wisdom of spending more time, "There's little chance of learning anything really significant: I just wanted a little background to add a touch of originality to my paper; but I am here". Aloud, she replied, "Yes, thank you, I will come back in an hour, if that's all right."

"Sure." As though afraid that Jane might not return without some enticement other than a meeting with Mr. Gregory, she added, "Would like to leave your brief case here while you have your coffee?

"No, thanks, let's say 10:15, shall we?

Fine Julie made a show of entering Jane's name and the time of her visitor's log, the empty page of the appointment book on the corner of her desk.

A small café down the block produced a cup of coffee and the morning paper, which occupied her until it was time to return.

As she re-entered the colorless room, she was having second thoughts. She had not prepared herself for th5e meeting and she had never paid any attention to the ASPCA before. She wasn't sure that she knew enough about the organization to even ask intelligent questions.

As it happened, she needn't have worried. When she entered the reception area, a bearded man arose from the only visitor's chair in the lobby. "You must be Miss Wilds. I'm Gregory. Please come into my office and have a seat."

Stepping aside, he opened the door for Jane to precede him. He was a huge man, at least six feet ten, heavyset, but with a solid healthy look. His straight hair, prematurely peppered with gray, flowed uninterruptedly over his ears, blending with facial hair forming a full thick beard. His dark eyes were shaded by heavy bushy eyebrows below a narrow forehead. She mused, "He's a giant, who would look more at home felling trees than anchoring a desk chair." His physical presence dominated the space of the office.

Entering, she noted that the bland style of his office was a continuation of the lobby: metal desk with vinyl top, metal bookcase jammed with journals and a few books few pictures, and a calendar. The sole exception to indifference, a once magnificently woven wall handing, was so faded and dusty that one had to imagine its original colors and intricate design.

"Please be seated. May I get you some coffee?"

"No, thanks, I really do appreciate your taking the time to see me.

Strange, every time she remembered her introduction to the Movement, she dwelt as much on the rooms as on the people. Repulsed by the total lack of character of the place, she had promised herself that, whatever lay ahead in her life, it did not, could not, include such an atmosphere. Yet, she had created just such a place for the Movement. Although he had talked for nearly two hours, she could not recall any of the first conversation with, in detail. He had begun slowly and quietly enough with the early history of the ASPCA and the obvious needs from which it grew.

"By treating animal experimentation with casual indifference, mankind insulted the order of things, his own humanity, and, yes, God. If we are immune to the suffering of nature's animals, can it be such a large step to become immune to human suffering? If the 'End,' a better life for human beings, justifies the 'Means', causing lower forms of life to suffer, is it beyond the realm of possibility to broaden the definition of 'lower forms' of life to include weaker and genetically warped or mutated human beings? Might not all of the old arguments for the necessity of animal experimentation, with but slight modification be applied to prove the need for human experimentation, with the same total lack of regard for the subject of the study?"

His voice had risen as this line of reasoning led him to recall the early part of the previous century.

"A European fanatic named Hitler had actually declared and that an entire race or religion (she wasn't sure which) should be declared subhuman. These people, the Jews, were used for experimentation, frequently without the benefit of anesthetics.

"From there it was a short step for these fanatics to conclude that the world would be better off without them." During this phase of his lecture he was persuasive and eloquent, if somewhat less than logically conclusive in establishing the causal connections between animal experimentation and Hitler's infectious brand of insanity. However, he certainly had at his disposal a large body of horrifying facts from which to formulate his arguments and there was no denying that millions had been killed or that millions more were persecuted.

The ASPCA organization had not been without influence. Significant legislation had been enacted in the United States and elsewhere. While animal experimentation was not forbidden, the more disgusting and painful practices were at least curtailed and controlled. His voice had softened and his color settled as he recalled the progress in educating humanity in the latter half o the twentieth century. Not enough had been achieved, but real progress had been made.

At this point, his voice had dropped almost to a whisper, but it still seemed to carry the full physical force of the huge from behind the desk. As she recalled the only other phrases from that meeting that she could actually remember verbatim, she could almost feel the pressure of that gentle giant's words burning into her memory. "Until, that is, the emergence of humanity's most disgusting affront to the sanctity of creation, the Morris Modeling technology. No longer is man satisfied to experiment with living beings. Now he mocks his Creator by modifying the very building blocks of life. Not content with evolving hybrid, man is now directly engineering living matter."

There had been more, much more; and Jane became so absorbed that she forgot her original question. It did not matter, however. As this gentle and sincere fighter reasoned his way from here to Judgment Day, he included the answer to her unspoken question. He had explained that the promise of Morris Modeling technology, to obviate the need for experimentation, had been fulfilled only for those reactions for which the entire chemical structure of all the reacting compounds were known. Even then, a tremendous amount of computing power was required to carry out a mathematical simulation of reactions with the complex molecules that are the building blocks of living matter.

Since only NAMBE had such a computer, everyone else still used experimentation with living organisms as the fastest form of "ANALOG COMPUTATION." Had the successful use of genetic engineering and its related breakthroughs eliminated the need for animal experimentation? On the contrary, the unqualified success of its programs had increased by a large multiple the need for such experimentation. More importantly, the success of these programs had created a social environment in which research was even more of a sacred cow than it had ever been before. Most of humanity actually considered it a sacrilege merely to question the necessity of providing whatever the scientists wanted.

She recalled the sudden, almost embarrassed way in which he had forced himself to stop speaking and acknowledge her presence. He apologized, and in spite of her assurances that he had more than answered her questions, he insisted that she pose them to him.

"I promise there will be no more sermons today?" He actually blushed, that giant of a man blushed. Of course she had complied by asking the question that had occurred to her as he spoke. True to his promise, he answered her questions in a concise and simple manner. There was a lot more: The lunch he had insisted on providing; her subsequent return on a number of a occasions to learn more of the impact of Bio-engineering; the inevitable personal involvement, the only real romance of her life . . . . The list went on endlessly. But she was reviewing the formation and evolution of the Movement, the ASPGH, not her love of Greg. With a struggle, she pulled thought back to the review that had launched this reverie.

Of course, Gregg was an inseparable part of the history of the Movement. Indeed, in the beginning he was the Movement. Dear Gregg. Strange, but he had no other name as fast as Jane was concerned. Mr. Gregory had become and she honestly did not know if he had another name.

Movement Dies; A Movement is Born

While Greg and many other socially motivated persons had long since begun to question the wisdom of bio-engineering and effectiveness of the SPCA in its battle to curb the applications of the new science, no one had anticipated the consequences of those considerations and the formation of a new movement which was to eventually empower the forces leading to The Outrage,. The process was significantly accelerated by the comments of a southern California college professor.

After Professor Thorens' reaction to her paper, she had dropped the sociology class. In fact, she had dropped the whole damned university. Who wouldn't have? Professor Thorens had not appreciated the touch of originality in her term paper. On the contrary he considered her arguments to be totally baseless. Trite, he called them.

He pointed out, in no uncertain terms, the unquestioned benefits to humanity of the fruits of the microbiologists' efforts. People lived longer more completer and more meaningful lives, as a result of the microbiologist's contributions. The broad based solution to the population control problem, through birth control could be accomplished by genetic engineering once the religious taboos were eliminated. One could still not convince all peoples everywhere of the need for controlled birth rates, but thanks to genetics,

"It is no longer necessary to convince the ignorant; it is only necessary to convince their leaders to use a particular crop to feed the masses. He had actually said that, referring to the recent announcement that a permanent sterility could be induced by eating a relatively small amount of a new genetically engineered grain. Even after all these months, she could still recall that scene in vivid, humiliating detail.

She had been leaving class two days after submitting her completed paper. The tiered lecture hall, with its varnished and slippery hardwood seating and deeply scored and initialed writing surfaces, had rapidly emptied as impatient students dashed t the next position in their computer ordered day. Looking forward to her free hour following Sociology 408, Jane had luxuriously wasted a few minutes arranging the contents of her Hartman leather briefcase, a gift from her father, commemorating her acceptance at Sand Diego's most prestigious university. As she looked up from her bag, she noticed the professor shuffling and reshuffling his notes; it appeared that he was waiting for her. Nonsense! He hadn't spoken twenty words to in all the weeks she had attended his class. Why now?" Still, as she reached the head of the aisle, just ten feet short of the door, he harrumphed. "Just like an old movie professor," she thought. She had noticed the shifting of his weight from foot to foot as he watched her descending from the center seat of the uppermost row, her favorite seat since the beginning of the year.

"He's behaving like a schoolboy. Is he coming on to me?" she wondered.

"No, that's not possible not Thorens. His nickname is Thorny, not Horny." She smiled at her silent pun and promptly ignored him, her thoughts turning to her previous week's inspirational meeting with Mr. Gregory. (He was still Mr. Gregory back then) She was pleased with herself for having had the idea of visiting the ASPCA. "A brilliant stroke, that. That's what old Thorny wants," she reflected. He's pleased at my initiative and is waiting for a chance to tell me so."

Smiling as shyly as she knew how, she had hurried the last few steps. The, as she neared the foot of the isle, her confidence faded; she wasn't sure. He had stopped fidgeting, but his features were set, stern, unsmiling. Something was wrong. Before she had a chance to speculate further, he made one last hurried survey of the room and spoke.

"Miss Wilds!" It was an exclamation, a command, a call to attention. Something was definitely awry. "This outline, this trash; I haven't seen such a trite argument since . . . . I can't remember ever seeing such a biased and patently ridiculous composition before! Of course there are still experiments with animals. Of course they are not only moral, ethical and necessary but obviously God's will. Man was created in the image of God. Man! Not rats, hamsters, or monkeys. The animals of the earth are here to please God and to serve man. Since man was created in the image of God, it is clear that what is good for man is good for God; in short it is moral. The very ability to understand the structure and forces of the building blocks of life is the result of "God's greatest gift to man, his intellect. Can there be any doubt that man's drive to question sand his ability to answer are the two most precious, most God like characteristics that he has? The exercise of that ability is the highest moral achievement attainable. Our atmosphere, our longevity, and the quality of human life are testimonials to that moral achievement."

He paused for a breath. "I have prepared a list of references for you to review. I want you to have them read and your term paper redrafted before class on Friday; that's forty eight hours. Slamming her paper into the battered waste basket at the side of the rostrum he continued "Reasoning such as this was responsible for the Dark Ages."

There had been more. He had not been content with supplying her with references. His tirade continued several more minutes. He recounted a few of the more dramatic achievements of bio-engineering: the elimination of diabetes and cancer, the virtual elimination of birth defects, the control of pests, the development of an endless variety of useful plant forms to mention just a few.

As though from physical exhaustion or exasperation, rather than from lack of more examples of biological engineering success, Thorens abruptly stopped speaking. He was aware of all of the developments mentioned by Jane; he mentioned most of the same ones. But Thorens was able to see only the surface effects of those developments. And he totally misunderstood the moral significance. How could he be so wrong, so blind" In spite of her efforts at self control, her own frustration streamed down her cheeks, embarrassing her further until she could no longer stand it. Shaking with suppressed sobs, she fled the lecture hall. Fuming she had turned her frustration into anger.

Even if he had been right and if society were better off and closer to God as a result of the Morris Modeling technology, this was a university, after all. Surely here, of all places, students should be permitted to ask searching questions and hold opposing views. Thorens was a travesty of a professor; this entire school is a travesty!

Her disenchantment with the university had been growing from some time. Now she realized it was not simply a case of Senior Blues, but rather one of having outgrown the institution. She never returned to class, nor indeed to any other part of the campus. She was adequately, though not lavishly, provided for by an annuity which her father had bestowed upon her as a twenty first birthday present. She decided to devote herself to the study of the issues raised. In time she was even able to acknowledge that Professor Thorens had made some good points. She was still convinced that he was wrong, but his questions did require answers. She had returned to. He gave her the answers and more.

It had not been an affair. They were in love, deeply so. No a wild, swing kind of romantic nonsense but a warm, comfortable, enduring love. It endured even now, two years after his death. It all seemed to happen so fast! She left school. A few days later, she returned to the ASPCA. agreed that not only did the university ring hollow, so also did the ASPCA, As its cause had become increasing less and less popular, its membership lost its will. Now only the facade remained. There was enough activity to satisfy the covenants on the various grants from the pas that still provided the funds for its operation, but no more. No new donations of significance had been made since the turn of the century.

"There are young people in the organization, but the movement has no youth, no vitality, no drive, no spine," had complained.

Two weeks later, spurred by his own arguments, he had abandoned his office, dust wall hanging and all; and in less time than she would have imagined possible, the American Society of the Preservation of God and Humanity had been born.

Those were golden days, highlighted by speaking engagements from one end of California to the other. Greg 's near hypnotic oratory had set fire to the latent tinder of belief, the need of humans for a higher authority, a reason for being. He did not question the benefits of those developments of this century; but he did suggest that there were ethical and moral limits. He was not fighting for the prevention of cruelty to animals but rather for the preservation of humanity and morality, for God! When spoke, everyone seemed to listen. Even his adversaries argued the issues with him on his own terms, or tried to do so. The ASPGH grew in two short years to become recognized and respected throughout the state. The end came out of nowhere and hit them. Even after the police had explained the entire incident, she could not recall seeing the car. She could not believe it had happened. A terrible, senseless accident ended the life that had become the center of her life and the rallying point for a statewide return to sanity. He was dead. That was almost the end of both Jane and ASPGH. The vision clouded over when the visionary died.

Help From an Unlikely Source

The tragic death of its founder, might very easily have been followed by the death of the ASPGH had it not been for Jane's, meeting Terry. Among other things Terry provided all the funding necessary to assure the survival of the organization. He had spotted immediately that is leadership and management suggestions were essential to its growth, and, therefore, essential to his plans.

Enter Terry. She had been introduced to him by Julie, the mousy little secretary. To Jane Terry was an enigma, a mysterious mixture of characteristics. He had none of Gregg's kindness and nothing like his physical presence. She had often thought his total contrast was one of the reasons for her attraction to him. Certainly, there was no way one could remind her of the other. A crude, wily, consummate rebel, constantly searching for a new adversary, Terry would never be described as a gentle giant with a mission. No, they were complete opposites; while 's speech had always been calm, educated and totally free of expletives, Terry rarely spoke without punctuating his sentences with curses, although when he chose to use it, his vocabulary was extensive and his grammar excellent; he did not curse out of ignorance of appropriate word but rather in defiance of society's accepted norms. When he got excited, angry, or apprehensive, his speech degenerated to a gutter dialect throughout which the single expletive, "fuck" was peppered generously. Even now, she was shocked when she recalled the incident at the open air restaurant when Terry picked up a menu and discovered a small harmless looking white spider scurrying back down the umbrella pole which punctured the table top. Terry had leaped from the table, brushing nonexistent spiders from his sleeves, knocking over his chair and cursing. 'Fuckin', goddamned bugs! I hate fuckin;' goddamned bugs!" After that, she noticed the way he always stayed as far from plants, trees and grass as possible.

Terry was opposed to everything in any way related to "them". "Them" included all persons or organs of authority. He seemed to enjoy rebellion for its own sake. It was being in opposition that counted with Terry, whatever the cause. Not far beneath the surface lay a cruel streak, as she had found to her own pain on more than one occasion. And yet there was a charisma about him also. While she could not identify the attraction, she was not the only to feel it; Terry was a leader. True, he lack's power to move crowds with his eloquent oratory. But, face to face, or in small groups he was captivating; people listened and followed. It was his eyes, Jane realized; they attracted and held people's attention with a magnetism that could not be denied. While their effective range was limited, those eyes were a captivating and compelling as 's voice.

As soon as he had learned of her affiliation with he Movement, he had seized the opportunity to attack NAMBE. "Of course, all this bullshit being developed and disseminated by NAMBE is detrimental to mankind.

"What the hell would you expect from the biggest government project in the world?" he had said. In his vulgar and dogmatic style he had gone on to explain that NAMBE was a necessary consequence of letting government get involved in anything. At first she had been repulsed by his vulgarity of style and language and had listened only out of courtesy to Julie. But before the evening had run out, she was captivated.

At the time of their first meeting, there was no doubt that the Movement was in the early stages of decay and that without some serious help it could not have lasted. Terry had cut through to the core of the problem immediately. "The members must be led; they must be sold the product and different salesmen use different styles. What works for one is not necessarily the right tool for the next. Apparently, this was an eloquent speaker; and apparently you are not. In any case, quiet speakers are okay only in the beginning. To attract and hold the masses, you need a crisis you can blame on someone else, an enemy to defeat. Every goddamned politician understands that. If you intend to beat them at anything, you need to know what they know. And to use that knowledge, you need money." Jane thought. "True, he is a cynic, but there is truth in what he says. Besides, didn't he demonstrate the validity of his arguments with the spring campaign last year?"

After their first meeting, she had somehow become caught up with Terry, seeing more and more of him. He in turn had adopted her cause as a battlefield upon which to challenge authority once again.

"We need funds and rallies and members, in that order" he had proclaimed.

Explaining that he had some wealthy friends in the Midwest and on the East Coast who would provide seed money, he had taken off for several weeks; and, when he returned, he brought with him donations of nearly one hundred thousand dollars. Together, they planned a statewide membership drive with marches and rallies in ten different locations across the state.

On that wild swing across the length and breadth of California, she had discovered that, while she could not speak effectively in a hall or auditorium, or convince people with the soft spoken appeal of logic, she could still be effective. She could excite crowds! The rally was her medium. Surrounded by placards and the great outdoors, her style was everything's was not: loud and passionate, punctuated with exaggerated gestures. She came alive before such groups, moved by a passion unlike anything she had ever known before.

The drive had been successful, or had it? They had attracted the attention of the national wire services, and the movement caught on the eastern states. She had been invited to speak at organizing rallies. There were now ten eastern chapters whose membership was still growing. But here, in her state, membership rolls had swollen last spring, only to shrivel and rink as spring passed relentlessly into summer and summer gave way to autumn. By the harvest moon it was almost as if spring had never been.

She complained to Terry, "The truths are still the same. Can't they see that . . . Idiots?"

With his language once again deteriorating, Terry replied, "Of course they're idiots and they don't care. Why the fuck do you think you had to tell them in the first place? Are you the only goddamned soul who can read and reason? The only one who can see through the horse shit put out by the goddamned NAMBE crowd? Of course not! You're just one of the few who give a shit."

He was off again. He had a new group to berate their own members. "Give'm action. You've got to keep selling the product. You can't hold people with moral outrage unless you can direct that outrage. Give them something to do as well as something to hate. Give them a mission. Show the gutless turkeys that you have courage as well as conviction. You have shown that you can inspire. Do you have the guts to lead? Give them more drama, nation and international recognition. Bring the video cameras of the world to focus on you objective.

Terry at his rational best; and he cut right to the core of the problem. He had been correct, of course. Her message was one of moral outrage. Morris Modeling technology was an affront to morality. It was not man's place to imitate God.

She had not taken the next step: tell them what to do about it. Shad mulled over Terry's tirade for two days before broaching the subject again.

"What can we do then? How can we get the attention we need and how do we focus it? She had expected another violent dressing down. Instead, a considered plan of action spilled forth in such detail that it was obvious that he had been thinking about it for sometime: longer, certainly, that the last two days. It would work; of course it would work, but is it really necessary?

Terry had left again two weeks ago. No explanations, no good-byes; he just did not come back one evening. It had twice before. The first had been the fund raising trip. For the second she had no explanation at all. She sighed, drained her glass, and lay back, closing her eyes.

Terry's plan is a major question mark? Yes, something dramatic was indeed necessary to save the Movement. And the Movement's cause was moral. But did a just cause truly justify any means? Were there other choices" That was the truly important question, and the answer was no. The plan was on. It had been virtually impossible to raise the money before Terry came along. But the plan would bring more national and international attention and focus than all the money she could hope to raise in twenty years.

Recollections Of The Security Chief

Like many parts of Entangled, some of the actual events reported in this section were never reported before. You will have noticed that I use the Chronicler's privilege of filling in with events that I feel are at least similar to the actual events. Considering what I later learned about Laurie Bass and her nephew, it is certainly likely that these events or some very similar occurred during the Ames and Terry visit to NAMBE. This incident provides some insight into the future actions of Laurie Bass.

While she had played an essential role in the life her nephew, she had seen him only once when he was still an infant. Though Laurie had been "watching over" Ames and cared and provided for him as much as she could manage, they had never spoken nor, even been in the same room since he was a few weeks old.

Hurrying through the intersection of the Ultra Atrium, UA, pathways, Laurie Bass glanced casually at the tour being led by Dr. Kim Newcombe. At least, she hoped her glance appeared casual. Surely, he was too absorbed in the tour to notice a single woman passing among the plants. Reassuring herself, she thought, "It doesn't matter in any case, he doesn't know me; on the other hand he's certainly an unusual young man. And, I was right. All of my choices for him have been right, including the very risky first one." Continuing past the Arctic Section of the UA to the exterior door, she silently observed. "Yes, he does look fine, but his color . . . . He's so tanned. I hope he isn't spending too much time in the unfiltered sunlight."

It was risky for her to take a chance of his recognizing her and she knew it; but she felt compelled to see him. She had the reports from Uncle Ben and Aunt Alice, their photographs, the local newspaper clippings, and his letters but a mother needs more.

That thought pulled her up short just outside the main entrance. "You are not his mother!" she admonished herself. "It's not possible for you to be anyone's mother! And if it were you'd have no part of it, the filthy animal like coupling required to conceive, some man's sweaty hands and slobbering lips and worse, possessing your body, contaminating it. Of course, God designed it so; but men are not content to engage in the act merely for reproductive purposes. No, they, and indeed many women too, wallow in panting total abandonment, moaning, groaning, and mixing body fluids in ways that go disgustingly beyond the requirements of procreation which was the intention of God. I know!"

She did know. In her earlier short career in law enforcement she had confiscated films and videos and had made more than a few busts in which the perpetrators were caught in the act, a vile disgusting act being recorded to undermine the morals of others. Indeed, her few involvements with vice busts had been responsible for her transferring from police work to security.

At first, it had surprised her that all manner of men and women from all levels of society were involved. The perversions of God's design were not limited to the poor, the wealthy, the ignorant, the indolent or the self indulgent. Nearly everyone, it seemed could fall victim to those temptations of the flesh. Her mother had been right. The only safe path to God was through celibacy. Yet the world was created for man, who was made in the image of God. But God didn't rut and sweat like some raging bull, depositing thousands of sperm cells in the blind hope that one would find its target. No, Christ was born of a Virgin Mary. Man was built in the image of God, but the image was not yet complete, not yet perfect. The developments here at the Facility are moving us closer to God, she reasoned. Procreation is now possible without sexual intercourse.

Of course, artificial insemination was possible decades ago; but now, through the techniques of the Facility's Project Nine, not only was it no longer necessary for two bodies to become entwined (she shivered at the very thought) it was not even necessary that they exist. The methods being developed not only eliminated the unspeakable filth associated with procreation, but it also eliminated all uncertainty and genetic accidents. 'Without the birth trauma' long known to complicate the psychic development of many humans, better human beings could be created in this way.

"Someday this will be the only way in which humanity is propagated;" she reflected wistfully. "Then the creation of man in the image of God will have been attained." While she knew well that such thoughts and motivations had nothing to do with the objectives of Project Nine, it seemed clear to that the result was inevitable considering what they were doing there; it was in fact equally clear that that result was the will of God. Yes, the technology does exist and she was confident that someday its true potential would be realized.

Letting her reverie drift on its own, she recalled the evening when she first learned the objectives of the research program. An emotional Mary Ann Bono had first explained the actual research going on in the level Nine Project. In an informal meeting between scientist and security officer, Mary, had disclosed the scientific details of the Project and unloaded all of her ethical concerns about the research she was asked to perform. Strangely, however, Mary Ann had never realized the essentially Christian implications of her work. Yet, she had been a part of it nearly from the beginning. In fact, had it not been for Mary Ann, Laurie might never have known any of the details of the project. "Protecting secrets had been and is my responsibility; it is not necessary for me to understand the technical details to fulfill my responsibilities; "she reasoned.

Shaking her head as if to rid herself of such thoughts, she returned to the present, "I am here today to catch a glimpse of my nephew, my only nephew, but one who must never know his Aunt Laurie as anything more than a distant and mysterious source of love and gifts." If she hurried she could see him once more as the tour gathered at the elevator for its trip to the seventh level. Her view would not be as good through the one way glass in the guardroom, but she would feel more secure, more sure of avoiding detection by her gifted nephew.

Through A Two Way Mirror

Proceeding at a normal pace, her outward calm belied the inner anxiety and excitement she felt. Entering the guard room without knocking, as was her custom ever since she had become the Director of Security, Laurie noticed both guards jerk to attention.

"As you were, boys; this is strictly an informal visit. As you both know, I like to have at least a brief look at each of these visiting s. Not that I've ever discovered anything that way, but old habits die hard." She sat down in one of the two unoccupied chairs.

The entire wall facing the hall before the elevator in which the visitors would descend was made of darkened, partially reflective glass. That glass, when combined with the subdued lighting in the guardroom and the bright lights of the hallway, essentially turned the wall into a one way window. Persons passing through the halls could be monitored without their being aware of it. From the hall side it looked quite decorative, a large mirror etched with images characteristic of the Facility's unclassified activities. Used extensively throughout Facility, the one way glass made it possible to maintain security observation without unduly disturbing visitors. Of course, like any one way mirror, the reflective glass did permit a small fraction of the guard room light to pass into the hall. However, the "leaked light" was minuscule compared to that within the hall itself. That fact combined with the reflective coating essentially rendered the guardroom invisible to those in the hall. On the whole, such devices are quite effective. In this instance, however, it failed to hide Laurie from Ames with his significantly enhanced visual acuity.

The designers of one way mirrors had not anticipated a need to reduce the transmission even further; no one had ever seen through mirrors from the wrong direction before.

Another Glimpse

As the small group of tourists was arranging itself for an orderly entry into the elevator, Ames glanced casually around. When they reached the one way glass, his eyes stopped momentarily. Scarcely inhibited by the trick window, his sharpened senses had no difficulty noticing the guard room and its occupants. Realizing that the system was part of the Facility's security system, he was neither alarmed nor annoyed by the use such devices. He was, however, surprised to see the central chair occupied by the stunning woman he had 'noticed' hurrying through the Ultra Atrium.

"There it is again, that twinge or flash! That woman is triggering something deep, very deep. Since to his certain knowledge he could never forget a single 'sensed observation,' nearly remembered events' were extremely rare in Ames's life and never failed to produced an eerie feeling when one occurred. Even as he turned his back on the one mirror, Ames carefully reviewed and studied the image he had just captured of the dark haired woman on the far side of the glass, cataloging her appearance in the minute detail that only he could have sensed. Even though she was seated, it was clear that she was tall. Her back was held straight and her shoulders square. Somehow her being built like an Amazon did not detract from her striking beauty enhanced by the Raven hair that spread over her left shoulder in a spill, ending at the peak of her breast.

Standing nearby and of course totally unaware of what Ames could see that he could not, Terry snickered to himself "Look at that fancy Dan," he thought, he 's dressed fit to kill and he can't pass a single mirror without pausing to primp. Bet he's a friggin' fairy.

Upon hearing Dr. Newcombe's "Please step to the rear of the elevator and face forward," both young men snapped back to the present as the tour continued to the lower levels.

Laurie's Memory Wanders as She Walks

Following Laurie's exploits during The Outrage, her life was studied in great detail by many trained reporters and I will not attempt to reconstruct it all here. But from the studies of her that I undertook, it is clear that the thoughts attributed to her in this incident must have been with her often. I include them at this point not because they necessarily occurred at this time but simply because the thoughts themselves are germane to our story and precisely when they occurred is not.

After some polite and meaningless conversation with her troops, Laurie left the guardroom. Maintained through regular, vigorous workouts and a sensible diet, her body's peak physical condition and physical prowess was a source of pride. She had no interest at all in trying to look diminutive, no flat shoes and slouching stances for her. No thank you! She was born large boned and destined to be tall; but being large was only a minor part of it. Gliding through the door into the now empty hall without apparent effort, her predator like movement was smooth and unhurried. On this occasion, as sometimes happened, she became aware of her movement, aware that on or off the mat she was always ready. At such moments, she derived a sensual pleasure from just walking. Invariably on such occasions, her mind would flash back, briefly recalling the stages of her physical development. Throughout her formative years, she had been larger than the girls; indeed, she had been larger than most of the boys. Intimidated by her size, most of her female acquaintances were reluctant to bond with her and she found it difficult to make friends. By the time she reached high school and understood what it was that occupied the minds of her female contemporaries, she was thankful that she had not formed close relationships with any of them.

However, the boys in her schools had been a different matter altogether. As she was growing up, they somehow perceived that she was as capable of any physical activity as they were. She participated actively in their games and sports. By the time she reached high school, they had long since ceased to think of her as "just a big girl. They didn't think of her as a girl at all. Good! They knew her as 'a good person to have on their side in any sport.' Such acceptance as an equal had been satisfying.

She had been the only female member of the varsity basketball and lacrosse teams. Still something had been missing. While she was certainly an unquestioned contributor in those team sports, she denied truly competitive areas; she was after, all just a big girl.

Excited and relieved when she discovered that the martial arts dojos, judo, karate and kung fu, accepted female members and trainees, she had quickly developed a keen interest in all of the techniques. True, she had had to begin in a women's class filled with secretaries and housewives interested in protecting themselves from imagined rapists. Actually, they were mostly interested in an occasional social hour and the fact that the class gave them another topic of conversation for their bridge club or cocktail hour. Laurie had quickly shown that she was a serious athlete. She had competed for the club in inter dojo matches and won a belt for her efforts. Not content with limited competition, she had inveigled her way into a number of matches normally reserved for men only and won far more of those than she lost. By such perseverance, she had removed the last equality barrier. However, discovering that she could win had proved to be a double edged sword. At first, there was the challenge, followed by the joy of success. Then, after she had proven to herself that she could win, the motivation was gone. There seemed to be no reason to continue to compete. She still worked out regularly, and once each month she had a one private lesson with her private coach Mako. But she no longer competed; the satisfaction of winning had waned. One on one combat with men was not what she needed. In fact she was convinced that she needed nothing from men.

"Still, I did join their teams and fight in their contests. What did I want? What did I truly expect from the martial arts competition?" She had always known that she could win. Had she been looking for something else, like physical contact? Nonsense! Expelling the entire topic, she squared her shoulders and increased her pace while shaking her head. She had been down that track a thousand times, and the end was always the same. Such flashes of insight when she thought the truth was near, were surrounded by an expanding a thickening fog of confusion that concealed not only the truth but direction but the questions themselves. Often such reverie had led to a heightened feeling of anxiety and a strange, distracting feeling that unused muscles were tensing for she knew not what. At such time, unwelcome desires, lurking just beneath the surface of her consciousness, strove to be recognized. Yes, frequently such thoughts disturbed her and never did they console. "Why then do I let them insinuate their way into mind so often?"

An Upcoming Meeting Pondered

On her way to a meeting which was not part of her normal routine, but rather one spontaneously scheduled by Dr. Q, Laurie worried that this tweak in Dr. Q's style might signify something amiss.

Glancing at her watch, she noted that there was still an hour before her meeting with Dr. Q. She could spend the time in her office completing the week's paperwork. Since that cold old man never wasted an hour during what he considered the working day, it was clear that the meeting with Dr. Q would not be a social chat. Though she had no idea what its purpose was.

"Something's on his mind—niggling at him; I wonder what?" Her slightly lifted eyebrows and furrowed brow evidenced her concentration. "What could it be? Security has had no significant problems in years, not since I've taken over. Well, yes, there had been that one serious security violation, but I'm absolutely the only living person in the world who is aware of that one and only serious event; furthermore, I'm the only one who will ever know."

At that thought and for a brief moment, she felt real fear slice its way into her consciousness as a palpable chill descended over her. She shivered. "Could Dr. Q possibly have found out? She consoled herself. No, of course he could not have! He only has an administrative clearance for Project Eight and he doesn't even know that Project Nine exists. Besides, if he had learned anything at all about that event, there certainly would not be a polite 'after lunch' meeting to discuss it." Drawing comfort from that conclusion, she gave a final shrug and continued to her office. "It's pointless to try to second guess Dr. Q," Laurie decided. "I'm certainly on edge today," she thought. "It's Ames of course. But I had to see him." She turned toward her office to at least make a start at catching up on her paperwork. Turning into her office suite, she smiled brightly at Susan, her frail looking blond secretary.

After a few futile attempts to find anything in the pile of routine papers with which to blot out her concerns about Dr. Q, Mary Ann, and Project Nine, she glanced at her watch. While it's too late for a swim, and too early to go to Dr. Q's office, there is just time enough for a brief walk through the Garden, she decided, using the staff's nickname for the Ultra Atrium. With twenty minutes to spare after completing her tour of the trophies of genetic engineering, she returned to her office.

A Luncheon Meeting

We do know from the NAMBE guest registration that Terry and Ames were on the same tour of the facility. From the way the final stages of The Outrage unfolded, we can be assured that these two very different men spent some time together. Absent any documented records of exactly when and where that meeting took place, I have once again taken literary license and I detail here the way I image such a meeting might have occurred and evolved.

While Laurie was rushing off to meet Dr. Q, another meeting although certainly not scheduled was in any case taking place.

Hoping to spend the lunch hour quietly analyzing his reaction to the two sightings of the dark haired woman, Ames selected an isolated table in a quiet corner of the cafeteria. Having reasoned that the other visitors would seek tables with a view of the Ultra Atrium, Ames selected a table with a minimal view of the UA.

Just as he was congratulating himself on his selection, he heard Terry Parker approaching his table. Ames did not need to look up to know it was, Terry Parker. His sense of hearing was much more sensitive, accurate and highly developed than that of the most accomplished blind persons, and he never forgot anything once he had sensed it with any one of his senses.

Terry and Ames had spoken to each other but a few times during the morning portion of the tour. While the conversations had been short, little more than an exchange of names and opinions about the tour arrangements, it was sufficient to plant the impressions of Terry firmly in Ames' mind. Ames had tried to discuss some of the developments described by Dr. Newcombe with Terry; but he had quickly discovered that Terry had no interest in the NAMBE's programs or its history. Terry seemed interested only in the physical layout of the Facility. Strange! However, Ames had not dwelt on this strangeness. He was very sensitive about his own privacy and carefully respected the privacy of others. Now, it seemed, he was going to have lunch with Terry, a prospect he did not anticipate with pleasure. Resigning himself, he looked up and smiled. "I see you've also spotted the only quiet corner. Please join me."

Actually, Terry had not looked forward to lunching with Ames either. He had not been at all taken with the soft spoken suntanned guy from No Place, New Hampshire. However, he had selected the corner table with the same rationale that had served him all morning, namely: Any white man's company is preferable to any "nig's" company.

"Don't mind if I do," he replied. "This food doesn't look bad for a cafeteria. Do you think it's what it appears to be or some freaky, artificial, imitation bioengineered protein?"

"It is tasty, whatever it is. The vegetables may be, probably are, a product of their bio-engineering effort. The meat, however, should be genuine; they do not engineer animals here. The act authorizing the formation of NAMBE specifically excluded raising animals at the Facility. The only exception permitted is the use of animals in secondary studies, to show the effect of feeding an engineered crop, corn, for instance."

"Slow down," Ames he cautioned himself just in time; "I very nearly rattled off the actual wording of the act." From past experience, where he had sometimes done so, he knew that long explanations of how he knew so much would then have been required. Ames was never comfortable trying to explain his unusual senses and memory. Over the years he had developed the defense mechanism of paraphrasing his references rather than quoting the original sources. Even so, he frequently conveyed too much information in casual conversation, and his detailed knowledge almost always led to raised eyebrows and suspicions. While it was a simple stratagem to conceal his differentness, it required his almost constant attention; but, Terry didn't seem to have noticed.

"The fresh fruit has a very different smell; pleasant, a sort of outdoor freshness, don't you think?"

"What a pompous ass he is", thought Terry. Aloud, he said, "I don't know about the outdoor freshness smell. I haven't been able to smell anything for years. Lost my sense of smell with some childhood disease, I think. I'm glad to hear the meat is real, though; I'm a meat and potatoes man. Maybe this time I'll skip the potatoes too. I'm not afraid of them. I just don't like the idea of people messing about in God's work, that's all."

This time it was Terry who put on the mental breaks. "What bullshit', he thought. "I sound just like some kook from the Movement. I'd better be careful I don't let that shit rub off on me".

The Conversation Takes a Curious Turn

While no particular friendship was established between them, Ames' prodigious memory inadvertently provided Terry with information pertinent to the formulation and staffing of world shocking operation he was planning.

Ames noticed the contradiction between Terry's words, as he sat down, and his behavior all morning. He didn't comment on it, of course; Terry's views and opinions, contradictory or not, were Terry's domain, and Ames certainly would not intrude uninvited into that area.

"This layout is really something," Terry observed as he began to cut into his roast beef. "You would think that with all this computers, chemicals, microbes, and I don't know what all they would have a strong security force here. It doesn't make any sense to me; looks like it's destined to be ripped off."

"Not really," Ames replied. "There is actually an extensive security force here, around five hundred employees, I think I read somewhere."

Ames knew exactly where and when he read this and that the <u>Newsweek</u> article had reported 543 employees in the security force at the Facility. At the time he read the article, he had wondered why such a security force was necessary. Neither that article nor any of the others, he had subsequently read, had provided a satisfactory answer to that question. He had pondered, "There are no secrets to protect. There are only a few entrances to guard and very little that an ordinary thief would find useful. Certainly, there is no need to have a large amount of cash or negotiable instruments around. To prevent vandalism, perhaps, but surely a much smaller force could protect against that. There is no reason to expect an organized march or siege; there were no mass movements opposed to the Facility. No that's not quite true." he corrected himself. "I read an article about the American Society for The Preservation of God and Humanity, which started in California and spread last year into the eastern states. The organization is given to talking and rallying but little else, according to the article. Of course, since I'm not particularly interested in the ASPGH, my reading on the subject has been cursory." He recalled that the Movement had been described briefly, incidentally really, in two <u>Boston Globe</u> articles.

Interrupting his woolgathering, Terry spoke, "Five hundred guards? That can't be right. I haven't seen a damned one, and I would've noticed. I can smell a cop from a mile away. Believe me. Shit, their goddamned town, Micro City, doesn't even have a single traffic cop. It's crazy, I admit, but you're flat assed wrong. There are no cops here."

Ames knew that his statement was correct in; his total recall was never wrong. "Furthermore," he mused silently, "I noticed them behind the one way mirror. His instincts told him to let the subject drop. However, he did not always listen to his instincts.

"They do not exactly have policemen: that may be what is misleading you. They are actually guards provided by a special branch of government service called simply Guards. The Guards was created in the early 1990s. Special guard duties, at embassies and facilities like this one, had been the responsibility of the U.S. Marines before a major scandal broke out in 1987 when marines guarding the U.S. embassy in Moscow were involved with a number of female Soviet spies. Part of the aftermath of that scandal was the creation of the Guards. In some circumstances they make a show of their presence, for instance at an embassy. Normally, their mode of operation is to meld into that which they are guarding and essentially become invisible. They are trained to be difficult to notice. But fear not, they are all around us."

"Damn! You mean to tell me they've got undercover men all over the place? It doesn't say anything about them in the handouts. I read them all, and I would've noticed things about police, invisible or not," Terry replied.

Having read the handouts himself, Ames knew Terry's first point was correct; none of the handouts mentioned the guards; but Ames had seen the article in NewsWeek. To Terry he said only, "They don't talk about security much. Their entire public relations campaign is aimed at promoting a "fully open, no secrets-no dangers-here policy."

"Ah, bullshit: Terry commented; "where the hell would they hide them?"

"Generally, they are hidden by putting them right out in the open letting them blend into the scenery so-to speak. I've noticed a number of wall mirrors, at least one on each floor we've visited. Some of them could be windows of one way glass," Ames replied. To himself, he added, "That's as close as I dare come to disclosure." Dropping the topic, he turned his attention to his meal.

After finishing his coffee, Terry brought it up again. "You mean they're trying to make a big goddamned secret out'a having a police force? That's crazy."

"No, it's no big secret. A number of newspaper and magazine articles have discussed the security measures here, including some rather bizarre sounding measures. The idea is that the presence of a large number of police makes some people uneasy; but, what you don't see is easy to ignore. You yourself failed to notice them and thought their absence was noteworthy. I think the system of inconspicuous security is sound. What puzzles me is the number of guards they feel they need. Maybe it's just a government form of featherbedding. The Facility is a certain size; regulations may say so many guards per square foot, whether you need them or not." Ames was not sure if he believed that argument, but he had never seen a more satisfactory one reported anywhere.

"Magazine articles, you say?" Terry asked. "Can you recommend any particular magazine? I might like to read about it."

Ames replied, "Any of the major nationals, Time or Newsweek, for instance."

An Exchange Of Useful Information

While continuing to "pick Ames' brains," Terry also provides Ames with information that at a later appropriate time will prove crucial to the evolving Outrage.

Filing the information away for later reference, Terry thought to himself, "You might be a shithead, Ames, but you're useful after all". To Ames he said, "Well maybe they have guards around here dressed up like regular people, but they're no good at guarding. Shit, man, look at this briefcase. I carried it completely un-opened right into the heart of the goddamned capital letter Facility. Who's to say I don't have some kind of automatic weapon in here all set to pull off a big holdup? That is, if there was shit worth stealing, that is."

"They may or may not be good guards, I don't know. I never really thought about it. However, I'm certain you did not bring any kind of loaded gun in here, automatic or otherwise."

"I'm not saying I did, but I might have, as far as they would know. They have no inspections, no X-ray machines, nothing. Not shit!"

"I told you before, everything here is not necessarily as it seems. Their weapons check is very sophisticated. They have bred a special strain of insect here, a derivative of the infamous African Killer Bee,

I seem to recall. This particular bug was developed as a sniffer of explosives. They are analogous to the dogs that used to be trained to sniff out drugs or high explosives, only these insects are considerably more effective. The Facility keeps them near every entrance through which people are admitted. At the slightest whiff of any one of the currently known explosive materials, those creatures swarm like bees onto the object or person carrying the stuff. In fact they are referred to as the SWARM. It's an acronym for Search for and Warn of Armaments. Anyway, that's why I'm sure you did not bring any weapon in here that contained bullets or any other explosives. The guards may or may not be effective, but those sniffing insects cannot be fooled. Since their effective range is limited to about twenty meters, they must be kept near each entrance, but that poses no serious problem. A strange side trait of these bugs is that, while they are specifically designed to detect explosives, they go berserk if they are exposed to raw gunpowder."

As his description of the SWARM unfolded, Ames noticed that Terry had begun to squirm in his seat and look around nervously. While scarcely noticeable to those with normal senses, Terry's nervousness was obvious to one with Ames's heightened awareness.

Shocked, Terry exclaimed, "No shit! Bugs for policemen! That's hard to believe. I guess you read about them in those magazines you talked about?"

Realizing that he had been shaken to his core by the revelation so casually delivered by Ames, Terry, who considered himself extremely good at hiding his feelings, was confident that Ames hadn't noticed. After all, as he had often pointed out to others, he now assured himself, "I'm the best damn poker player I ever met."

Aloud he said, "I hope they don't have a lot of experimental bugs running around this place." As if to assure himself that he was not being attacked, he looked anxiously around his plate and at the floor near his chair. "I can't stand bugs. Not since I was in the army fighting in that friggin' jungle in Central America. They had these bloodsucking little bastards down there got into everything! Ever since I left there, I get itchy all over from a single damned bug. Some goddamned army psychiatrist would have a field day with my head if I told him about the bugs. They're not going to take us through a bug section, are they?" he asked.

Noticing the Terry's face pale, Ames replied, "No danger. Insect developments are very rare here and much more closely controlled than the vegetable experiments. Visitors are never permitted into the insect labs. However, the SWARM has been declared safe for use outside the Facility and the first shipments for an outside test will be made sometime at the end of this summer."

Feeling that the conversation has gone far enough but not wanting to appear impolite, Ames tried a ploy that usually worked: he asked Terry about himself.

"Are you interested in security generally, say, as part of your business, or is it only the security here at the Facility that interests you?" Recalling an article he had read in the Boston Globe, Ames felt certain that Terry should be interested in police matters in generally; "Still", he mused, "it seems at this point that Terry's questions are specifically aimed at the Facility's security systems. But there's nothing here that could interest a thief with Terry's record."

A Crime Spree Recalled

Terry boasts of his planning prowess and illustrates it with an example of his first extensive crime wave crediting the Army as the principle source of the honing of those skills. While Ames had very little interest in those escapades, the useful characteristic Terry had revealed a few minutes earlier was strongly re-enforced and by the an additional trait which was about to emerge in Terry's ranting.

Terry was never bashful about his arrest record; it was public knowledge after all, thanks to press coverage of his trial. In fact he often, boasted about his criminal prowess, particularly to strangers he never expected to see again. Looking across the table at his 'prissy' companion, Terry decided, "It would shock the hell out of that prick if he knew he was sitting at the table with a man whom the press had described as 'a callous, self centered social misfit, totally without honor, among thieves or otherwise'."

Aloud he said to Ames, "You might say I'm generally interested in security. You see I'm a thief." As he spoke, he looked carefully at the other man's face to enjoy the shock he was sure would appear. It didn't! "Did you hear what I said?"

"Yes, you're Terry Parker. I read an article about you sometime back. You were arrested and then released. Insufficient evidence, wasn't it?" Of course Ames knew that it was plea deal not lack of evidence; but the little lie helped mask his total recall; "Besides," he reasoned "Terry would rather boast about outsmarting the police than turning in his partners."

"Yeah, that's me. Them dumb bastards have never been able to hold me. I've been nabbed six times. They always had to let me go. The stupid shits either forget to follow their own rules so their evidence is thrown out; or they just plain have insufficient evidence in the first place."

As Ames had expected, Terry started on his favorite subject, Terry. With an audible sigh Ames relaxed into the contemplation of his own problems, letting the other man's words flow directly into storage after checking for cues that would require a response. Terry continued to expound on the general stupidity of anyone sucker enough to join a police force. ". . . risk their lives for a pittance . . . looked down upon by nearly everybody else . . . easy to fool them even with their modern computers and cross referencing bullshit . . . . I know it will work. Shit, I've done it myself, twice, just to fund my plan." The last word was stressed ever-so-slightly.

Noticing the emphasis on the word plan, Ames wondered if Terry was currently formulating a plan involving the Facility. Ames mused, "Interesting thought; but based on the articles I read, he is strictly small time and the Facility is the biggest of big time."

Across the table, Terry continued his boastful monologue. "The idea is that you want a diversion, just like an army strategy. But the diversion must be carefully selected; if the diversion involves too large a target or objective, the bastards will get you during the diversion. If it's too small, it won't work; they'll just ignore it. So here's how you do it. You pick some simple crime that by itself won't attract too much heat: say, you knock off a gas station, small liquor store, somethin' like that. You do it with some trademark, some easily recognizable method of operation and dress; if you're too subtle, the pigs won't notice it at all. To make sure they get the picture you pull the same job, you know, same MO, say three nights in a row. They're all planned out in advance, see? Yeah. Well, what do the coppers do? I'll tell you. They feed all the shit into their computers and bingo! They got an MO. They don't know who you are, but the notorious Gas Station Mob is born. Two days later the Gas Station Mob strikes in, say, Erie or Buffalo but not in Peoria, where it was before; after three quick hits, the cops know they're hot now. The MO's been put on a computer net work and the computers all talk to one another; that's important. The most important part though is that it ain't you in Erie. No, you're sitting on your ass back in Peoria with your buddies and being seen and building a computer solid diversion and at the same time creating an alibi. Get it? They know that the guys in Erie, your buddies by-the-way, who are pulling the job with the same MO showed on the computers are the same guys that hit in Peoria. The Gas Station Mob is on the move. Next, some other buddies in a couple different cities repeat the caper. In the end the police are looking for a mob with a computer MO, the Gas Station Mob that's been rippin' off stations halfway across the country.

You get the papers to talk about this roving gang even if you phone in the tips yourself, 'cause that's your diversion. Now, with all the computers talking and the papers reporting, four big jobs, nothin' to do with gas stations, happen all at once in those different towns and the mob dissolves. Nobody runs away; they all just go quietly back to being the nothings they were. After say six months to a year, they move quietly on and enjoy their share of the loot in some new hometown. See, you can use all that hi tech shit the police have against the police themselves if you know how. It works. I've done it! So I guess you could say that I'm how would you say it 'professionally interested in security'?"

Alerted by his mental monitor, Ames's decided that some response, however innocuous, was called for at this point in the narrative. Since the whole tale has passed into his consciousness, this time he had no difficulty expressing surprise. "Can this guy be for real?" He wondered. 'I'm no expert on criminal techniques, but on the face of it, I don't see any reason the scheme might not work, depending on the rest of the details. But what a colossal ego, to describe a series of crimes in such depth to a total stranger! If not crazy, this man is so supremely arrogant, so cocky confident that his trail is suitably covered that even with this hint the police can't apprehend him. Or else his need to receive praise is so great that he'll take the risk. Or he's lying, or all of the above. I don't know or even care. But I'm into it now".

Aloud, he said "That's interesting. You were in the army? Is that where you learned to plan so thoroughly?

"Yeah, I was in the army, that last fracas in Central America. I stomped around those bug infested jungles for over two years, hot and wet. Goddamned jungle's all I ever saw there. Who the hell would want to fight over it's gotta be outa his mind. It's all useless trees, not good for shit but hidin' snakes and bugs slimy, bloodsucking, stinging, flying, crawling, fuckin' bugs. 'Bug capital of the the whole goddamned world', that place is." Recalling his time in the jungle, plagued with all manner of insect life, always disturbed Terry. And when disturbed and agitated, his speech invariably degenerated. At such times his temper was never far beneath the surface and his self control was tenuous.

While noticing Terry's barely suppressed shuddering and his nervous scanning of the table and floor at the mention of bugs, Ames also noted the degeneration of his speech.

"Yeah," Terry continued, "I did a lot of planning in the army. I led a hit 'n' run squad of foot soldiers. Our job was to sneak inta one o' the insurg's smelly fuckin' camps and blow away anything they had that might be worth a shit. You know weapons and ammunition, shit like that. Then we had to shag ass outa there without gettin' our own asses shot off. My job was to see we got there and back. I never lost nobody in them fuckin' swamps. None o' my guys was left for the fuckin' bugs. I was the best goddamned hit 'n run planner in the whole damned Army."

Noting the slight trembling of Terry's hand, Ames thought, "That's a rather extreme reaction. I believe he's actually frightened."

"Outfit I was in, you didn' make no friends. 'Attrition rate was too high'. That's a fancy assed way to say we got our asses shot off. In my squad nobody ever had a second name. One name was all you got, nickname, mother given name, whatever but just one. Nobody wanted to get close to nobody else. But I brought all their asses back. It did take a lotta plannin'. Those goddamned Indians down there were born and raised in the jungle. They could smell a white man, given half a chance. Trick was, you don't give 'em half a chance. You gotta make sure they're lookin' and sniffin' in some other direction when you make your move. Just like them cops with their computers."

"Yeah, I hadn't thought about it before, but you're right; plannin' for them slobs in the army was probably good practice for me in outwitting the cops."

"Yes, it's true, there does seem to be an interesting correlation," Ames replied. "But I don't see how it relates to the Facility."

"It doen't, really. But you can bet I could crack this place too. Not much point though, since there's nothin' here worth stealing. Nothin' you could fence after you got it out. You're dead right; no need for all those pigs in a place no one wants to knock off."

Ames stood up to leave. He nodded across the table. "Nice talking to you. I'm sure I'll see you again during the remainder of the tour. Right now, however, I've got to visit the men's room. Excuse me." He turned and left.

Terry remained seated. "Strange one, that guy." he thought. "He knows a lot about this place, or he lies good. Still, it's good I talked to him. Think of it. Five hundred cops in the place, and God knows how many bugs. I'd better learn more about those cops; they could queer the whole deal. How do I handle five hundred of the bastards?"

Dr. Newcombe Continues Her Tour

Continuing her tour of the facilities, Dr. Newcombe includes a rather mundane seeming visit to the warehouse facility. A single fact provided by her proved interesting to Terry, solving a crucial problem that Terry's conversation with Ames had disclosed in Terry's plan.

The tour continued with Ames successfully avoiding further discussion with Terry. Along the last corridor of Level Zero, to which they returned at the end of the tour, one of the students asked about supplies for the Facility. "In such a remote location as this, far from the industrialized parts of the country, it must take a lot of planning to supply the laboratories and feed the staff."

"Yes," Dr. Newcombe replied. "We have the most sophisticated ASRS, Automatic Storage and Retrieval System, in the country, and it is truly fully automated. A special purpose computer keeps track of inventory levels and requirements. Material, including food, is ordered automatically, and upon arrival it is received, marked, and stored without the intervention of human beings. Indeed, except for routine inspection and maintenance, there are never any people in the automated warehouse area. There are not even any entrances to the warehouse, except from within the Facility. I mean, there are no entrances for people. Clearly, the contents of trucks and boxcars are unloaded through automated loading bays, but there is no need or provision for people to enter the Facility that way."

Bringing supplies into the Facility was not of interest to anyone on the tour, except one. Sensing this, Dr. Newcombe moved the along and continued her standard briefing. Only Terry had paid careful attention to the ASRS description. His air of total concentration as he carefully listened to Dr. Newcombe surprised Ames.

A Frustrated Director Considers

Dr. Q was the head of NAMBE with administrative control over all operations, plans and budgets of both the NAMBE facility and Micro City. That is, he was in control of everything except for the "Carve Out Operations" on level Eight. Access to all matters in

Level Eight was controlled on a strict "Need to Know" basis and since its inception Level Eight Programs had been tightly controlled from Washington, DC. While he could accept the logic at the intellectual level, it grated his soul every time he was reminded that Level Eight existed. Of course he was not even aware of the existence of a Level Nine Operation, nor of the physical Level 9. On this occasion a planned future meeting was the cause of his frustration.

"Damn! Damn!" Dr. Q said to himself, naturally; Dr. Quincy would never give voice to frustration, not the always in control, always composed Dr. Quincy. Engrossed in the frustrating consideration of the upcoming visit, he had gone directly past Margaret's desk as though she were not there. Since he rarely spoke to her unnecessarily, there was nothing really unusual about that. When he remembered to smile or nod upon entering his office, such actions were not really for Margret, but rather a simple matter of convention. Like all of Dr. Q's interpersonal relationships, his treatment of Margaret was directed entirely by convention, not conviction; one was expected to greet one's secretary upon entering his office.

On this occasion he was distracted. Disturbed would not have been too strong a word; except, of course, Dr. Q did not get disturbed. He was always in control.

Just inside his massive oaken door, he paused and surveyed his spacious office. No, this space should not be called an office; it was rather a domain, a lair. Carefully arranged furniture gave an impression of randomness and relaxation; The feeling was enhanced by the foliage that divided the space into distinct functional areas without giving the impression that there was any master plan in mind. Forming a private corner area with a vast view, a large curved section of window joined the two outer walls and formed his private corner. Seated in his high backed leather chair, he was facing north, away from the partially reflecting windows. The sun could be counted on to illuminate his desk over his right shoulder in the morning, switching predictably to the left shoulder every afternoon. He liked predictability.

Stretching like an unruffled sea to the base of the distant Cortez Mountains, standing in stark clarity with the sharpness of their outlines belying their distance, an uninterrupted panoramic view of the desert was revealed by an easy pivot of his high backed swivel chair. Two centuries earlier, the stark clarity of the distant mountains had produced an illusion of nearness that had deceived unsuspecting travelers and had seduced and persuaded to them undertake impossible treks.

Without even glancing at the marble surface of his desk he swiveled to take in the view. It was not that he hadn't seen the view before. On the contrary, he never began a day in the office without deliberately reveling in the view, soaking it up like a sponge. Raising his eyes slightly, he focused his attention on those remembered sensory stimuli of the cool springs that still broke through the surface beside his favorite mountain trails.

With great reluctance he swiveled about and dragging himself from his reverie and with a conscious exertion of will, brought his attention to focus on his forthcoming meeting with the Security Director. Fundamentally, he objected to the very concept of a need for a Security Director. Though he accepted the ordinary precautions required for building security, he was strongly averse to all the additional security fuss necessitated by that damn Project Eight, whatever that is.

He fumed, "What right had anyone to put a classified project in the heart of the world's most open Facility? Even the existence of Level Eight was top secret; imagine hiding a whole level! Admittedly, the very openness of NAMBE was what qualified it as an ideal home for a secret project, but what damn secret project and why is it necessary to hide and deny its very existence?"

Remembering that in its twenty five year existence there had been not a single security incident, he had to admit that the security was good, excellent really; furthermore, the security precautions were unobtrusive, nearly invisible; but the measures did seem extreme. "Even I don't know what the hell is going on down there on the bottom level, and no one who wasn't cleared had any idea that there has been a classified project here for twenty five years. For nineteen of those years the security arrangements had been under the directorship of Laurie Bass. She was only twenty two when she joined us and only twenty six when she took over as Director. Yes, she's performed well", he conceded. As far as he could see, she had no other interest in life, no men, no family and no social life. As far as he knew, her only outside interest was that karate, or whatever one called the sport in which she was said to excel, was called.

Thinking that he had already spent more time thinking about security than the topic merited, he picked up the memo on the top of his pile and reread it. The buzz of the intercom on his desk pulled him up short.

"Yes?" he addressed the intercom in the same formal tone that he normally used in Margaret's presence.

"Miss Bass is here to see you, Dr. Quincy." Margaret's equally formal reply issued from the oak colored box on the corner of his desk.

In the lobby, Laurie thought, "Margret is the only person who works with him every day, and yet she is also the only one who calls him Dr. Quincy instead of Dr. Q. They were made for each other, the two most formal people I know".

"Please send her in. By the way, Margaret, I do not wish to be interrupted regardless of the subject until after Miss Bass leaves."

With the smooth and easy stride developed over years of martial arts practice, Laurie strode gracefully into the room. It was the way she moved more than her trim body and dark wavy hair that created her illusion of perpetual youth; strangers and newcomers invariably put her age in the late twenties. As happened every time she entered this office, she noted that its size and the ostentatious furnishings suited Dr. Q to a tee. It was no more and no less than she would have expected of him.

"Please sit down, Miss Bass."

"Thank you, Dr. Q," she replied. Wishing to express her confidence and individuality, she deliberately took the comfortable chair against the wall, near the large oval coffee table, rather than the more Spartan wooden chair directly in front of the desk. She had long since given up all hope of any degree of informality from him, and it appealed to some inner mischievous streak to depart from the expected action occasionally. She waited for a response and was not disappointed.

"Don't you think you would be more comfortable nearer the desk?"

Replying, "No, this is fine, thank you. I find it easier to be attentive if I am not distracted by your lovely view," she settled back and relaxed into the supple leather.

Arrangements, For a Formal Visit

Having considered whether her insubordination merited a reprimand and reluctantly rejecting the idea, Dr. Q went directly to the point of the meeting. "I've just received word from Duncan McPherson. He is delaying his visit for three months, and then he's bringing his entire NAGWAD committee."

He sat back and sighed as though he had just made a monumental announcement. If he had expected to shock Laurie, he should have known better. Since visits of McPherson's committee are always classified, and since no classified visits can be arranged without the Director of Security being fully informed. In this case McPherson was bringing Dr. Cochran, the Washington representative of Project Eight, the program so classified that Dr. Q was not permitted to know about it

"Yes, I know. I received a telex from McPherson last week," Laurie replied. Before Dr. Q could ask, Laurie answered, "I couldn't reach to you on Friday. You will recall that you were away from the Facility. This morning I thought we each had more pressing things on our plates, with the visitors' tour scheduled for today. I had intended to raise the topic at tomorrow's staff meeting. As far as I can tell, it is just a routine visit and nothing to be concerned about. I will, of course, take care of all of the security arrangements, including accommodations and transportation. I have had no information regarding an agenda. Presumably, they will arrange that with you."

"Yes, I'll arrange the agenda, all of it except for the special agenda for Dr. Cochran and his associates. As you well know, I still don't consider it reasonable that an entire floor of this establishment is given over to a project classified beyond the Executive Director's clearance level." As Laurie started to reply, he raised his hand motioning her to silence. "No, I don't need you to explain to me again that it is simply a question of Need to Know. That still does not make it reasonable." Having been over this ground a number of times, there was really nothing more to say; and facing Dr. Q on this topic always made Laurie uncomfortable on two counts. First, she understood his point of view and sympathized with it; there was simply nothing she could do about that. Secondly, the situation was even worse than Dr. Q thought; the Facility also had an additional level whose very existence was unknown to him. Project Nine was not only another classified program of which he was totally unaware, it used an entire Facility level, Level 9, which Dr. Q did not even know existed.

"I'm sorry, sir, but we both know we are powerless to change the arrangement and must just make the best of it. McPherson and his staff rarely visit more than once a year, and except for his visits, you have no other indications of the presence of the Project Eight programs. This time, however, he seems to be bringing his entire Washington office. I have received clearances for six scientists besides McPherson himself. Considering his attitude about publicity, I intend to book the entire guest house for the seven of them, if you don't mind."

"Of course, those arrangements are your responsibility and I will not interfere. However, it will mean that McPherson and his staff will have rooms in the city. That in turn will mean an hour a day in extra travel time for them. I guess they can tolerate that for the sake of their precious security, and in some ways it will simplify our lives.

"I asked you up here not to discuss arrangements or to complain about the security requirements again, but rather to discuss the significance of their changing their plans. They were just here in March, and as you say they rarely visit more than once every twelve months. Then they schedule a visit only three months after their last one, cancel it out, and then reschedule. Have you heard of anything amiss in the Project Eight programs? I know you can't tell me any details. But if there were any difficulties of some sort there, I would like to believe that I would hear about it from you first, rather than from McPherson." Laurie grew thoughtful. She too had wondered at the change in visit frequency and the unexpected rescheduling on short notice. She could not, however, share her questions about the mysterious Beta 4 project with Dr. Q, since he was not cleared. Instead, she sought to reassure him.

"Frankly, I don't know. I confess that I too was surprised at a visit coming this close to the last one. However, that visit has now been moved thirteen weeks into the future; that really is a mystery to me. If anything were seriously wrong they would not wait so long. Put your mind at ease regarding trouble on Project Eight. I know of no reason for concern down there. Dr. Cochran has two new additions to committee, and they will be accompanying him. Perhaps that is the purpose of the trip, to provide an orientation for the new members. It would also account for the shift in the date if there has been some delay in obtaining one of the clearances. I really don't know. I am only told of those matters that directly affect or are affected by security."

The entire conversation was unsatisfactory. Dr. Q always felt uneasy talking to his Director of Security. "Why did I call this meeting anyway? It is humiliating to know she knew so much about Project Eight and that he knew nothing except that they existed. "Damn McPherson and Cochran anyway," thought silently. The truth of the matter was that Dr. Q did not like being anything but number one. During the periods between McPherson's visits, he was the Executive Director. During their visits, he was treated almost like a hired hand. They were polite to him and his staff who presented status reports on the various programs the unclassified programs, naturally. But he always felt there was too much going on that he didn't know about. It was almost as if Level Zero through Seven existed solely as a cover for Level Eight. He, Dr. Quincy, was merely tolerated in his own Facility.

Following the meeting with Dr. Q, Laurie returned to her office and called Susan in to work out the schedule of the visits. Because of her position as the Security Director's secretary, Susan was cleared administratively for both projects Eight and Nine. That is, she was not cleared to know the contents of the programs, which she would not have understood in any case; but she was cleared to know of their existence and the code words used in referring to them.

"Well, Susan, as you no doubt learned from the telex, McPherson and his entire committee are coming for the next review meeting. I think we'll take over the entire guesthouse for them. Please arrange it, and make sure Personnel and Public Relations are aware that the place is fully booked for that time. The dinner arrangements you made last time were excellent. I'll leave them to your good judgment again. We'll need the usual transportation arrangements as well."

"Yes, I thought so, Laurie. I've already booked the guesthouse. I figured it'd be better to cancel it if you wanted me to make a different arrangement rather than to take a chance on the PR people booking some VIP in before we got to it. The new manager, Jerry, still kicks up a fuss at being asked to cancel someone's reservation after he's sent out an acknowledgment."

"And I suppose you've already made the dinner arrangements as well" Laurie smiled. "Susan, you're a gem. Sometimes I feel totally superfluous around here. Please don't let Dr. Q know that you don't need me. Okay, scat and let me get on with the rest of this paper Pile; unless you've handled everything in there also."

"Not a chance," Susan replied as she picked up her shorthand pad and left the office.

Laurie settled back in her chair, closed her eyes, and thought about her meeting with Dr. Q. Clearly, her trepidations preceding the meeting had been unfounded. In spite of everything she felt sorry for him: all these projects going on in his Facility, and he's not allowed to know what they're about. In particular she recalled the story Mary Ann told of her disclosing the full extent of the research Level 9 and of the momentous implications of Dr. Peter's research.

As it developed, the planned visit was destined to coincide with the onset of the Outrage and the presence of those very visitors at that place at that time significantly increased the severity of the aggressive action.

An Old Comrade Is Recruited, Tiny Meets With Terry

In the years since their Army service Terry and Tiny had had no contact at all. Each had somehow brought their Army skills to bear in civilian life. Terry had turned his planning skills to crime. Tiny had found a perfectly legal profession that let him utilize and further hone his destructive skills. Then out of the blue a request for this meeting. Tiny was puzzled but he was certain that Terry had not requested a meeting to reminisce about the old days.

Standing only five feet two inches (if his shoes were sufficiently new; they rarely were), Tiny was aptly nicknamed. In a woman, his bone structure would be described as delicate. However, no one would ever have used the word to describe Tiny. Small? Yes. Wiry? Yes. However, there was never anything delicate about Tiny, neither in his appearance or his mannerism. Unruly red hair tumbled over his forehead, threatening to obscure his pale brown eyes. Now, preparing for his meeting with Terry, Tiny realized he had not seen him since they left the service. "What the hell does Terry want with me?" He wondered. "Well there's only one way to find out." Grabbing his coat, he turned and left the flat early enough to arrive at the appointed time and avoid a ration of shit from Terry.

Twenty minutes after leaving, he slouched on the bench across the table from Terry. Tiny's sprawling posture managed to take up an entire side of the booth despite his diminutive frame. Intertwining his disproportionately long fingers around a tall glass of scotch and water, he stared at Terry with unblinking eyes. "Let's see if I got this straight."

He paused, his eyes never leaving Terry's. "You want to rig an explosive charge so it can be freely and safely transported in some goddamned bouncing eighteen wheeled juggernaut. Then on the user's command you want this same rig to become so delicate and sensitive that any sort of movement, however slight, will set it off. On the next command you want the process reversed and the bomb made harmless again. Have I got it right?"

"Right on. Give the man a big cuddly Kewpie doll," Terry replied.

"What the hell for??" Tiny asked incredulously.

"There's a hell of a lot of ground to cover before I answer that question. The first question is, can it be done? What's so tough about that; either it can be done or it can't be?"

"If I'm the rigger, of course it can be done. You know that. That's why we're here, for chrissake. Who do ya think you're shittin'? But ya got it wrong. The question is not 'Can it be done?', but 'Will Tiny do it?' And the answer to that one depends on two other questions: What's in it for Tiny and what the hell do you intend to do with the rig? If you're not ready to discuss that, it's Thanks for the drink and I'll see ya around."

While far from wealthy, Tiny had finally reached a place in life where he felt at home, almost comfortable. Did he really want to risk his simple but satisfying existence on some hair brined Terry Plan?

Terry did not respond immediately, and Tiny sipped slowly at his drink and thought, "I'll give the bastard a couple of minutes. Then either he opens up or screw him. Who needs one of his complicated schemes, anyway?"

Sitting patiently, Tiny, who considered himself a no nonsense guy who took pride in demonstrating what he considered his unique ability to cut through the horseshit and get to the heart of the matter, reflected upon the factors leading up to this meeting.

Orphaned early, Tiny had learned expect nothing to come easily. He could not remember ever having had real parents. "I was born an orphan," he used to say to anyone who asked him about his family. At first, when he was quite young, deep bonds would form between his foster parents and himself. But then, for reasons he never understood, he would find himself in a new home.

"I'm sure you will be happy here, Tiny. Won't he, Papa?" These were the first words uttered by each new set of foster parents. For the first two or three this might in fact have been true; but then he learned that as soon as he was comfortable or formed any sort of bond, someone would manage somehow to destroy it and he would be whisked off to another set, also sure he would be very happy there.

Friendships formed with children his own age from his 'neighborhood of the moment' were no different. Invariably, or so it seemed, a change in parents meant a change in neighborhood and a

whole new set of kids. Having always been the 'new kid on the block
and of course always the smallest, Tiny had never been comfortable
with deep or lasting relationships. New areas of town or entire new
towns meant a new round of challenges and taunts centering on
his size and origins. At first he had accepted the physical challenges
and attempted to compensate for his size with ferocity. It rarely
worked, and after a time he quit trying to win acceptance. "Fuck
'em" became his response long before he had any concept of what
the phrase meant.

He had retreated to books. He was an avid reader who would
read anything simply because it was there; but for all his reading
and his retreat into study, he was only an average student. His
best subject was science, but on the whole he did not attract the
attention of his teachers, as he quietly accumulated B's and A's, with
an occasional C.

Long after he had quit trying to be accepted, his bitterness
smoldered. Against the sociological odds, he finished high school.
But then what? Without consciously thinking about it, he knew
anything he built up would surely be torn down by the shadowy
"them" who invariably shoved him from pillar to post all his life.
After graduation, he spent his first summer drifting from one odd
job to another, looking for something but knowing he wouldn't find
anything.

He might have continued in that manner indefinitely had it
not been for the army: the perpetual international chess game in
which the major powers sought to purchase influence, ideological
conformity, and territorial expansion with vast military aid and
a handful of grain was still in progress. One of its periodic crises
was about to peak as another Central American rebellion and
accompanying border conflict threatened to get out of hand. The
chance of U.S. advisers being sent in and exercises being staged in
the area were increasing daily.

Half crocked one evening at his favorite watering hole, he
watched the evening news. "Silly bastards, they need their asses
kicked." Later it was not clear to him which side needed their asses
kicked or why. But by then it didn't matter; someone else was making

his decisions for him. He had enlisted in the Army, where he was accepted, abused through boot camp, and then became a volunteer for assignment to a Special Forces. Expecting his size to exclude him, he fully expected to be rejected; possibly he even hoped for yet another demonstration that 'they' were always against him. To his surprise, he was accepted.

If boot camp had been abusive, this new training center could only be described as torturous. He was singled out for particular attention because of his undersized frame. Reversing the habits he had built up over his final years of school, he set out to prove that he could damn well make it if anyone could. By then, whatever reasons he might have had for joining up in the first place and for volunteering in the second place were long since forgotten. However, he had been determined finish. He did. "Guess I showed the big bastards," he congratulated himself at the ceremony marking the end of the torture camp.

The Central American situation had indeed progressed as forecast by the news media. The United States was sending troops under some politically acceptable guise to participate in the gallant struggle against the further encroachment of communism. Packed into the latest version of military air transport, Tiny had been shocked to find himself actually bound for a combat zone on the border of two countries he hadn't ever heard of before this current crisis arose.

"I didn't lose a goddamn thing in that goddamned jungle. Why the hell am I here?" he thought. "You spent a stupid, booze soaked evening in front of a goddamn TV news broadcast, that's why," he admonished himself. But even as the thought entered his mind, he realized it as a gross oversimplification. The scotch and the television had nothing to do with it. "I was just running away; but from what?

"Who the hell knows or cares? What am I, some kind of goddamn psychiatrist or something? Maybe my mother hated me, whoever she was. Maybe I don't like myself. What's the difference? I'm here and I'd better start paying attention or I'm liable to be planted here. Forget the goddamn introspection and concentrate on staying alive and getting out of this mess. I can figure out why later."

Tiny followed only part of his own advice. The how he had gotten into the mess, and he ignored the second part of his private counsel; he had not concentrated on staying alive. He volunteered again and eventually found himself part of an infiltration team. He had specialized in demolition and soon earned himself a considerable reputation.

The other team members carried the heavy stuff and provided protection. Tiny destroyed. He had found his calling. A few handfuls of plastic, some wires, a battery, a radio, a trip wire, a mechanical trigger, or whatever, Tiny brought down buildings, bridges, airplane hangars or anything at all. No structure was impervious to his skills. He took equal pleasure blasting a munitions store, demolishing a bridge, or destroying a plane. He had the knack, and, somehow, the risk did not seem to matter.

Tiny Remembers Terry

For the first time in years, Tiny thought about Terry and recalled his first impressions. Accustomed to always feeling like an outsider and 'different,' Tiny always silently accepted differences in others. Over the years, that attitude made him increasingly critical of the prejudice of others. It is not surprising that he was suspicious of Terry

The leader, a tall sullen kid from somewhere down south, was a buck sergeant named Terry. The members of the infiltration were, in fact, all rather sullen; each had his own very private reasons for being in such a team. Not surprisingly, Tiny couldn't remember Terry's last name; no squad member ever used more than one name. And in their rare off duty times they separated, each to his own private escape. Tiny remembered Terry as a planner. He made no pretense at bravery or idealistic motivation. All he ever wanted from a mission was to return, and he was surprisingly successful at getting his squad in and out alive. They had been caught in the open and fired upon only once that Tiny could remember. That time two guys were hit, but the wounds were so minor they were treated only by the medic.

On those rare occasions when he thought about his army days at all, Tiny could picture only one other member of the team, Albert. The grandson of an English immigrant, Albert was a tall slender guy (of course, by Tiny's standards nearly everyone was tall) with dark hair and a rodent like appearance. The most remarkable thing about Albert, however, was not his physical appearance but his obsession with gambling.

The tour ended and the team split up, going their separate ways with no vows to get together some time or stay in touch. It had not been that kind of squad. Tiny had bummed around a bit, dabbled in petty crime, and managed to avoid involvement with the authorities. Uninterested in penny ante crime and aware that he lacked the planning skills for the big time, he had returned to the "odd job routine."

By chance, answering an advertisement for casual labor, he found his place at Corpella's Demolition Services. Corpella quickly recognized Tiny's skills. He accepted his Tiny's sullenness as a small price to pay for someone who could drop a building with such predictability. Happy to be destroying things, Tiny had no desire to grow in the job or to manage. Interrupting his reverie to finish his drink, Tiny scraped himself together and began to get up, "Thanks for the drink, see ya around."

"Sit down and order up another drink. I'll tell you about it." Terry carefully outlined his plan, at least the part the little creep needed to know. Enough to get him hooked and to demonstrate the importance of his particular talents.

When he reached the end of the scheme and the size of the payoff, Terry paused to let it sink in. Then he went on, "So you see, we need the device to be quite safe, both during its initial delivery and during this placement by unskilled guys under less than ideal conditions, who will not be told what they're handling. Then it will be transported by truck halfway across the country and stored in a warehouse for a couple of months. Then we need to activate and permit the detonation of only a small charge, just large enough to demonstrate that we're not full of shit; certainly not large enough to do any damage or to set off the rest of the explosives. Then the remaining explosives are activated, and the fun begins. At the appropriate time we shut the entire thing down, turn it all off."

"Yeah, I see. I'd need some special electronic gadgets. This rig will be in a building. I need to be sure I can communicate with it." He paused and contemplated his glass again. After a moment he nodded and rose. "Yeah, I can do it. Count me in. After everything else is arranged, look me up again. If you can convince me you got it wired, I'll do it." Without waiting for any further discussion, he turned and left.

Terry's successful recruitment of Tiny filled the most single most critical staffing position in his entire plan.

Satisfied with his evening's work, Terry waved the waiter over, paid the check and left. Tiny was a conceited little son of a bitch, but goddamn good.

Terry also remembered Albert Stamp! Like Tiny, Terry had not had any contact with the old members of his squad, but he had followed newspaper accounts of Albert's rise to prominence in the Bahamas branch of the Colosimo family, which controlled all gambling in the Western Hemisphere. Recently, he had read that Albert had bought into some large real estate deals in southern Canada. The papers had suggested it was another part of his complex money-laundering operations.

When Tiny was well out of the room, Terry rose and went to the phone.

Brian Anticipates the Meeting

Brian, was not a part of Terry's army squad but was friendly with Lefty, who had been part of the squad. Lefty had introduced Brian to Terry for the first of the gas station jobs.

Tossing and turning, Brian Taylor had not really rested all night. Sleep had completely eluded him. Considering that the long awaited meeting was set to take place this morning, not a moment too soon for the Peoria contingent.

The din of his boarding house had long since pulled and jerked Brian from his restless sleep; his crumpled bedding was bunched up under his shoulders, exposing his feet to errant drafts. Determined to get some rest, he thumped onto his side. In the process the sheets and blankets were twisted further. Brian gave up. "What the hell! Who needs sleep anyhow?"

Throwing the bedclothes back, he dropped his feet onto the bare linoleum floor of his colorless one room flat. Through the gaps surrounding the ill fitting shade and curtain, the harsh violet tinted light of the street lamp seeped into the room, casting a blue pallor over the sparse furnishings. The eerie illumination seemed to lower the temperature of the room. Brian shivered again. Hunching his shoulders against the pervasive chill, he shuffled into the bathroom. Switching on the light, he flinched at the painful contrast between the glare of the bare bulb and the gloomy half light he had just left. As his eyes adjusted, he stared at the scruffy face greeting him from the mirror. In the vain hope that some warmth could be coaxed from them, he fussed with the faucets. Giving up, he splashed cold water onto his face, cupping some of it to his mouth to complete his morning freshening up. Glancing again at his image in the mirror, he ran the fingers of both hands through his stringy dirty brown hair. Worn somewhat longer than was the current custom, his hair more or less covered his out sized ears. Hurrying back to the pile of clothes heaped at the side of his bed, Brian shook his head to shed the remnants of his sleepless night. The action served only to sharpen the dull pain forming behind his eyes.

"Christ," he mumbled, shaking a cigarette from a crumpled package and rummaging through the clutter on his night table in search of a match. He found a greasy, stained cardboard book of matches and lit up. Inhaling deeply, he closed his eyes, momentarily savoring the effects of this first smoke of the day. Reaching down and pulling his trousers from the heap of clothing at his feet, he blinked his eyes against the irritation of the acrid smoke drifting up from his cigarette into his eyes. It seemed to Brian that he had always lived like this; he barely remembered a time when he had

slept in a comfortable bed in a warm room and arose in the morning
to a shower and a clean set of clothes provided by Gail.

Gail had left him. Dead, they'd said. Now, Gail was but a faded
memory, and memory had never been his strong point. Recollections
of his life before the orphanage and the subsequent string of foster
parents were particularly vague. Though he had only lived with three
foster families, his memories of them were very vague and jumbled.
He couldn't even arrange their names in chronological sequence.
Hell, he couldn't even recall all their names. In his mind, they had
taken him in only to get their hands on the state's support money.
Who gives a shit? He'd soon be rolling in money, thanks to Terry.
Unaware of the snags and pills mottling his army surplus sweater,
he pulled it over his head. He was suddenly struck by the smell, an
acrid, musty odor, pungent but somehow not totally repulsive. It
was, after all, his own smell. "What the hell else do I own?"

He did not regard his depressed self pity as noteworthy; it was
his normal state of mind. Opening the door to face the morning,
he grabbed his coat, a faded windbreaker. Not only would it be cold
outside, he was sure that if he left it one of the neighborhood creeps
would pinch the damn thing. It did not occur to him that in its
present threadbare condition it was less tempting for others than it
had been for him a year ago, when he had stolen it. That had been
before he met Terry.

A moment later, fully dressed and taking a long pull at his
cigarette, he stepped through his apartment door. In the hallway,
he paused and glanced both ways as though expecting to find some
threat lurking in the corridor. Then, grinding the remains of his
cigarette into the floor, he hurried out. Today would be different; it
would not be another endless day of waiting for word from Terry.
Today is the day.

Meandering slowly, he turned left onto a walk that followed
the riverbank at a safe distance. His wandering took him a full eight
blocks from his room to a bend in the river. The river was wide at
this point, and the width, combined with the bend, created the
effect of a small bay, known by the locals, as Pirates Cove.

Too small to have commercial significance, this sheltered area had long ago been abandoned. Its location, on Peoria's poor South Side, forbade its use as a resort or club site. The neighborhood kids once swam here, but that was before beer bottles and other trash had rendered the water, and the muddy bottom it concealed, unfit for any human activity.

At the head of the decaying wharf, Brian turned aimlessly to the right, facing the east. Loose and broken planking stretched twenty feet in front of him, crumbling and decaying into the stagnant water, trapped there in 'Pirates Cove'. Barely obscuring the banks on the north and south sides of the bay, the mist rose as gently from the surface as steam from a slowly simmering Salvation Army stew. At random intervals, here and there wisps of mist seemed to struggle free and strain upward. High above, a brilliantly cerise sky, overlaid with a complex tangle of whiter wisps, stretched as far as the eye could see in all directions. The breathtaking scene was totally wasted on Brian. In the vivid sky he saw only a reminder that he had missed an entire night's sleep.

Brian Recalls Meeting Terry

While Brian was a member of the offensive team at the center of The Outrage, not many would consider him an important factor or central character. But that illustrates an important characteristic of chaos theory. It is not Brian himself that is central to the story; rather, the important factor is that someone with the traits of Brain exists at the proper place at the proper time to become an integral part of Terry's final team. Hence, it is not Brian himself that is central but rather the character traits that have to exist in a single person at the right time and the right place. I included him here to introduce those traits into the mix.

Brian had first met Terry a year ago in Dan's Corner, a small dimly lit bar on Peoria's South Side. It had been a hot night without a hint of breeze to provide even the illusion of relief from the oppressive humidity. As was his nightly custom, Brian had sat quietly in the dark corner farthest from the door, staring aimlessly at the interlocking circles of moisture that formed every time his cool bottle rested even momentarily on the table's stained Formica surface. In spite of the humidity there were sections of the table that seemed to resist the puddling of condensation. Why? he wondered. Was it an imperfection in the plastic coating or simply a greasy leftover from a previous customer? Carefully shaking the ashes from his cigarette on the questionable areas and blowing them across the surface, he attempted to settle this important question by observing the behavior of the ash. These weighty deliberations were rudely interrupted by a hoarse "There you are!" from Lefty.

"Where the hell else would I be?" he retorted. He had known the chain smoking Lefty all his life, at least all it that he could remember. "Sit down and buy me a beer, you old horseshit."

It was only as Lefty was sliding into the other side of the booth that Brian noticed the other man with him. "Terry, Brian. Brian, Terry," Lefty said by way of introduction. Terry merely nodded an acknowledgment as he slid silently in beside Lefty. Lefty spent nearly as much time at Dan's Corner as Brian. Shirley, the overly endowed and under attired waitress, wasted no time in bringing him a cold Pabst with a double Four Roses on the side. "What'll your friend have?" she asked, shamelessly examining the newcomer, while leaning with studied carelessness over Brian's shoulder to place the drinks within Lefty's reach. It was impossible for Terry not to notice her ample breasts.

"Beer," the expressionless reply revealed Terry's complete indifference to Shirley's exposed flesh. Rather, his green eyes never left Brian's. They seemed to bore into him. Brian squirmed uncomfortably under the unwavering stare. At length he caved in. Picking up his glass, he drained it in an attempt to hide his discomfort. An issue important to him but never mentioned had been satisfactorily settled. The details of that first meeting were difficult for Brian to recall, except for Terry's eyes, the most unusual and penetrating eyes Brian had ever seen. There was no forgetting, however, that before the evening had ended, the first plan had been formulated and agreed upon.

Two nights later the three of them pulled the first of the quick hits, a modest liquor store in the North End. It had gone as smoothly as Terry had said it would; they were out of the store almost immediately with the contents of its cash register stuffed into their pockets. His task was to drive without attracting attention the "borrowed" neighborhood car safely and quickly to their own vehicle; or in the unlikely event that they were noticed by the police, to lose them before ditching the loaner and picking up their own wheels. Twice more in the following evening they had pulled the same job at two separate locations.

"That's all for that plan," Terry had explained. "There is now an MO established in the minds of the Peoria police. The same MO will appear in Chicago next week and in Buffalo the following week. By then the police of three cities will be sure a gang of liquor store bandits is on the move, drifting northeast. In the following week the gang will strike again, this time in Boston. The simpleminded pigs will then be damn sure they are right and will mount an all out dragnet. Then we strike right here in Peoria where we will have been all the time, drinking at Dan's and staring at Shirley's boobs."

It had all gone precisely as Terry had said. The only surprise was that their and last job in Peoria was not another liquor store but three widely separated suburban supermarkets, all struck within a period of two hours. After that night Terry vanished, having explained that this was merely a warm up, a demonstration of Terry's planning and organization. Their next job, he said, would set the world on its ear.

From this point onwards a number of different plans emerge at different points in time and space. The plan that resulted in the Outrage was Terry's Plan with a capital and from this point on, I shall use the capital P to indicate Terry' Plan central plan. The first step of Terry' Plan had been a complete success; and, only he knew that there was a Plkan and that this action had been the first step thereof.

Brian and Lefty were allowed to keep two thirds of the loot and were told that if they attracted no attention to themselves, they would soon be part of the largest, most sensational heist ever pulled anywhere on the face of the earth. No other explanation. No arrangements for keeping in touch. No indication of when the next job might be. No nothing. Terry just left.

For a month everything had gone just as he said, not only in Peoria but in four other cities. The multiple city story played out exactly as Terry had predicted. "What could Terry have in mind for the next job? Would it be a single job or a national sweep? It had been a year since the last jobs, a year of waiting and watching the money supply dwindle to near nothing. And where the hell is Lefty?" Lefty had left town three days ago and then he simply vanished.

Turning north into the wind, he put both men out of his mind and contemplated his day. There was enough change in his pocket to eat breakfast Joe's diner just ahead its location indicated by the sputtering neon, "Joe's Real Eats for Real Folk." Brian entered. After the chill of the morning air, the heated atmosphere of the diner, pregnant with the odors of frying breakfasts, flushed his cheeks, and all thoughts of Terry and Lefty slipped from his mind. As he sank into an empty booth at the back, he lit another cigarette and nodded to Marie, the only communication necessary to arrange his standard breakfast. Since his five foot five frame did not quite fit the booth, he squirmed around until his feet could rest on the bottom of the table leg. He savored the heavy odors of the diner. Like so many very thin people, Brian had an insatiable appetite.

Across town at the newly opened bus station, Lefty stepped down from the eastbound bus and carrying his canvas bag over his shoulder, he headed south. Contemplating his upcoming meeting, he thought "Brian, the poor slob whose routine never varies will be having breakfast at Joe's. Well, he is sure as hell is in for a shock today."

Lefty still found it hard to believe that Terry really intended to attempt such a caper. "Sure, he had baffled the police of several states with his last plan. (At least he thought it had been Terry's last plan.) But is he really serious about taking on the Feds? Yeh, he's serious, and so am I. Goddamn right I am." He hurried on, hunching his shoulders and bunching his coat against the cold. He was looking forward to telling Brian. Wait until that simpleton hears this.

Terry Return's from Europe

Abuzz with more diverse tongues than the Tower of Babel, Heathrow's Terminal 3 bustled with crushing crowds, attired in every conceivable costume from blue jeans to saris, swarming around the arrival gates, waving arms and signs and calling out the names of loved ones. Standing discreetly at the back of the mob-like scene, corporate drivers quietly displayed their company names or those of the passengers they had been delegated to meet. The din and the confusion were maddening to those uninitiated in the rites of the International Arrivals area of London's Heathrow Airport.

Arriving from the United States Two days ago, on his way through Heathrow to Switzerland, Terry had elbowed through the crush of 'gooks and niggers' and using his small shoulder bag as a combination battering-ram and shield, and quickly passed through to the bus for Terminal 2. Yes, he had been through the 'Arrivals" routine, but it had not really prepared him for the Departures scene he encountered on his way back to the States.

He had convinced himself that the seething mob of humanity was characteristic of Arrivals only; surely the Departures would be more civilized, more British. Wrong! The throngs that had greeted the arriving passengers were back, sending them off with kisses, tears, and a cacophony of babbling. Only the quiet, courteous corporate drivers were missing. If anything, the confusion was worse.

The lower level, a sea of humanity washing back and forth along the spillways formed by the ticket counters, were clogged with a hodgepodge of luggage, boxes, clothing and children, tied to or constantly chased by harried parents. There was no relief on the upper level. Further blocking and delaying the pressing crowds as they sought a few inches of horizontal surface on which to write, were departing passengers who had suddenly discovered that departure cards had to be completed in order to gain admission to the Departure Lounge. They'd so piled and scattered their carryon luggage on the floor beside them as to render passage nearly impossible without risking life and limb. Armed as he had been two days before on his way through to Switzerland, Terry fought his way through to the Departure Lounge. The situation was no better there; if anything it was more confusing and noisy. True, there were tables at which a variety of drinks were consumed; and off to the left, a cafeteria counter dispensed hot, milky tea and a variety of stale biscuits and greasy food. Of course, there was no such thing as a vacant table or chair. "Screw it!" Terry muttered.

At the rear of the lounge, the largest single flight display board Terry had ever seen finally revealed the gate number for his flight. Shaking his head in disgust at the mob scene, Terry passed into the hallway and began the long walk to the waiting area from which the articulated bus would pick up the passengers and deliver them to the plane.

After protracted waits and delays, mercifully he found himself airborne. It had been a useful trip. He patted the breast pocket wallet that held the two account numbers.

Another step along the road to the success of a brilliant scheme, the Plan, had been successfully completed.

Terry Reviews His Strong Men

With the cabin darkened for the in flight film, the drone of the jets, barely audible above the music, soothing his imagination, Terry thoughtfully reviewed his muscle men. "Herm is a real son of a bitch, just exactly what I need, at the right moment" he reflected. "His eyes alone will scare the shit out of most people." Terry had known Herm for a long time, ever since Terry had dropped out of college in the middle of his junior year. "Who the hell needs a goddamn degree anyway?" he had thought and went out that evening and tied one on.

It turned out to be a drunk to end all drunks. He hadn't been sloshed since. The next day he woke up in the stinking 'tank' with a bunch of dirty, smelly winos. When he was able to sit up without setting off an earthquake, he managed to pull his eyelids apart, even though the glare of the naked overhead light, a 500watt bulb shielded only by its wire cage, physically abused his eyes. Despite the pain, he surveyed his companions. One of them was Herm. Six feet six at least, and all of 280 pounds of hard case, wearing a stained sweatshirt and beltless, faded jeans that sagged spilling his outsized abdomen, he simply stood there. His forearms were covered with tattoos of large snakes. From where Terry sat, hunched over, it was impossible to tell if the big bastard was asleep or awake. But he stood absolutely immobile with his head slumped forward onto his massive chest. Jet black, tightly curled hair grew in thick profusion over his head, jowls and chin. His shoulders drooped forward, pulled down by the weight of his huge hands and massive arms.

His back pressed against the bars to maintain his balance, Herm had been standing immobile for two hours. Unlike Terry, Herm had been here before and was fully aware of the stages of misery through which he had to pass following a binge. Unfortunately for the rest of the world, he was not a regular drunk; for when Herm drank he became steadily more quiet and subdued. He was mean and dangerous only when sober.

Somehow, the men got through the morning formalities and were released after a only a minimal amount of hassle. Despite the inevitability of their return, the police seemed pleased to be rid of them. Terry and Herm, the last to be processed, found themselves slumped side by side on the bus stop bench just outside the tank.

"Goddamn sun. It's vaporizing my goddamn retinas." Terry groaned as he turned and narrowed his eyes in a vain attempt to escape the sun's onslaught.

"Yeah, it's a bitch," was Herm's considered response. "It'd help if my head would hold still until my guts had a chance to settle down." He grunted. "What we need is a good stiff drink, the hair of the dog."

"Can't do any harm," Terry agreed. "If the goddamn bus ever gets here we can ride down to the College Tap, get that drink, and pick up my car. After that . . . ." his voice trailed off. It was just too much effort to think further than that.

"Yeah, I damn sure got no place else to go." It developed that Herm had quit his job the day before. "Just hadda get the hell outa this college town." Since Terry wasn't really interested, he didn't pursue the matter, and the cause of Herm's bitterness was never discussed again.

Having retrieved Terry's car from the police, and ingesting a breakfast of beer and hamburgers, they drove out to the edge of town and spent the rest of the morning sitting on a park bench, alternately dozing and watching the two swans patrolling the pond. Lunch, consumed on the same park bench, was another round of hamburgers, garnished with French fries and washed down with beer.

Stumbling through the recovery stages of their hangovers and not letting the hair of the dog cure lead them to a repeat of the previous day's consumption, they managed to survive the day. With nothing more in common than a night in the tank and colossal hangovers, the two men had bonded. As the day wore on, the alliance was strengthened by the unspoken realization that each man had cut himself loose from his previous life without any plan. For each of them it had been sufficient to just get the hell out. At nightfall, they split up after agreeing to meet the next day and leave town. Neither of them had a very clear idea of a destination. "Away from this hellhole" was a sufficient goal.

For a couple of months that summer they bummed around together, working as casual day laborers with a road construction gang. It was hot and dirty work, but neither had any intention of staying with it very long, so they were not bothered by the dead end nature of the job. While each was sure in his own mind that he would soon be moving on, neither had any idea where or when. They were content, for a time, to drift. Their days were filled with sweat and the loose and casual camaraderie of the work crews with whom they were thrown together. Their nights were occupied with beer and eight ball, punctuated by an occasional romp with a local prostitute.

A Frightening Explosion

The side of Herm that he now considered important to the Plan had been unknown until a cheap pool game provided the perfect showcase for the brutality of the man for whom Terry now had a specific use.

Terry had first seen the explosive cruel streak in Herm's makeup when, in the middle of a $2 pool game, an opponent had suggested that Herm had nudged a ball in front of a pocket. The accusation was scarcely made before Herm had delivered a shattering backhand to his opponent's lower jaw. A sickening crack was followed immediately by a pain filled groan. Carelessly, without haste or comment, Herm picked up the money that had been placed on the table to cover the wager, pocketed the bills, and hung up his cue. In all that time he had not looked at his victim or spoken a word. The entire pool hall had gone silent, except for the choked back sobs of the downed player. All faces turned toward Herm. With the slightest of nods to Terry, and moving as though there were no one else in the building, Herm started casually toward the door.

"Whoa ya big bastard; where the fuck ya think you're going?" The voice belonged to one of the three men who had come in with the now nearly unconscious pool player, who, slumped over on the floor, was looking in disbelief at the blood that spilled between his fingers.

Without a word, Herm turned to face the voice. He simply stood and looked down at the three friends, who separated slightly from one another, forming a semicircle in front of him. His demeanor and stance were still relaxed and casual and completely contemptuous of the implied threat; neither the verbal challenge nor by the tactical formation were worrisome to him. He was totally unconcerned with the trio threatening him. Shocked by Herm's complete indifference to the beating he was sure to receive, Terry edged back, waiting for the attack to begin and wondering what his own role would be in the disaster about to befall his companion.

Before he could decide, he was struck by the hush in the bar. There should have been an active brawl going on by now, with a lot of cursing and accusing. But no one was moving a muscle.

Terry looked from the trio to Herm and gasped, knowing that if the men moved, Herm would kill them somehow. The men knew it too. It was in Herm's goddamned eyes. They didn't waver; they didn't move. They're like windows into hell.

Terry was as riveted to his position as were the men ringing Herm. He stared open mouthed as they parted, opening the way for Herm's departure. Silently and still nonchalantly, Herm strolled toward the door. The other players in the hall also moved aside as he passed. Nervously, unsure of how much longer Herm's hypnotic stare could hold back the onslaught, Terry followed in his wake, through the hall and out the door, careful not to look back.

Without discussing the incident or a destination, they left town the next day and drifted westward, from one large development project to another. Twice more in their travels together, Herm's explosive temper had resulted in confrontation and injury. Twice more, a numerically superior opposition backed down in the face of Herm's mesmerizing stare. The third incident had been the last straw. A comment, so innocuous that Terry could no longer even remember what it, had earned a local barroom ruffian a badly smashed nose. Reeling from one of Herm's furious backhands, the startled loudmouth fell across a table, shattering a chair and seriously injuring his back. As usual, Herm calmly stepped back, glowered around the room, and left without comment.

Watching nervously from the sidelines, Terry decided to split. The bastard would go too far one day and kill somebody. Or worse yet, some of local toughs would decide to take him on, and he'd kill the lot of them. The next morning, while Herm slept in, Terry took off.

Terry Enlists

The Central American problem was filling the news. For a change, the anticipated US involvement had a lot of popular support. For no good reason Terry enlisted in the army. He hadn't even tried to rationalize his action. He just enlisted. It did occur to him at the time that his actions were ill thought out and without any positive motive or objectives. He was not overly disturbed by the fact, he simply observed it and filed it away.

A Pointless Vandal Raid Just South of Chicago

This event did occur in Era 2 but some months later than Terry's discharge from the service. At the time of its occurrence, the raid of the glassware company, Chemglass, just south of Chicago, Illinois, had been extensively reported and discussed as an example of meaningless and wasteful vandalism. Its relationship to The Outrage was not suspected until weeks into the investigation of the assault on NAMBE. It was by no means meaningless vandalism in relationship to Terry's plan. On the contrary it was an essential step in his overall plan and it had just been successfully completed.

The night was cloudless and, thanks to the tireless MAJ cleaners, absolutely clear. With no pollutants to impede the earth's radiant cooling, the temperature had fallen sharply after sundown, reminding all who were out and about of the winter nights of just a few weeks earlier. There had been cool spring nights long before the MAJ, but they were more common now. The night sky was magnificent. The Milky Way swept from horizon to horizon, its distant mistiness dotted her and there with individual bright starts that refused to be obscured. The blackness of the surrounding firmament seemed to amplify the brilliance of those heavenly bodies outside the mainstream of the misty veil. Three men in black moved silently across the poorly lit parking lot of Chemglass, Inc., a manufacturer of laboratory glassware just south of Chicago. Two of them, bent under heavily laden black sacks, shuffled along behind the leader, who carried the least lethal load of the three, a 12gauge pump shotgun.

All three men had been assured by Terry that the shipping area would be totally deserted for a full two hours before the night watchman hastily keyed in his 2 A.M. check of the security system. They had also been assured that the night watchman with his archaic clock punch was the only security system that the warehouse had. Indeed the products produced by Chemglass were of little interest to thieves, and the relatively remote location of the warehouse made it virtually immune to vandalism. Terry had told them this and they had no reason to doubt him. However, none of them drew any comfort from that knowledge.

"Terry's really flipped his lid this time," George muttered. What they were about to do made no sense at all to either one of them. They had each expressed the same thought directly to Terry with but slight variations.

"Trust me," he had always replied. Then he laid out his plans. There was absolutely no doubt that he had cased this place well. He had been correct in every detail. He would be right about the guard and the lack of an alarm system, too. They did not expect to be caught, though each man knew that being picked up with the loads they were carrying would be disastrous; each had been in and out of the joint more than once. The fuzz would throw the book at them just for carrying this stuff? It didn't bear thinking about. No, their real concern had been voiced by Skip. "Even if we don't get caught, what the hell do we gain? It doesn't make sense."

That thought, or similar ones, had passed through each man's mind more than once since the evening had begun. Sure, Terry could make it sound like a game. But Terry could sell a dead man a new shirt. The fact was, it didn't make sense. As usual, Terry paid well. But, why pull this silly stunt? Shifting the shotgun to his left arm, George raised his right hand, a signal to stop. They listened. Silence. They crept forward. As Terry had said, the door was ancient and opened easily with the simple tools from George's pocket.

Craziest thing I ever heard of thought George. Pick the lock on the way in and break the door in on the way out. Of the three only he understood the reasoning behind that tactic; even so it was still a crazy mission.

Once inside, they moved quickly to the back of the cases stacked up for tomorrow's shipment. George checked over the papers, taking care to select only those marked for the correct destination.

Settling his load quietly on a nearby table, Skip cautiously offloaded the top tier of cases from the middle pallet. Then he and Don carefully slit the masking tape holding the cases closed and began to extract part of the contents. When a suitable cavity had been created within the cases, they transferred the contents of their tote bags into the cases. George carefully resealed the boxes using a roll of tape from a nearby workstation. It was a neat job. The new tape had to be precisely aligned with the original strips. Only a very thorough examination would ever reveal the resealing, and even then it might not give cause for alarm. Besides, they would have plenty to think about around here tomorrow without examining the tape on a few unbroken cases. Turning from the pallet, George joined Skip and Don, and the trio set about systematically destroying cases of glassware. Still operating quietly, they added the contents of several cases to the glassware they had removed from the resealed boxes, forming random heaps scattered around the floor. The cases themselves were flattened or torn. Packing materials, from the cases and from the storage bins, were scattered haphazardly among the piles of glassware.

By 1:10 A.M. they were ready for the final stage of the evening's activity. Taking up the pipes they had carried, they began noisily breaking glass and smashing cases still on the pallets, carefully avoiding the selected pallet and the one just behind it. The rear door was now smashed in from the outside. As expected, the noise carried throughout the factory and brought the hoped for reaction.

Startled, Pete Mallick, the elderly watchman, dropped his thermos and half filled cup, spilling sugary coffee across the manager's desk. (It was his custom to "borrow" the manager's office as his nightly resting spot.) Flustered, he was torn between mopping up the coffee and attending to the noise in the warehouse. Not that he was about to charge into that din in the dark!

"Not on a bet!" he thought. "They don't pay me for heroics. Goddamned gun probably won't shoot anyways; but I gotta do something: mop up the coffee, check on the ruckus, something. 'Ol' man Murphy'll have my ass either way."

Reflexively, he grabbed a handful of papers and began a futile attempt at mopping up. Too late he realized he had taken the papers from the in basket on the corner of the desk. Before he could quite absorb the magnitude of his transgression, a loud crash from the rear of the building assaulted his senses. Goddamn! What the hell were they doing back there?"

Forgetting the coffee, he hastened as fast as his arthritic joints would permit to the master switch for the warehouse lighting. With trembling fingers he pressed the large green button. Then with a shaking hand on the warehouse doorknob, he drew the heavy weapon from its holster and placed his ear against the door. Only then did it occur to him that he had never actually handled the gun before.

"Is it loaded? I hope not," he thought.

The lights were the signal for which the three out back had been waiting. Dropping their pipes, they took off through the smashed door. George grabbed up the shotgun as he ran by the worktable. Skip dropped a lighted match on a pile of packing material that had been carefully chosen and isolated to assure that the fire would not, in fact, spread too easily or too far.

Tentatively, Pete Mallick peered around the warehouse door just in time to see their backs as they hastened into the darkness. "No, I didn't see their faces. They turned tail before I opened the door," he would explain over and over again to the sheriff and local reporters.

Relieved but still apprehensive, he stepped into the big room and looked around, searching for stragglers and hoping against hope he wouldn't find any. Only when he caught a whiff of burning wood did he notice the flaming packing material. Reacting with a speed born of fear, he grabbed the extinguisher near the door and attacked the blaze. The carbon dioxide cloud quickly smothered the tiny blaze before it had a chance to spread to any other materials or to the building itself.

This quick response, with the resultant lack of fire damage, won him praise the next day so much praise that his earlier mishap in the manager's office was completely ignored. Pete was a minor celebrity around Chemglass for several days. No one seemed to notice that the placement of the fire was such that it would have been nearly impossible for it to have spread very fast.

George and the other two were, of course, never caught or even suspected. "Malicious, senseless vandalism" was the verdict, not only of old Murphy but also of the local police. The necessary insurance forms were filed. The local population cursed the vandals from the big city up north, and, after a perfunctory investigation, the police dropped the case, relegating it to the unsolved cases file.

One more example of pointless vandalism entered the record books and to be soon forgotten. However, pointless act was the completion of another important step in Terry's Plan.

Puddles and Streaks on A Window

Some time after Ames's visit to NAMBE and subsequent graduation, Ames is still having trouble trying to see where and how he fits into the world. His need to find himself, whatever that really means, was a major factor in his life at that time and continued to be so until after The Outrage.

"For four days now there had been drizzle, drizzle and more drizzle. No, not drizzle. Mist? No, it's more than mist, but less than drizzle."

Ames was fascinated by the seemingly random gyrations of the droplets outside working their way relentlessly down his window, there to be joined by others that had successfully fought their way down different but equally circuitous paths. At the bottom of the pane they accumulated like an army mustering for a final attack. In this case the objective was simply the bottom of the window frame. Soon their consolidated mass could not be denied even by the forces of surface tension. In a rush perhaps a teaspoonful of water broke out, would spill over the edge of the frame and splash onto the sill, where it joined an existing puddle. The combined weights proved unstoppable. The water would stream over the edge of the sill and out of Ames's sight. In his mind he could see it falling thirty or so feet to the ground below. He visualized a mushrooming splash with all the detail of the high speed stop action photograph Dr. Eggerton took in the 1900s. Reluctantly, he turned away from the window and ambled back into his dorm room.

Time to Contemplate the Facility, And My Place In It

"It's nearly time to leave this university and exchange it for another place with new problems, NAMBE. How will I fit in there? The same as every else, I guess, not at all."

Graduation was history, completed yesterday. Like all commencement ceremonies, this one had been too long, too hot and too boring: four hollow, seemingly endless speeches followed by the individual reading of 375 names. Each nominee had stepped forward, shaken hands and accepted a diploma.

After finishing high school at the age of 14, Ames had been accepted at State, where he was enrolled in biology. He had not expected much of a social life because of his age, but he was used to that and thought he would have had no trouble adjusting. He had been wrong. The differences between high school and college were vast. The first few weeks were a whirl, a montage of jumbled images from registration and rush week to the beginning of classes. Ames's achievements had not been insignificant by any standard, except his own. You read, you listened, you remembered and you regurgitated on command. The professor gave you an A. Whoopee! It was always same.

It had been some time before he realized that his memory concealed an IQ, that, while above average, was well within normal bounds. "Is there any test known to man that separates memory from IQ?" he wondered.

His deductive powers were average. He managed mathematics more because of his memory than his ability to reason logically. He played chess and checkers with no more than average skill except, of course, that he never forgot a mistake or an advantage after having once seen it. At the university he found he could learn to read and listen to different languages by a single pass through appropriate books and tapes. However, he had great difficulty learning to speak new languages. His mind was always ahead of his tongue; his accent was terrible. He had not been surprised. He had long since learned to be objective about himself. He had unusual abilities in three areas: his memory was like a recording, his senses had several times the average sensitivity and acuity, and his reflexes were significantly faster than those of anyone else he had ever met.

Beyond these three traits he was an average guy. Actually, in several ways he was less than average. His stamina was low. He participated in some sports, but only individual ones, such as tennis and judo. His quick reactions seemed to his opponents to be an uncanny ability to anticipate their actions. He felt sure it was simply his ability to sense small motions, a nod of the head, or the shift of a foot or a change in stance, that gave him an edge. However, if the edge did not enable him to win quickly, he was likely to tire and lose the match. His speed nearly always stood him in good stead for a first encounter; but after his lack of endurance was detected, he was frequently defeated in subsequent matches.

It was the same with board games. He could play a classic chess game unerringly and, because of his memory, usually be counted on to win. A really good opponent who could deviate from the classic approaches could often defeat him. Without the edge provided by his ability to recall, he was quite average.

He let his mind drift back, tracing the experiences that had led to his present feelings of isolation and loneliness. As a toddler he had had the normal amount of difficulties learning to pronounce words. When he had gained some ability to speak, he had, like all children, been taught to count. Of course, once he heard a sequence, he could repeat it at will any time. On the other hand, he had not been so quick to learn the secrets of generating the further members in the set. This was the first evidence of his prodigious memory, but no one noticed.

He began to sense that something was wrong only after he had learned to talk as well as understand. Everyone with whom he came in contact kept asking him the same questions. He was not to understand this peculiar behavior until he was in school and learned that most people required such repetitions to implant facts in their minds. Until that time he continued to feel a frustration he could not understand or explain.

He had demonstrated no particular skills with toys or crayons and pencils or other childhood activities. His capacious memory and heightened senses went largely unnoticed throughout his preschool years.

School and More Disappointments

School was a shock. Up to that point he had met few other children, and he had not appreciated his uniqueness. He watched in amazement as other children gave incorrect responses to questions. At first it did not occur to him that they did not know the correct answers, because in all cases the teacher requested information that she herself had already given them. And the teachers were so obviously pleased at receiving correct answers that Ames could not understand the reluctance of the other children to provide them. Was it some great joke that he had missed? During recess, he asked some of them what the joke was. They did not understand the question. Indeed, some of them seemed confused, as though he were teasing them. Then, observing the obvious discomfort experienced by his classmates when they failed to give the correct answers, it suddenly occurred to him that it was not a joke; they just did not know the answers! How was that possible? They were present when the lesson was given. They had heard the same things he had. Grownups often said "Pay attention," an admonition that Ames also found completely puzzling. Apparently it meant the same as "listen." How could they not listen. Of course, sometimes it meant the same as "look," and he did understand it was possible to look away. Grownups are funny, he had decided. Some of those kids must know how to not pay attention.

Soon he had to abandon that explanation also. A number of the other kids really seemed to want to do well. They seemed to be listening and watching all the time, and still they would give the wrong answer.

"They don't know!" The shocking thought burst into his consciousness like an explosion. "They had heard the answers and they can't remember!" The thought was totally incomprehensible to the six year old. He watched and listened. He was right. They did not know!

He had asked his dad about it that evening. "Dad, why is it that the other children don't seem to learn things when the teacher tells them?" He had lacked the vocabulary to express the extent of his confusion, and his father did not appreciate the depth of his concern. How could he? He did not realize that his son literally never forgot anything.

"Not everyone is as bright as you are, son," his father had explained. Thus, innocently, a major misconception had been born, which was never recognized by most people and not understood by Ames himself until much later. At the time, however, he accepted his father's explanation. In school Ames finally came to accept that teachers spend a lot of time testing and measuring the students' ability to learn. He did not really understand why but he participated. Since essentially all the tests simply measured memory, his classmates and teachers soon considered Ames a genius. His family and his teachers fussed over him, and his fellow students mistrusted him, feared him, and, as a consequence, avoid him. He, in turn, did not really understand the other children either.

In particular he was bothered by their loud behavior, whether petulant and crying or happily yelling and cheering. Such loud noises were physically painful to him. Until he learned that his own ears were much more sensitive, he had found it incredible that children would deliberately create such painful noise.

His heightened senses were not always a disadvantage in childhood. They were, in fact, a distinct advantage in some activities such as hide and seek. His ability to notice even slight disturbances, detect small sounds, and even sniff out the presence of the other participants were very real advantages, until he proved so efficient that the other children accused him of cheating.

He had had equally unsatisfactory experiences with Easter egg hunts. In an attempt to win acceptance, he learned to pretend that he could not find more than a fraction of the hidden treasures. But it was too late. By the time he understood that other children objected to his always winning such games, there were too many hard feelings for him to gain acceptance simply by allowing others to win.

Those were his earliest memories of rejection by his peers. They were by no means the only ones. Each new class and each new game of skill or strategy found him either winning or deliberately losing. When his classmates discovered that he was deliberately throwing the game or slowing down to give others a chance, they were unhappy with that also. Ames had attempted to lose himself in study. If he could not have peer acceptance, he would at least have adult acceptance and approval.

School might have been different in a larger community where there were provisions for the unusual student, but not at Harrison High School. The teachers did suggest boarding school or busing Ames to another town, but his parents would have none of it;

their own reluctance was reinforced by that of his mysterious Aunt Laurie. He had never met her, but she had always been a factor in his life. More important than her presents and cards were her letters. While they came irregularly:, there were many of them. Sometimes there would be several in a single month followed by several weeks in which he received no mail at all. Certainly the average was more than two a month.

Aunt Laurie never spoke of herself. She was always interested in Ames; his activities, his achievements, his dreams. She could never seem to get enough pictures of him, but she sent none of herself. Threatening to withhold his own didn't work because his mom and dad would send them anyway. Her love and concern were genuine, but she never visited. She was a mystery, but still an important part of his life.

The three adults seemed determined to minimize the attention that Ames attracted. They particularly did not want attention drawn to his special abilities. He never understood why, and they steadfastly refused to discuss it. Instead they pretended not to understand what he was driving at and assured him there was no need for concern.

The only way his parents had ever disappointed him or behaved in any way that he could consider the least bit cruel or objectionable was the treatment the subject of his background. Even before being told, he had guessed that he was adopted.

The Questions Continue Into University

The first most obvious genetic difference from his parents, his slightly tan coloring, might be overlooked or attributed to some forgotten ancestor. However, enhanced memory, heightened senses and quickened reactions were unique in his experience. He had never met anyone else, including both his parents, who possessed more than one of these characteristics, never mind all three. He was unusual: not just a little unusual but virtually a sideshow attraction. They were not. They were, in fact, the most normal, average people he had ever met, Norman Rockwell models. Beyond acknowledging that they were not his parents, they had refused to discuss his genealogy.

They said they had made a solemn promise to his real parents whom they had not, in fact, met. His Aunt Laurie was the go between and had insisted on absolute secrecy. There are no rotten limbs on your family tree. You have nothing to be ashamed of, but there were some irregular shortcuts in the adoption process." his father said.

Later, during a university vacation, when he had pressed the point he had learned that "irregular" meant he had never been legally adopted at all. Beyond that startling revelation, he had not been able to learn anything either about the procedure or about the role of his Aunt Laurie had played.

The next semester he had taken a course in comparative anthropology in an effort to learn if there a group of people anywhere in the world who had a genetic makeup like his own. He had not found one; but he was well aware of the limitations of his study. Despite his having read everything he could find that related in any way to unusual memory, quickened reflexes, or heightened senses, he could not be and not locating a particular tribe he could not be sure that there was not a clue to be found.

For the last thirty years, genetics and bio-engineering had been the most active and heavily funded scientific activity on earth, and there was an enormous body of data to be found in the libraries. Unfortunately, it dealt almost exclusively with bacteria, plants and lower animals. There was virtually no research on the genetic structure of humans except when related to genetic disease and abnormality. In time he had come to accept that he was a genetic accident. Even if he were able to find his natural parents, they would probably turn out to be quite normal.

His protracted search left its mark on him. He was very widely read in anthropology, genetics, and bio-engineering; all those books were permanently recorded in his memory. He had developed a genuine interest, and this had led to his choice of specialization at the university. His performance there had resulted in his receiving an appointment at NAMBE. He would leave campus for the Facility in two days. Am I ready? he asked himself. Am I ready to leave this place? Certainly! Am I ready for NAMBE? That's another question entirely.

Certainly, he knew the subject matter well enough, and obviously he could learn whatever else he might need to know in very short order. But was he ready for another bunch of people with whom he would not fit? It was an entirely adult world. The age differences would be the greatest he had ever had to adjust to. Most of his coworkers would be old enough to be his parents.

The thought was frightening. He would be out of place wherever I went. At least at the Facility there will be common intellectual interests. I might find friends on that basis alone. Well, not friends, maybe, but acquaintances who can accept me for what I seem to be: a "bright young lad" who is very interested in bio-engineering.

Turning again to the window, he let his vision take in the dark, boiling underside of the clouds that hung low over the campus. Concentrating on the changing, drifting shapes had a calming, almost hypnotic effect on him. The Facility and the challenges of a new life seemed to be swallowed up and obscured by the soothing, pervasive gray mass.

Ben Fromme Reflects On His Son's Life

It had been a long and convoluted road that brought Ben and his wife Alice to position of congratulating their son upon his graduation. And yes they both thought of him only as their son not their adopted son.

The graduation ceremony last week had been solemn and impressive, Ben Fromme thought. Think of it! 375 graduates! Ames had looked so young. Of course he <u>was</u> young, only eighteen years old. Yet he had stood there among all those other graduates, and he was the only one to complete both a bachelor's and a master's degree in four years. Only eighteen years old and he's valedictorian of the class. He's such a serious boy. No, he's no longer a boy; he's a man and such a man. Today he would report to NAMBE to begin his professional career. Ben and Alice Fromme were bursting with pride.

Who could have guessed all of those years ago, after her fourth failure to give birth, that Alice would ever be congratulating her son at a university commencement? It could never have happened without Laurie.

Ben's thoughts urned to the evening he always thought of as Ames's birthday. Rising from his favorite chair and walking to the front window, he recalled another trip to that same window on a winter's night years ago. It had been snowing that night, he remembered (. . . and I stood here . . ")

Ben had stood at the bay window, his back toward the room. Behind him, the squeak clunk of Alice's rocker was barely audible above the crackling of the log fire, was the only evidence of her presence. He did not need to turn around to know that she was reading another novel. He didn't object to her reading. She had both always enjoyed books. But in the past it had been a supplement to their other activities, a means of expanding their interests or enlarging their experience. Lately, reading had become Alice's sole refuge. She did not read in addition to her other interests in life, but instead of other interests. Everything had lost meaning for her when their last baby was stillborn. It was inexcusable for a child to be stillborn in this day and age. "This is the twenty first century, for chrissake!" he thought for at least the hundredth time since Alice's discharge from the hospital. Of course it was traumatic for any woman and perhaps more so in her case, considering her age and the three miscarriages that she had already been through. He should have insisted on giving up after the third failure. But he hadn't.

In the hope that a complete change of lifestyle would snap her out of it, he had given up his position and sold their home in the city to accept an appointment at a minor small town college in New Hampshire. In the past she would have been excited by the process of selecting and decorating a new house. This time she had gone listlessly through the motions. The psychiatrists and counselors were no help. She'd tried three of them.

Briefly, the high beams of a passing car lit up the falling snow, which was silently remolding the contours of his property. The flash of lights drew his attention to the outside. Now that he had noticed the snow, the soft yellow glow leaking outward into the night from his own windows was adequate to illuminate a small area around the house. Just beyond the arc of illumination, total darkness hung like a curtain. It was as if the rest of the world had vanished, abandoning Ben and Alice to their own soft cocoon of light. Captivated by the falling snow, he started when the telephone's ring roused him.

"Hello," he mumbled, not quite recovered from the hypnotic power of the falling snow.

"Uncle Ben, is that you?" "It's me, Laurie."

"Yes, of course. I'm sorry you caught me daydreaming, mesmerized by the falling snow flakes I guess. Where are you? We haven't heard from you in some time. What are you up to these days?" He regained his customary staccato manner. "Are you going to be able to visit this holiday season? Who"

"Whoa, wait a minute." She went on in a choppy imitation of her uncle's rapid fire style. "I'm at Logan airport. It's been only a few months, actually. I'd like to visit and tell you what I'm doing. There! How do you like that for brevity?"

"You win," her uncle conceded, good naturedly. "Yes, you may visit if you promise there'll be no more of these compressed conversations. Shall I come pick you up? Why didn't you let me know you were coming? I can pick you up in half an hour."

"Whoa, again. Thank you, but no, please. I've rented a car, I have a lot to tell you, but it will have to wait until I get there. Please put on a large pot of coffee and warn Aunt Alice that I'm coming. See you in a bit."

Ben dropped the phone into its cradle and turned toward Alice, who had placed her book face down and was looking up at Ben questioningly.

"It was our Laurie. She's at the airport and is coming for a visit, she didn't say how long. We better check the spare bedroom. She asked to have a pot of coffee brewed for her."

As Laurie had done, Alice interrupted him. "Slow down, Ben. There's no need to get everything said in such a rush. She'll be at least an hour getting here in this snow. I'm surprised that they even landed in this weather. Ben smiled. That's the most he'd heard Alice say in a long time. Laurie's visit would be good for her. Aloud he announced, "I'll make coffee while you check the spare bedroom.

You wouldn't trust my judgment on matters of cleanliness and readiness, but I can brew coffee."

In such a prosaic way had the most momentous night of their lives begun. Laurie arrived, as she always did, with virtually no advance notice, and the usual hugs and kisses were exchanged. Then, over the first cup of coffee, Laurie's expression became serious and she suddenly fell silent, staring blankly into her mug. "Earth to Laurie," Ben called, to recapture her attention as he had done when as a child she occasionally seemed lost in her own reverie. It worked. She looked up.

"I'm sorry. I'm just looking for a place to begin. Please, Uncle Ben, don't advise me to start at the beginning. I really don't know the beginning. I've come to ask something of you, something important to me and something important to the government. The situation is complex and many of your questions I simply won't be able to answer, either because of my ignorance or due to government regulations. I don't mean to make this sound ominous or cloak and dagger like, but there are questions of security involved. Furthermore, there are certain aspects about which even I am not completely clear. I believe that I am acting everyone's best interests but there are questions. I honestly believe this is an opportunity for both of you, particularly for Aunt Alice; though I'm sure you both will find it satisfying. I am sure it will add joy to your lives. I am equally sure that after tonight your lives will never be the same."

Alice could refrain from interrupting no longer. "Wait a minute. You sound like you've been taking speech lessons from Ben. What are you talking about? Start as near the beginning as you can. And, please, take a breath now and then."

With a visible effort, Laurie brought herself under control. "I've tried to find a smooth way to slide into this. I can't, so here goes. At the center of this is a child no, a baby, virtually a newborn infant, a few weeks old. This child needs a home not a temporary home, an orphanage, or a foster home but a permanent, loving home. The child needs a genuine, normal family, and I'm hopping you two will provide it. You will both love him. I'm sure you will." She paused.

They both spoke at once, bombarding her with questions. Laurie waited patiently until even Ben had run down. "I told you I will not be able to answer most of your questions, even though they are reasonable. But I can reassure you on several points.

There is no way that his parents or any other relatives can enter your lives later or make any claim on the child. He has no living relatives, and there are no direct links with his past.

He is physically normal and, as far as can be determined at his age, mentally sound. There is no reason to expect problems in either of those areas. On the contrary, I believe he will develop into a remarkable child and adult.

All the legal questions you asked, Uncle Ben, can be treated at once. Should you agree to accept him, the boy's birth certificate and all hospital and other records will show him to be your natural son, born to Aunt Alice. Please don't ask how that can be done. Believe me, there will be no loose ends. Paper trails are one of my specialties. In the unlikely event of an extensive investigation in the future, all trails will lead to the conclusion that he was born to Ben and Alice Fromme.

"Why, you asked, am I involved in this thing? I'm not allowed to fully answer that. There are two considerations, one professional and one personal. On the professional side are national security issues. "On the personal side, I made a promise to a dying friend, whose name I cannot give you. She pleaded that all circumstances surrounding his birth be held in the closest confidence. I promised to do that." She paused and became momentarily introspective. She was misleading her aunt and uncle, not by what she said but by what she did not say. They believe that your dying friend was the mother and that the child was illegitimate, she thought, but there was no other way.

The conversation went on for some time but Laurie steadfastly refused to provide more information about either the mother, the circumstances of the child's birth, or the nature of the national security issues. She repeated her assurances that there were no clouds hanging over the parents and no reason to expect that the child harbored any faulty genes. Laurie had been quite emphatic on both those points.

Without anyone realizing it or consciously directing it, the conversation changed course. They were no longer discussing why the child needed a new home or where it came from; they were not discussing whether or not they would accept the child. They were discussing more practical matters. "Will we be allowed to see him before we make up our minds? How will we explain his existence to friends and neighbors? Do we have adequate space for him? Is there time to redecorate the guest room?"

Of course they would accept the child. They would have done so under far less agreeable circumstances than those offered by their favorite niece. Ben had looked into adoption; it took such a long time, and in Alice's present state he had felt it better that she not be submitted to a long process that might end in more disappointment. He had also considered becoming foster parents and decided that was even more risky. Laurie's proposition was nothing short of a godsend. A miracle that would save Alice's life!

Laurie's arrangements for them to see and hold the child seemed to be overly complicated, but they had accepted her assurances that these precautions were necessary. As Laurie had known it would be, it was love at first sight. The child would be good for them and they for him. Her pledge to Mary Ann was satisfied. A week later the infant had an identity; Ames Andrew Fromme was "born."

Events had gone much more smoothly than either Ben or Alice had dreamed possible. Laurie took care of everything. The only thing she asked them to sign had been a government security form that required them to respect the secrecy of Ames' origin; she had taken that form with her. She left them nothing that could ever prove that Ames was not their natural son.

She had simply arrived one evening with Ames and all the records that were required to verify his birth as their child. Like the fabled stork, she delivered the baby and vanished into the night. Only much later did it occur to them that they had no evidence of his true background; on the other hand, they had impeccable evidence that he was their legitimate son.

However, there had been one price for this "gift" a non-insignificant price. Laurie insisted that the child never know of her at all except as his Auntie Laurie. She would be an eccentric, wealthy old aunt who, though interested in everything he did, would never visit him or send pictures of herself to him.

"Say I travel a lot; even you haven't seen me since I was quite young and you're never sure where I am. I don't really care how you handle it. But he must not know who I am or where I work. I promised his mother that I would never lose track of him. Were it not for that promise I would fade out of his life completely. He will receive gifts from me at all the usual times and a trust fund has been set up that will mature when he reaches twenty one. Please handle this request in any way you see fit. He must never learn who I really am or how to find me.

You will have guessed by now that this condition means we will never see each other again. I really do love you both, but you already know that. You will hear from Auntie Laurie with no last name and no fixed address."

Even the old pictures they had of her were to be destroyed before Ames could see them. They had both viewed these measures as extreme, but were so overcome with gratitude that they acquiesced with little complaint.

As time passed, Alice and Ben thought less and less about the origins of their son. Ames was indeed a healthy child, suffering only childhood diseases and complaints, and seemed quite average in all respects for the first four years of his life. Even after their early realization that he was different, they considered the difference to be only a matter of degree: Ames had a phenomenal memory. Outwardly, the only evidence of any difference at all was that as he approached adolescence his pigmentation darkened slightly. At first they thought he had simply tanned, but the tan never fully left him.

Snapping out of his reverie, Ben said aloud, "He Is a very bright young man."

ERA 3

the Outrage

At this point all of the early independent events and separate individuals have been introduced and some of the early interconnections, intertwining, of those deep roots have been glimpsed. In this the final Era the pieces are all in place; and the most important personalities have been revealed. The events in this Era will be reported more or less in chronological order. Furthermore, the events in this Era will require fewer asides by the Chronicler.

Plans

A siege, a full frontal attack on NAMBE was planned by two co-planners. However, while they openly cooperated on the development of the attack, they did not actually share the same motivations and they certainly did not share the same objectives. One of the planners totally unaware of this conflict and was to learn it only well after it was too late to rectify the error.

The ASPGH Plan

With a huge sigh, Jane Wilds settled back against the pillows she had propped up at the head of the bed and pulled her feet back until she was sitting in an almost fetal position. With both hands wrapped around the steaming cup of tea resting on her knees, she caressed the cup, drinking in its warmth through her fingers. It was a comforting sensuous contrast to the characterless motel room with the cold rain driving against the window.

The room was chill. Like motel rooms everywhere, its thermostat had been turned down when the previous occupant checked out. Soon, of course, the temperature would rise to the comfortable level she had selected on the small Honeywell control unit on the wall near the door. Already she could feel the warm air issuing from the combination heater and air conditioner against the wall. The do it yourself coffee service across the room was still making the popping and hissing noises, reminders of the water she had just boiled. It could be worse, she thought.

Sipping the tea, she consciously listened to the rain. It was not the hypnotic pitter patter that quietly lulls one to sleep but rather the pelting sound of a driving, angry rain pounding steadily against the panes. Occasionally, a momentary increase in the wind rattled the frame and the raindrops seemed to increase in hardness, sounding like shovels full of fine gravel suddenly thrown against the windows. She listened. Perhaps they are hailstones, she thought. A bright flash was followed, quickly by a loud clap of thunder, the force of which overrode even the pounding of the rain.

"That was damn close," she thought. As if the nearby crash had been a signal, smaller flashes darted at random across the underside of the low hanging clouds, a pyrotechnic ballet danced to a thunderous score. She sat captivated, wriggling her toes under the edge of the blanket she had turned down before settling onto the bed. She had intended to relax quietly, read herself to sleep. But now . . . .

She leaned over, turned off the lamp, and settled back, again caressing her teacup and drinking in the display as though it were being provided for her personal entertainment. As bright and exciting as the storm's display was, it could not prevent the events of the last three months from intruding into Jane's consciousness.

The plans were in place. It had gone well, easier than she had expected or could have hoped. Everyone was eager to get started, to "do something". She was frankly surprised. What she had asked the directors of ASPGH to approve was not without considerable hardship, expense and risk. The Board's Lawyer, Tom Hanson, had described at length just what the potential consequences of their actions might be. With a clear and concise cynicism born of years of successful legal practice, he had explained that, even if they avoided incarceration, there was only a slim chance they would attain any marked success in their quest. "At best," he had said, "we may start a few people thinking and hope that they, in turn, influence their representatives in government. It will be a long road from here to some sort of moral sanity. This protest barely constitutes a beginning."

Yet without exception the regional Directors had not only agreed but had wholeheartedly supported the entire plan. All sixty buses would arrive from their separate chapters. In addition to the buses, others would arrive in cars, RVs, trucks, and vans. To expose the NAMBE fraud for the evil it represents all of these believers and supporters are prepared to stay the course, including arrest and incarceration, if necessary. She could close her eyes and visualize the tent city that would spring up in Micro City and on the grounds of BioPark itself. Her euphoria was boundless. Then silently she caught herself.

Calm down, Jane! Pace yourself. Review the plan. It's your last chance to make any alterations. Their enthusiastic support is necessary but, as they say in math class, not sufficient. We are not planning a simple camping trip or jamboree. This is a national expose'.

She closed her eyes to shut out the distraction of the storm's pyrotechnic display and deliberately set aside her enthusiasm. As was her custom, she began her introspective review as objectively as she could.

The occupation will last as long as necessary. Though truthfully, she could not imagine holding the siege in place for more than a few days, two weeks at the outside. A siege? She stooped herself. Yes, call a spade a spade. She had always felt very strongly on the issue of being honest with oneself. He was fond of quoting Polonius's advice to Laertes, "This above all, to thy own self be true." Yes, it will be a siege.

Each chapter across the country had staged its own series of rallies and protests aimed at raising local awareness to a point where the population was at least receptive to listening to the views and arguments of the ASPGH. Gregg had always said that all they had a right to ask was that people listen to them.

Early summer was a propitious time. By the end of spring the entire population of the country was be in a receptive mood, wallowing in goodwill and love of nature. If there was any time when the arguments for leaving nature to nature were easy to sell in this age of M-cubed technology, it was the height of spring would say, "Any fool can see the truth in the spring." Now, wait, Jane, this is not just a memorial to Mr. Gregory. However, it does include honoring his memory. is dead, damn it, but his dreams were not.

She continued her analysis. After having created a fuss and attracted all of the attention they could manage, the East Coast s go silent the first week in June and begin their trek west by chartered bus, their objective to arrive in Nevada as nearly unnoticed as possible. During this time, the West Coast brings its activities to the maximum exposure level. This raises the attention level of the s most likely to be able to attend rallies to the highest levels just before announcing the siege, and at the same time attracts attention away from the East Coast s quietly wending their way toward Micro City. The West Coast marches and other activities reach their peak, and the major local rallies are held two days before the occupation is scheduled. The concluding half of the gatherings all staged for the same evening. Free transportation is offered to all who can attend.

She paused in her analysis to settle herself more comfortably. Thank God for Terry's rich friends back east. She had never met these folks. In fact, she did not even know their names. But they certainly delivered. Not once, but twice, Terry had recognized the Society's need for funds but explained that she had no need know about fund raising or to waste her time on the topic. Raising money was to be his sole responsibility. The first trip he had been gone for several weeks. However, he did return with the cash without which the Movement would surely have died. Then, within three months he had made a second trip and again returned with funds for the full operation, including the trek across country. No doubt about it, the contributions of Terry's friends were as important to the longevity of the ASPGH as was's vision to its creation. "So, yes there is no doubt that the buses will converge on BioPark in the heart of Micro City at the appointed time.

The very existence of this park, with its virtually endless variety of plants "adapted from naturally occurring vegetation" was both a testimony to the success of NAMBE and an effrontery and threat to the very humanity of mankind. There was no doubt that the Park was beautiful, and a miracle of sorts. Those photographs Terry brought back would have been incredible had anyone other than Terry, World Champion Cynic, attested to their authenticity.

Never mind, most of the buses will converge on the Park. Two busloads will be taken directly to the Facility to join the regularly scheduled June tour. There will be one load from each coast, and the third will carry participants from Midwest locations. When the cameras and reporters arrive at the Facility, they will find members protesting from all across the country. The Society must not be viewed as just another local aberration from California.

The members will sign in and blend with the rest of the day's visitors. There will not be many others since the two busloads of ASPGH members is nearly equal to the maximum allowed tour for a single day. After the visiting badges have been issued and the coffee and doughnuts consumed, Dr. Q will arrive for his welcoming address.

Then two of our men will move to the rear doors to act as guards. Two more men head for front of the auditorium. Terry will leap to the stage and announce that there is a new agenda for the day. Walt and his two friends, who elected to skip the formal tour, will place themselves strategically around the Reception Area and the entrance to the UltraAtrium. The building is ours!

Before they can decide whether we represent a real threat or are just a bunch of psychos, Randy and Donna will have made a national television announcement.

How to make the national statement had been a matter of serious concern. The threatening takeover of the Facility had been considered risky enough without invading a national broadcasting network, radio, or television. Randy's solution had been a stroke of genius.

The world will know that there are at least some human beings with a conscience. From there on it's a matter of who has the most determination, the most staying power. There's more, of course. If the occupation persists, extends in time, there are questions of provisions and rest periods, shifts, and other practical details. Such matters are by no means unimportant if the quest is to succeed. However, given that the initial stages go according to plan, then the details, while numerous, will certainly be well taken care of by the people assigned, good solid citizens all.

Yes, she thought everything depended on those first few minutes after the men moved to the rear doors and Terry took over the stage.

Terry again! He was a random ensemble of contradictions. His language was coarse and arrogant. He was intelligent, but randomly educated. His vocabulary can indicated the scope of his reading and schooling; but it is all too frequently punctuated with vulgarity more characteristic of the streets. And his mood swings sometimes make it frightening just to be around him. He could be riding high one minute, pleased with himself and the world, speaking and behaving reasonably; and then suddenly, at some minor setback he would crash into a depressed state and punctuate every phrase with that disgusting gutter talk.

He is cynical in the extreme; and yet, he is compassionate enough not only to devote all his spare time over the past year to the Society's business but also to convince his friends to devote considerable quantities of cash to its causes.

But who are these friends? "Important businessmen with genuine moral concerns, but whose positions in society obviate their openly involving themselves in this cause." Recalling old Thorny's reaction to her term paper, she could well understand their concern. But did Terry know people to whom social position and acceptance was a matter of concern? Clearly he did. They deliver the goods, Jane reminded herself for the hundredth time.

She had been over this ground before, many times. It always ended the same way, with the same conclusion and the same uneasy feeling that something she could not see was very wrong, whatever the contributions; maybe the contributions themselves were cause of her nagging concerns. In any case such doubts must be put aside. The die is cast. There was no possibility of turning back. Not only would the inertia of the program at this time tear the organization apart if there were any attempt to stop the program, the Society needed this confrontation.

For some time now, even before the present project was planned and formalized, she had sensed that either she had to find an outlet for the drive and emotions of the membership or watch the ASPGH, 's movement, fold up and fade away.

The Same Plan Reviewed

A thousand miles away, Terry also sat in a motel room.

Accompanied only by a bottle of Jack Daniels and a bucket of ice, he too was reviewing his plans for the upcoming visit to NAMBE.

It was almost three months since Terry had visited the Facility. Most of that time, he had spent laying his plans and selecting his team. In the areas of muscle and guts he had had a wide variety of options available. The requirements in this area were simple, after all; blind obedience to his orders and the guts or simplemindedness to be brutal, if necessary. He did not expect any need for brutality, except as a threat. There would be no need for weapons skills. The sheer size of the army of ASPGH fruitcakes and fanatics would surely discourage any serious counterassault by the NAMBE security forces. However, in the unlikely event of a fracas, he wanted to be able to count on prompt decisive action by his men.

Convergence, the Travelers Arrive

As envisioned by Jane's plan, the travelers from all across the country converge. A few other travelers also part of the planned siege but whose very existence is totally unknown to the members of the ASPGH also converge on the planned rallying point.

Liz Blaine sat behind the wheel of her customized van, her eyes staring at the endless ribbon of black stretching across the valley opening before her. Up, over and beyond the tree fringed hill that formed the horizon of her view, the divided highway beckoned. As though programmed, her eyes continuously roamed between the lane markings and the roadside signs. The monotonous countryside flashed past. The fences, bridge railings, Jersey barriers, and occasional trees formed an unresolved blur in her peripheral vision, the color changing formlessly as the simple features slid past. Well removed from the highway, perched on higher ground, an occasional farm. Their distance from the road reduced the speed with which they disappeared from view, making it possible to examine those remote scenes more closely than the roadside blurs. Such breaks in the sameness were so welcome that they captured her attention, momentarily diverting her from her inner thoughts. She drank in every detail of each homestead. Not that she really cared about the barns, silos, honeysuckle-covered trestles, grazing cows, or rooting pigs. She simply welcomed the relief from the miles and miles of monotonous miles and miles that had characterized the drive all morning. She actually caught herself cataloguing the different structures, noting the various types of grain elevators and farm buildings.

Her taciturn manner portrayed the impression of total concentration on the mechanics of driving, of holding the hurtling van within her chosen lane. In fact, although she was cruising along at fifteen or twenty miles per hour over the speed limit, her driving was nonetheless almost a totally subconscious effort controlled by long established neural patterns. Her concentration was on the implications of the trip.

As Director of the New England chapter of the ASPGH, she had accepted the responsibility of leading her members on this trip and had prepared herself for the responsibility by carefully planning each stop. She had booked reservations with Kampgrounds of America all the way from the East Coast. Camps, what a misnomer!

At each stop the two RVs in her group hooked up to water, electricity, and sewage drains. Even the van, station wagon, and automobile travelers had showers and reasonable cooking arrangements.

She had subdivided her forty members into four sections of ten each and appointed a leader for each. These leaders were to assure that their individual teams left on time and stayed with the main body. They would also handle whatever logistical problems should arise during the course of the trip. They met Liz each evening to report on the day just past and review the plans for the next one. She had few concerns for the actual trip, which would last only another day and a half.

The adventure and camaraderie of traveling over countryside new to most of them and camping out together was keeping everyone enthusiastic and in line. Her concern was for the days following their arrival. That would be a whole new ball game; the full impact of what they were embarking on would be felt.

Days of the occupation and siege loomed ahead. By that time control might be more of a problem. Planning the occupation of a national institution is heady stuff. A of concerned friends, long frustrated in their attempts to get the world to listen to their arguments, to share their genuine concern, can find a release for their frustrations. Surrounded by people who share your beliefs and whose enthusiasm feeds off your own, it is easy to develop a belief in the invulnerability of your plan and the inevitability of your success. At such times "failure" and "adverse consequences" are not a part of your vocabulary. When legality is totally submerged in moral indignation, there is no room for fears and second thoughts.

To actually take over the Facility and, like a band of terrorists, to carry out the rest of Jane's plan was likely to prove more complex than simply a summer's outing and a few inspiring speeches. With an international of world famous scientists involved it was quite possible, perhaps even likely, for things to get out of hand. The disease of reality could set in, bringing with it a realization that this venture would certainly produce more consequences than those that were so carefully planned. None of our lives will ever be the same after this event, Liz thought. How will we control our members when they all realize just how serious this is?"

Looking over at her sleeping companion, Tom Hanson, senior partner of a prestigious Boston law firm, it occurred to her that she had first heard that question raised by Tom. Not that he withheld his support for even a moment. Indeed, he was more exposed than most of the. Conservative Boston lawyers wore pinstripe suits, shirts with starched collars, and club ties and carried slightly worn leather briefcases. They did not don bleached jeans and Tshirts, hoist a protest flag, and march on a national institute; but Tom Hanson was doing just that.

The Director Drones On Again

As Dr. Q drones his way through his 'short' Welcoming Speech, the minds of his audience began to wander.

Ames

Three months after his first visit, Ames found himself again in the main auditorium of the Facility as part of another tour. It was his last day before officially joining the NAMBE research team. Of course he did not need another guided tour to find his way around, anymore than he would need tomorrow's tour as part of the new employee orientation program. He was not exactly sure why he had come. Perhaps, after NAMBE's acceptance of him, he just could not wait. More likely, he simply did not want to spend another day at the university, nor could he think of any other place he wanted to visit or people he wanted to see. For whatever reason, here he was.

Laurie walked casually down the Central Corridor, the two new members of the NAGWAD Committee into the Main Auditorium.

Of course, Ames noticed the three people as they came in. The short, balding, rolly polly man in the tweed coat was smiling and bobbing his head in a nervous acknowledgment of the tall woman's comments. The other man with the graying hair still spiced with the cinnamon coloring of his youth, was walking quietly a few steps behind them and seemed engrossed in trying to absorb the entire Facility on his first trip through.

The flash of anxiety that had bothered Ames the first time he saw the tall brunette returned. The intensity of the feeling was somewhat reduced through familiarity, but it bothered him nonetheless. Since she was employed at the Facility, there was a chance that he might officially meet her and be able to place her properly in his past. He no longer had any doubt that she belonged there, but her remarks to her guests provided no further useful clues.

Meanwhile Dr. Q continues, "This is the Main Auditorium. We are quite proud of it. It seats nine hundred people. Each seat is equipped with a headset and a selector with which to choose any one of eight different languages to listen to the presentations. Each seat also has its own microphone, to facilitate questioning. Excuse me; here I am, rattling on like a tour guide. Dr. Newcombe and her staff are much better at it than I, and you will be getting the full treatment in a few minutes." Laurie and Dr. Q had decided that the standard tour was an efficient way to introduce the new committee members to the Facility. It was Laurie's intention to leave the in half an hour and return to her preparations for the classified meeting to be held that afternoon.

Jane

Jane Wilde's attendance at today' meeting had been long planed and was an essential part of the planned activities. She was to tense to waste time on Dr. Q's drone.

In addition to the Director of Security and her guests, there was a full tour this Monday morning. Of the ninety people gathered, eighty were with the ASPGH. This included Jane Wilds and seventy two members, plus Terry and eight of his friends, who had come along to assist in the planned activities.

Jane had been confident that she could raise a large enough following from the Movement's members alone and would not need the assistance of outsiders. Terry had pointed out that he was an outsider and that without him there would not be a plan at all. He wanted some help he could count on, and that was all there was to it. He had become quite angry, in fact; not wishing to risk a major confrontation, Jane had acquiesced. However, she had been uncomfortable ever since she met Terry's friends.

Herm Miller, a large brute of a man, always seemed remote and bored at their meetings. Worse, he seemed to exude a quiet hatred. When she was around him, she always sensed that danger and violence lurked just below the surface of his sullen demeanor. Then there was Brian Taylor. He was a simple soul, not a simpleminded person, though he did seem to be much less well educated than any of Terry's other friends, who had all finished high school at least. Several of them had actually attended college, but none of them had graduated. Brian seemed to follow Terry around like a trained spaniel, waiting for a chance to please. He never seemed to think for himself; he always waited for Terry or Lefty to tell him what to do.

Lefty Williams: she gathered that Lefty and Brian were close, but they were not exactly friends. Lefty seemed to look after Brian, who seemed to accept his attention and guidance grudgingly. They both came from Peoria and had attended the Chicago ASPGH meeting together.

Then there were three from back east; George Weatherby, Skip O'Hara, and Don Turner. They kept themselves pretty much apart from the members of the Movement, as well as from Terry's other friends. Mike Morris and Brad Thomas; there was a pair, mutes. They never say anything, never smile, just watch and wait content to perform whatever is asked. In fact, now that she thought about it, Terry's friends were a collection of misfits. They didn't fit with the ASPGH or with each other, nor did they want to. They didn't seem to want to know anyone or become known themselves. There were only eight of them but they formed three distinct s: Herm, by himself; Brian and Lefty; and George, Skip, Rick, and Don; and Mike and Brad. Jane already knew all of them; hence her scan of their section of the hall was perfunctory and did little to relieve her nervousness.

She glanced over at a young, dark skinned, light haired young man in the rear, sitting completely alone and seemingly totally absorbed by some internal analysis. Strange coloring, she thought, but a handsome guy for all of that. Strange that he would be here alone.

Off to the right, she noticed a striking brunette, speaking to a balding butterball of a man sitting beside her. His hair, snow white, long, and wispy, was combed back from the tufts growing above his ears, a much better way to handle baldness than stretching a few strands across a shiny dome.

Laurie

Sitting quietly, apart from the tour, Laurie recalled the first time Mary Ann had told her about SEMSs. Though she had nothing like Ames' memory, that late evening conversation with Mary Ann had so changed her life that she could recall its every detail, not just the words but the facial expressions and inner emotions, shock, disgust, fear, and compassion. She had relived that evening innumerable times over the past eighteen years. She did so now.

The Truth about Level Nine

"Dr. Peters has devoted his professional life to the study of human genetics," Mary Ann had said. "He doesn't give a damn about people. But the hundreds of thousands of genes in a human chromosome represent a challenge. This man is the biggest egotist in the world. He has always been sure that he represents the ultimate in human intellectual evolution. He knows in his soul, if he has one, that he can solve any puzzle God can create. The man is megalomaniac.

"But that's enough about Dr. Peters," she continued. "To understand what he's doing down there on Level Nine, you must have a little background in the science of biology and genetics and"

"Whoa, Mary Ann, I don't really have a Need to Know on

Project Nine. Of course I'm cleared, but I don't do anything that requires me to know the details of the work."

"Relax, Laurie, I'm not going to violate your precious security regulations. You already know the objectives of Dr. Peters' research from your own standard briefing material. Besides, several thing have happened that not only give you a Need to Know but make it absolutely essential that you know a great deal.

"Please be patient with me, even if the explanations a bit longwinded at first. The basic idea is that all traits of plants and animals are carried by genes. Genes are complex organic molecules. Each gene carries a code that dictates the particular properties for which that gene is responsible. To begin with there are DNA molecules of specific length. The code is actually made up of four simple molecules, called code-characters; these are distributed up and down the DNA molecule in a particular way, different for each trait. The distribution of these four code characters determines the way in which amino acids are combined to form the complex proteins that are the very stuff of life."

Mary Ann paused, but her friend had not really understood enough of her "simple explanation" to have any questions.

"The genes, each carrying its particular code or set of codes, are linked together to form a chain of molecules called a chromosome. Every living thing, plant or animal, has a specific number of paired chromosomes. Human beings, for instance, have twenty-three pairs of chromosomes in every one of their nucleated cells. These twenty three pairs of chromosomes contain all the genes, hundreds of thousands of them, necessary to build a complete human. Thus every cell contains the blueprint necessary to build a copy of the entire organism. That is the basic premise of cloning. We use a cloning process to replicate plants for the UltraAtrium. Once we have found a plant that is particularly pleasing, we can use any one of its cells as the blueprint to produce endless replicas.

"The process is not new. Actually, cloning was practiced long before the Facility was even conceived. Its use revolutionized ranching in this country by totally eliminating chance from the breeding of livestock. However, for all the certainty associated with the cloning process, it is limited to the chance formation of the first thing that is to be cloned. That is, natural evolution or selective breeding must produce the desired specimen before it can be replicated. There is no way to assure that the desired specimen being will ever evolve. Is that clear so far?"

"Oh sure," Laurie replied. "Clear as mud. But the gist, I gather, is that we must rely on random evolution or our own kind of cross breeding to make the first of something and then by cloning we can copy it. Is that it?"

` "Yes, that's just what I said."

"It sounded easier when I said it."

"Okay, I'll try harder. The breakthrough produced by the M-cubed technology is that we can now predict the effect of making changes to the basic genetic code. It is quite possible, using modern computers and the Morris theory, to postulate a change in the pattern of the elemental coding molecules of the gene and then to calculate the effects produced by such a change. That is, we can predict precisely what the altered properties of the organism will be from a knowledge of the changes that are made to the genetic patterns. From earlier research we know which genes control which characteristics. Thus we can systematically produce new life forms by using the computer to model the effects of altering genetic structure. When useful effects are predicted for the traits being studied, we can actually produce the organism to see if one or more of its other traits that we have not calculated were affected. All the projects in levels One through Seven follow this general process of genetic engineering as applied to plants."

Mary Ann paused here to organize her thoughts before proceeding and to see if she still had her audience.

"Are you with me?" Laurie nodded and she continued. "In Project Eight we employ those same methods to develop particularly virulent strains of bacteria and viruses, as well as some nasty strains of plants. As you know, there are a relatively large number of people cleared for that project and its results. A much smaller group has a "need to know" that the results reported from Project Eight have all been demonstrated on living human tissue.

Laurie was aghast, "Tested on people? No, Mary Ann, surely you're joking . . ." Her voice trailed off. There was no way Her friend would joke about a matter like this. "We can't test that horrible stuff on human beings, surely."

"No, Laurie, I didn't say it was tested on humans. I said 'demonstrated on living human tissue.' We can determine all we need to know from testing our weapons with tissue samples as long as it is living tissue of the appropriate kind. However, it is reactions such as yours that keep the details of Project Eight so classified. Besides yourself, there are only twenty people cleared to know what I just told you. One of them is the President. Only six people know how that living human tissue is obtained. You are about to become the seventh. But first let me tell you a little more about Dr. Peters and Project Nine."

"Dr. Peters developed two theories about human genetics. His first theory related only to the physical characteristics, Here he believed he could build an entire chromosome from scratch, without a human chromosome to start with. Figuratively speaking, he could and design a gene, splice it into a chromosome or splice it onto another gene he had designed and evolve the entire chromosome. He could create whatever sort of person he wanted a blond giant or a dark dwarf, for instance.

"His work on physical traits went a step further. He and his technicians proceeded to produce all the tissue necessary by simply designing a person with certain physical characteristics, producing samples thereof, and at the appropriate time providing fetal tissue to the investigators of Project Eight. Those investigators were in need of tissue and were not curious about where it came from. I know; I was one of them once."

She stopped. It still amazed her that she and the others had been so ready to bury their heads in the sand. Shaking off such introspection, the young scientist resumed her tale.

"Soon, however, the great scientist became discontent with simply designing bodies. He wanted to design minds. His second theory evolved until he was ready to tackle the design the sensors and the brain itself. His earlier model, Total Test Tube Specimens,

TOTTS as he liked to call them, had senses and brains of course but their composition had simply been left to chance. Now he was convinced that he could specify them as easily as he could specify the length of the femur or the color of hair.

There was a catch, however. To prove his theory correct with respect to physical characteristics, the TOTTS fetuses did not need to age beyond a few weeks. He made the necessary simple measurements and then had his technicians prepare tissue samples to be used in Project Eight." She paused to let Laurie absorb the full implications of what she had just said.

"You can't mean . . . ; but of course you do. He simply killed them! All those unborn babies! He just cut them up like so much meat to . . . to experiment with!"

"Settle down, Laurie. It is true that you can view it n that light, but there's a more accurate point of view. The work of Project Eight is important. Not just from a military point of view, though that is the government opinion, because it does provide basic research into the effects of disease. This research could not be performed under open programs, precisely because it does involve working with human tissue. When Project Eight began, the source of tissue for these studies was aborted fetuses. In spite of the scientific advances of the last twenty years, abortion is still fairly widely practiced as retroactive birth control.

"Well, for some time now, aborting mothers have been asked to sign papers making the fetus the responsibility and property of the hospital. The alternative is that the mother assumes responsibility for its disposal herself. Most women who are resorting to abortion do not want to assume such a responsibility.

"Such a practice is widely followed and tacitly accepted by the vast majority of the population. However, most of us don't like to discuss it. Well, the Peters approach is a step farther up the ladder of acceptability. His fetuses are completely the creation of his own test tubes. There is no conception involved. No woman carries these embryos. In fact, no woman or man ever carried the seeds from which they sprang." Mary Ann paused here, momentarily. That argument had converted her to become a supporter of Project Nine, and she hoped her friend would find it equally compelling.

Laurie found the thought of test tube conception without the need for sexual contact, months of discomfort, and the agonies of birth to be more than a simple way to justify Dr. Peters's action in taking fetuses. For her it represented a major step in bringing man closer to God. Christ had been born without sexual intercourse; now maybe man, too, could be freed from the disgusting practice. She didn't voice these views to Mary Ann. She knew full well that most people engaged in some kind of sexual activity, but she could not reconcile that knowledge with her own deeply felt convictions.

While they had never discussed the topic, Mary Ann was aware of Laurie's aversion to matters sexual. She did not date, although she as attractive and had an easygoing confidence around people. There certainly was no indication that Laurie had homosexual tendencies; it was just that sex was not a part of her life. Since coming to the Facility, Mary Ann had also avoided sexual involvements, though not through any particularly conscious effort. She just seemed to have lost interest

"It is certainly easier to accept the test tube produced fetal material.

"I'm sorry, Laurie, I didn't intend to spend so much time on details and philosophy, but you need some background so you won't judge me too harshly." She began to shake with silent sobs, and tears began to puddle in her dark eyes.

Laurie had attempted to console her. I would never judge you harshly; I wouldn't judge you at all. You didn't design the world or Project Nine."

SEMA Disclosed

Mary Ann sobbed, "No, you don't understand. I stole one! I took one of them home to rear as my own child. That's what I've been doing since I started working with Dr. Peters: raising them. It was a relatively easy matter for me to duplicate the setup at home. I took an SEMA"

"Whoa! Slower please. You took a what?" Laurie asked.

"Sorry. There I go again forgetting that you aren't familiar with all of the acronyms," Mary apologized. She continued, "Each embryo has a set of initials, an acronym, designed to help remember which genes are being controlled. In the case of physical characteristics, TAFF is used to denote tall fair female, while BEM denoted simply a blue eyed male. "One example of mental genes being controlled was SEMA, which stands for Sensors Enhanced Memory Amplified.

"SEMA is normal in all respects except these two. He will never forget anything, if Dr. Peters theories are right, and he hasn't been wrong yet. Also, his senses will be several times more sensitive than normal. Dr. Peters predicts that a person with enhanced sensory abilities will be aware of numerous subtle changes that normally go unnoticed, and this awareness could result in the development of any number of extra abilities, such as apparently shortened reflex time because he would notice things much sooner than others, or some apparently psychic abilities, because he can actually see, smell, hear, and feel things that normal people are totally unaware of. There is a slight chance that muscular actions would speed up and stamina be somewhat reduced. However, those effects if they exist at all will apparently be so slight as to escape notice by others.

Mary Ann had gone on to explain the details to her shocked friend. She described the equipment she had purchased and built for her home. She described in detail her plans to leave the Facility and simply vanish as soon as the time was right. She had her savings and her small inheritance. They would have survived. Maybe she would even have gotten a job after he grew older. She did not attempt to explain why she had done such a thing, nor did Laurie ask. Such was her respect for her friend that she could not bring herself to pry. Mary Ann would tell her what she wanted her to know. Mary Ann explained that she had been successful. The fetus had matured to a fine eight pound baby boy. She had gone on to explain the significance of his name.

"I don't know about that. I only know I have come to love my SEMA as though he were truly my child, the child I could ever give birth to because of some stupid childhood disease. Now I shall lose even him." For a few moments she sobbed uncontrollably. Laurie put her long arms around Mary Ann, patted her on the shoulder, and consoled her, again for the wrong reason. "You have nothing to fear from me, Mary Ann. Your secret is safe."

"Of course, I trust you, Laurie," sobbed Mary, regaining control with a struggle. "But I still lose. I guess it would be more accurate to say that SEMA loses. How selfish we are to put our own losses first." She paused, her face contorted with the strain of what she was going through. At last she had burst out with it. "I'm dying, Laurie. I only have a few weeks left, two months at the outside. No, before you say it, there is no mistake. I reran the tests myself. It's a rare disease not so uncommon as to be unknown, just uncommon enough to attract very little effort to find a treatment—or a cure. We give it the Sister Kenny treatment: treat the symptoms as they arise and pray. Unlike polio, however, no one has ever recovered from this one." She stopped speaking and struggled visibly to hold back new tears.

"Look, Laurie, I have only two or three weeks of rationality left before the pain requires mind fogging drugs. I've got to find a home for SEMA, a home where he has a chance to live a normal life, full of love and pain, successes and failures. I can't expose him to any official channels. I don't want him to be regarded as an experiment. I don't want Dr. Peters know he exists. You've got to help me."

Laurie had helped her friend. She had, in fact, become as emotionally involved with her SEMA as Mary Ann was. It had taken some doing, but by calling in various favors she had obtained a birth, certificate under an assumed name, that proclaimed for all the world to know that the SEMA was a real person with a right to live.

Thus, had the only crime to occur on Laurie's watch been committed with Laurie, herself, aiding and abetting the crime. It was that crime that she had feared Dr. Q may have discovered. It was a crime destined to have a major impact on the Outrage.

By now, he is a grownup young man, on the threshold of a new and promising career.

Terry Ignores Dr. Q

Terry, who had heard the welcoming address before, completely ignored Dr. Q from the moment he heard "Ladies and gentlemen, welcome to the Facility. I am Dr. Quincy. All of us here at NAMBE are very pleased to have you visit us," and looked casually around, reviewing the details of the large room. It sloped only slightly toward the stage, which filled most of the front wall. Five double doors were equally spaced along the rear wall. On this occasion four of those doors were closed and locked as they had been on his previous visit. Good, he thought.

At the front of the auditorium, the stage was flanked on both sides by emergency exits. These, he observed, were also closed as before. These bastards are consistent; excellent, he told himself.

From his study of the handout material he knew that the main communications center of the Facility was located just next door to the Auditorium. Although its main entrance was through a door opening onto the second ring corridor, it could also be entered through a side door that opened onto the back of the stage. That location had been chosen in anticipation of the numerous occasions when all or portions of a NAMBE-sponsored conference would be televised around the world.

Broadcast cameras were arranged to provide discreet coverage of both the entire audience and the stage. A teleconference studio was located in an adjacent room, also reached through a door off the same side of the stage. Teleportation, as visualized in <u>Star</u> <u>Trek</u> and other science fiction dramas, did not exist; but teleconferencing studios, with their wall sized television screens and Surround Sound audio systems, could give the illusion of joining two rooms thousands of miles apart. Also located in the communications center were the central telephone exchange and the primary controls for the Facility's emergency systems. It couldn't be a better setup if I designed it myself, Terry concluded.

Venue for Terry's Announcement

The objectives sought by Jane and those involved in the Terry's plan both required a wide far reaching forum for their respective announcements. Fortunately, it proved possible to find a single announcement method that satisfied the needs in both cases thus avoiding any need to acknowledge that there were in fact two contradictory objectives for the siege.

In Chicago an enthusiastic whispering snickering crowd settled, into the TV studio's comfortable chairs. The show was about to begin. Martin Hayes, its popular host, stood in the wings awaiting the director's nod to make his entrance. In spite of the number of talk shows already in existence, had been an immediate success. Its rapid rise to become the top-rated morning show in the country had been analyzed by many who sought to emulate or compete with it. There seemed to be no simple explanation, either in format, content, or style. All were agreed that the show worked because of Martin himself, but none were sure exactly why. Martin's healthy good looks were not the only thing that endeared him to his loyal morning following. Certainly, another factor was his honest and simplistic moral stance on all issues. This was reflected not only in his introductions and monologues but also in his straightforward manner of questioning his guests. Turning his audience loose might better describe his style. He was content to let them ask what they liked, and in many cases to let them answer their own questions. There were no trick questions from Martin, no carefully constructed sequences designed to entrap or embarrass. It was not that Martin did not have a well developed sense of humor. Indeed, his quick wit was widely considered to be a main attraction. However, he was extremely careful to assure that none of the laughs he inspired were at the expense of his audience or guests. There seemed to be one significant exception to Martin's rule of never ridiculing any member of his show. That exception was the show itself. The very selection of topics for his daily invasion of the nation suggested that, in fact, his entire show was a tongue-in-cheek satire on the whole concept of talk shows in general and on his predecessors and peers who hosted them. Almost from their inception, such shows had been the sounding boards for the most extreme liberal views. They had served up an amalgam of topics ranging from the problems of being a transvestite in a straight world through dating your mother's boyfriends to the right of convicted murderers to weekend passes. At first glance Martin appeared to adhere to this general format. But while he conducted his show with an evenhanded good humor in which his personal views were always suppressed, his friends knew Martin to be extremely conservative. Yet he continued the same general format of presenting guests with flagrantly liberal sentiments. He screened all the news bulletins in search of someone who could legitimately be considered a spokesman for subjects guaranteed to outrage those who shared his own beliefs. The more-far out the thesis, the more likely Martin was to seek out its proponent for an appearance on his show.

Today's guest was no exception. As Martin stood offstage, just out of the field of vision of the morning's audience, he looked through the small one-way window set to the right of the stage entrance. Martin had had the special window installed to give himself a head start on the crowd. Looking the audience over before facing them helped him prepare. "I've got the usual mixed bag this morning", he thought. "There are two young black couples sitting in the front row to the right. They look like typical, hard working, conservative, middle class Americans. I wonder if they will find today's topic worth the effort. That big fellow with muscles straining for release from his newly pressed suit looks uncomfortable, almost nervous. I doubt if he has much patience for explaining away people's problems. His perky little wife seems completely at home, talking right past him to her friend on his other side. She's not likely to be very receptive, either. The other fellow looks a little older, a little more settled. Perhaps he and his wife will be somewhat more liberal in their views. I don't think those four will be very enthusiastic supporters of our visiting doctor, but they won't be any trouble. The five young girls taking up the second row on the right side of the aisle, who look like high school seniors, I'll bet will be considerably more sympathetic to this morning's topic. It will be something that they can immediately relate to." In this manner he worked his way up the right hand side of the aisle to the fourth and last row of the first level. It was indeed the usual mixture of guests. Most of them were tourists who included a visit to a television studio in their itinerary simply because they did not have one in their home town. Most of them came to his show to be seen by friends back home, rather than to see him or participate in the discussions. Their reservations were made and their tickets issued before he had even selected his guest for their particular date, so it was certainly not an interest in the topic that brought them here." He moved to the last row on the left and worked his way down that side. Full house, he noted. The studio's first level only held an audience of thirty-two in widely spaced chairs that made it easy for the host to move freely about among them, passing the microphone to each visitor who wished to comment. Three short steps at the rear of that level led to thirty-two more seats on the second level. There were his retirees in the top row, trying to escape attention, no doubt with some bus tour. In the next two rows were four housewives traveling together from a PTA or some such organization. Look at that, he thought when his attention got to the front row on the left.

That is the reddest hair I have ever seen!

The solemn blonde next to him would be striking in her own right were it not for her companion. I wonder what they're doing here? They are more intense, somehow strained, than anyone I've seen in my audience for a long time. Those four must have come in together. It's not likely that two such agitated young couples would meet by chance in the front row of my studio. The signal from the show director disrupted his analysis.

He nodded to his guest speaker, Dr. Annabelle Greenlee, a short plump woman with gray hair. Together, they entered the studio. He led her to two chairs at center stage and casually picked up the microphone. "Good morning, ladies and gentlemen. Before anything else, let me thank you all for sharing a part of your morning with me, whether here in the studio or out there in your homes. It is my sincere hope that the investment of your time will earn abundant interest this morning. Our purpose is not to inform; such an objective belongs to a news program or an educational series. As always, our objective is to provide an hour of lively discussion with as unstructured and free-flowing a format as the federal regulations allow.

"Clearly for a show such as this to work, it is necessary that its guests, both speakers and audience, provide most of the ideas and energy. This morning is no exception, and the burden of getting us off to a good start falls into very capable hands. It gives me considerable pleasure to introduce to you Dr. Annabelle Greenlee. Dr. Greenlee received her PhD in Sociology from North State University for her research into the demonstrable relationships between specific childhood experiences and adult malfeasance. A specific example was chosen from her studies and used as the basis for her widely read book which adorned Boston's best-seller list for three months. She is a widely traveled and well-known speaker on this topic, and it is indeed a privilege to welcome her to and to ask her to introduce this morning's subject."

Accepting the microphone, Dr. Greenlee began. "Thank you, Mr. Hayes. Good morning, ladies and gentlemen. Let me join Mr. Hayes in thanking you for sharing a portion of your morning with us. It is a rare privilege for me to have the opportunity to speak to so many of you at once. She paused for a breath and looked around at the studio audience. She noticed that a young man in the front row, one with bright red hair, kept looking from his watch to the wall clock over the exit door. He's very uptight. I wonder where it is he wants to be at this time? She continued aloud, "My topic for this morning arises, as Mr. Hayes has explained, from my doctoral research. "Hold on a minute, Annabelle." Martin leaned forward in his chair. That is twice you have referred to me as Mr. Hayes. "I bet over half of the audience doesn't even know I have a last name. They'll all think they've tuned into the wrong channel." "I'm truly sorry . . . Martin." She turned once more to face the audience.

"As I was saying, this morning's topic grew out of my early research. In 2015 I began to be interested in the connection between childhood trauma and specific sociological behavior . . . ." Dr. Greenlee was off and running begun.

The Occupation of BioPark Begins

The members of the ASPGH arrive at BioPark in accordance with Jane's plan to occupy the entire park as part of the siege of NAMBE. Once there, they prepare their for a long stay; but the high point of the day is the anticipated national television announcement of the other members arrival at NAMBE itself and the first public airing of the ASPGH demands.

Liz Blaine pulled her van the first visitor's parking area on the south side of the main gate of the National Monument known as BioPark,. There, she carefully pulled up to the parking space that two members of her team had roped off the night before. She switched off the engine, leaned heavily back against the seat, and exhaled audibly. The sudden quiet left her feeling momentarily disoriented. The drone of the engine and the slight vibrations that communicated the road surface texture throughout the van had had a soporific effect. Their sudden absence added to her feelings of discomfort. For nearly five days she had guided her caravan across the country. The entire focus of her daily activities had been to arrive at this point, at this time, on this morning. Now, here she was. Somehow, it was a letdown. She needed to shift roles from driver and caravan leader to protestor and marcher. She looked around. A row of chartered buses lined the back of the southern section of the large asphalt covered area. Movable rope fences and painted yellow lines divided the lot into sections appropriate to the day's expected use. Without counting she knew there were at least fifty-seven chartered buses in the group. In the left or western section of the lot in the space reserved for such vehicles, was a collection of RVs of every description, ranging from modified pickups to thirty-eight-foot Winnebagos and Gulfstreams. Both sections were quiet now, deserted. Even before being parked, the buses had discharged their passengers at the gate. The RV occupants had long since made their way into the verdant man-made oasis. Beyond the parking lot opposite BioPark, miles of sand stretched toward the a jagged ridge on the horizon, which seemed near enough to be included in an afternoon's walk but was, of course, a considerable distance away. "The air out here does not require the tireless activity of that disgusting manmade bug to keep it clean. It stays the way it was created because man has not yet polluted it, not because he's come back and scrubbed it with some mutated affront to God's order. What unknown disaster would follow in the wake of the MAJ?" she wondered. "Will there be another episode like the one a couple of decades ago when the Killer Bee was defeated? Perhaps there had been no other such incidents, or perhaps the government has simply succeeded in covering them up." Without conscious effort, she was warming to the next stage of the program, the protest. She looked at her watch, 9:37. In thirty minutes the announcement would be made nationally and the posters would be unfurled and mounted. The flags and signs will be hoisted and the march to the Park Administration building would begin. She turned to Tom Hanson, dozing on the seat beside her.

"Hey, wake up and join the party."

"After four and half days of driving, here we are," she thought.

Tom groaned and commented, "No one's noticed us yet. We could still change our minds, just leave and forget the whole thing."

"There's not a chance! Come on, you lazy lawyer," she scolded, raising her voices lightly, reaching over and shaking his shoulder. Exhaling deeply, she opened the door and jumped down. The effect of the dry heat was immediate, like a physical pressure. "And it's still early morning! What will it be like when the sun really gets up? Come on, Tom."

With a huge yawn and a stretch, Tom dragged himself back to consciousness. Removing his glasses with his left hand, he rubbed his eyes with the thumb and forefinger of his right hand, pinching at the bridge of his nose. Tom was a big man and rarely comfortable in contrivances designed for average people. However, sleeping was one of his chief talents. He had long since mastered the art of sleeping soundly, even in cramped quarters and when only short periods of rest were permitted. Resigned, and mostly awake now, Tom opened his door and stepped out onto the hot tarmac. The entire van shook as its suspension adjusted to compensate for the sudden removal of his two hundred and fifty pounds. After the air-conditioning of the van's interior, the atmosphere felt like a sauna. "Are you sure you've brought us to the right place?" Tom asked. "Can't we reform the world from some place cooler than this?"

"You're lucky the government at least chose a dry climate for the location of its abomination," Liz retorted. "Can you image this temperature in some place like Miami?"

"Anything cold left in that container?" Tom opened the rear door of the van and lifted the lid of the cooler and after sloshing his hand around in the icy water, came up with a can of beer. He raised it over his head to let the frigid runoff dribble onto the top of his bald head. It ran down into his bushy eyebrows, which seemed totally out of place on an otherwise hairless head. When the dripping stopped, he rolled the can around on his forehead.

"How you do carry on, Tom," Liz noted. "What will you do when the sun really gets up? And how can you possibly look at a beer before ten in the morning?"

"Liz, I thought I explained to you before that the beauty of a can of Coors transcends the limits of time and space. Besides, it's afternoon in Boston, and my biological clock does not acknowledge the existence of other monitors of time." He hooked his finger through the loop of the aluminum can and popped the top. He tipped his head back and swallowed half of it in a single swig. Wiping the back of his hand across his mouth, he exhaled loudly.

"Disgusting," was Liz's only comment.

After emptying the can in a second long pull, Tom turned back from contemplating the distant mountains. "Well, where do we start?"

"As we planned in the van, I would like you to take charge here while I go over to the Facility and get things ready for the big exodus. You know what to do. We basically want to empty the Park of all none members and then use the Park's own protective devices to keep everyone out except ASPGH members and television crews. Actually, the grounds should already be secure if the others have done their jobs ; and from the small number of vehicles parked here I assume that they have. But please verify that. Then set up the rear screen projection system on the truck bed we're using for a stage.

You have only a half hour to get ready before the show starts. I'll leave as soon as I make a quick check to make sure everyone got here all right." She was referring to a projection TV, which had been brought along so that all the protesters would be able to track the national coverage generated by the day's action.

"You got it. I think everything will go smoothly, at least initially. After the government realizes that we have emptied the Facility and its showpiece of an arboretum, there is no doubt that we will have gotten their attention . . . and then some. It's the 'and then some' that I worry about.' Up to the time of the first considered federal response, I believe we are in good shape; but after that, who knows? Well, who knows? In any case, you can go on as you feel you should. I'm ready, and as I said I'm sure the first stage will go smoothly."

"You're right on all counts, Tom. Take care of yourself, you fat indolent mouthpiece," Liz said affectionately. Bending over, Tom retied his shoes, which had been loosened for the drive; then with an agility and speed surprising for one of his bulk, he ran off toward the crew engaged in moving the ropes so as to close off the entrance to the parking lot.

"Hey Bill, find any problems so far?" he called out as he approached the nearest.

"No sweat," Bill replied. "This is going to be as smooth as silk."

"Yeah, I think the morning will go all right. I'm not so sanguine about the afternoon, though. Are you sure that there are no non-members in here?"

"Oh, it's clean all right. The Guards or Rangers or whatever the hell they are come by at six a.m. and open the gates. Then they take off and return around ten-thirty a.m. and stay for the rest of the day. When we passed through there was nobody here at all. I posted Jake down by the entrance to prevent tourists from entering. He's invented some line of shit that's plausible enough if you don't question it too closely. By the time the guards get back here, the Movement's national TV announcement will have been made. After that, we can just tell them they better keep the hell out. Don't worry, Tom, I can handle the entrance. You may as well go get the TV set up."

Turning slowly, Tom started towards the flatbed truck. He trusted both Bill and Jake and was confident that their portion of the day's activity was in good hands. The second major consideration was the TV show. That was important for the overall morale; certainly morale merited consideration. With the pressures and strains that Tom was certain would be brought to bear, he knew the determination of the members would be tested to the limit. As he approached the flatbed, the first thing he noticed was the placement of the truck. The TV cameras would be forced to face due west. The site selection was perfect. The jagged, imposing Cortez Mountains provided a dramatic backdrop. "Who could gaze, however briefly, at their awesome beauty and not believe in the sanctity of God's plan? Who could doubt that there were some matters best left to God," he mused.

"Hey there, Tom," a small girl called from atop the truck bed. Everyone referred to Barbara as a girl, despite her thirty-five years. Her small frame, tiny features and high-pitched voice seemed totally inconsistent with the fact that she was an extremely competent electronics engineer.

"Yo," Tom called back. How're you doing? Is there anything I can do to help?"

"I hope not. If I ever need the services of an attorney, especially one as renowned as Thomas Jefferson Hanson, the Third, I'll consider myself in deep yogurt. Come to think of it, I suppose I'm not too far from there at the moment. Seriously, Tom, this is some heavy stuff we're about to undertake."

"Yes, but we've been through all that a dozen times. Still, if you feel at all unsure, then my advice, as a friend and as the senior partner of Hanson, Bliss and Courtney, is to leave this job to someone else and scat." He looked at his watch. "You have about seventeen minutes to associate yourself. However, I was not really offering you legal advice. I was asking in case you needed my help as the charge hand. Shall I rustle up a couple of strong guys to help you lift and install those speakers or connect the wires or whatever? If it's relatively simple grunt work, I might even be able to handle it myself."

"I was sure that's what you had in mind. No. This is pretty straightforward stuff and I can hook it up in less time than it would take to explain. In fact, I've just made the last connection and I'm about to switch on. Also, thanks for the advice; but as you say we have been over that ground many times, and I'm not about to back out. Turning away, Tom headed for the last checkpoint. Just inside the park was a large gazebo like structure that served as a shelter from the sun and was the site of the licensed refreshment vendors. It was here that the ASPGH would hold meetings and serve food during their stay at BioPark. It was also here that Tom had feared there could be trouble early. The concessions were normally manned not by civil servants but by employees of commercial concerns. It was possible that some of them would feel it necessary to arrive early and get their booths set up ahead of the crowds.

Just as the last tables had been arranged in the prearranged pattern, he reached the gazebo. Stopping just beneath the slatted roof, he looked around for Grant, who was to have been in charge of this setup. Grant was not to be seen, nor was there any reason for concern. There were no shuffling or arguing sounds. Apparently, either none of the vendors had arrived early or Grant had succeeded in sending them away with some innocuous lie. He turned and ambled back toward Barbara

Occupation of NAMBE

The moment to unleash the full impact of Jane's plan had arrived. With BioPark fully occupied and her members ready to preempt a national television program for their announcement, they were ready to enter the final and definitive stage. Take over the entire NAMBE Facility; announce it to the world and inform the President of the United States of their demands. While the operation was considered to be Jane's plan, Terry's role and that of his few select friends were essential if often repugnant to Jane. The President would receive his surprise this day; so also would many others who thought that they were fully informed in advance.

The Take Over

In the Main Auditorium Dr. Q was addressing the latest
of visitors. Following long-established practice, he had paused
momentarily after his first sentence of welcome. This moment of
silence gave the audience a chance to terminate their conversations
and private reveries so they could give him their undivided attention.
It always worked. It was a matter of the appropriate volume for the
amplifier and the correct timing. The first comment had to be short
and simple so that it could be absorbed without concentration. The
pause had to be long enough to finish a sentence but not long enough
to begin another thought and Dr. Q was a master at such timing.

"At this point in your visit," he continued, "it is my custom
to present you with a brief history of NAMBE. I try to make my
introductory remarks both brief and informative. Such an objective
necessitates that I make some choices as to which topics I include
and which I omit. Clearly, these choices reflect my own prejudices,
which may differ from yours. However, this is your visit; and
therefore, I encourage you to ask questions as they occur to you so
that we may be sure to include topics of particular interest to you.
Are there any questions before I begin?"

"The pompous ass hasn't changed a bit in three months.
Which by itself is reason enough for our taking today's action,"
Terry whispered to Herm.

"Now!" Terry continued aloud, rising from his seat in the first
row. Waving his arm in the universal manner of a student with a
question, Terry approached the stage. Stepping to the side of the
podium, Dr. Q leaned forward.

"There is no need for you to approach the stage. There is a
microphone built into the arm of your seat. Simply lifting it will
activate the transmitter. In that way everyone in the room will hear
your question." Of course Terry, knew this, but was not about to
speak from his seat like some ordinary visitor; he was Taking Over.
Grabbing the microphone from Dr. Q's hand, he leapt to the stage.
The startled Dr. Q stepped back.

"There is a change in today's agenda, Dr. Quincy. You will please notice my two friends who are joining us on this stage." As he spoke, Herm and Brad rushed to the podium from opposite sides. Dr. Q was trapped. Brad, who had quickly withdrawn a large ceramic hunting knife from beneath his jacket, now aimed it casually but threateningly in the general direction of his host's throat; he said nothing. Herm simply turned his cold eyes on the audience and silently stared. Shock glued the occupants of the hall to their seats and held their tongues as Terry hastened to seize the moment. He began to speak even as he approached the podium. He had rehearsed this moment a thousand times.

In a calm and controlled and considerate voice he softly intoned, "Nice and easy, now. Smooth and quiet, and no one in the room will be harmed. We have just taken over full control of the Facility. As Dr. Quincy might put it, our reasons for doing so will be made clear to you in due course. For the moment it is enough for you observe the actions of my friends." Terry was in complete control of the audience and himself. Kim Newcombe had been standing just behind and to the left of the podium, awaiting her part in the morning's tour; she would call in the other tour guides at the conclusion of Dr. Q's introductory remarks. Now Herm reached out a long arm and roughly dragged her forward to a position beside Dr. Q. His angry eyes never left the audience, never wavered. Terry waited a moment for the full implication of Herm's act to sink in.

"Before we go on, I would like you all to look around. There are two doors at the rear of the auditorium and one at the rear of the stage. The two men at either side of the left rear door are George and Mike. Their last names are unimportant. So are their first names since they are not the names, they were born with anyway. At the other doors are Skip and Don, or whatever you would like to call them. They are there to keep the doors closed. The stage door is locked from the inside and the only way to it is to pass Herm." He signaled toward the brute holding Dr. Newcombe with his large hand and immobilizing the audience with his eyes. Herm made a sarcastic bow to acknowledge the introduction. "The visitors here this morning may be divided into two groupss: those who are a part of my team and those who are not. In order to help those in the second to assess the odds of whatever foolish action you may be considering, the members of my team will please stand up?" The seventy-five ASPGH members rose as a body and looked around at the four who were still seated. "Thank you. Those of you who do not have specific tasks for the moment may sit down.

Terry Explains The Plan, Most of It, To Dr. Q And His Staff

"All right, by now you have the idea. Even if we were not armed, resistance would be foolhardy. We are likely to be here for some time, so it's important that we understand each other. Before we settle down, there are a few simple matters to take care of. First, Dr. Q will declare a C-Zero Emergency. Thanks to an employee manual I borrowed three months ago, my friends and I know what this means. For the four at the back who may not, I'll explain. Dr. Quincy and the other eggheads in this Facility are fooling around with some pretty potent stuff: very dangerous little bugs or germs, whatever you want to call them. These little microbes can be so lethal that very special precautions were taken in designing the Facility. In order to contain the little bastards, should an accident occur, the Facility was built with special seals, hermetic seals, so that if necessary each level of this Facility can be totally isolated from all other levels and from the outside world. The possible problems requiring isolation were divided into three classes, A, B, and C. A Class A emergency arises when a microbe known to have serious effects on humans has been somehow released, say somebody drops a test tube or whatever. In that case the entire Facility is sealed and the people are literally locked in by a system which, according to the employee manual, is so well designed that even if a scientist panics and wants to place his safety above the possible release of a serious biological agent, he will be unable to get out. There are arrangements for getting air, food, and water to the trapped staff, so you see they can stay there indefinitely. "If an accident occurs involving a microbe with no known adverse effects on humans but not as yet approved by the National Biological Safety Council, or

NABSAC, we have a Class B emergency. In a Class B emergency only the level on which the accident occurred is sealed off. These seals are very important, and therefore an automatic system was installed to monitor them. If one of the seals fails its routine test, the entire level protected by that seal is evacuated and the adjacent level is sealed off.

"Regardless of which class of emergency is declared, the first step is to follow the appropriate seal procedure and then institute a rescue operation. Now, I'm sure you will all see the reason for the Class C-Zero emergency. The Zero means that the emergency is with the Level Zero seals, so the entire ground floor will be evacuated in an orderly fashion. Also Level One and all of the rest will be sealed off, and several hundred scientists and their helpers will be securely locked in. The best minds in the country have devised a perfect jail. Thank you, Dr. Quincy."

Confidently, he paused again to let the message be absorbed. To those who knew him, Terry's manner and vocabulary were clear indications that he was winning, and he was flying high as a result. "No one will be able to get into this level from outside the building or from a lower level. Of course you need not be concerned for the eggheads on the lower levels who will be temporarily trapped underground. They'll be comfortable enough, at least for a while. Isn't that so, Dr. Quincy?"

"You young hoodlum, you know you cannot get away with this," Dr. Q, managed to appear unruffled in the face of all that was going on. Terry became mildly agitated.

"Cut the bullshit, Doc! You know as well as I do that what I said is absolutely true. It's right out of your own fucking employee manual." Sitting in the first row, Jane cringed. I wish he wouldn't talk like that, she thought. He sounds so reasonable, so mature and educated, and then after a single sentence from Dr. Quincy his gutter vocabulary emerges and he sounds like a slob."

"Of course the safety system works. That is not what I mean and you know it" Dr. Q spoke up again. "It is your scheme, whatever it is, that will not work. You cannot hold the entire Facility as hostage. Even if you could, whatever do you expect to gain? There is nothing here you could sell even if you succeeded in stealing it and getting away. What is the meaning of this?"

"All things will become clear in good time, my good doctor. Jane, the young lady sitting to the right of my seat, and her friends have gone to great lengths to arrange for the answer to that question to be provided on national television." Terry relaxed, enjoying the argument. "Pardon me, while I explain another feature of your Facility to the people in the audience who have not been here before. Among the controls to be found on this rostrum is a switch for the largest television set most of you will ever see. A touch of a button will bring down a twenty-foot square screen which will be covered by a projection TV's image. Pausing to look at his watch he added, "When the national announcement is made in approximately ten minutes, you will all be able to see and hear. Once again, Doc, we owe a 'thank you' to your technology.

"But I'm getting ahead of myself. First, we must clear the building. Now, I am sure you would prefer to give the appropriate instructions for a Class C-Zero Emergency while Dr. Newcombe's face is still intact. For me it is a matter of complete indifference whether or not Herm has to modify her appearance to win your compliance. He, I can assure you, would rather that you forced him to convince you of the sincerity of our intentions."

Terry turned toward Dr. Q who stood resolute and silent. If only there were some other way to get past this point, Jane thought miserably. I know we agreed that this is the most crucial step; if he declares the emergency, the game is won. But still, I wish there were another way.

Small Secret Is Withheld From Terry

Seven rows behind, sitting in an aisle seat, Laurie Bass felt her stomach muscles tighten. She had previously chosen the aisle position to facilitate a quiet retreat after the formal proceedings had started. Now, as her pulse rate elevated in response to her adrenal signals, she thought only of the ease with which she would be able to make her move. Calm yourself, old girl, she thought. Dr. Q will not let any harm come to Kim at this point. "He will concede. Your best card is surprise, and to use it you must be patient. At the right time you may be able to save the situation, but only if you are free to act. Other than Kim, Dr. Q and the two visiting firemen, no one knows who or what I am. I'll keep it that way as long as I can. I may get a chance to act from a position of anonymity but never as the Director of Security. Though she knew her logic was sound, Laurie was not consoled. Kim was a friend of hers; and for that matter, so was Dr. Q in his own standoffish way. Easy she told herself. There is no immediate danger. Laurie's analysis was interrupted by Dr. Franklin's whisper, "What the hell is going on? Is this guy for real or is this a security demonstration of some kind?"

Sitting alone off to one side in the rear Ames admonished himself; "I sure misjudged Terry. I thought of him as a punk of some sort whose idea of a big deal would be to steal the petty cash. I sure was wrong. I wonder what he's really up to. The woman in the front row is, of course, Jane Wilds, current President and co-founder of the ASPGH. I've seen any number of articles about her. What has she to do with the likes of Terry Parker? The connection does not make sense. I'm sure he doesn't care an iota for the principles of the ASPGH, in spite of his comments at lunch three months ago. I wonder. Just be patient and observe," he advised himself. "Perhaps there will be a way to help soon." With an effort he settled back to watch and wait. Of course he had not failed to notice the attractive brunette he'd seen on his previous visit. The same disturbing emotions had set in, but he forced them aside for the moment and concentrated his attention on the stage.

Terry's amplified voice boomed from the stage. "Hey, you, back there, the stuffed shirt with the dark haired broad. Yeah, you. Shut up! For now, I'm doing the talking. After I finish, Jane has her turn, then the TV announcement, and then maybe I'll let some of you have a word. But for now, silence! You got that?"

Turning his attention back to Dr. Q. "Now, have you considered your options? I assume you would prefer to make the necessary phone call to establish the Class C-Zero Emergency before Herm performs on Dr. Kim. I don't know the precise procedures. But I will be listening carefully to everything you say. I probably don't need to tell you that if anyone opens either door, the Facility will need a new Executive Director and distinguished tour guide. You can use the phone that I know is built into the rostrum."

"You're an animal! Whatever the hell you're after, you're not going to succeed. But yes, I'll make the call." Dr. Q picked up the telephone, his hand steady, belying the turbulence in his mind.

The phone rang only once before it was answered. "Main Station, Andrews here."

"This is Dr. Quincy and I'd like to speak to Lieutenant Bradley. Immediately, please. It's a qualified emergency." He spoke the phrase that indicated that he was dealing with a genuine crisis, not a practice or drill. "Yes, sir, right away, sir."

After only a short pause, a familiar voice roared in his ear. "Bradley here, what's up?"

"Class C-Zero emergency rules go into effect now," was Dr. Q's reply. To his credit Bradley turned to Andrews and barked the necessary commands before asking any questions of Dr. Q. Issuing the orders required less than two minutes while Dr. Q remained on the phone awaiting the questions that he thought would pour forth any minute. To his surprise, there was only one question. "Whom do you want for your Action Team?"

Did Dr. Q Send A Message? What Does It Mean

"I have all the help I need here already, David. There is no need to inform Bass. The Security Director is away from the building with out-of-state visitors. Consider yourself in charge until Bass's return. I expect this level cleared and the others sealed off in less than fifteen minutes. Call me back on the Main Auditorium extension just before you leave yourself."

At the other end of the line Lieutenant Bradley replaced the receiver. "I could have sworn I saw Laurie return with those two guys an hour ago." he said to Andrews. "And when did Dr. Q start referring to Laurie as Bass? Ms. Bass, Director Bass or Laurie, but Dr. Q never refers to anyone by the last name only. It's not his style."

Telling himself to stop wool-gathering and get the damned Facility cleared and sealed, he hurried out to oversee the evacuation. Twelve minutes later, after the alarms had quieted and the flashing of the lights had abated, the tense silence of the auditorium was broken by the buzzing of the rostrum phone. Dr. Q grabbed the phone; Terry leaned his ear next to the receiver and listened.

"It's Bradley here! The building is cleared and sealed, except for me. However, the receptionist's records show that eighty seven visitors are still in the building. They're in the auditorium with you, as I understand it. What shall I do about them?"

Before Dr. Q could speak, Terry grabbed the phone placing his hand over the mouthpiece. "Tell him to lock the final door and come in here. Unarmed," he whispered into the scientist's ear.

"What's the matter? I can't hear you," Bradley's voice sounded anxious. "Nothing's a matter; I just had a minor cough. Please lock the final door and come to the auditorium. We'll discuss the visitors when you get here." Dr. Quincy hung up. Terry nodded with an ostentatious. "Thank you, doc. That was fine. I hope for Dr. Kim's benefit he arrives here unarmed."

"Don't worry. Our guards do not carry weapons." Meanwhile, Bradley hurried down the hall toward the auditorium. It was the first chance he had to turn his full attention to Dr. Q's strange behavior. First, he refers to Laurie as Bass; second, he holds eighty-seven tourists in the auditorium during a Class C-Zero Emergency. No sense to that at all. "Is the old boy is cracking up," he asked himself. I'd better be prepared and watch my step. He passed the UltraAtrium entrance, turned right, and rapped loudly on the door. Inside, Terry was finishing his warning.

"I'll bet Dr. Kim hopes you're right." There was a sharp knock at the left—hand rear door. Terry nodded to George. "Open it."

David Understands The Code, But . . .

"Come in, David," Dr. Q called from the stage. Lieutenant Bradley strode casually through the door, convinced by now that something was very much amiss. Lifting his eyes to the stage, a single glance was sufficient to take in the entire tableau; Herm with his cold eyes staring into the back row and his large hand wrapped around Kim's upper arm and Brad with the large ceramic blade still pointed at Dr. Q's throat and Terry at the podium. Like Laurie, he was professional enough to know that he had no immediate choice but to follow instructions and wait for an opportunity. While glancing casually about the room, he continued to walk slowly toward the stage noticing that Laurie and her visitors were seated in the audience. Obviously, Dr. Q's message was that these hoodlums don't know who they have back there. That's an advantage for our side, a small one, but nonetheless an edge, important or not depending on what the demands are and how this thing plays out. He stopped far enough from the stage to indicate that he was no threat but near enough to hear and be heard. Addressing Dr. Q in a voice loud enough to be heard by Bradley, Terry said "We are now ready for step two. But before the TV show we must make one further point clear to you. For this I will require the services of the capable Lieutenant Bradley."

He turned to the security officer. "Lieutenant, I would like you to accompany Brian and Lefty to the ASRS facility. It won't be necessary for you to lead them. They know the way from the excellent maps the Facility provides its visitors. While you are there, you will witness a small demonstration that Lefty will put on. After that you will report to Dr. Q the nature of the demonstration and then you are free to leave. In fact, we will insist that you leave. Lefty, Brian, hurry back, please. I don't want you to miss the TV show."

As Bradley and his escorts left the auditorium, Jane shook her head. "What the hell is Terry up to now," she wondered." We never talked about any demonstration, except of the members outside.

"Doc, things are going so smoothly, that I don't think you need stand there with a knife at your throat any longer. You and Dr. Kim may be seated-here on the stage, of course. Also, I think it would be more convenient for all of us if the four nonmembers at the back were to come up on the stage and join us. There is no need for you to be alarmed. I have no intention of harming you, or anyone else for that matter. Our objectives are nonviolent, unless of course we are compelled to resort to force. Perhaps you can introduce yourself as you step forward."

"You are stark raving mad." Dr. Q spoke up. "That woman is Laurie Bass, another of our guides, and the two gentlemen with her are no doubt visitors. They are certainly not a part of the Facility staff."

"Shut your face, Doc. I didn't ask you to introduce them. I asked that they introduce themselves. Your interruption only serves to make me suspicious. Welcome, Dr. Laurie," Terry continued, tacitly assuming that, like the other guides, Laurie was part of the scientific staff. Laurie and her visitors reluctantly rose from their seats and came forward. Laurie moved slowly, hesitantly, trying to portray the impression of a nervous, frightened female scientist, and all three remained silent after they took their new seats. Several minutes after Laurie and her guests mounted the stage a small explosion was heard. Every head in the conference hall turned toward the rear doors. Everyone sat—listening. There were no further explosions. After letting the tension hold for nearly a minute, Terry picked up the microphone.

The Chicago Vandalism Was Successful

"There is nothing to be concerned about. That was just part of Lefty's demonstration. The good lieutenant will be right here to explain all in a few more minutes." After what seemed like hours but was probably no more than five minutes, Lt. Bradley entered the room, followed by Lefty and Brian, each carrying automatic pistols in both hands. They stopped at the foot of the stage and Bradley spoke. "Dr. Q, these men have succeeded in smuggling three cases of explosives and one case of weapons into the Facility. Before you say this is impossible because of the SWARM, I'll explain how it was accomplished. The weapons didn't come through any of the personnel entrances, which are all guarded. Instead they were shipped into the automatic warehouse, the ASRS. The explosives and weapons were concealed in cases of glassware and shipped as part of a routine order of beakers, Petrie dishes, and test tubes. I don't have any idea how they got the stuff into the cases. The noise you heard was the result of setting off a small bomb, no more than a large firecracker, actually. The charge was attached to the most sensitive electronic accelerometer switch I've ever seen. I simply tapped the case with a pencil tip and the charge went off. Lefty claims that the two other cases marked X contain twenty pounds of plastic explosives each connected to similar switches, and I have no reason to doubt his word. If those cases contain a total of forty pounds of plastic attached to switches like the one I set off, we have a serious problem. As it happens, the cases are stored within a few yards of the main ventilation system for the lower levels. We have to assume that simply touching those cases, or moving them ever so slightly, would result in an explosion that would terminate the air supply to the lower levels. When I reach the Director of Security, I'll report that in my opinion we have no option but to concede whatever it is these turkeys want. Apparently, I'm expected to leave here and report to external law enforcement agencies what I think the chances are of disarming those boxes. If so, I'll state that it cannot be done. I don't know what these people want, but you'll have to give it to them."

"You got it," said Terry. "Now get the hell out of here. Escort him, Brian, and make sure you lock the door behind him."

Squirming in her seat, Jane could contain herself no longer. She leapt to her feet. "Terry, what the hell are you doing? We don't need bombs, we just need exposure. We want thinking American people to hear our story, our arguments. When they've seen the evidence, they will act. I know we need to be prepared to take some extreme measures. That's why we're here. But we didn't plan on knives, guns, and bombs. For God's sake, Terry, what the hell is going on?" Behind her, seventy-five sets of feet began to shuffle. Whispers rose. Onstage Ames had been reviewing everything he knew about the ASPGH and its leadership. He had never done any particular research on the topic, but he had come across articles in newspapers and national magazines. Violence was never mentioned or even hinted. "Miss Wilds seems to be having serious second thoughts. Perhaps it represents my second break."

The natives are growing restless, thought Dr. Q. "Now, now, Jane settle down. You don't understand these things as well as I; and you know it. It's my job to establish and maintain control. It's your job to seize the opportunity to make your case. Now, please get up here and explain to the Doc exactly what's going down and what's next."

"I just don't know," Jane stammered. "I guess you're right, but please be careful." She turned to Dr. Q. "Dr. Quincy, I am truly sorry it has to be done this way. But believe me, we have been trying for five years now to get people to understand that the M-cubed technology represents a serious affront to God and humanity." She had begun. Within a minute 'Jane the crowd mover' had emerged. She began softly using the reasoned arguments she had learned from. Then, she increased the tempo. She was no longer merely addressing Dr. Q, she was teaching the members of the Movement. She sure can sway a crowd.

"What a waste!" Terry thought. He settled back. He'd let her have her moment. She'll get her rude awakening soon enough. Jane was winding down to a pause, just in time for Randy. Yes, she surely was good at crowd control.

"So you see, Dr. Q, this action is necessary. It was necessitated by your own insensitivity and that of our government. Now, if you will throw the switch and reveal the screen, we will see the show begin on a national level."

The Truth of the Outrage Explodes Into The Facility Auditorium

The hall was quiet except for the swish of opening curtains. "Press the buttons for channel two, Doctor." Terry called. The screen filled with fuzzy colored images that slowly sharpened as the sound emerged from the bank of speakers encircling the auditorium. A pedantic female voice filled the hall, ". . . dramatic trauma such as parental rape or cruelty but rather the little understood but equally disruptive and shattering experience of broken toys. I w-"

"Pardon me, Dr. Greenlee." A good-looking young man with bright red hair strode forward and took a microphone from the outstretched hand of the famous philologist. "I have an announcement of national-no international—importance to make and I am afraid I that I will have to preempt a portion of your time. When I have finished perhaps you will want to continue; but as I understand the widely advertised format of this show, I am permitted to discuss any topic. Is that correct, Martin?"

"Yes, but it is customary to let the speaker at least get started. However, go ahead. I hope you have something of interest for us."

"As I explained, I have an announcement to make. At this very moment, the national abomination known to the world as NAMBE has been occupied by the members of the ASPGH. All staff members on the ground floor, referred to as Level Zero, have been evacuated. The staff of the lower levels has been locked in. For those of you who doubt this is possible, let me point out that these mad scientists are without soul but not without brains. They know the monstrosities with which they they experiment can be dangerous, and they have designed their Facility in such a way as to make it possible to seal it off in sections. Our members have simply used the Facility excellent safety systems to contain them. The message I have been asked to read today is intended for the world; however, I have a specific message for the President of the United States. First-" Terry reached over and switched the set off. Silence returned to the hall, again broken only by the swish of the curtains.

A call came from the front row, "Hey, what the hell are you doing?" This was followed immediately by a chorus of similar shouts from the membership, who felt they were being deprived of their moment in the sun. "You can't do that!"

Stepping to Jane's side, Terry stared down at the crowd. "I wish you fucking people would quit telling me what I can and can't do. It should be patently obvious to you all that I can do it, and in fact I just have. If any of you dumb shits think the purpose of this exercise is to prevent these egghead bastards from fucking around with genetic bullshit, you're crazier than I thought you were. You don't honestly think that plain Jane here has the brains to imagine, let alone plan and organize, a major EVENT such as this, do you? Without me you wouldn't even have a goddamn organization left. Look at her, standing there with her mouth open. This operation has just moved into its most important phase. 'What's it about?' you might ask. I'll tell you. It's about money, lots of it. Not money to buy more protests, but money to buy freedom and pleasure, mine and that of my boys. I want no more shit out of anyone about what I can and cannot do. What Lieutenant. Bradley told you, and by now has no doubt told the authorities, is still true. "Now we will really divide this into those who are with me and those who are not." Lefty stepped up to Jane's side and raised his automatic pistol to the level of her abdomen.

A Celebration's Called For Liz and Tim Check On The Evacuation of NAMBE Staff

The fact that the NAMBE scientists exited en masse was taken as an indication that all was going as planned. Liz and Tim were confident that the counter intelligence scheme to track government's response would also go smoothly. Accordingly, after a brief at the Facility parking area, they returned to the main ASPGH at BioPark. Hence, they missed the second mass exodus of the Facility when their own members were forced to leave also abandoning the entire Facility to Terry and a handful of his men.

It was still early when Liz pulled into the visitor's parking lot in front of the UltraAtrium. Carefully picking a spot where could park facing due East and checking the van's dashboard clock, she noticed it was switched on the console that Barbara had installed for her. From the roof of the van a collapsible antenna emerged, expanded, and rotated to the preset compass heading. A small panel on the dashboard slid back revealing a six-inch television screen. As the set warmed up, she checked her watch again; it was still showing 9:50. She glanced at the entrance to the Facility, anxiously searching for the exodus that would indicate the successful completion of the first phase of the takeover. There were only twenty minutes to go. "They're cutting it pretty damn close," she said aloud. She was alone in the van. She glanced at the news program that was winding down and, leaving the television playing, hopped down from the van and set off to make her brief rounds. Here, unlike at BioPark, there was just a small contingent of ASPGH members here. Their only purpose at this stage was to provide reconnaissance. Jane and Terry were to stay inside the Facility and thus would have no way of knowing what sort of forces the government might be mustering on the grounds outside. Liz's small team was to blend in with other tourists and curious onlookers and pass information about the government's activities on to Jane by tight radio beam-whatever the hell that was-she thought. But, Barbara had said it would work and be nearly undetectable except by very sophisticated equipment which the feds of course owned but would not be expected to use at a gathering of a bunch of protestors who were considered weird but harmless. If Barbra said so that was good enough for Liz. At the opposite side of the parking lot, she found Tim looking at his watch and shaking his head.

"Hi, Liz, good to see you," he called as she approached. "They're sure taking their time in there."

"Yeah, they better get with it or we're going to have an announcement before we have an occupation. I wonder-"

"There they are. Hot damn! We've done it . . . they've done it . . . someone's done it! They're filing out! Liz turned. "You're right. Here they come." She heaved a large sigh: relief or fear? She was not sure as she noted an orderly procession of NAMBE staff streaming out of the main entrance of the facility, was. "There are hundreds of them," Tim noted.

"Yes, well, now the fun begins. Let's go to the van and see what's playing on the television," Liz said. The emerging NAMBE staff moved off about thirty yards from the entrance before stopping and turning to face the Facility. They broke into small s, where in animated discussions they sought to decipher Dr. Q's cryptic announcement. "What the hell are the rules for a Class C emergency?" someone asked.

"You have to empty the affected level and seal all of the other levels," replied a perky little secretary from Personnel. "I know the actions required in response to the call. What I don't know is what it implies. What kind of emergency justifies the use of Class C? Have we all been exposed to a horrible disease or virulent poison? What the hell is going on?"

"No, Class C is used when there has been no release of any agent of any kind, but a leaky seal or something has been discovered. So that if some other level has a problem we would be exposed. Or if we leaked something we would not be able to contain it."

"That's what I thought; but we don't have any biological agents on Level Zero. We don't have any chemicals more sinister than salt and sugar. How can we be a threat to anyone? There must be a threat to us." The same conversation in perhaps a hundred variations was taking place in the small impromptu s that had formed.

Liz and Tim retreated to the interior of the van and settled back to watch the national announcement. In the BioPark lot, Barbra had finished setting up the television system and she and Tom Hanson were impatiently looking forward to the popular talk show. "This damn waiting is driving me wild, Tom. What time is it now?" Barbara looked at her own watch for the answer.

"You've got to learn to relax," Tom Hanson replied. Then, as though taking her question literally, he continued, "Five more minutes. I guess we can turn the set on and let it warm up. Will that ease your anxiety?"

"Of course I will not. You know as well as I that this baby does not require a warm-up," she replied affectionately, patting the projection TV that was the focus of her morning's s activities. "But what the hell, let's turn it on anyway." She leapt back up onto the bed of the truck with an agility that promoted her young girl image. As she had predicted, the screen immediately sprang to life. The credits for the situation comedy that had just ended scrolled up the face of the five-foot square screen. As the theme music swelled to its conclusion and the credits faded to the beginning of the inevitable commercials, Barbara reflexively pressed the mute button on the remote control unit she had retrieved. The commercial continued, silently. Barbara glanced around again, taking in the wonders visible from her vantage point. Even though the flatbed truck had been parked fifty feet from the entrance to the park, the botanical wonders within view were breathtaking, not only for their beauty but for their seemingly endless variety. Beyond the sectors of the patio garden, the park displayed further wonders of bio-engineering that Barbara had not as yet had a chance to see. "Tomorrow, maybe," she thought. Standing beside her and also ignoring the television commercial, Tom Hanson was completely absorbed in his analysis of the current situation and the likely developments as the day wore on. The morning's activities had certainly gone smoothly. From the arrival and arrangement of the buses, vans, RVs, and cars to the quiet sealing off of the entrance and placing of the large projection system in the shade near the park entrance, there had been no hitches, no mistakes and no trouble. Tom was well aware that such a tranquil state of affairs would not last once the authorities were aware of the Movement's intentions. He was prepared for trouble. Indeed, that was why he was here. The legal arguments he had prepared to justify their actions were at best only adequate to delay their forcible ejection and arrest. They were violating a number of laws, state and federal and the best he would be able to do by demanding full preservation of their constitutional rights would be to buy a little time. Everything should go smoothly enough until sometime tomorrow at the earliest, he assured himself.

Aloud he said to Barbara, "Here it comes. Turn the volume up; let's hear what they have to say." A crowd gathered within seconds of Barbara's turning up the volume, talking quietly while they awaited the appearance of their red-headed star. The minute Randy's long arm reached out toward the microphone, there was complete silence; as though someone had thrown a switch. By the time Randy had finished, the excitement had built to a fever pitch. "Thank you, Martin, for the opportunity to express our views. We will be in touch with the President's office directly to discuss the arrangements for providing our Movement an international forum for our formal statement. After that statement has been made, we will return the Facility and its staff, unharmed." Cheers exploded in the BioPark lot. Everyone was slapping backs, shaking hands, kissing cheeks, lifting someone up or otherwise enthusiastically expressing excitement. Chilled bottles of champagne appeared as if by magic, and corks popped like of firecrackers on the Fourth of July. The release of pent-up tensions was complete. The members of course knew nothing of the change in plans at this stage.

A Very Systematic and Organized Man Is Interrupted

I always remembered Prescott as a fastidious and systematic student and those traits followed him undiminished all the way to his Presidency where his reputation for 'order and method' was legendary. On this occasion his order would give way to chaos and Outrage.

Buzz Cochran Calls

Comfortably ensconced in his leather wing backed chair, Charles Prescott Winters, President of the United States, gazed across the green marble table that served as his desk. As he readied himself to tackle the rest of the day's paperwork, he was satisfied with the orderly array before him. He had no need for drawers or in and out baskets or any other indicators of disorder. Never more than one subject at a time occupied his mind nor his desk. The expansive polished surface of the table provided adequate room for whatever reports or white papers were necessary for the current task but not one scrap more. Just outside the massive hand-carved door he had had installed shortly after his inauguration sat Martha, the Ever-Efficient *as he sometimes affectionately referred to her.* The last item of his day in the office was the scheduling and sequencing of the next day's activities. Martha orchestrated this task and had long since learned to gauge the amount of work the President could get through in a day. Among her virtually infinite list of responsibilities was the task of assuring that whatever he needed at any given instant was there in easy view on the green marble surface. No paper was left there once it had served its purpose; no required report, or summary thereof, was ever missing at the time he needed it. At the conclusion of each task or review, Martha entered in response to the subdued buzz of their private signal. She invariably placed the papers required for the next project on the upper left-hand corner of the table and retrieved the stack from the last one from the upper right-hand corner. Prescott Winters was not the most creative or charismatic of presidents, but he was arguably the most systematic administrator ever to hold that office. As most of the world knew, he took his first break from paperwork at 10:00 a.m. each morning. At that time he received visitors, held meetings, briefed staff, heard pleas, and made awards or whatever the tireless, unflappable Martha had scheduled. Whatever the requirements of the day, the period from four p.m. to six p.m. was also reserved for paperwork. In the center of the marble expanse was a recessed computer terminal. When activated either by a concealed switch at Martha's desk or a foot switch near the President's left shoe, a section of the marble dropped and slid to one side. The terminal screen, a full color LCD, eight and one half by eleven inches, popped up and a keyboard with an attached microphone slid forward from beneath the surface of the desk. With this terminal he could not only communicate directly with Martha's electronic files, he could also access a number of selected national computer systems. While it was possible for him to use the microphone and communicate verbally with the computer, he was an excellent typist and usually preferred communicating with the computer through the keyboard. Secure communication links connected his terminal to systems at the NSA and the CIA, as well as a seemingly endless number of less classified agencies. While Martha prepared the final copy of all typed material that left his office, the President himself often initiated the documents which she then edited and cleaned up. On this occasion, the morning paper period had been extended, running until 1:00 p.m. At that time he had scheduled a luncheon meeting, to be held in the Oval Office, to review his comments on this year's budget with the Secretary of State. His attention to detail was not limited to administrative matters. The President paid equal attention to his own well-being. His daily exercise pattern followed exactly the schedule and amount prescribed by his personal physician, Dr. Howard Brown, and his diet was optimized by a well-known dietician. Each morning, Dr. Brown learned the day's schedule from Martha and obtained a summary of the previous day's activity from Harold Fibbs, the President's social secretary. This latter precaution was necessitated by the fact that occasionally it was necessary for the President to deviate from his carefully arranged schedule. This was rare, to be sure, but when it occurred it was Dr. Brown's task to get the President back on course. Organization and schedule were not just questions of technique and style to Prescott Winters. They were constitutionally essential. He could handle any kind of crisis as long as it fit a pattern. The largest international crisis would not ruffle his feathers if the perpetrators were acting predictably-that is, in accordance with their own policies, either as stated publicly or inferred from CIA, FBI and other investigations. The buzz of the intercom startled him; he was not to be disturbed during his "paper time." It was a strict rule of the Oval Office that he called Martha when he was ready for the next set, and she did not call him at all. Could it be time for his first appointment? No, it was only a quarter to ten," according to the digital clock above the mantel. The buzzer sounded again. Pulsing repeatedly, it sounded more strident, impatient. What the hell is the meaning of this" he wondered? He paused momentarily to take a deep breath and settle himself. Regardless of the break in protocol, he did not want to convey the impression that he was ruffled. "Yes, Martha? There must be a matter of extreme concern to the nation, or you certainly would not call me at this time." His tone conveyed a mild reprimand.

"I'm sorry to bother you, Charles." Martha was the only person in Washington who referred to the President as Charles. He was President Winters to most, and Prescott to his friends and advisers. This single peculiar aberration of was a small price to pay for efficiency, devotion, and tolerance of his own eccentricities. "Dr. Cochran is on the line and insists that we do, in fact, have a national crisis on our hands. He further insists that developments over the next ninety minutes are crucial and could produce disastrous effects on the international front. He has either gone totally bonkers or there is, in reality, a matter requiring your attention. Shall I put him through?"

"Yes, for God's sake. After an introduction like that, how can I refuse? But keep him on hold until I signal you, please." It always took a moment or two to get ready for Buzz, to shift gears from reality, so to speak. The President considered Dr. Benton Cochran to be a good friend. He admired him for his brilliance, but there was more to it than that. Years ago they had been together at graduate school and as members of the same fraternity, one a biophysicist and the other a political science major. Together they had boozed a little, caroused a little, and then gone their separate ways. While they had seldom met during the following years, they had stayed in touch and Prescott had followed his friend's career closely. Three and a half decades later when Prescott Winters was elected President and took over the activities of Projects Eight and Nine, he had thought immediately of Buzz Cochran, by then a full professor of biophysics in a small Midwestern university. Prescott Winters and Benton Cochran were opposites in many ways, in addition to their academic interests. Prescott was a slender six feet tall, weighing 180 pounds and in good physical condition. He was an immaculate dresser, given to three piece suits, heavy applications of starch and French cuffs links. He eschewed jewelry, except for his cuff links which were a simple gold signet in design. Buzz, on the other hand, was a chubby five feet ten and weighed considerably more than the President. He had given up weight lifting years ago, and it showed. From his mop of thick salt-and-pepper hair to the toes of his scuffed shoes, he was a living stereotype of the disheveled college professor. He hated starch. In fact, any ironing of his clothes at all was done in spite of him, rather than because of him. He owned few ties. And on the rare few occasions that he could be persuaded to wear one, a tightly formed Windsor knot would be seen pulled down the front of his shirt. His gaping shirt revealed a collection of gold medals, lost in a forest of graying hair. Regardless of the weather, Buzz's idea of dress suitable for formal occasions—from dining at expensive restaurants, to being granted an audience with the President of the United States-never varied. Oh, the colors might change, but "dressed up" was invariably an imported Harris tweed sports jacket, worsted wool trousers, and a one hundred percent cotton white shirt, oxford cloth with a button-down collar, of course. He always wore expensive cordovan loafers, shined by the manufacturer and never afterward. "I wonder what's on the old boy's mind this time? It's not going to help my budget problems, but it won't be trivial either." The President touched the contact beneath the front edge of his desk, and the brief flash on Martha's console indicated that he was ready. There was a slight click as Martha pressed the button, transferred the call, and switched on the recorder that would preserve the entire conversation.

"If you're going to tell me those clowns at NAMBE have created a monstrosity, I'm not surprised. If you're about to tell me that they let the damn thing escape, you'd better have the names of the heads that are going to roll. Of course, yours will head the list," Prescott began, good-naturedly needling his old friend. "If it's not at least one of those, then it's inexcusable. It's probably inexcusable anyway, you old reprobate."

"Excuse me, Mr. President, sir." Buzz interrupted with mock reverence. "Normally, I find your sense of humor amusing, not for its wit, rather for its existence. However, this is too serious a matter for even a President to joke about. Whatever you have on for the rest of the day, no, for the rest of the week, cancel it. This is the big one. This is why you were elected President. I know you like an orderly world, but a collection of fruitcakes has just upset your schedule."

"What the hell are you babbling about?" the President interrupted in turn, wondering if his old friend had flipped.

"I'm sorry. Of course you will not have seen the television program that broadcast that just a short time ago, or heard any of the radio coverage that was hastily thrown together to interpret the action and rebroadcast the audio portions of the TV show. And naturally, no one on your staff would interrupt your precious schedule.

"Lieutenant Bradley reports that NAMBE has been taken over! Hijacked, occupied, put under siege, whatever term you feel is appropriate. Every NAMBE official or other occupant of Level Zero has been expelled except three: Dr. Q, the cute, chubby Dr.

Newcombe; and that Amazon of a security director, Laurie Bass. My two new committee members are in there also, along with a kid who is supposed to start work next week as a graduate fellow, some prodigy who graduated with a master's degree in microbiology at age eighteen. Everyone else inside seems to be a member of the ASPGH. There are, I believe, seventy-five members, led by a madman. He claims to want nothing but the opportunity to tell the world of all the heinous crimes against "God and humanity" that are being committed by bio—engineering in general and at the Facility scientists in particular. So far, we have had no indications of what those crimes are." He paused for a breath.

Buzz continued before Prescott could comment, "Oh yes, I forgot to tell you. All lower levels from One through Nine have been sealed, complete with staff. That staff includes two hundred and fifty of the world's leading microbiologists, over fifty of whom are from currently friendly nations. I use the term advisedly. When the implications of that goddamn television announcement are understood, there will be no friendly nations."

Again he paused for a breath, and this time the President seized the opening. "All right, you win. The matter is important. But surely you exaggerate the gravity of the situation. We have an extensive, highly trained Guard force there-over five hundred, if I recall correctly. In any case, no half-crazy, simple-minded fanatic can take over NAMBE. He and his protestors would have be unarmed and would certainly be outnumbered. He can't simply seal up the whole damn Facility. You've always been prone to hyperbole."

"I'm sorry, Prescott, but what I told you is the simple unblemished truth. The nutcase is a man named Terry. I'm told we'll have his full name shortly, not that it will matter all that much. He will still have the Facility. He has got to be crazy to pull a stunt like this, but I can assure you that he is not simpleminded. He holds all the aces at the moment, even more than he realizes-at least I hope he has never heard of Level Eight or Level Nine. There is no way to empty that place from the outside. And as it stands now, there is no way to empty it from the inside without Mr. Terry's help. I could explain the situation more fully, but trust me: your time and energy will be best spent by ordering one of the Air Force supersonics to get me to DC, post haste and then calling together the appropriate of experts. You know who they are. While I'm in route, Duncan McPherson can fill you in. There has been no word from within the Facility since they expelled Lieutenant Bradley, the number two security officer. This Terry, on the other hand, holds machine pistols and has explosives wired to very sensitive accelerometers. That means they'll blow up if you move them at a velocity greater than one centimeter a week. He's got us, Prescott."

"Now I know you exaggerate. Explosives cannot be gotten past the SWARM. I've seen that demonstration myself a number of times. Those damn bugs are incredibly sensitive."

"As always your memory is excellent. When you listen you don't forget. Sometimes, however, you just don't listen. Terry is in there. He has guns and explosives. He did not bring them in past an entrance guarded by the SWARM. In fact, he did not bring them in at all. A supplier unknowingly shipped them in for him. I assure you, we are wasting time and you should get on with the program I suggested. But since you either don't trust my judgment or just plain don't mind wasting time to satisfy your curiosity, I'll explain the explosives. Then we need to get started. Lieutenant Bradley was given a demonstration of the sensitivity of the accelerometer switch. He was asked to move a large carton, loaded with scientific glassware. He was to move it by using a rubber eraser to erase a pencil mark made lightly with a hard lead pencil. When he rubbed the top corner of the box-gently he claims-there was an explosion at the rear. According to Lieutenant Bradley, it sounded like a large firecracker. He was then shown two other cases containing glassware from ChemGlass, a company in Bitville, Illinois, just north of Joliet, that manufactures test tubes, volumetric flasks, condensers, and other such paraphernalia. He was told that each of these cartons contains similar switches and fuses attached to large quantities of plastic explosive. I called ChemGlass the moment I heard Bradley's story. It seems there was a break-in at ChemGlass a few weeks ago: vandalism, or so everyone thought at the time. With the excellent vision of hindsight it is clear that the vandals were in fact Terry's boys-or Terry himself, for all we know. In the confusion created by a small fire, no one checked the contents of the cases that had already been packed for shipment to NAMBE. He must have opened the cases, inserted radio and accelerometer controlled switches and explosives, then resealed the cases. These cases were then shipped to NAMBE, where they were taken in through the ASRS entrance, Automatic Storage and Retrieval System. Since people are never admitted through that entrance, it is not guarded by the SWARM. It is clear that this lad has had his operation in mind for some time. I hope that gives you some idea of what we are dealing with. I confess I'm scared. That's your old buddy giving you the straight scoop. One last point, and then you really better get moving. I don't believe for a moment that this is an ASPGH operation. Oh, I believe that they are crazy enough. God knows I've cursed them a thousand times. Not one member has a clue about the realities of life. But while they are crazy, they are none of them violent. They would not play with explosives and guns. I have met and talked with Jane Wilds, who presently runs the Society, and her predecessor, something or other Gregory; I have no idea who this Terry is or what he is up to. But it's not about selling the 'leave evolution to nature' message."

The President Reacts

"You're right. It's totally outrageous. . . . By the time you get to the Micro City airport, the Air Force will be ready. I think it's just over an hour's flight on their latest bird. Come directly here, Buzz. Don't stop for anything." As if to punctuate the urgency he hung up without a salutation. He touched a second contact under the lip of his desk, and Martha's voice erupted from the intercom. "Yes, sir; I gather your old friend has a real emergency; you were on the phone quite some time. What's up?"

"I'm not at all sure that I know. But here's what I want you to do. First, find General Macmillan. I want him on the phone in less time than it takes to explain. While you locate him, I'll clean up this mess. Then bring in your pad."

"Hey we're in luck," the *Ever Efficient* interrupted. Macmillan was in his office, just closing his briefcase, preparing to depart. I got him just in time."

Without preamble Prescott began, "Mac, no time to explain now. I want something supersonic, the fastest two-seater you can muster, to pick up Dr. Cochran at the Micro City airport. Ten minutes from now would not be too early and twenty minutes from now may be awfully late. Can do?"

"Can do. It's only a small miracle. My wife called ten minutes ago with a tale about some nut taking over the show out in Chicago. I guess she wasn't lying! Don't worry; Buzz will be here before you can gather up the rest of your Tiger Team. You can fill me in later. So long;" Prescott had scarcely hung up the phone, before Martha entered the room, shorthand pad in hand. Listing them in the order they should arrive and indicating the intervals between arrival times in those cases where a private discussion was in order, he quickly rattled off the names of Cabinet members he wanted at his meeting. Martha had, in fact, already listed the names while he was on the phone, even though she had not known exactly what the budding emergency was. Among the Presidential staff and advisers he requested, there were no surprises. But she was not prepared for his next request. "Find out what local station carries Martin in the Morning and give them a call. I want a complete copy of today's show. If possible, have it beamed directly into my office on a tight beam. I want to see it immediately, certainly before Buzz gets here, which should be just over two hours from now. Get in touch with the Research Department, Domestic News Section. I want someone here within the hour to give me an up-to-date briefing on an organization calling itself the ASPGH and its leader, Jane Wilds. I'll take the next twenty-one minutes to get my thoughts in order and my questions lined up. Then I want Research's presentation."

The Situation At the Facility Develops

While she was familiar with Terry's mood swings and unpredictability, Jane had absolutely no inkling, no preparation for what was about to become of her grand plan. In a few words it was exposed as nothing but a cover for Terry's very detailed and carefully executed plan to lay siege to the Facility for sole purpose of blackmailing the President of the United States. The whole exercise of raising money (he probably stole it) for the ASPGH and carefully planning its national announcement was a sham, a cover for an awful crime.

The Invaders Split Up.

Laurie Bass and the two new members of the NAGWAD committee, Dr. Edward Franklin and Senator Frank Morse, were still sitting quietly on the stage, trying to make some sense of the situation in which they found themselves. Dr. Franklin was internationally known in the scientific community as an authority on human genetic disorders and was more popularly known for his work with SWARM. He had only recently accepted an appointment to the Oversight Committee. He had been cleared for access to the Level Eight and Nine programs just the previous week and had come to NAMBE expecting to be thoroughly briefed. Of necessity his overview briefing, upon receipt of his clearance, had been limited to a mere statement of the objectives and an Executive Summary presentation of some of the earliest results of the Level Eight programs. It had been interesting and even somewhat frightening, but for a scientist of his capability, it was far from complete, having raised many more questions than had it answered. In consequence, he had arrived at the Facility full of enthusiasm and interest, almost as if there were a graduate student again. He had been prepared to learn, to be amazed even, but not to be hijacked or kidnapped or whatever the appropriate description of his current situation was. Dr. Franklin was a quiet, serious man. He was in many respects a stereotypical college professor, of medium height and totally except for long tufts of snow white hair perched above his ears. His cheerful light gray eyes were constantly darting about, cataloging whatever there was to observe. His intellectual curiosity was boundless and almost totally undisciplined. He applied the analytical training of his profession with equal vigor to whatever topic was presented, either in casual conversation or as a result of extensive research. His soft round appearance was not limited to his face. His sedentary life style had taken its toll of his waistline and the general muscle tone of his body. His only form of exercise was walking, and he spent a lot of time at it. He derived little aerobic benefit, however, since his insatiable curiosity and darting eyes invariably found more than enough material along the way to turn any vigorous walk into a contemplative stroll. Senator Morse was an entirely different personality. He was the complete intuitivist. He was widely read, but his reading had no order or objective. He simply read whatever was available when he sat down, wherever he sat down. At home his bathroom contained a small bookcase that was always overflowing with magazines and novels. More magazines, newspapers, and books could be found scattered throughout the house. He formed his opinions and views quickly, and without any conscious train of logic to support his choice. Having leapt to a conclusion, his extensive reading and better than average memory enabled him to construct an elaborate string of arguments to rationalize his selection. Like Dr. Franklin, Senator Morse had just been briefed the previous week. Unlike Dr. Franklin, he had not engaged in any study of the pertinent technology since being briefed. It was not his style; and since there had been no related articles in his magazine or newspaper supply in that time, he had read no further on the subject since the briefing. He was a slender man, six feet tall, who was given to running and bicycling to maintain his trim physique. While he considered himself in good physical condition, he had no illusions about his physical ability to overcome the threat posed by this hijacking. He sat quietly, wondering if this collection of fanatics could have learned of the classified projects. He hoped not. he political consequences of such a leak were too frightening to contemplate. They were both rudely jerked from their thoughts by Terry's electronically amplified voice.

There was only a short moment when the control of the situation at the Facility was in doubt. Terry's calm, quick and heartless measures quickly put the end to any questions of who was in control.

"Now, Jane, I guess it's time for you to grow up," Terry said with a snarl." He had paced impatiently back and forth across the stage as the Facility employees were removed, the Class C-Zero emergency put in place, and his other instructions followed. Until these steps were completed there was always a chance, however remote, that one or more of the NAMBE staff would decide to take a chance and overpower Terry's men. Except for Herm, his men were not fighters. They could be overpowered. He had grown steadily more agitated throughout the process of implementing the emergency procedures. When the NAMBE personnel were finally out and the emergency seals were in place he relieved his frustration with an explosion of obscenities and verbal abuse.

"That's right, Jane, you. You can't really believe that I went to all this goddamn fucking trouble just so the goddamn bugs and plants could evolve in their own fucking time and fashion! Why the hell should I care? Let the bugs screw or not screw. Frankly, I don't give a shit. And if the good Dr. Q and his white-coated clowns want to design their own vegetables, I couldn't care less. I don't even care if they have to experiment on a few animals to test the friggin' purple striped potatoes or whatever. They can engineer their own fucking animals as far as I'm concerned. Dr. Q's sponsor, the federal government, is going to buy me my own private island, safe from whatever freaks they want to design here. 'Course the President doesn't know that yet, but he will!

"Now for you and your turkey friends out there . . . ." Suddenly turning sharply to the right to face two large football types, who had just risen, he changed his topic briefly. "You two there, sit your big asses back down or you will be treated to the biggest mess of guts you ever saw." He turned to Lefty, whose machine pistol was still pointed threateningly at Jane's midsection and continued. "Lefty," he said in a voice that was picked up by his hand-held mike, amplified, and heard throughout the auditorium, "If you see anyone stand up before I say okay, just squeeze the trigger. Don't ask any questions, just squeeze the trigger. Ya got that?"

He was certain there was no chance in hell that Lefty would carry out that order; but he hoped no one in the audience realized that. "Yeah, I got ya." Lefty spoke quickly, before the fear he felt welling up had a chance to reach his voice. To himself he added, "Terry, you've gone completely nuts. Hijack the goddamn Facility! Okay, that's the sort of thing legends are made of, and it's great to be in on it even if it doesn't work. But murder: a machine pistol in someone's guts as a roomful of people watch? Go to hell Terry. They got the death penalty in this state."

The audience all made a show of settling down into their seats. The sight of machine pistols and knives unnerved them. No one wanted even to consider the question of whether or not Lefty would follow instructions.

"You lose, suckers," Terry thought. "You just blew it. You had your chance. If the bunch of you had risen and walked toward the stage, just quietly walked, it would all have been over. Lefty would have shit his pants and dropped the gun."

Then he noticed Herm. His grip on Dr. Newcombe had tightened, and he had drawn his own ceramic hunting knife, the twin of Brad's, and placed it near Kim's throat. That son of a bitch would not have held back. Terry heaved a sigh of relief. He was in Control; there was just one last stabilizing step to take. His mood switched; he was calm again and his speech improved. He raised his mike to his mouth and squarely faced the audience.

"All right, now that that is settled, we can continue. First, we are going to split this little group up. Most of you are leaving. That's right, you are about to join Dr. Q's friends and associates outside. There are, naturally, a few exceptions. Everyone who is not a member of the ASPGH is an exception. Other than that, Jane will stay, and the rest of you protesters will leave. Is that clear? The good-looking Amazon up here with her two friends stays, as does my good friend Ames; we've done lunch. Isn't that right, Ames? Don't answer. Lefty might get nervous if you stand up and grab the mike. For those of you who are leaving, I don't need to tell you why Jane is staying behind, do I?"

He paused and looked around as though patiently searching for a questioner. "I thought not. Now stand and, in orderly fashion, please file out of here. Oh, one last thing: when you leave you will undoubtedly be asked many questions. Answer them. You can also carry a message from me. I am well aware that there will be professionally trained assholes sent to sweet-talk me out of this action or to stall the operation. The message is this: I will speak to no one except the President of the United States. He will not need a negotiator, trained or otherwise. There will be no negotiations. The President and I will speak, and he will damn well do as I tell him to. There is no need to wait while he checks with a higher authority; he is the higher authority. Now, go on file quietly out through the rear door and march along to the exit. Brian, you run along with them and lock up like you did before. I'll stay here with the rest of the men and keep our remaining guests company.

At this point Terry sends his first message to the President, indirectly." Oh, yes, you can tell the President, before he calls me, that I know what's going on here, and I'll talk only to him or to the world television audience."

A Momentary Face Off, But An Important Secret Maintained

Heads hanging and feet shuffling, the defeated and disillusioned members of the ASPGH walked out of the auditorium. They were stunned by the sudden turn of events. One minute they had been flying high, their mission a success. Then just at the peak of their success came disaster. Jane's life was threatened, their entire effort of the past months ridiculed. It was more than most of them could stand. Silent tears of shock and defeat streamed down several faces. Terry turned his back to the seats to address those who had been left behind. They were loosely assembled into two groups. Nearer to him, only a couple of steps away, they more or less formed a semicircle. On his left stood Drs. Q and Newcombe; Herm's large hand was still wrapped around Kim's upper arm and the ceramic knife was still poised at her throat. Directly in front of him, Jane stood frozen into immobility by some inner chill. Lefty's automatic pistol was still held inches from her waist. Looking bored or withdrawn, Ames stood on his right. ed together several yards farther back and closely hemmed in by the rest of his team, were the Bass woman and the two visiting firemen. Brad, who had sheathed his knife when he had stepped back, was just behind Dr. Q. George, Mike, Skip and Don had joined them onstage, carrying the rest of the guns. When Brian returned, the team would be complete and ready to move into the next stage. "Nine of us," he thought, "it doesn't sound like a lot to take over the whole Facility, but we did it."

Aloud, he said "Now, as soon as Brian returns, I will explain all you need to know about the upcoming festivities." As if on cue, the rear door opened and Brian entered and came directly to the stage. "Okay," Terry continued, "We are all convened. Some of you may have noticed this small black box resting on the podium beside me. It has two buttons. The green one is the one which I will use to deactivate the accelerometer switches on the bombs in the ChemGlass cartons down in the ASRS warehouse. The red button can be used to detonate the fuses by remote control. As Lieutenant Bradley explained to you, the consequences of exploding those bombs are significant. I tell you this just in case you should contemplate some foolish activity. I have no desire to harm any of you. In fact, it pleases me to think I've taken over Dr. Q's whole Facility without a fight. It pleases me, but don't misunderstand. I will blow this fucking place into the mess Jane thinks it is if you give me half an excuse." At the mention of her name, Jane seemed to stiffen further and tremble slightly from some inner tension. The change was slight, imperceptible to all but Ames. She's about to blow, Ames was thinking, as her hatred and frustration exploded to the surface.

"You are an arrogant, filthy-mouthed son of a bitch!" Jane screamed and leapt at Terry with her hands curled into claws and aimed directly toward his eyes. Ames 'noticed' Herm's tightened facial muscles, the first indication of his intent to act. Even as the big man's left arm started forward, Ames was in motion, and with a single move the blow that could have broken Jane's jaw was deflected harmlessly over her head. Ames had simultaneously noticed Terry's preparation to strike, but deflecting Herm's blow, which he correctly sensed as the more damaging, had consumed too much time for him to block Terry effectively. Terry's right hand balled into a fist, shot over Ames's arm just before it connected with his elbow, and landed squarely on Jane's nose. Blood streamed almost immediately from both nostrils. A fraction of a second later, Ames' upward swinging fist caught Terry's elbow, driving his arm into the air and drawing a curse. "You bastard," Terry growled as he swung a round house left at Ames' head. His reactions were too slow and his untrained and wasted motions had telegraphed his blow, which sailed harmlessly over Ames's right shoulder, having been helped along by a slight but well-placed nudge. Lefty jumped back, confused, managing to avoid Jane as she collapsed from Terry's solid punch. Recovering his senses, he leveled the machine pistol at Laurie and her guests. Herm had been turned almost completely around when the force of his blow was skillfully redirected by Ames's counter. Now he turned, breathing fire. "No one pulls that shit on me," he grunted, as he turned to attack Ames. then he stopped. Watching Terry square off as though to fight amused him, in a twisted way. He had fought for and around Terry on many occasions, but he had never seen Terry so much as raise a fist. Now perhaps it would be Herm's turn to watch. "What the hell? It don't matter ta me who kicks the shit outa that little bastard Ames long as that suntanned punk gets his ass kicked too," he thought. The momentum of Terry's missed blow had thrown him momentarily off balance. He turned back, with murder in his eyes. Ames had not moved forward to press his advantage. Instead, he moved over to the fallen Jane and was bending to help her back to her feet. Terry called, "You son of a bitch, Ames! I'll kick the living shit out of ya!" But, some internal switch was thrown and cooled the situation; his agitation and frustration had returned. He sensed his control slipping. With a visible effort he managed to pull himself together thinking, "The fucker needed to be stomped, but I have more important things to take care of. Piss on him; there is too much at stake." As he stepped forward to make good his threat, these thoughts reduced his anger to manageable proportions. Fighting was never very high on Terry's list of priorities. He liked to control by brains, not brawn. He stopped just in front of Ames.

"Shit, you ain't worth the fucking effort. Pick the bitch up and drag her ass back there to that in the rear," he raised his voice slightly to address the entire assembly" All right, everyone, settle down. I've got a lot more important things on my mind than fucking brawling. Any more shit out of anyone and I turn the boys loose with the fucking pistols. I don't really need more than one of you alive to achieve my objective. Shit, maybe I don't even need one."

Terry's rapid mood switch had so distracted everyone that no one took notice of the lightning speed of Ames's reactions. *The preservation of that secret would be an important factor later.* Actually, one person noticed the speed of Ames's reflexes and filed it away.

Laurie, standing in the rear and surrounded by four drawn weapons, was too far back to have prevented the blow she too had sensed was going to be leveled at Jane. Laurie had observed the short-lived fight with a cool professional eye. She liked what she saw of Ames's quickness The way he had moved indicated sound training. But he had acted hastily. He was lucky Terry was more greedy than vicious. Still, he had inadvertently given her an opportunity to study the reactions of the gang that held them. Certain that everything about her captives would prove important at some point in this crazy incident, she reviewed what she had just learned.

"Herm is not only vicious but unhesitant and uninhibited. His punch would have broken several bones in that poor girl's face; she may have a broken nose anyway. Terry is much more dangerous. He's not given to knee jerk actions. His is a cold and calculating bastard, dangerous. I also think he's a little afraid of Herm. Lefty and the others are just average run-of-the-mill hoodlums who are in way over their heads. One of them might pull the trigger in an unthinking response to a sudden order from Terry or out of sheer fright, but they don't share Herm's viciousness or Terry's determination. If I can break this gang into smaller pieces I can take them out, weapons or not but Ames had better settle down. I don't want him hurt." Her evaluation finished she turned her attention back to Terry. He was just beginning his latest round of instructions.

"Now, boys and girls, we're going to get this operation organized. I need you two with me." He pointed to Dr. Q and Dr. Newcombe. "Your services will be needed from time to time. I have no need for a guide or visitors. So, Dr. Bass, you and your guests there can join Ames and Jane." Jane sniffled and choked back a sob. Blood was still dripping from her nose. Her hand was pressed across her mouth as if to hold back the sobs. Her index finger stroked the side of her nose to help ease the pain. The leaking blood slowly tracked down the back of her hand, forming a thickening red trail down her forearm and gathering into drops at the end of her elbow. Occasionally, a drop broke loose and fell to the stage, where a small puddle was beginning to coagulate. At the sound of the suppressed snuffle, Terry turned back to Jane.

"You're a fucking mess, girl. On your way out of here stop at the drinking fountain and wash your face. And stop that goddamn blubbering!" He returned his attention to the others. "To simplify keeping track of you all, I'm splitting you into two s. Herm and Brian will take charge of you five, Ames, Dr. Bass, the two lucky visitors, and Jane, if she can quit sniveling. George, you go along with that. That gives you two guns and your knife, Herm. Think you can handle two females, a couple of middle-aged farts and Kid Judo here, or do you want more help? Remember, I don't want these fuckers killed, not even messed, up unless it's absolutely necessary. We might be able to use them for some deal, but damaged goods don't trade as high."

"Fuck you, Terry," retorted Herm. "I'll handle them, but don't expect me to back off from Sonny boy if he starts some shit with me again. You'll just have to trade some badly shattered merchandise."

"Got that, shithead?" he asked Ames menacingly, as he turned to face him. Sensing that Herm was only posturing verbally, not preparing to attack, Ames continued to stand quietly and showed no emotion at all.

Terry continued his instructions, "down the hall to the right, about a hundred yards on your the left, you'll find a much smaller conference room, built to handle about twenty people. Hold them in one of those rooms. When you're all settled in, let me know.

The extension of this phone is 1009. I'll hold my crowd in here because of the television and communication setup. I think I read somewhere that there is a two-way TV setup in that anteroom at the back of the stage. If so, Dr. Q is going to teach me how to use it and we will be one more major step towards wealthy."

"Awright," Herm replied. He turned to his party of captives. "Okay, you turds, get moving. You heard the man: out the door and down the hall to the right." Led by Brian, they slowly left the stage. In single file they walked out of the room, appearing only slightly less crushed than the ASPGH membership had been. The two members of the Presidential Oversight Committee were seething but each remained quiet. The best thing for them was anonymity. As long as they were simply two frightened tourists, they were likely to be ignored. If that madman, Terry, were to realize that he was holding two US Officials, there was no telling how he might react.

An Opportunity Presented and Recognized

A master combatant, Laurie takes delight it the further splintering of the mob ever smaller, more isolatable segments. She immediately starts playing her chosen role. An as yet vague plan begins to form and in fact to begins to take shape even before it's fully formulated. This is a break, Laurie thought. Perfect! It couldn't have been better if I chose the split myself. It's going to work out.

Still trying to convey the impression of a helpless female tour guide Laurie stammered, "Sir, Mr. Herm, sir. Would it be possible to take a small detour? There is a first aid room just beyond the first bend in the corridor. I think Miss Wilds should have some first aid and I am qualified to provide it."

"Shut the fuck up, broad. You heard what Terry said; get into the Goddamn conference room. Now, move your frigging ass and guide us there. It's your job, ain't it?

Seemingly defeated, she edged along, her head bowed. Just outside the door to the conference room, she stood aside and waved the others forward: first Jane and then the visitors.

Action!

Finally, as Ames was about to enter the room, Laurie acted. So quick and unannounced were her movements that even Ames did not realize what was happening until Brian and George stood disarmed and doubled over. George's lowest two ribs on his left side were broken and Brian was gasping for breath, the result of a well-directed elbow that carried the full leverage of Laurie's large and well-trained frame. As a result of two perfectly placed and simultaneously thrown blows from the knife edges of her hands, both men had essentially paralyzed hands. "Get their guns, Ames, and move those two into the conference room," she said calmly. The action had been so quick she was not even breathing hard. She turned her attention to Herm, who at last had realized what happened. She stood relaxed and staring into his cold and threatening eyes. Her own eyes never wavered. She had assumed no particular fighting stance. Her arms hung loosely at her side. Her feet were spread comfortably wide apart with her weight resting slightly more heavily on the balls of her feet. Her attitude bespoke of contempt for the huge hulk before her. Not only was she not afraid, she did not even require any particular preparation to handle an attack if he were to launch one. In her mind she was sure he would. If necessary she would goad him into moving, and quickly too. She wanted him as confused as possible by what he had just witnessed.

"I would like you to step inside also," she told him quietly, with no particular threat in her voice. It was as if she were inviting him to stay for coffee.

"How about that shit?" Herm snarled. "So you would like me to step inside would you? Look, you dumb broad, I ain't the least bit impressed by your fuckin' Kung Fu or whatever the hell it is you think you pulled on those two turds in there. This is Herm talking now."

Herm, did not know his antagonist and would not have understood her if he had. Probably it would not have mattered. The arrogance of a bully is rarely tempered by reason. In any case, his next comments could not have been more poorly chosen.

"After I cold-cock you and get this mess straightened out, I'm taking your ass down to that first aid room you talked about. You and me are gonna make whoopee, lady. I like 'em big and sassy. But first you're gonna suffer a bit. If it'll help at all, you can think about the screwing you're gonna get. It'll help you bear the pain now, knowing all the pleasure you're going to have later."

Trying hard to look frightened, Laurie thought, "You just wrote yourself off, you loud-mouthed, arrogant slug."

Aloud she said nervously, "Please, Mr.-ah, Mr. Herm." He lunged. Both big arms were in motion. A roundhouse of a right hand was looping up, over and crashing down toward Laurie's left ear. As part of the same motion, his left arm was rotating back and down, cocking the left arm for a crippling upper cut intended to meet the descending head of his antagonist. Herm was big and strong. There was nothing subtle about his approach. Hammer and thrust was all he knew. It was all he had ever needed. Few people had to be hit twice by Herm, and none had ever required a different approach. This time both blows connected with air. With a grunt he turned to locate Laurie, who was standing quietly, relaxing, having slipped two feet to her right, well ahead of the arrival of either blow. She did not need Ames's unusual perceptive skills to know what Herm had intended, and her hours in the gym facing trained opponents had more than prepared her to handle him. Convinced that all he needed to do was to get one hand on the dumb bitch and she was dog meat, Herm took a deep breath and changed his attack. This time he spread both arms wide, to keep her from escaping to the side, and charged forward. Before he had completed the first step, his world became a blur punctuated by a series of sharp pains that seemed to flash out of nowhere. All the blows appeared to land simultaneously. It was impossible for him even to work out the order in which they fell. A smashing knife edge to the bridge of his nose was followed by stiff fingers that drove deeply into his solar plexus. Two hands crashed like cymbals over his ears. The heel of another hand smashed into the underside of his nose. Two more stiff fingers found his eyes. In spite of all that punishment, which he absorbed in seconds, his body continued forward, blindly. Using a single fluid motion to direct the full momentum of his huge meaty frame, Laurie dropped Herm heavily against the wall. The impact produced a loud thud, accompanied by a cracking noise. Herm collapsed in a heap. He lay still without a sound save a shallow troubled breathing.

"Will someone please drag this trash in from the hall?" Laurie called to the men. "Find something to tie him up with. I don't know how long he will be out nor how badly he's hurt. However, you can bet he'll be angry as a hornet if he ever does come out of it." In a few moments Herm was tightly bound to a table leg by his belt and gagged loosely with his handkerchief. Laurie moved to the front of the small conference room to address the small group. Though they had worked in stunned silence as they had gone about the task of immobilizing Herm's unconscious body, everyone now began to speak all at once, mixing praise and wonder

"You sure as hell handled him. I never saw anything like it," Senator Morse complimented her.

"Who the hell are you, lady?" said Brian.

"I am Laurie Bass, Director of Security here at the Facility. Yes, Herm is no longer a factor for us to contend with. However, don't fool yourselves. Our nightmare is not over by a long shot. This Terry, whoever he is, is still very much in control. He has five more armed hoodlums and two important hostages. He also has the little black box. We can't afford to rush him or anything heroic like that, but we have a few aces of our own. First we need to decide about these two." She indicated George and Brian, who sat in silent shock, scarcely able to comprehend the events of the last few minutes. Brian had recovered enough for his pain to be replaced by fear that the whole thing was coming apart. After all the clever plans and their complete success up to this point, it did not seem possible that they could fail. Yet surely Terry's entire operation had been shattered by the lightning speed of that woman's hands. He had never seen anything like it. Crumpled in the seat next to him, George had hardly noticed the fight between Laurie and Herm. He was in excruciating pain, and it took all his concentration and determination to hold back the tears that were welling up. He was sure that he had at least one broken rib. And though the pain in his right wrist was subsiding, he was not at all sure that something was not broken in there also.

As they pondered their situation, Ames recalled a casual lunch meeting and believes he can formulate an effective plan but concluded that for now, we must wait."

"We do need to make some decisions and lay some plans fairly smartly," Laurie went on. "I suggest that we secure the others just like we secured Herm, at least temporarily." She looked at George and Brian. "Then we can move next door and discuss our options. While we're tying them up, it would be wise not to talk. There is no point letting these two hear any of our ideas before we've had a chance to consider them ourselves."

From Ames and the injured Jane to the two committee members, all were pleased to have someone assume a leadership role, particularly someone as capable as Laurie Bass. They all complied without hesitation, silently binding the two hijackers and tipping their chairs. Then Ames helped Jane to her feet, and the four former captives followed Laurie into the next room. Dr. Franklin was the first to speak.

"Does anyone know what is taking place? I was sufficiently upset by the prospect of being held captive while some near-fanatic misinformed protestors who made inflammatory speeches to a world audience. Such activity goes well beyond any reasonable definition of free speech. However, that does not appear to be the issue any longer. This poor girl-we really must do something about her nose—is definitely not in control, and the protest seems to have degenerated into a simple hijacking for ransom. But surely there is no way for such an action to succeed?"

"Your summation is accurate except for two important points," Laurie said. "There is nothing simple about this hijacking. It is very well thought out. Also, it could very well succeed; it has so far. Don't let's fool ourselves. If Terry remains in charge of the Facility, it is highly likely that President Winters will have to agree to his terms. We may be in a position to change that, if we can find some weakness to exploit. At this point, we have only surprise on our side. It worked once, but when Herm doesn't call in at the specified time, the element of surprise will be gone and Terry will be alerted. Now, what do we know about this madman? Ames, he claims some sort of friendship with you. Can there possibly be any truth to that? Jane clearly knows him, but she's in no condition to talk; I agree with Dr. Franklin that we must attend to her nose. But we must decide first what to do about Herm's phone call or else time will make that decision for us. Ames?"

"Well, I did actually meet Terry three months ago, when I visited NAMBE for the first time; he was also here on tour. He must have been looking over the Facility, 'casing the place,' I guess he would call it. We went around in the same, one led by Dr. Newcombe." Ames went on to report the details of his conversations with Terry

"There's not much there to help us, is there?" Laurie asked.

"Oh yes, there is," Ames said. "I think I have an idea that will make Terry lose control. I will explain later; but now we must hurry. To save time let me explain just the first phase and I will explain the whole plan later."

Cooperation In The Parking Lot

Unable to contain themselves, several of the ASPGH members who had tasks to perform back at BioPark crowded into a corner of the Facility parking lot to observe and celebrate the first evidence of their initial success, the exodus of the Facility staff. Of course they were totally unprepared for the second exodus.

The Facility was built at the edge of a large plain. The ground sloped gently upward as one moved from the main entrance across the spacious patio toward the parking lots, which were on two levels, one about ten feet above the other. On each level the lots were curved, fanning out to the east and converging toward a common center, the Facility. The site had been chosen to keep the bright sunlight, cutting through the pellucid atmosphere, to the backs of the staff, both on their way into the Facility in the morning and on their way out in the evening.

The ASPGH observers had been waiting outside the Facility onto the upper level. It did not matter that they could not see or participate in the action taking place inside; just being physically near had provided a kind of vicarious sense of collaboration in the hijacking that they knew was taking place. Their numbers had swollen to more than twice the fifty that were considered adequate for the anticipated TV news cameras. Many of those who had been assigned to stay at BioPark had left their assigned places just to be nearer the action. A loud cheer had gone up when the building emptied on schedule, evidence that the first phase of the occupation had succeeded.

The departing NAMBE staff had been completely bewildered and surprised at the chanting. The unfurling of the ASPGH banners did little to relieve their confusion. Most of them knew what the ASPGH was; the organization had recently received considerable press. It was understandable that the fanatics, as the ASPGH membership was universally viewed by the Facility staff, would be pleased to see the Facility involved in a crisis; but there was no way that they could possibly know that a Class C-Zero emergency had just been declared—unless they had caused it. But wasn't that was too preposterous to contemplate? As the staff discussed the presence of the cheering crowd, their misgivings turned first to concern, then to suspicion, then to certainty, then to anger. The inescapable conclusion was that these zealots had somehow managed to cause serious enough damage to the Facility to result in its evacuation. David Bradley had climbed up on the marble railing that formed a semicircular arc partially enclosing the entry patio. He waved his arms as he shouted for attention, his voice amplified by a loud hailer.

"Hold on. I'll tell you everything I know in a moment. First, I want all Guards to make themselves known and form a line between Facility staff, who are to stay on the lower level, and the ASPGH membership, to be kept on the upper level."

The guards removed their badges from their pockets and, using integral magnetic clips, attached them to their shirts and blouses. The crowds on both levels were surprised at the number of badges that were displayed. The realization that there ware over a hundred Guards in their midst had a sobering effect on both crowds. One serious complication of the day's activities, a potentially dangerous and injurious riot, had been averted.

"All right," Bradley began, "here it is, as far as I know it. The ASPGH has occupied the Facility-hijacked it would be a more accurate term. They are nominally led by Jane Wilds, of whom you have no doubt read. However, the real power behind the hijacking is a man named Terry, who is supported by a number of thugs who may or may not be ASPGH members. I personally believe that they are not and that Terry has duped the whole Movement.

"In any case these men have smuggled weapons into the Facility by shipping them through the ASRS entrance in ChemGlass cases. I don't know how the weapons came to be in the cases. The entire Level Zero is now empty except for the hijackers and their captives: Jane Wilds, Drs. Q and Newcombe, Laurie Bass, two government visitors from Washington, and our newest member of the scientific staff, a young man named Ames Fromme. Terry has, as allies in the auditorium, seventy-five people, presumably members of the ASPGH,; though I would not be surprised to find that a number of them are ringers.

"Bombs were also brought in through the warehouse and are are located there now, near the ventilation shafts. "The lower levels are sealed off, with the staff trapped inside. Of course the levels can only be opened when the emergency is cleared from the Level Zero. As things stand, Mr. Terry controls the only means of clearing the emergency. The hijackers are demanding a forum from which to launch their complaints about NAMBE and bio-engineering projects in general. They apparently made some plans for a television announcement.

"That is all I can tell you at this time. I would like all staff except for Guards to go home. There is no chemical or biological emergency. There is nothing that any of you can do to help. I have your phone numbers, and you will be notified when it makes sense for you to return. You will, of course, be called if there is any chance that you can be of assistance. My staff will help you if you have any problems in getting away.

"After the lower lot has been cleared, I would appreciate it if the ASPGH members would disperse quietly. Guards are to use no force to remove visitors. However, they will take whatever measures are necessary to assure that any members of the Movement who do remain stay in the upper lot. Thank you all for your help."

He had turned and hastened toward his car, confident that his staff would carry out his orders in a systematic fashion. There had been a swirl of activity on both levels, accompanied by cheers and catcalls from above. Bradley paused beside his automobile and turned once more to survey the crowds. Satisfied that his people could handle the situation, he looked wistfully toward the Facility. To his surprise, the entrance door opened and seventy-odd members of the ASPGH filed out.

"It's started already: the breakup of the conspirators," he thought and walked forward to meet the emerging throng. As he approached, a short, thin man had stepped forward. His words poured out in a continuous rapid-fire stream without pause or emphasis, a delivery style that might be expected from a high school student who had memorized a speech someone else had written for him.

"I'm Henry Johnson, an attorney for the ASPGH. I came to protect the rights of the Movement's members. In the present circumstance, however our interests coincide. I am advising our members to cooperate fully with your investigation. This man Terry-I don't know his last name—has abandoned the just cause of the ASPGH and, acting entirely on his own, is now holding for ransom. not only the Facility but also for the return of three visitors, and God knows how many scientists Furthermore, he is also holding the leader of our Movement, Miss Jane Wilds. He holds her not only for additional ransom but to hold a knife to her throat to assure our cooperation. The reign of terror and violence has already begun. The brute named Herm, who threatened Dr. Kim Newcombe, has already seriously injured Jane. That occurred before we were forced, at gunpoint, to leave the auditorium and join you here. The man is quite mad, but he is in control. He will talk only with the President of the United States. He will not negotiate, not even with the President, but will simply present his demands, which are to be complied with in their entirety."

Now he's not talking like a lawyer, rather than a protester, Bradley thought. Interrupting before the attorney could launch another volley, Bradley assured him, "Thank you for your offer of assistance. I can assure you I will report your cooperation to the authorities, who may, look more favorably on the arguments for clemency that I am sure you will make on behalf of yourself and your clients."

"Now, Mr. Johnson, if you will divide your members into smaller groups along the north wall, I will send some of my staff over to begin the questioning of them; we want to learn as much as we possibly can, since you are the only ones who know this madman and have heard his latest pronouncements."

Each member of the Movement was identified and questioned. In the half hour required to reconstruct the activities in the auditorium following Bradley's departure, the NAMBE staff quietly dispersed. Many of the ASPGH members had left also, but a small remained, waiting to question their friends who had been inside. As each member had been dismissed by the security force, he was absorbed by the growing of disillusioned idealists. David Bradley with more than enough information to assess the situation had hurried off to meet the Senator.

David Evaluates The Situation

It was clear that Terry had carefully studied the NAMBE handout after his first visit to the facility. His plans perfectly used the Facilities own defenses and protections against it. There is really no option except to concede to his demands and wait him out.

"Yes, Mr. President," Duncan McPherson held the telephone firmly. "Lieutenant Bradley is right here, and we're reviewing his plan of action. It does appear that anything he can do is being done. I can give you a partial report now and fill in the details later, or simply wait to give you a complete report when our review is finished, whichever you prefer."

"Call me back; that will be fine. I don't want to delay any action that has even a remote chance of being effective. But in any case I want as full a report as you can provide before my staff meeting in another seventy minutes," Prescott Winters replied.

Hanging up the phone, McPherson turned to Bradley and said, "Talk about a fishbowl situation, Lieutenant. This is certain to be the most microscopically examined operation either you or I have ever been involved in."

"I'm nervous enough without the added pressure of President Winters tracking our activities on an hourly basis, but I guess there is nothing we can do about that. It's a big advantage having you here, sir. I'm sure I'd be tongue-tied and incoherent if I had to deal with the President directly. By the way, since we will be working closely together, I wonder would it be possible to do so on a first name basis? I don't mean to be presumptuous but we're very informal out here, and every time you say 'Lieutenant I want to look around to see if someone else is in the room."

"Yes, of course. We're not really all that stuffy in D.C., either. I didn't mean to sound overly formal. My name is Duncan, pure Scots; let's make it Dunc."

"And I'm David. Pleased to meet you Dunc. Now, as to this review, I'm afraid there's not all that much going on. You are likely to have a slim report to the President. We don't yet know who this Terry is, but we're running a check of the Computerized Mug book, CompMug. It accepts verbal descriptions-height, weight, hair color, and so on—then processes it through a series of geographically distributed data bases. We help this along with data on such things as organizational affiliation, etc. The result is usually a tremendous listing. In this case, since Terry's such an average looking guy, the list was especially long. I have three men working to see if they can trim it down to a reasonable size. It would save a lot of time if one of the ASPGH crowd would just tell us who the hell he is; but, as they see it, either there is some confusion and Terry is still on their side, or he really is threatening their leader's life. Either way, they don't want to risk angering him, in spite of the advice of their attorney. I've got the other names going through CompMug too, but I'm no more bullish about results. Actually, knowing who they are may not do us much good in any case. They hold all the cards at the moment. There is very little to be accomplished by those of us outside as long as he has all of those hostages on the lower levels. There is absolutely no entrance to that Facility during a Class Zero emergency except to blast your way in. The Facility is designed to provide as perfect a containment as is possible in case of an accident. Any entrance that was operable from the outside would be a potentially dangerous release point if some uninformed person should enter at an inappropriate time. No, we cannot force our way in. We will have to wait for Terry to open the doors.

We have only one ace on our side: our security director, Laurie Bass. Terry thinks she is only a tour guide; she has surprise on her side. She is also one damn competent lady. If anyone can turn a small advantage into a capture or escape, it's Laurie Bass. However, I'm not sure that even she can do much. She's our only hope. Don't think we can send in the Marines or do something equally dramatic. Even if we were to blow down the outside door, we would find ourselves in a sealed section. We would then have to blast our way through one protective seal after another to get to a particular segment. To reach the auditorium, assuming that they stay there, we would have to blast through no less than six seals. That would give him ample time to move, and since he has the controls he can move quickly and freely. I think we can take it is a given that Terry is in there for as long as he wants to stay.

"Our best chance for an overt action is probably when he leaves. I have no idea how he expects to get out of there after his demands are met. Don't shake your head, Dunc. Like all of his predecessors, this President refuses even to consider giving in to pressure. But either Laurie will find a miracle or we will pay that damned Terry whatever he asks."

Noting the look of incredulity on the senator's face, Bradley continued, "We are not just talking about American citizens. There are maybe two hundred foreign scientists in there. Are we likely to risk their lives to satisfy our President's moral and ethical convictions? You would know better than I, but I doubt it." The senator did not reply. "Then there are other factors that dare not be denied. There are microbes, plant seeds, mushroom spores, and I don't know what all that have not yet been tested. While nearly everything is intended to be safe for use in the open, I'm sure I needn't remind you that until they have been fully field-tested they are considered dangerous and in fact in some cases they have proven to be deadly.

"I am convinced our only hope is to take this bastard when he leaves. We can't really prepare a plan for that phase until we learn something about what he has in mind. While I'm sure he can hold the Facility, I can't see how he can affect a safe getaway, even if he plans on taking hostages with him. Once he's outside, we have significantly more options. I've sent for a SWAT team, including an extra contingent of marksmen. I've also arranged for tracking aircraft, fixed wing and helicopter. Flying and driving are the only realistic ways out of here. We can stop him at that stage, but there is nothing that we can do to end his occupation."

Senator McPherson considered his arguments, "You're sure there are no ways to get in that are unaffected by Class Zero? We can't descend an air shaft or sewage drain or something of that sort."

"Not a chance. The designers were determined to contain insects, microbes, and spores," Bradley said with finality. "There is no way into the complex with using explosives, and even then it would not be easy. We're trying to determine what his escape plans are. At this stage though, it's a purely routine legwork."

"You have a team working the Society members?" the senator asked.

"Those few who are willing to cooperate are being worked, yes. The others out here fall into two groups: those who carried signs in BioPark and outside the Facility; and those who were inside with Jane and Terry. The first group has broken no laws though I'm convinced they would have if Terry had not aborted their program. The second group came closer to committing a crime; they were inside the building with Terry and Jane and are probably guilty of conspiracy, but I can't prove it.

To top it off, each has a lawyer. Henry Johnson was inside and a man named Tom Hanson, a senior partner of a respectable law firm back East, was outside, Hanson is giving instant courses in how to demand your full constitutional protection, and how to advise others to do so. His improvised staff is circulating through the crowd faster than my men can manage, and essentially advising everyone to play it quiet. That is, don't interfere with the authorities but don't do anything to help them either."

"You certainly make a good case for patience. However, on the other end of that phone line is Prescott Winters. Standing around until some hoodlum gives him orders is not likely to sit well with him. What about that TV program? Any leads there? Can we arrest the studio contingent? They appear to be pretty far away from their lawyer."

"No, they are absolutely not! What they did is not only illegal, it also fits the advertised format of the show they used to make their announcement. The network is more likely to pay them for more interviews than to press charges. This is the sort of stuff their viewers lap up. Indeed, the flaming redhead who made the announcement is also an attorney-not nearly as well known as Tom Hanson, but adequate to the present task. I've called the Chicago police, and they have two detectives standing by the studio just in case they're needed. But I don't expect much concrete help from that quarter either."

"You certainly seem to be on top of things, David," Senator McPherson said. "I can only hope your pessimism is or unfounded. Now, what do we know of Terry's demands? I take it there is no longer any question of getting out of this with a promise of extended TV and radio exposure?"

"Not by a long way. This guy Terry used the ASPGH only as a cover, an army for the first act of his takeover. He couldn't have known how many security guards would be in the hall this morning; usually there are three in plain clothes."

"As it happened, he didn't need his army at all, but he couldn't have known that. This morning the auditorium doors were closed when the guards arrived. They had detoured to check out the gathering crowd in the parking lot. It is unusual to have a large number of visitors other than those who come for the tour. When the guards arrived, they stood in the hall waiting, rather than face Dr. Q's wrath, which surely would have been aroused had their entrance distracted his audience.

In any case, Terry was able to mount a show of force consisting of seventy-five people, which would have been enough to discourage me even if I had had my three men in there. Once he had used the society members he dismissed them-threw them out is a better description. That reduced his audience to a number much easier to control. He certainly has no desire to help the cause; he never did have. No, as he said, he wants money and lots of it; we don't know how much. We do know he will deal only with the President of the United States."

"He what?" spluttered McPherson. "Some goddamn hoodlum, a cheap crook of a hijacker, wants to negotiate directly with the President? Fat chance! No one with any idea of what Prescott Winters is and believes in could even contemplate his negotiating with a cheap crook like that!"

"I didn't say negotiate," Bradley replied. "Terry is explicit. He will make his demands known only to the President, and he will not negotiate. His last crack to the departing Society members was, 'Tell the President that I know what's going on here, and I'll talk only to him or to the world television audience.' I have no idea what he meant."

McPherson was too beside himself with anxiety and indignation to speak clearly. "That arrogant son of a bitch!" he managed to say at last. "Get on with what you are doing, and please let me know the minute there is any break or any additional information. I'll stay here, and in close touch with the President. Thank you, David."

"Don't worry, Dunc. If anything happens, I'll be in touch." Bradley hurried out.

Micro City had a City Manager form of government. By charter the titular city manager of the city, was the Executive Director of NAMBE, Dr. Q. He was supported in this position by a staff of elected councilmen. Dr. Q maintained an office on the top floor of the town hall, at three stories the tallest building in the city. While not as ostentatious as his NAMBE office, it was more than adequate for the two half-days a week he spent there. Now, Duncan McPherson sat behind the massive oak desk that was the focal point of the office. Since Dr. Q had expected to spend the day at the Facility, the desk, like the appointment calendar, was clear. The day's plan had been that McPherson and Dr. Cochran would spend the morning here, going over the financial reports on NAMBE's operation in preparation for the Administrative Review, which was scheduled in Dr. Q's NAMBE office immediately after lunch. The two new members of the Committee would spend the day with the tour as part of their orientation. The remaining members had been scheduled to arrive that evening, and the In-Depth Technical Review would take place tomorrow and the next day. Terry had changed all that. Dr. Cochran had gone back to Washington, and the other two members had been called and their trips canceled. Now, alone with Lt. Bradley's analysis and his own thoughts, McPherson began to contemplate the consequences of what had taken place this morning and what was in fact still taking place even as he sat there at Dr. Q's pretentious desk? In David's mind, the situation was serious and in David's mind it was getting more so by the minute. But David did not know the half of it. He was not cleared for Projects Eight and Nine. Senator McPherson was a man of action, known for his boundless energy and unwavering drive. In the present circumstance his was clearly a reporting role: sit and wait for David or Ms. Bass to generate some news worth reporting. He knew Bradley was not cleared for the SAR programs. Of all of the security force, only Laurie Bass and her secretary were cleared. This was not usual, but in this case all had agreed that it was necessary. Even Dr. Q was not cleared. Nathan Peters was, of course, but he was trapped in the Facility. Dr. Peters had shunned the financial meeting saying "I've got no time for bean counting" and had intended to spend the day in his laboratory. Well, it looked like he'd get lots of time in the lab today. What exactly did this guy Terry mean by "Tell the President that I know what's going on here, and I'll talk only to him or to the world television audience"? If that son of a bitch had discovered Level Eight and Level Nine, it would be a disaster even if he didn't know what was going on there. The governments of the world would not require much time to arrive at a pretty close guess as to the type of research being done in a laboratory over twenty-five percent as large as the entire known Facility and buried forty feet below it a laboratory we pretended didn't exist. That the United States had a biological warfare studies under way would surprise no one. Some programs were so mildly classified as to assure that every nation on earth could discover them. Those were, of course, only studies and not very encouraging ones at that. But could some half-baked hoodlum uncover the most highly guarded secret in the country? Careful, McPherson cautioned himself. This fellow has already demonstrated that he should not be underestimated. He has hijacked the most prized laboratory in the country and is holding captive several hundred of the world's best bio—engineering minds, all without firing a shot or otherwise causing an injury. We had better take as a working assumption that he does know what's going on. But how? He turned to the computer console at the side of the desk and keyed in the code to activate the word processor. It was time to organize his thoughts in preparation for his call to the President. Prescott would want to hear everything I know, little as that is, and he will want at least a summary chart or two faxed to him in time for Martha to prepare vu-graphs for his meeting. Even though he knew that Martha would redo his charts, he formatted them as he typed.

TOP SECRET NAGWAD

Handle via Glitter Channels Only Slide 1 of 3

NAMBE Siege Facts, Speculations, Recommendations

1) A group of 9 hoodlums in complete control of the Facility
2) Explosives and weapons were brought into the Facility in concealed in ChemGlass cases
3) Entry had been through the automatic warehouse entrance which is not protected by SWARM
4) Entire Facility is under hijacker's control with all of its technical staff, domestic and foreign are trapped below Level Zero
5) Drs. Q and Newcombe, Security Director Bass, two new Committee members the ASPGH leader, and Fromme, a new and young NAMBE scientist, are trapped on Level Zero and held as hostages
6) Two hundred scientists from around the world are trapped on the lower levels.
7) There is no way into the Facility without explosives,
8) Because of multiple locks and seals, any attempt to blast in would require near total destruction of the Facility
9) Leader of the siege, Terry, will speak only with President

Terry sent the following message "tell the President that I know what's going on here, and I'll talk only to him or the world television audience"

TOP SECRET NAGWAD

Handle via Glitter Channels Only Slide 2 of 3

Speculation

Terry knows of the existence of the lower levels He does not know of Projects Eight and Nine, but may have accurate guesses
Terry and company will be more exposed at escape time
Laurie Bass on the inside is a potential advantage (Bradley feels strongly on this point)

TOP SECRET NAGWAD

Handle via Glitter Channels Only Slide 3 of 3

NAMBE Siege Recommendations

1) Leave physical security and crowd control to Bradley
2) Get a terrorist specialty team in place as Presidential adviser
3) President will have to deal with Terry

McPherson stopped typing and stared at the word processor screen. He had just produced the poorest report and recommendations he had ever made in his career. Three charts that boiled down to "We're in trouble, Mr. President; I suggest that you talk to the hijackers."

All the rest was window dressing, and not very good window dressing at that. Even the grammar was poor. But damn it all, he thought, what else is there? We certainly cannot risk the international consequences of disclosure even if the price of avoidance is compromise with hoodlums and hijackers. We can't raid the place and kill the bastard. We can't even gas him out; that place is built to be isolated. Old Nathan Peters's collection of minority builders did a damned good job of it, too good under the present circumstances. There simply are no other choices.

Heaving a sigh of disgust, he glanced at his watch: he had twenty more minutes before he had to call Prescott. "What will be any different in twenty minutes?" he asked himself aloud. "Nothing," he said out loud and reached for the phone to which Bradley had attached the scrambler and dialed the President's private secure line

The Gambler Brings A Needed Set Of Skills

While waiting for Presidential contact, Terry reviewed the later stages of the Plan. His trip to Europe had satisfied him that the Swiss banking system would accept, store and protect his money as well as his identity. However, to take advantage of the Swiss banking system he had to get the money over there. The transportation of cash in the quantities that are involved is a non-trivial challenge. He could demand an electronic transfer but he knew damned well that you cannot trust 'them.' No, he would demand physical cash and then transport it physically to Switzerland. It was easy to state that goal but it required plans and schemes. For that task Terry had recruited another army buddy, Albert Stamp, the Gambler. Now, for the hundredth time he reviewed his meeting with the "Rat".

Albert Stamp sat beneath a large, brightly colored sunshade at an outdoor table at the Patio Cafe in Niagara Falls. At his left hand, steam rose from a large mug of frothy cappuccino. Though his mind was preoccupied with other matters, his long fingers were busily engaged in the ritual like opening of the fresh warm croissant on the plate before him. With his fingertips touching along a section of the outer edge of the roll, his thumbs met precisely halfway up the inner edge. With short, deliberate motions he methodically split the bun for the length of a quarter inch and then, shifting his grip a little farther around the arc, repeated the process. He progressed in this way until the flaky bread was neatly halved yielding two white crescents mirror images of each other. Continuing his absentminded ritual, he systematically applied butter, uniformly covering the freshly exposed inner surfaces. After adding marmalade, he leaned back and, momentarily ignoring the roll, lifted the hot mug. After a number of short, nervous sips, he replaced the coffee and began eating the roll, breaking off precise, bite-sized pieces. His eyes were in constant motion, darting first in one direction and then another. Thus, alternating between sipping coffee and breaking bread, he continued his meal in silence, seeming to ignore his companion. In fact, however, it was his complete concentration on his brunch guest that accounted for his absentminded demeanor. The little runt hasn't grown an inch since Central America, he thought. He doesn't seem to have changed at all. He sits there calmly, sure of himself, not the least upset by my ignoring him. Strange, you spend months with a bunch of guys tramping around in some Godforsaken jungle with your lives completely interwoven and interdependent, your very day-to-day survival was dependent on one another. Then suddenly it ends. You're split off, cut loose. They are your whole life one day, they simply don't exist the next.

To himself he mused, "Until that call from Terry month ago, I'd have sworn I had totally forgotten those guys and simply had suppressed the entire experience, as the shrinks would say."

Ames Develops A Plan

Based on his total recall of his previous meeting with Terry, Ames develops a plan to end the siege and apprehend Terry and his gang. In addition to the facts recalled from that meeting Ames's plan requires a feint. Terry must be convinced of the existence of a secondary release mechanism for freeing the scientist.

After reviewing his plan twice, Ames spoke, "I believe there is a way out of this mess. I think that I have the basis of a plan." Laurie felt a mixture of emotions: anxiety, fear, love, admiration and concern. She had admired the attempt he had made to intercede for Jane, even though her professional evaluation was critical of the timing. Without gaining an advantage, Ames had disclosed that he was trained in combative measures. He would not be given another chance to surprise his adversaries. This mixture of skill and impatience was not really surprising in one so young, but she was too involved to acknowledge such excuses. Her association with Ames clouded her objectivity.

"You say you have a plan? We'll all listen; but remember, there are hundreds of scientists trapped on the lower levels. I can't think about leaving unless I can free them."

"No, ma'am, I'm not referring to the possibility of our escaping alone. I believe I can see a way out for all of us, including the scientists. My idea may sound like a round about game, but I assure you it is based on certain knowledge. Perhaps we could step out into the hall and discuss it?"

Laurie opened the door and looked at the tightly bound hoodlums and from there to the bleeding and still sobbing Jane. She addressed Dr. Franklin. "Sir could you and Senator Morse can keep an eye on these three bundles of trash and try to provide some comfort to Miss Wilds for a few minutes? I have reason to trust this young man's judgment, and if he has an idea that should be kept from those three, I'll at least listen."

In discussing the Ames plan, Laurie reveals her first name and thereby clears up a major mystery for Ames.

As all three nodded their agreement, she led Ames into the hall. Ames had been growing steadily more restless and uneasy over the last few moments and welcomed even the simple activity of walking to the hall. "I don't mean to seem mysterious, Miss Bass-is that correct, or should I call you Director or something?"

"You may call me Laurie if you like; everyone does. Besides, Director is such a-" she stopped. Ames had gone suddenly pale. He stared at her. His senses were drinking her in. She was being recorded. Never again would she be simply a disturbing, nearly forgotten image.

"Auntie Laurie," he said flatly. Startled, she asked, "How long have you known?"

"Just now! Your first name was the needed clue. Bass, of course, meant nothing to me. But I was here three months ago, in the spring, and I saw you then. You matched an image; but I couldn't place it. You can't know how rare that is for me. I never forget anything that my senses detect, so I must have seen you before, but when? It eluded me. But seeing you again and hearing the name, the connection was made. I'm still not sure how or where, but I'm sure that you are from my before time, before Mom and Dad-your Aunt Alice and Uncle Ben. His tone was analytic, dispassionate. He was describing an interesting revelation. The explanation relieved the confusion and tension that had arisen the first time her saw her. He was thankful for that, anyway. He would like to feel more-love maybe. But it was not to be. He shook his head briefly as if to clear it and then began to outline his plan.

Ames Reveals his plan.

"There are certain things I learned about Terry at our lunch three months ago, and things I have read about the security system here, which I'm sure can be combined to provide a way out of this mess. Let me explain." He went on to outline his plan in some detail. Laurie was moved by the revelation that Ames knew who she was but she was also a professional and such thoughts would have to wait. She turned her full attention to Ames's recounting of the pertinent parts of his conversations with Terry. He then explained the role of the Facility's security systems in his plan. She had to agree that his plan made sense. She knew that the security systems worked exactly as Ames said.

"Good. I believe it will work for Mr. Terry, but there are still five other men in there with him. We have to split them up. We should have Terry alone when we put your plan to action. Also, it's going to take time to get everything arranged, and Jane needs some first aid. When we split up, I'll take Jane to the First Aid room. It's located down the tan spoke-"

"I know. I've seen the floor plan," Ames commented drily. "Okay, here we go. Once we're back inside, I'll explain the false plan and after that we can dismiss Brian." He and Laurie reentered the room.

"Well, Jane, gentlemen, Ames has a good idea. Put simply, he sees that the main threat to the United States government is not that the Facility will be out of commission for a time, or even that the Facility might be somewhat damaged. The real threat is that should, any harm come to our visiting scientists from around the world, it would prove highly embarrassing to the President. The President's position regarding blackmail and terror is well known. There is no way he would pay a ransom to avoid inconvenience for or damage to the Facility. However, where citizens of other countries are involved, particularly citizens as important as those locked below, we feel certain he will have to concede. In short, it looks like Terry has a fairly well-founded plan.

Sitting comfortably at the side of the room, Dr. Franklin had been considering their predicament. His coolly analytical mind had come to the same conclusion. Not only was there the very real pressure that Ms. Bass had just reviewed, there was the equally compelling pressure that she could not discuss projects Eight and Nine. Yes, the conclusion that the President had to give in was inescapable. There was no way for the trapped scientists to release themselves. Sitting next to Dr. Franklin, Senator Morse had also reached the same conclusion. He had not read the technical briefing yet, but the security arrangements as described were too logical not to be correct. He had no trouble visualizing a lot of scientists, security officers, and politicians dreaming up such a system as a sop to a nervous populace. Of course the President could not allow harm to come to those distinguished visitors; nor could he permit the existence of Projects Eight and Nine to become generally known.

Laurie's task in the Ames plan is to sell the feint.

Laurie noticed both men silently and solemnly nodding agreement. She also noticed the more gleeful nods of the two bound but conscious hoodlums. "As I was saying," she continued, "the President will be forced to comply with whatever demands the terrorists, or kidnappers, if you prefer will make."

"You bet your sweet ass, lady. And there ain't nothin' you can do about it," snarled George, his cracked ribs making the effort of speaking painful.

"Yeah, he's got that right. You can't do shit about it, Miss Black Belt, or what the hell ever you are," Brian added.

Laurie ignored both outbursts and directed her attention to Dr. Franklin and Senator Morse. "What Mr. Terry the Terrorist doesn't know is that, while it is not possible for the trapped scientists to release themselves, it is possible for me to release them. The locking system normally controlled by Dr. Q and currently in Terry's hands, has a backup, an additional release mechanism in the Security Director's office, my office. Unfortunately, my office is located over on the far side of the Facility. It will, therefore, be necessary for us to walk all the way over there in order to effect the release. It is possible, I suppose, that he knows of the second system. He certainly has seemed well prepared and well informed so far."

"You got that right, smart-ass cop. Terry's the best planner in the goddamn world. He's had the floor plan of this place for months. Ain't nothing he don't know about this place. Your ass is grass; just admit it and let us up from here. You ain't releasing nobody." Brian was beaming with pride at having put the big broad in her place. Laurie continued to ignore him.

"My working assumption is that Terry is unaware of the backup system or he would have boasted about sending someone to deactivate it. Ames, here, is a new employee at the Facility and has already had his orientation session; he is therefore familiar with the layout. He will take the two of you directly there. I will take Jane to the infirmary first and join the three of you as soon as I've patched her up. We can leave the trash there in the corner for the janitors to clean up in the morning." She indicated the trussed forms of Brian, George, and Herm.

"What about some first aid for us, lady? You hurt Herm real bad, and I bet you broke George's ribs. What about us, huh?" Brian's confidence of a few moments ago was beginning to wane. In his soul he knew that Laurie was right. If that conceited bastard, Terry, knew about her backup system, he would never have passed up the opportunity to rub Dr. Q's nose in it.

Dr. Franklin, however, had read the arguments for the establishment of the one release only system very carefully and he knew the Security Director was bluffing. He could not figure out why. Senator Morse had not read the technical briefing, but he had discussed the security issue with Dr. Franklin at some length during the flight out from Washington. He also knew the Security Director was bluffing. Obviously, she wanted Terry to believe that there was a second way to release the imprisoned scientists. His instinct also told him that she wanted Brian or George to carry the word of its existence to Terry because he would be more likely to believe it then. The Security Director at last acknowledged the existence of Brian and George. It was important to her plans that they escape their bonds and report to Terry, and she had sensed that they would respond best to insults.

"I am having trouble imagining anything less important to me than your problems but I'll give you some free advice. There are two first-aid rooms on this level, the small one we passed on our way here from the auditorium, and the main infirmary to which I'm taking Jane. You are neither one so tightly bound that you can't work loose, though doing so will be extremely painful for your companion", she looked at Brian "George, if that's what he's called, certainly has at least two broken ribs. That crumpled cockroach in the corner is seriously injured. Under no circumstance should he be moved by anyone other than a trained medical professional." After a pause to let Brian catch on she added, "If I were you, I'd work myself free as soon as we leave and then run down to the first aid for some aspirin to give to George; you might take a couple yourself. Then I'd ask Terry for some real medical help. I know you won't do that; it would show good sense, a characteristic totally lacking in your actions thus far. We'll take your weapons with us, and I promise you that it will be very unhealthy for you to attempt to interfere with my treatment of Jane's wounds. I've considered tying you more tightly, but frankly you're not worth the effort. It would certainly kill Herm if you try to move him; I obviously don't care, he's no threat either way, and certainly the world will not miss him. A good doctor could tape George up to a point that he could at least walk and maybe carry a pistol. You don't have such a doctor, and as he is, George is no threat to anyone except himself; if he moves around too much before getting proper care he will at best permanently injure himself. As for you, you are simply not a threat under any circumstance. So get loose if you can, but stay out of my way."

She turned to Senator Morse, "Are you two ready for a long walk?"

"Yes, of course," he replied, wondering what she was up to. "Let's go, Edward, a little walk will be good for you."

Placing a supporting arm around Jane's shoulders, Laurie led the way. Outside in the corridor, Ames handed the automatic pistols to the two older men. He had picked them up along with the ceramic knife on his way out of the room. Both recipients proclaimed that they had never seen an automatic pistol before and had certainly never fired one.

"I'm sure you won't have to fire one today either," Laurie said. "But let me show you, just in case. This is the safety switch. It should never be in the on position unless you are about to fire the weapon. If you must fire it, point low and squeeze the trigger. I have set the auto/single switch to single. Under no circumstances move that switch. Used in the automatic mode that weapon is more dangerous to your friends than it is to your foes unless you're well trained. Ames will explain the details of his plan to you as you proceed along the Yellow Spoke. I'll meet you later, after I've seen to Jane. Good luck." And the little split up and went their separate

The Meeting In The Oval Office Is Convened

In response to the NAMBE President convened his first meeting. This meeting was attended only by the only other four persons who were cleared for and managed the Level Eight and Level Nine programs. The

actual danger associated with The Outrageous occupation of the Facility was vastly worse than Terry could possibly imagine. Indeed he was not aware nor had he even guessed at a real biological threat; however, those convened could not be sure of that and their choices were thus very few indeed.

Finally the meeting was convened. Dr. Cochran had just arrived and taken the vacant seat at the foot of the coffin—shaped table, the end opposite and farthest from the President. On the President's right sat the Secretary of State, flanked by the Secretary of the Interior. To the left of the Chief Executive sat the Secretary of Defense. Buzz thought there was very little reason for the Defense Department to be represented at this meeting. "At least," he thought, "I sincerely hope there isn't."

The rest of the table was empty. The vacant seats would be occupied by other officials and their aides the minute the security level of the meeting could be lowered enough to permit their inclusion. The present contained everyone in Washington, who at the moment was briefed on Projects Eight and Nine. The President began, "Gentlemen and lady." He directed a nod to the Secretary of the Interior, Louise Nuffield. "I have given you copies of Senator McPherson's report. I assume it is accurate; but as you know the conclusion to which he comes has always been totally unacceptable to this Office and absolutely repugnant to me personally. The President of the United States will not pay ransom money to some cheap hoodlum. I am ready to hear views, opinions, and recommendations from each of you. Please feel free to speak openly. But I don't want to hear any more of this nonsense about acceding to the demands. I want those scientists out of there and I want that bastard behind bars. Okay, let's talk."

There was a heavy silence. Finally, Buzz Cochran, loosening his already dangling tie still farther, cleared his throat and expressed the sentiments of them all. "You'll notice, Prescott, that you aren't being inundated with alternate suggestions. The simple reason is that none of us have any under the ground rules you just established. McPherson is right. Either this guy is terribly clever and has breached the un-breach able, or he is just plain lucky and has fallen into the only fool proof hijacking scheme in this country. I'm inclined to think the latter, though McPherson leans toward the former. In either case, the only reasonable course of action is to assume that his crack about knowing what is going on is true. Like I said, I don't personally think he does know, but even if I'm right, even if he has no idea that there is a Level Eight or a Level Nine, let alone two highly classified projects being conducted there, the risk is still too high. Treat with him and you invite the scorn of our allies; don't, and lose the life of even one of their precious biologists, and you invite even more scorn.

I don't have any idea for getting them out of there, and I assume no one else has either. I suggest that we get in touch with him, find out his demands, arrange to meet them, stall him long enough to put in place a foolproof trap and nail him the minute the hostages are free. If nailing him were accomplished with a rifle, I'm sure none of us in this room would object. I know your views; I share them; but you really don't have any choice."

He loosened his tie still further, completely undoing the knot. There was another silence. It seemed all the more awkward this time, since Dr. Cochran had given voice to the considered opinions of them all and had forced a reluctant acceptance upon them and it was one thing to come to such conclusions on your own; there was always the chance that you had made a mistake, overlooked an important, ignored an alternate strategy. The list could go on endlessly. But when your most eminent authority tells you that his conclusion is the same as yours, you are left looking reality in the face.

The President, too, felt the impact of Dr. Cochran's summation. He had read the McPherson report as Buzz had; and like Buzz, he could find no holes in the Senator's arguments. However, he was well aware of his own limitations in understanding the details of the NAMBE security arrangements and had allowed himself to hope that his friend and chief technical adviser could give him some fact, however small, on which he and the others could base a plan of attack. The realization that even Buzz could see no flaw in the hijacker's scheme was even more disheartening to Prescott than to the others in the room. He, after all, was the one who would have to make the decision to deal with the kidnappers. He slowly surveyed the table one last time, his gaze resting for a few seconds on each face in turn.

Then he straightened the already neat stack of papers on the table before him. Interlacing his fingers as he rested his hands on the notes, he sat quietly for nearly a minute and a half. He had all of the facts; no pleasant situation altering new datum was going to be pulled from Cochran's bulging brief—case. Now that he could quit hoping, he could start thinking, making decisions. "That's what I'm paid for", he thought. His decision made, the President spoke, "Okay. One last question before we begin to plan the exit trap."

Everyone in the room knew the horrible emotional price Prescott Winters was paying for the decision he had just made, though not a trace of strain showed on his face. "Louise, what do we know about Lieutenant Bradley and the Director of Security, Laurie Bass? Who is she? Why does Bradley place such significance on her being there incognito, so to speak?"

In this computer age Prescott Winters still considered individual personal effort to be an important commodity. He didn't believe in miracles or Superman-or Superwoman in this case-but Bradley seemed to have a lot of confidence in her. The President had directed his question to the Secretary of the Interior, whose department controlled the Guard for the past twenty years. Louise Nuffield removed two folders from the pile of papers on the table before her. "Sir, I've only met the Director a few times. She was appointed by one of my predecessors, so I don't have as much first-hand knowledge as I would had I appointed her. However, after I read McPherson's report and before Buzz arrived, I called the office for the files on Bradley and Bass.

"I spoke to First, Lieutenant Bradley. He came to us from the CIA, where he had been an accomplished investigator. His psychological profile describes a stable, mature individual. He is thought of by his peers as intelligent and realistic, a 'both feet on the ground' person. He is certainly not given to the use of drugs or excesses of alcohol. He is number two in the NAMBE security system nationally. Normally, there would be no reason to doubt his judgment in security matters. Of course, this is not a normal situation. Nonetheless, I consider it highly unlikely that the Bradley described here would behave irrationally even in these circumstances. He believes and will have some objective or at least rational reason for so believing, that Ms. Laurie Bass, Security Director and his boss, is a force difficult to contend with." After looking around the table, Louise Nuffield picked up the second folder.

"Based on her personnel file, that would certainly be true if it were a question of a purely physical contest. This young lady, and by my standards the term still applies to those in their forties, is an outstanding athlete. Our records show her as having black belts in Karate and three other martial arts. She has held one National and several State and Regional titles.

"She has a degree in sociology and three years' experience in law enforcement prior to joining NAMBE. She obtained her bachelor's degree at the age of twenty. Her psychological profile describes a loner interested in sports and physical conditioning. She does not date, either men or women. "She's a good administrator, well liked by her staff. There has never been a security problem since she took charge nineteen years ago. On her record she could gone further in the Department for example, she was suggested for a senior appointment when I started building my staff—ut she turned it down out of hand, without even interviewing.

In summary, she appears to be a competent woman whose metal has never been tested in a dire emergency. I'm sure she would be flattered by her subordinate's faith in her; but I don't see anything in these folders from which we can draw any particular hope. If in fact she comes up with a scheme and we can help her in any way, I believe we should. However, I don't think her presence in the Facility is reason enough for us to change or delay our decision."

She removed her Ben Franklin glasses and began the quite unnecessary task of polishing the already spotless half lenses. She was obviously uncomfortable in bursting the last bubble of hope, but she was used to uncomfortable situations and tasks. In fact, in this case the discomfort was somewhat relieved by the fact that no one had really expected anything different. One unarmed woman faced by nine men carrying automatic pistols and explosives did not really represent even a slender thread, Bradley's faith notwithstanding.

Sensing her discomfort, the President reassured her as he addressed the, "I didn't expect any more than that. I simply could not pass up any chance of avoiding our apparently inevitable but highly undesirable conclusion."

He turned to Herbert Aldauer, Secretary of State. "How about your helping, Herb; you could relieve some of the pressure by assuring me that our allies would not react all that negatively at losing a few scientists or finding out about Projects Eight and Nine. Tell me they would be pleased at our standing firm, even if the cost was partially borne by them."

"Not a chance, Prescott, and you damn well know it. Even less of a chance than Louise has of producing Wonder Woman to bail you out. Every nation in the world, including our closest allies, can be counted on to condemn you for dealing with these damned hijackers. That's a given. It is also a fact that nearly all of those same countries have senior scientists at the NAMBE Facility as a part of our international free exchange of technology. While they will all censure you for complying, not one of them, with the possible exception of the U.K., will be willing to risk their share of the consequences. As to their reaction at finding that we have serious genetic weapons research going on in the center of the highly visible Facility, which we are constantly touting as an example of open international cooperation, I'm sure you don't need me to discourse on that."

Before the President could answer, Buzz Cochran stepped in, "I'm sure these high blown diplomatic concerns are genuine matters for concern. But if you are really looking to weigh all the facts for one last time before issuing the orders we all know you don't want to issue, why not lay the big ace on the table right away and put an end to this time—wasting exercise? I'll do it for you, since I guess it would be my turn next anyway. Everyone at this table is cleared and briefed on Project Eight. Dr. Peters and his merry men have produced what they call the Beta 4 virus. That probably signifies nothing more than the fact that the fourth variant of the second experimental strain produced the desired results. The name is not significant; the desired results are. According to Dr. Peters, this virus makes a direct and extremely virulent attack on the human nervous system. His estimates are frightening, but I've never known him to be wrong in estimating biological effects on human beings. According to those estimates, ninety-five percent of those infected could be expected to die within forty-eight hours. Of those who survived, ninety-five percent would be mindless idiots.

"Furthermore, this Beta 4 virus is virtually unstoppable once loose. It multiplies very rapidly at any temperature above freezing. It will quite happily survive and be carried by air or water. It will accept a wide range of conditions in either media. Finally, it can find its way into bloodstreams and nervous systems through the lungs, eyes, or digestive system. The stuff is unbelievable. I'd say it is as close as I can imagine to being a biological doomsday weapon. To date, there is no known cure or vaccine.

"There are four small vials of the stuff in Peters' laboratory. The quantities involved are microscopic. They're just residuals from the evaluation run. They are, of course, properly stored and perfectly safe where they are. The vaulted lab that contains them is entirely robot operated and nothing that enters that lab can leave, except through the special incinerator system. Even after incineration, the residue is subjected to high temperature and intense hard—radiation sterilization. It is perfectly safe: that is, as long as the systems function and qualified personnel use them. But if some turkey brain blew up the wrong power supply and its backup, in an effort to demonstrate how tough he was, there would be no way to contain the runaway multiplication of the virus. If that same idiot, by chance or design, opened a seal or by accidental destruction of another circuit caused one or more seals to be opened, perhaps to release a hostage or two to shoot or torture, the effects would be incalculable. Under those conditions we could not be sure of containing the virus at all. At a minimum Level Eight and every person on it would be sacrificed; at a maximum the entire Facility could be forfeited or, even worse, a few of those hostile little life forms might escape into the atmosphere. I don't need to paint the rest of the picture, surely."

Silence! Dead silence! The stillness was palpable. The Secretary of State was the first to speak. Breathing deeply as if to emphasize his disbelief, he asked, "Who the hell authorized such-"

He knew, of course. He knew, as they all did, that the only authority for "any Project Eight or Project Nine program was the committee presently convened, of which each and every person in the room, except the President, a non-voting Chairman, was an equal voting member. There was no 'casting vote.' The membership was always held to an even number. On some occasions it had been six; on others, as now, it was four; but it was always an even number. In either case if more than one person objected to a program it was not authorized. Such was the rule governing the development of bioengineered weapons; in practice, no project had ever been started with less than unanimous concurrence. The Beta 4 program was no exception. The specific virus of Beta 4 had not, of course, been authorized; but the broad viral project, VAGNEFF, Viral Agents with Neurological Effects, was one of the earliest programs of Project Eight. It was annually renewed without a single objection that the Secretary could recall. Raising both hands in mock defense and silent apology to his colleagues, he continued. "I'm sorry for that sanctimonious outburst. Of course we all authorized it. It is somehow different to say 'I agree to spend so many millions of dollars on the development of bio-agents' than to hear from a learned and respected colleague that breaking a vial containing a microscopic amount of contaminated fluid could spell the end of American civilization as we know.

"Surely you are exaggerating slightly for effect, Buzz, engaging in a little hyperbole." It was a faint hope. In his heart he knew that Buzz was not prone to exaggeration.

"No, I'm not at all, Herbert. If anything I erred on the mild side, I'm afraid. If that damned 'contaminated fluid' as you call it were released, I can't assure you that the effects would be limited to the hemisphere. Left to its own devices Beta 4 would have trouble crossing the oceans; and in the time it took, it is highly likely that a vaccine could be developed. We know absolutely everything there is to know about the structure of this damned thing. We designed it, after all. In the normal course of events, we'll design the vaccine that will conquer it. "However, evaluate the odds of two possible scenarios for me, please. Let us assume that the thing is accidentally released from the Facility. In forty-eight hours people start dying and most of the survivors turn into blithering idiots. Do we quarantine the entire country west of the Mississippi and immediately stop all foreign intercourse, travel, export and even mail? Do we announce to the world that our borders are closed and that air and water that has passed through the U.S.A. is hopelessly polluted? Do we publish for the world the details of the Beta 4 virus while the Facility still has a resident with enough brains left to operate the telephone or the faxs machine? Do we admit quickly, while we still can, that we have a classified experiment buried in the Facility that has gone berserk and could endanger major parts of the human population? Do we take not one but all of those actions promptly, while there is some chance of containing the thing?

Or do we procrastinate while we try to determine if the stuff is as bad as Dr. Peters says it is? Do we try to sugar coat the pill? And while we engage in all the delaying and ass-covering tactics we can imagine, what does our friend Beta 4 do? It hitches a ride on everything leaving the country, that's what: Tourists, businessmen, stamps licked by victims, fruits and vegetables rained on by infected water: all these things become ambassadors of death.

"Well, Herbert, Louise, Prescott; do any of you believe that the second scenario is less likely than the first?

"No, Herbert, I am not engaging in a little hyperbole to get my way. All of you want to save the country's face. You want to hush up the whole incident, hide our duplicity in using the Facility as a cover for classified operations. I don't mean to belittle those objectives. If it were not for Beta 4, I would be as worried over those issues as the three of you, perhaps more so. But there is a Beta 4, and therefore, there is no choice." He banged the table for emphasis.

"Calm down, Buzz, don't break up the furniture. I might not be able to afford a new table for some time." The President smiled in a vain attempt to break the spell of gloom that was falling on his committee; he could feel it himself.

"I am forced to agree. Goddamn him to hell, I am forced to agree." The frustrated President withdrew a handkerchief and mopped his forehead. "You each have my apologies. A president is not supposed to lose his cool, and this one never resorts to obscenities. Let's get on with it then. Buzz, you get hold of Dr. Peters. I understand that he is among the trapped, but he still has a phone and his laboratory. Is that correct?" Prescott Winters asked. "Okay. I want him to get started now on the development of a vaccine for Beta 4. He can conscript whatever help he needs from among those trapped in the Facility." The instructions continued. Louise, I want you to get in touch with Bradley. Find out if there is any way to get in touch with that Security Director. If not, ask if there is any way at all that we can be of assistance. I believe in individual effort, but I don't want that woman doing something precipitous and inadvertently causing the release of that damned bug.

"Herbert, you are the diplomat, the negotiator. Your first task is to get in touch with this Terry. Find out what the price is."

Ames's Plan Begins To Unfold

While Laurie and Jane hurried down the wide corridor of the Tan Spoke toward the clinic, Ames paused just outside the small conference room door, all his senses alert as always. He recorded sounds from within, the whispered conversation, the scraping of chairs and feet as the two bound men struggled to free themselves. George groaned and soon stopped moving. Brian's efforts continued, though his conversation stopped. From the sounds Ames could visualize Brian's frenzied struggle. Even as he monitored the activities within the room behind him, he also followed the progress of the two women down the tan spoke by following the sounds of their footsteps. As he listened, he recalled the expanded floor plan he had been sent in his New Employee information package. The women had just turned left; they would be going around Ring Three. Halfway around that ring they would come to the larger of the two First Aid rooms, the one referred to as the Infirmary. They were making good time; they would be safe. From the sounds

within, Ames deduced that Brian was finally loose and getting ready
to leave. It was time for Ames and his companions to move on also.
He turned to his two charges.

Ames Explains On The Fly

"I think we had better be getting on with our part of the plan.
When Brian leaves this room, we want to be at the next intersection
of corridors, and he'll be coming out any minute. Let's go."

Without question both men followed him down the hall.
When they reached the intersection, Ames paused to explain the
layout of the Facility to the two visitors. "You are, of course, aware
that the Facility is octagonal in shape and that there are eight levels.
Where we are standing is referred to as level Zero, and there are
seven levels below this. The building extends below ground level
rather than above for the simple reason that security is easier. "Each
level has eight octagonal corridors that ring the Facility at that level;
each of those octagonal rings of course has eight corners. There are
also eight radial halls that go out from the central lobby, each Level
has one. Those radial hallways lead through the corners of each
ring. The sectors colors are all matched to the radial corridors. The
corridor along which we're proceeding is a spoke corridor and leads
to the center of the building. The eight concentric ring corridors
are placed at fixed intervals of forty feet. "This basic plan is straight
forward. But adapting the building to changing needs resulted
in numerous extra internal halls leading in various directions
crisscrossing the sectors differently in every sector of every level.
Since each was constructed according to the needs and whims of the
manager controlling that section, there is no correlation between the
patterns of these auxiliary corridors. New employees are supplied
with a map so that they can find their way to and from different
sections of the Facility."

"I apologize for the long-winded explanation, but the intricacies
of the hallways play a significant role in our plan. Neither Terry nor
any of his men will be familiar with the layout. Ms. Bass of course
knows the passages well, and I saw the employee's map yesterday

evening. The plan depends in part on taking advantage of Terry and his men being ignorant of the floor plan. The door of the room occupied by Brian, George, and the still unconscious Herm had not yet opened. With his keen hearing Ames could listen to the muffled conversation within.

"You've got to stay here," he heard Brian explaining. "Look at you, for Chrissake. You're a wreck! It's all you can do to sit up, and you think you can go running down those halls? It's over a mile from here to the auditorium. You heard the big broad, you got broken ribs. You need help and I don't know how to fix no broken ribs. No, you haf'ta stay here with Herm. That's all there is to it."

"But he's all busted up," George protested. "What the hell am I gonna do for him? What if he dies or somethin'? That dumb bitch! Just wait till I get her."

"Yeah, you get her and she'll break your ass in two," Brian retorted. "That'll really teach her a lesson. No, you stay here. Just ignore Herm unless he wakes up. Then do whatever you can without moving him. I'll get on back to Terry." Brian continued. "We got more guys with guns back there. I'm sure Terry will know what to do with those assholes out there running the halls. We'll kick their asses or crack their heads or whatever and come back for you. Just take it easy." He walked toward the door.

"Now," said Ames as he turned and started slowly down the Green Spoke. He noticed Brian hesitate and duck back into the room when he saw Ames and the two visitors. Ames continued on his preselected path. From the sounds reaching him from around the corner, he noted with satisfaction that Brian had stepped back into the hall, closed the, door and started off in the opposite direction. So far, everything was going according to plan.

As they walked, Ames explained. "A few more yards down this spoke and we will turn into Ring Three. Just along that hall about twenty more yards is a concealed guardroom. Almost the entire wall is a one-way mirror, and the door is blended into the decor of the hall in such a way as to be essentially undetectable. Actually, the hall door would only be used in an emergency. The guardroom is normally entered and exited through a door from an adjacent room, one of those inner passages I told you about.

There are similar guardrooms placed strategically throughout the Facility. The idea behind the design is that the building should be secure but neither the staff nor the visitors should be made to feel uncomfortable by the presence of security people. It seems a little extreme. However, you must remember that at any given time there is a large contingent of foreigners here. They tend to be suspicious of a surfeit of guards anywhere, particularly in an open and unclassified operation such as this one."

Of course both Senator Morse and Dr. Franklin knew in a general way what the security arrangements were, though Ames was unaware of their official status. He had taken them at face value as important visitors, but not officially connected to NAMBE. They were both surprised that Ames should know of concealed guardrooms if he was really a new employee. Even if he were an old time employee, it would be surprising, since a major reason for concealing the stations was to hide their existence from the Facility staff. Surely, their existence would not be described in the briefing of a new employee. Similar thoughts ran through both of the men's minds.

"There was something unusual about this young man. Was he a new security employee? No, he was described as a young scientist." Senator Morse, the intuitivist, gave expression to their common thoughts.

"You seem to know a lot about the Facility for a young man who hasn't even started to work yet. I don't see your New Employee Map in your shirt pocket, yet you certainly seem to know your way around. Furthermore, I shouldn't imagine that your pre-employment briefing would include a description of the concealed guardrooms. Unless that is you are to be a part of the Guard service?"

"No," Ames replied, "I am not a part of the guard service. And it is true that I am not carrying a map. But at my pre-employment briefing I was issued a map showing the layout of the Facility. I studied it yesterday. Also I was here once before on a general public tour; and that tour, went past a few of the guardrooms, no doubt to provide a chance for us to be observed, I saw the Gaurds observing us. In fact, the Director of Security herself was observing us from one of the guardrooms. Having seen the stations and noticed how carefully the hallway doors were hidden, it was an easy to deduce that the principle entrance must be from an adjoining office. Otherwise, the chance of being seen entering or leaving the guard station would be too high, you see."

Dr. Franklin did not see at all. For him Ames's explanation raised as many questions as it answered. To the intuitive Senator Morse, however, the explanation made perfectly good sense. Ames was a young man with a photographic memory. Well, that explained most of it. He wasn't quite sure how a photographic memory helped him notice that a decorative mirror was, in fact, a one-way mirror, but he felt sure the new NAMBE scientist had, in fact noticed the one-way mirror and seen the attractive Director of Security in the room beyond it. This young man merits some close watching, he thought. Having accepted Ames's explanation, the Senator felt sure he now understood how Ames had developed his rescue plan.

"I see," he said. "So you noticed from reading the new employee's guide that there were two sets of controls, and that's how you were able to suggest the rescue plan you and Ms. Bass worked out. Am I right?"

Ames replied, "No. I wish that were so. That was a complete bluff, Senator. There is no Security Director's control panel. There is only one way to release the people on the lower levels; Terry has the only key in this Facility. There is but one alternate key and it is held by the President of the United States. In an emergency arising from the levels being accidentally sealed, the control panel locked, and with Dr. Q away with no one delegated to have key control, the backup key would be flown in from Washington. In such a case the staff of the lower levels might be inconvenienced by the delay, but no real harm would be done. In the present case we might arrange to smuggle the President's key in if it were available, but it would be very tricky, with Terry controlling the switches to the outside doors. I can't think how we would go about it, actually. The same control panel that controls the exterior door controls the seals of the lower levels. It is logical, since the only reasons for locking the exterior doors are the same as the reasons for sealing the lower levels. No, there is no way we can release the staff."

He paused to be sure they had understood. Then he added, in a frail attempt at humor, "Before you ask, I must admit that I did not know that until Ms. Bass explained it while we were in the hall together. There are some limits to the new employee's manual, after all."

"But," said Dr. Franklin, "you said . . . why would say you were going to rush to the Security Director's office and release the people on the lower levels if that is not possible? You will simply anger this Terry fellow, and who knows what he might do?"

"I'm sure it is simple enough, doctor," Senator Morse inserted. "We are to be used as bait. Is that not so, my young man with the amazing memory?"

Somewhat nervously, Ames replied, "I wouldn't exactly put it that way, sir. We do have a plan for obtaining the release of the scientists below without compromising the entire NAMBE operation, a plan that requires splitting Terry's gang down into smaller units. Remember, he and his men are armed; some of them may even know how to use those weapons. We have two guns and no one who knows how to use them. Surely you agree, Senator, that we could not win a shoot-out under those circumstances?"

"No, of course we could not. I'm way ahead of you there. You and Ms. Bass were deliberately baiting Terry through that robot of his, Brian. You want Terry to send his men out in search of us. That will break them into at least two groups. You took pains to assure that Brian knew we were going one way while Director Bass was going another."

"In that sense, I guess we are bait," Ames conceded. "It simply seemed logical to break the gang down into smaller pieces if we were to prevail. In any case, if we can get them parted into small groups spread out a bit, perhaps lost in the network of halls and corridors, we may be able to stop Terry without having to face him and his men in a gun fight."

"How is that, Mr.-ah, is it Mr. Ames?" asked Dr. Franklin.

"No, it's simply Ames. My full name is Ames Fromme. The plan requires a rather long and detailed explanation even though it is in fact a simple one," he continued, as he turned into an office door that opened in the rear to an inner hall. He led the way to the guardroom.

"Please sit, gentlemen." He indicated the chairs near the desk. Ames stood by the one-way window and peered down the corridor for several seconds before turning back to face into the room. "They are, of course, nowhere near us at the moment. My guess is that it will take Brian another five minutes just to reach the auditorium. After that he will need five to ten minutes to convince Terry that Ms. Bass actually put Herm out of action. We have, let's say, ten minutes before we need to watch and listen. Actually, as long as I stand near the window I will know if anyone enters either end of this corridor.

Feeling that he may have too far already, raised too many questions in the minds of his companions, Ames did not explain his last remark.

Meanwhile, Laurie and Jane had reached the infirmary, "Here, Jane," Laurie said gently, "let me clean this wound and see what's required to get you shipshape again."

Still in a daze, Jane hadn't spoken since they left the auditorium. She allowed herself to be led over to the sink and stood silently as Laurie washed the blood from her face and hands. Fortunately, the cuts were superficial. Laurie applied a mild antiseptic salve and led Jane over to the chair near the examination table. Attending to simple wounds was well within Laurie's experience. As an athlete she had seen a large number of cuts, bruises, and broken bones. She was a lot less comfortable with shock, from which she feared her young companion was suffering. She searched her memory for an appropriate treatment, but all she could remember was to keep the patient warm. She found a lightweight blanket and wrapped it around Jane's shoulders.

Still without speaking or looking up at her benefactor, the young woman shivered slightly and pulled the blanket tighter. The Security Director was encouraged by even this limited voluntary action. If Brian had succeeded in releasing himself quickly, they had perhaps ten minutes before Terry's guys began their search. The

Infirmary would be among the first places searched. She herself had planted that thought firmly in Brian's head. She pulled another chair over and sat down near Jane, an arm around her shoulder.

"Do you want to talk about it?" she asked. "You needn't, but if you think it will help, I can be a good listener."

Jane sobbed, her shoulders began to shake, then her sobs began to come more quickly. She shook more violently, and leaning her head against Laurie's shoulder, she started to cry without restraint. Awkwardly, the older woman hugged her.

"That's okay. Go ahead and cry." For some minutes Jane did just that. Then, though not clearly at first, she began to speak through still heavy sobs.

"How could he? Oh, I've failed . . . that bastard . . . he never cared, never . . . laughing at me . . . laughing at me. I hate him!"

Laurie spoke softly, comfortingly, "There, there now. That's okay. Go ahead and have a good cry. Just let go, no need to hold back." Laurie had very little experience with any of the emotions associated with the love of another person. Her one friend had been Mary Ann Bovonio, and Mary Ann had died just as the friendship matured. Now, when she needed her wits about her, she found herself distracted and confused by emotions she did not understand. The danger to herself did not overly concern her; she felt sure that she could handle it. Her concern was for the others; Franklin, Morse, Dr. Q, Kim, all the people trapped in the lower levels, and for Ames. Ames, the person to whom the feelings she had developed for Mary Ann had been transferred. Ames was more than just her only nephew. Ames, the closest thing to a son she would ever know. Ames, who until today she had seen only once when he was a very young infant had been the focus of love for eighteen years. Ames was now a man.

"Eight minutes gone; time to get moving. She spoke softly, "Come now, Jane, we must get away. Do you feel up to walking? Would you rather have that wheelchair?"

"No . . . I'm all right, really. I . . . I can walk okay. I won't need a chair. But may I keep the blanket?"

"Of course you may. Here, let's put it like a shawl." With Laurie leading the way they emerged in the corridor and turned inward. While she kept them moving steadily, they did not run. In the first place, Jane probably could not have managed it, and in the second Laurie felt no need. They had only a short walk to Ring Four, and she was confident that Terry had not yet gotten himself organized. They reached Ring Four, turned right and proceeded down the corridor past several doors to the Women's Lounge. The outer room of the lounge area was designed as a quiet place for female staff to escape for a few minutes and rest. There was such a lounge on each ring of the Facility. Once inside, Laurie seated Jane on the couch.

"Why don't you lie down for a while and get some rest? I have to be gone for some time, but you're safe here. I'll fix the door to lock. Don't you open it for anyone you do not recognize."

Jane's response was immediate, "I'm all right, really. Let me come with you. I honestly don't need to rest."

"You certainly do, young lady. You've had a bad shock. Don't worry. I'll be back as quickly as I can." Reluctantly, Jane stretched out on the couch and allowed the blanket to be tucked in around her, and Laurie turned and left the lounge.

Back in the Auditorium

In the main Auditorium Terry's reaction to Brian's story was exactly what Ames and Laurie had expected. "What the fucking hell are you talking about, you dumb—ass? That dark-haired old broad took Herm? You are totally fucking full of shit! I've seen village bullies melt from just having Herm look at them. Now cut the bullshit and tell me where the fuck ya been. And why'n the hell are you holding your arm that way?" To calm himself Terry waited a moment and caught his breath before again weighing in on the unfortunate bearer of ill tidings. "Come on, out with it, for Chrissake. What the fuck is going on? And don't gimme some shit about a broad knocking Herm around." He punctuated this last instruction with a backhand to Brian's face.

"Goddamn it all, I told ya. Herm never laid a hand on her! She was saying shit like 'don't be too hard on us' an 'please don't hurt us' and more shit like that. Well, Herm, he says how he's gonna tie the men up, then he's gonna rape the shit outa the big broad; you know he's telling her how she's gonna enjoy it, and that kinda shit. George and me, we're standin' there with guns and Herm's issuing orders, like some top sergeant. Then, wham! Man, there is like a blur! It's all over. Like that!" He snapped his fingers. "There's George with at least one broken rib, maybe more. Then there's me with a totally useless goddamn arm, maybe somethin' broke for all I know. And there's Herm, smack up against the wall, blood streaming from his nose. And his eyes . . . shit, man, I swear it looked like that woman's fingers went clean inta his eyes." He'd been speaking as fast as he knew how, hoping to finish the tale before Terry came down on him again.

"This shithead Ames, he picks up the two guns and gives them to those two old guys. Well, that was that. I mean shit, man. We got two guys crippled up and me with no hand; them, they got the guns. I mean the fight was over before anybody even knew there was one."

Terry was becoming more convinced and more agitated by the minute. Shaking his head in disbelief, he interrupted, "You're too fuckin' dumb-assed stupid and scared of me to make up shit like that. "She really took Herm out? What did he do to her? How badly is she hurt?" Brian relaxed, sensing that Terry had at last accepted his story.

"Man, you didn't listen to me! He didn't have time to put up no kind of fight! Nobody did. The big broad just made like Wonder Woman for a few seconds, and then Ames started picking up the pieces. That's all there was to it." Terry stood silently, staring at Brian until chills ran up his spine.

As Brian began shifting his weight nervously from foot to foot, afraid his boss would, after all, kill the messenger, Terry spoke, "All right, so the fucking Amazon is big and quick and some kinda fuckin' black belt. Herm's ass is grass. I find that hard to believe, but let's say you are tellin' the truth. How the fuck did you get out and drag your pitiful ass in here?" Making an extreme effort to maintain control, Terry's hands shook, and the veins on his neck pulsed visibly. Brian sensed that Terry was on the verge of an explosion and hastened to divert it.

"George and I worked our way loose, but he's too hurt to come all this way without some help. Herm's out cold; he ain't goin' nowhere." "How'd you work your fucking knots loose with those heavily armed old men standin' over you" Terry asked.

"They weren't standin' there. They went to release the people from the lower levels and to fix up Jane. They-"

"What the fuck are talkin' about?" Terry screamed. "There is no goddamn way to let those fucking eggheads out of the lower levels except to release the fucking seals, and I got the only fucking key to the control console! Ain't that right, Dr. Q?"

Sensing that the Security Director seemed to have another bluff going, Dr. Q replied, "You have the only key to that control console, yes," choosing the words and emphasis of his answer carefully. Brian was reporting what the Director of Security wanted him to report. Dr. Q would go on once he found out what it was that she was claiming. Until then, the best he could do was to be vague.

Terry did not miss the significance of Dr. Q's qualifier. "What the fuck you mean by that crack? The only key to the 'that console', are you suggesting that there is another fucking console or somethin'? Don't try to mess with me, jackass."

Dr. Q cleared his throat, but before he had to answer Brian interrupted, "That's what I'm trying to tell you. That woman is Director of Security at this place. She has a backup console in her office, keeps a key in her desk, and is on her way there to throw the switch or whatever. That's what I been try to tell ya, for chrissake! What we gonna do if she lets alla the prisoners go? Huh, what we gonna do then?"

"Shut the fuck up, shit face," Terry shouted. He was visibly shaking. More than his language was deteriorating. "You, Mr. Famous Doctor, is there anything to this shit? Is that fuckin' big broad really the Director of Security? Did you lie to me, you son of a bitch?"

He started toward Dr. Q with his fist cocked. "Y-Yes, she is the Director of Security. And yes, she probably did break your friend in two before he knew what hit him. And yes, of course she has a backup console. Think about it for a minute. Could the Facility have been designed with only one way to release scientific staff from all around the world? What would happen if there were an accidental malfunction? What if my office were to burn? What if I went mad? What if, what if, what if. The list is endless." The Executive Director still had no idea why Laurie wanted them to believe this story, but clearly that was her wish and he would go along.

"Why the fuck didn't you tell me, you lying fucking bastard?" Terry stepped forward and slapped Dr. Q on both sides of the face and sent him stumbling backwards.

"You never asked me." Dr. Q feebly replied. "I would have told-" He was interrupted by another slap in the face and another verbal outburst from Terry.

"Shut the fuck up! You speak only when I ask you to from now on. Not another fuckin' word!" Terry was near the breaking point, and his men knew it. Fortunately for Terry, so did he. Taking a deep breath and exhaling slowly, he turned back to Brian. "Okay, shit-for-brains. Go on, slowly this time. I want to understand, and I only want to listen to your sniveling voice once. That part where Herm is knocked out and you and George are standing around wetting your pants while two old farts, a pansy, a bloodied idealist, along with a mighty Amazon calmly tie you up. Have I got that part right?" He looked over at Brian who nodded, defeated. "So after they tied you, then what happened?"

As carefully and as accurately as he could, Brian reviewed in detail the events following Herm's defeat. "She knew that we could work our way loose," he concluded. "She just didn't care. They're headed for her office, wherever the hell that is, by two different routes. Jane still looks a mess, so the lady cop was taking her to the Infirmary. Ames and the visitors went on alone."

Terry had been listening carefully. "You mean they have split up?" he asked. "Who took the guns?"

"Yeah, they split up. The guns went with Ames and the old guys. The ceramic knife, before you ask, was picked up by the kid."

"The dumb broad has out-foxed herself this time, Brian my boy. Now it's her ass that's in a sling. Here's what we're going to do.

First, I really don't give a shit if those stupid eggheads get out or not." Having found what he believed to be a fatal flaw in Laurie's plans, his arrogance swept away all feelings of doubt and his spirits lifted rapidly. With the mood swing he began to regain a measure of control of his voice and vocabulary.

"This whole action is about money, and this Facility is worth more than what we're asking, to say nothing of these two prize scientists. Do you believe the President of the United States will stand by and let Drs. Q and Newcombe be shot and then watch his precious Facility be blown apart? Who knows what untested bugs might be released? No, those eggheads down there were nice insurance, but we don't really need them." His mood swing continued. He was, after all, the world's best pl Annr and his plan was solid.

"So the Amazon can fight. Big deal." He could out plan anyone. "But guess what? We're going to keep the scientists anyway. 'Cause you guys are gonna nail their asses, Laurie Bass, that fairy-faced Ames, and those two goddamn visitors. I don't need more than two of you here. Brian, your ass is already draggin'; you stay with me. Skip, keep one machine pistol and give one to Brian; you're staying here too. The rest of you split into two teams and get your asses out there in the corridors and nail those idiots. Remember, don't get too close to that black-belted Amazon, just shoot her. Shoot all of them in the legs if possible." He continued his instructions, "There are visitor's maps by the door. Brad, see if they show the locations of the Security Office and the Infirmary. If not, I'm sure that Dr. Q or Dr. Kim will be pleased to mark the locations for you."

Telephone Edicts

The phone rang stridently, interrupting Terry's train of thought. He snatched the receiver, "Yeah, who the hell are you?" He listened briefly. His face lit up and a relaxed smile began to form. For the first time since Brian's return, Terry felt elation return. His confidence soared to new extremes. "Oh, this is the White House, is it? Well, you don't say . . . . Yes, this is Terry, Terrence Parker to you. Put me through to the President and quit wasting my time with needless questions." He stood straighter as if to gain stature, importance. Mimicking the exasperated expression of executives the world over, at least as portrayed by films and videos, he stood with the phone to his ear and tapped his foot. His earlier shaking had stopped: his features relaxed. His mood had rocketed from an extreme low to unprecedented heights.

"Yes. Hello. Who is this speaking?" He listened briefly, then for the second time this day he lost his cool. The veins again popped up in his neck; his face flushed, and his hands shook. "Who the fuck are you? I don't want to talk to some fucking lackey, some lowly goddamn secretary! I want to talk to the fucking President of the fucking United States of America. Is that fucking clear enough? And don't you start any of that 'please calm down' shit with me! I have no intention of calming down! . . . . Yes, you better fucking believe I'm wound up tight! I would love to start shipping you horseshits pieces of your precious fucking Doctors wrapped in pieces of your Goddamn Facility! How about for openers I just create a few cracks in some well-selected walls and seals? Would you like that?"

He paused briefly. His mood was darkening further. Mike and Brad, the only two of his companions left who knew him well, sensed the double reversal in his mood. In the past such quick changes in moods from one extreme to another frequently presaged an uncontrolled outburst. They were both becoming uncomfortable. A calm and calculating Terry was a keen strategist and tactician. Out of control he was a disaster looking for a place to happen. Terry was listening to a very experienced negotiator, the Secretary of State, who had quickly sensed Terry's state of mind and was offering up profuse and soothing apologies. Terry thrived on subservience, and as he listened to one of the nation's most famous politicians kowtowing to him, his calm returned and his confidence again began to soar.

"Never mind all that shit. Here's the game plan, see.

"First, I ain't talking to you no more, nor to none of the other flunkies, either.

"Second, the price of this Facility and its contents is fifty million dollars in cash. I want the money delivered to an address I will give to the President and to the President only. I want it delivered twelve hours from now. That is important; the clock is running as we speak. I want the money in hundred dollar bills packed in suitcases, three-suiters. Remember, the clock is already running.

"Third, I will not negotiate. The terms you just heard will not vary.

"Fourth, I will not talk or listen to anyone except the President of the United States. Stalling around or trying to get me to talk to some goddamn head shrink or terrorist specialist will just get you that much closer to the time when I start pushing buttons here. The clock is running and the delivery instructions will be fairly complex. Got all that? Of course you have; you got a fuckin' recorder going!

"Fifth, I want the President personally, remember I don't talk to anyone else again-to call me back within thirty minutes from now. I'm just setting a second clock to time his call. If he's late, I push buttons. You guys can guess which ones.

"That is all-shut the hell up, lackey. As I was saying, that is all for now. I will wait for the President." Dropping the telephone receiver dramatically into its cradle, he turned cheerfully back to his men. His eyes glistened with success. He had them. He was winning, hands down.

"You guys hear that? That was the Secretary of State on the line! Not bad, huh? We got those bastards by the short and curlies. The big Amazon can just go to hell."

He had soared to the other extreme again. The swings were getting more frequent and the extremes more pronounced. For now he was winning. The world would know he was the greatest.

"Okay, Brad, you and Lefty head for the broad's office by the shortest route and nail that damned Ames and the two old geezers. I'd prefer them wounded and alive, but it isn't necessary." He turned to the other two men. "Mike, you and Don will go after the two broads. Try the Infirmary first, but watch out. She's apparently tough as nails and tricky as a fox. If what Brian says is only half true, you'd better not get too close. Just find her and blast her legs. Now, beat it the hell out of here."

After they left, he turned his attention to his two captives. "Are either of you specialists in Karate or Kung Fu or any such shit as that? Don't answer; I intend to tie your asses to those chairs over there anyway." He indicated the chairs surrounding the conference table. "They're anchored to the floor for your TV conferences. If I get any shit out of the President we're going to have a television conference with him-just a one-way conference. He gets to see your asses shot off if he doesn't listen to me."

Turning to Skip with further instructions, he continued "Skip, tie the eggheads up. Brian, shoot either one of those bastards that moves. Try for the feet or lower legs if you have to shoot. I want the merchandise to look presentable, at least for a while." Exasperated, Dr. Q had sat and listened through it all with his mind in a whirl. "What could be on Laurie's mind? Was there any way to help? Dr. Newcombe was absolutely white with shock and fear. How much more could she take. Aloud, he addressed Terry. "Look here. Neither of us knows anything about fighting, nor are we dangerous to you in any other way. You have our word that we will not attack you or cause you any trouble. There are three of you, after all, and, you are all armed. It would be foolhardy in the extreme for us to rush three armed men. Please show at least a modicum of compassion for poor Dr. Newcombe. She is on the verge of passing out. She needs a blanket and a chance to relax. Tie me up if you must, but at least let her sit relaxed in the indicated chair. What harm can that do?"

Concern for the well being of another human being was totally foreign to Dr. Q, and he was surprised at his reaction. Terry's response shot back almost before the request was completed. "Shut your face. I can't stand to hear your high-toned sniveling and fancy-assed vocabulary. Why in the name of hell would I believe you? You're a lying bastard; it was you who told me that big broad of a Security Chief was just another tour guide, remember? You don't get to shaft old Terry more'n once. And that harmless, chubby, nearly freaked-out broad with you, poor, stunned Dr. Kim, is nothing to worry about, huh? Well, that's what Herm thought about your black-haired Security Director. She broke his ass up good." With a flourish he turned to Skip.

"Tie them the hell up."

Brian and Lefty Locate Ames

The Auditorium was on the outermost corridor, Ring Eight in the Blue Sector. It was diametrically opposite the Security Director's office, on Ring Eight in the Red Sector. It was of course for this reason that Ames and Laurie had declared the Director's office to be the location of the backup control console. The team that was sent to disrupt or destroy that console would have a long way to travel. The visitor's map would show the location of the office, but it would not indicate any of the internal hallways that could be used to shorten the journey. Even if Terry had instantly accepted Brian's tale and quickly dispatched a team to stop Ames, they would have found it impossible to reach there before he did. Ames had the much more detailed new employee map, which showed all of the inner passages as well as the major corridors. Therefore, he knew the shortest possible route, and he had started out significantly closer. Thus, even after stopping to settle Dr. Franklin and Senator Morse in the guardroom, he arrived in Laurie's office ten minutes ahead of Brian and Lefty.

Just down the hall from the Security Director's office, another guardroom was located. Ames waited behind the one—way glass, scanning the halls and listening intently for early signs of the arrival of Terry's men. He had left one of the machine pistols with Senator Morse; Dr. Franklin wanted nothing to do with it. The other was lying on the table beside him. He sincerely hoped he would not have to fire it. He was not at all sure he could, even though Laurie had shown him how to release the safety and squeeze the trigger. There was no danger that he would forget those instructions. But he had serious doubts about being emotionally capable of bringing himself to follow them with a man at the other end of the barrel. His plan was to surprise them and bluff them into dropping their weapons. He wasn't at all sure how he was going to bring that about; but it was essential to succeed here if his plan was to work.

Snapping out of his reflections, he heard slow, quiet footsteps and whispered voices down the corridor. The two men had not yet turned the last corner, but he could distinguish two separate voices.

One of them belonged to Lefty, whom he'd heard speak in the Auditorium. He had not heard the other voice before. Easing around the corner, the two men pressed to opposite sides of the corridor. They examined the hallway in each direction before moving into the Blue section of Ring Eight. One man rushed swiftly forward beyond the Security Director's office and started back slowly at a pace designed to arrive at one edge of the office door at the same time Lefty arrived at the other. From Terry's sarcastic introduction Ames knew the man was Brad. Okay, so now they have names," he thought. "So what good does that do you?"

He watched as they approached the closed door. Standing well clear of the actual doorway, Brad rapped the barrel of the machine pistol on the upper panel of the solid door. There was, of course, no response from within. Again Brad knocked; no answer. He nodded to Lefty.

"No need to be quiet," Lefty said. "Either the jerk's not here yet, or he's been and gone, or he's hidin' in there waitin' for us. If he's in there, he knows we're out here. If he ain't, there ain't no reason to be quiet. Let's make in like the movies." He lowered his voice, "I'll roll in to the left and you roll right."

Lefty reached down and slowly tried the doorknob. It turned easily and quietly. "Ready?" he asked. Brad nodded, and Lefty swung the door open and dived to the left. Brad followed, diving to the right and rolling to his feet. Their entrance was met with silence. They stood up.

"He ain't here yet," Brad announced. Lefty looked around. They were in an outer office. "Secretary probably sits out here," he commented. There were two doors into the secretary's office. The larger solid—looking door was located at the rear, "No doubt the Amazon's office," he said, indicating that one. "Check the closet." He pointed to the smaller door on the right.

Brad spoke up. "I still don't see anyone in the hall. I can't hear anyone, either. Maybe the three turkeys got lost. The console's probably in the big broad's office; you want to look around in there? I'll guard the door here an' check out the hall."

"Fine," Lefty said. "Bastards might come along any minute. Tell you what. They won't know how many of us are in here. You watch from the hall door like you said, and I'll go into the big office and close the door. Then if anyone gives you a hard time, I'll step in and sort them out. Okay?"

"Check," Brad replied. Lefty turned and entered Laurie's office and closed the door behind him. Ames had, of course, overheard their entire conversation. The minute they had opened the door and lunged from the corridor into the Security Director's office, Ames had stepped out of the guardroom into an inner hall. Two steps down this inner hall had taken him to a second door into Laurie's office. He had partially opened the door and waited, listening to the conversation in the outer office. He could hardly believe his good fortune. Lefty had actually arranged that they separate and close the door between them. To ordinary ears the closed door would significantly muffle the sound. Ordinary conversation would not be easily heard. He waited. The door on the opposite wall opened and Lefty stepped in, talking.

"I got no idea where the goddamn console's gonna be. I might be awhile, Brad. You hold the fort, right?"

"You got it," Brad's reply came as Lefty pulled the door closed. With his ears Ames followed Lefty's movements around the room. There was a credenza on the wall to the right of the door where Ames stood. As Lefty leaned down to open the sliding front panel, Ames stepped quietly forward and placed the barrel of the machine pistol against the back of Lefty's head. He wanted to give the impression that he was uptight, dangerously tense. "Considering all the butterflies in my stomach at the moment that should be easy enough", he thought. "Aloud he spoke softly, with as much quivering nervousness as he could manage in a half whisper. "Quietly please, Lefty. I am nervous enough with this gun. I can't be sure what would happen if you startled me, any loud noise, like calling Brad, would certainly startle me. Now, keeping that pistol in your right hand, lay it gently the top of the credenza in front of you. Do that quietly and I'll feel better." As he waited, holding his breath, Lefty gently lowered the machine pistol onto the highly polished surface.

Lefty had seen nervous guys in the service, guys who couldn't hold a gun of any kind without starting to shake. More than once some green kid accidentally discharged a weapon. He had no delusions about surviving if the nervous kid behind him squeezed the trigger.

"Be Goddamned careful with that thing," he whispered. "I ain't got a gun no more; and I ain't saying nothin' except in a whisper. Okay? You just back off a little. That gun's dangerous."

"Not y-y-yet," Ames stammered, he hoped convincingly. "Your f-friend is still out there. That makes me nervous too. I want you to call him in here. Please don't warn him or call out too loudly. Just tell him it's all clear, and ask him to come in here for a minute. You can sit behind the desk. That way I can stand behind you and rest the pistol on the top of the chair just behind your head. It'll keep me from shaking too much."

Lefty complied, and in a few moments Brad stood before them. He had not noticed Ames until he had almost reached the desk. When recognition did show in his face, Lefty was quick to speak. "Easy, Brad. This son of a bitch has a machine pistol at my head, and he's nervous as a cat." Brad could see the accuracy of that summary.

Laying his own pistol on the desk and stepping back, he said "Okay." He was not too comfortable with the idea of shooting people anyway. The guns were just supposed to scare hell out of a bunch of weird scientists and civil servants. He had never expected to be called on to fire one. Anyway, it was clear that Lefty was a dead man if that funny-looking guy should shoot. Brad wanted no part of that. He had thought of nothing but how to get out of this mess ever since Brian had returned. Ames could sense that there was more fear in Brad than Lefty. Lefty's actions were more calculated. Ames could not explain his reasons to anyone else, but he was sure Brad would not put up a fight and Lefty might.

Following his instincts, as always, he addressed his two new captives. "Brad, I would like you to stand over there to the left of the main door."

He waited while Brad complied. "Lefty, you and I are going to walk over there next to Brad. I'll hold this pistol against your spine, and we'll walk slowly in deference to my nervousness. When we reach the wall, you will stop a couple of feet from it, spread your feet slightly, and then lean forward, touching the wall with your head and hands, just like in the movies." After that had been accomplished, he said, "Now, slowly pass your hands behind your back. You won't fall if you keep your head pressed hard against the wall. Brad, use your belt and strap his hands tightly behind him." Brad complied, and Ames repeated the process, tying Brad's hands securely behind him. A few minutes later, they had both been bound and Ames had used his own belt to knot their elbows together, forcing them to stand back to back and to move as a unit. It made walking awkward and slow, but it effectively kept them from surprising him. Carrying all three guns, he took them to the guardroom where Senator Morse and Dr. Franklin were waiting. Upon their arrival, the two prisoners were securely bound to chairs, using handcuffs that the inquisitive Dr. Franklin had found in a desk. Fortunately, the cuffs had been found open, for the key was nowhere around. It had all gone smoothly, much more smoothly than Ames had dared hope. He was bothered by a premonition that the remaining stages would not be as easy. Leaving the two hijackers bound and locked in the guardroom, Ames led the two visitors toward their next destination. As they walked along, he explained the next stage of the operation. At the same time he was wondering how Laurie's first phase was going. Would they actually come out of this alive? He had found his Auntie Laurie at last. He was sure he had known her, probably only briefly, before he had been adopted by the Frommes. What was significant about finding her here? He felt sure that he was at last near the core of the biggest mystery of his short life.

Don and Mike Find Laurie

Back in the Green Sector, Laurie left the Women's Lounge with Jane covered and nestled comfortably on the couch. If Brian has gotten loose as pl Annd and carried the tale to Terry, one or more armed men would be searching for her.

Reasoning that they would probably start their search at the Infirmary back on Ring Eight, she turned in that direction. In case they had moved faster than she expected, she used the inner halls whenever possible to reduce the chance of being seen. A small office used by an accounting clerk had a wall in common with the Infirmary. When she reached that room, she crept quietly to the common wall and listened. There were no sounds. She looked again at her watch. Sufficient time had passed. "They should be here by now," she thought. "I wonder if something has gone wrong. Maybe I misjudged this Terry. Perhaps he is so confident of his position that he doesn't mind if a few of us run around loose. What harm can we do? None if he doesn't buy the story about a backup console in my office. Even if he does, that could be all he cares about. Will he just send a few guys to stop Ames from releasing the seals and let me wander around the Facility? No, not with that ego. When he learns about Herm, he'll be fuming at Dr. Q and even more so at me. I don't believe he cares about Herm. But Dr. Q lied to him when he described me as a guide. Then, if he believes a woman took out his bully boy, he'll demand my head just to show his superiority. Finally, if he believes I have the means to destroy his whole plan, there is no way he cannot demand my head." She shook her head and sighed. "If he believes the story."

Looking at her watch again, she decided to give them five more minutes, and then go to her office and try to intercept them there. Just then, she heard a sound from next door. Softly, she crept to the wall and placed her ear against it. "The bitches ain't here," said one voice.

"So", she reasoned, "there are at least two of them in the Infirmary." To establish an exact count she listened carefully.

"Where the hell ya think they went, Don?," said another voice.

These two were thieves, not killers, Laurie thought. They had not expected to be involved in some kind of OK Corral showdown. Waving guns at unarmed people was one thing; searching for five people armed with two automatic pistols was quite another. Besides that, there was Brian's account of Herm's injuries to be considered; they had probably taken their time as they meandered over here to the Infirmary, considering and discussing that episode.

"I dunno. Let that son of a bitch go find the broad," Don said. "I say we look for her, but not too hard. We won't take no big chances, right?"

"Okay," Mike said. "We got here, we looked, and they ain't here. Whatta ya wanna do now?"

"Me? I wanna get the hell outa here and forget I ever saw this fuckin' Facility. But we can't get out any more than the people on the lower levels can. So here's what we do. We head back to the Auditorium slowly. We tell Terry we can't find her. He can go get her if he wants to. At least back there we got a chance. She would have to come to us, and Terry's got the remote trigger for those bombs of Tiny's."

Laurie listened with mixed emotions. The collapse of Terry's team was good news, but she did not want them to regroup. Don was right. If they gathered in the Auditorium there would be nothing she could do but hide and wait. She had to stop them from getting back. Reducing the size of Terry's gang in the Auditorium to three or fewer was an essential feature of the plan she and Ames had developed. "All right," she thought, "I become the hunter instead of the hunted." With that she pounded her fist on the desk beside her and stepped quickly into the next office. Once there, she again pressed her ear against the door and was rewarded by Mike's reaction.

"What's that, Don?"

She listened as they nervously discussed the situation. Planning their route back was their primary concern. The main corridors were twelve feet wide and their plan was simple. Stick to those corridors, one man down each side, and head as directly as possible for the Auditorium. She pounded again. Again Mike reacted.

"Goddamn it, Don, there's someone next door, on the other side of that wall. What if they're all in there? We can't just go prancing down those big halls and wait for them to ambush us! Fire a burst at that wall. Then I'm headin' the hell outta here! I'll go right. You go left."

"No. Hang on, Rick," Don replied. "There's no point splitting up. We should use the same hallways, one behind the other. You go first or I'll go first. Then, say half a minute later, the other guy follows. If they stop one of us, the other guy comes on like the cavalry and rescues him. Whattaya think?"

"Shit, Don, I don't know. I ain't the big planner. That's Terry's job, and this time he blew it. We can't just stay here. That broad probably knows this Facility inside out. She's liable to show up anywhere. What if she's got a gun too? Ya heard what she did to Herm without one, and he had a knife! Shit!"

"Calm down. I think the Amazon's alone. I think Brian was tellin' it straight. She took off with Jane, who's all busted up from that crack in the mouth. The kid, Ames, he takes off with those two old farts to let the eggheads out. Then Wonder Woman, she puts Jane to bed somewhere and takes off after us. Those old farts, they stayed with Ames. That's what I think. I say she's out there somewhere, all by herself. Probably ain't even got a gun. Shit, they only had two and she'd be sure to think she don't need one." Don paused and weighed his own arguments. Satisfied that they were sound he continued. "I'm telling you, Mike, that broad's out there alone."

Don was talking for his own benefit. He needed reassurance, even if he had to supply it himself. "She can't follow us both. I'm going alone. Which side you want?" Rick did not answer. Laurie, sensing the breakout was near, left hurriedly and headed out to intercept Don, whom she felt sure would go right as he had originally said. She was barely in place when her judgment was vindicated. There he was. She turned into an inner hall and raced forward. She planned to intercept him at the next intersection. She arrived well ahead of her prey and pushed two chairs, each equipped with five silent casters, from a small conference room near the door. Don could be heard pounding down the spoke corridor. She waited for him to come near before sending the first chair rolling directly into his path. Too late, Don saw the obstacle. Sliding to a stop to avoid colliding with the chair, he briefly lost his balance. That was all she needed. Laurie struck. Don dropped, unconscious, to the floor. Grasping his collar, she dragged him into the conference room. She looked around for something with which to restrain him. Finding nothing, she stripped him to his underwear and tied him quickly and securely, using his trousers and belt. Then closing the door to the conference room, she jammed a chair under the door handle for good measure and turned left in pursuit of the other one. As she passed, she had picked up the automatic pistol. However, realizing that she had never been trained in its use and was more alarmed than comforted by its weight, she paused and removed the clip, then deposited the gun in a drawer in a nearby desk. She closed the drawer and dropped the clip into the next wastebasket she passed on her way back to the Infirmary.

Mike had hesitated. He was sure she was out there. She would stop Don; Don had been right. She was alone, he felt sure of that, but she didn't need any help. Don was finished. She would nail his ass. "What about me?" he said out loud. He felt his control slipping. He had to do something; but what? Then he heard a crash. Without thinking, he was immediately galvanized into action. Cocking the automatic and jacking a cartridge into the chamber, he made for the door as quickly as he could manage. For no particular reason he turned left, away from the noise he'd heard, the noise he was sure spelled the end of Don as a force in the present action.

He ran. Conditioning was not one of Mike's strong points, and by the time he had passed the second ring corridor, he was panting heavily and beginning to rationalize his slowing down.

"She can't be anywhere near here", he thought. "She's back there taking care of Don. She can't just leave him there. She's got to take care of him somehow. I got lotsa time. There's only two more rings and one more spoke. Take your time, settle down. What the hell was that?" he gasped as he thought he noticed, a flash of yellow ahead. She had been wearing a yellow blouse above an off-white skirt. How the hell? He stopped. She was between him and the Auditorium. What is she up to? "What's that?" he asked aloud, turning toward a noise behind him. There it was again, the yellow flash. Guessing blindly at the next appearance, he turned quickly back up the corridor. No! The noise came from the other direction in back of him. She was crossing the corridor behind him again, in the opposite direction this time.

"What the hell are you up to, bitch?" he yelled. Unconsciously, he snapped the cocking lever of the automatic again. This time the previously chambered shell was ejected and rattled to the floor, echoing through the empty corridors. Rick's self control was rapidly receding. He turned back and forth, pointing the automatic first down the corridor toward the center of the Facility, then up the corridor toward the outermost ring. His search went unrewarded. He could feel the tension rising. With conscious effort he stopped his spasmodic searching and steadied his hands. Then, breathing deeply, he considered his situation as coolly as he could manage. "She's out here in these goddamn halls and she's after my ass he thought. The bitch is sure to know her way around this place without a friggin' map like I gotta use. She took out Herm, unarmed, bare-handed. What the fuck is she anyway? She took Herm. Then somehow she took Don. He had a goddamn gun like this one." He raised his right hand, feeling the weight of the weapon. Looking at it brought another jarring thought, "Now, that fucking bitch has got one too! Jesus H Christ!"

The thought of being stalked by that woman had been bad enough before; now it was more than he could bear. "Come on, bitch!" he screamed. "Come and get me! I ain't scared of no bitch! Fuck you! Here I am!" His outburst was greeted by silence. Again, he began jerking his pistol up and down the hall in a vain search for a target. It occurred to him that he could see in four different directions rather than two if he took a few steps back down the hall to the intersection of the corridors. He did so. With his back pressed firmly against the wall, he checked out each direction, the weapon in his right hand tracking the direction of his search. Nothing!

Less than thirty feet down the spoke corridor, Laurie stood just inside an office door. She had heard him rush to the intersection after screaming out his challenge. She had heard the panic in his voice and knew a mixed blessing. His loss of control would reduce his ability to consider his alternatives rationally. On the other hand, it increased the chance of an irrational firing of his automatic weapon. "Perhaps I should have kept Don's pistol," she thought. Even before she completed the thought, she had dismissed it. Not only was she untrained in its use, she was positive she could not fire one at a human being. Calmly, she stepped farther back into the office and kicked the door shut, then turned immediately and ran to the rear door of the office. Mike heard the door slam and reflexively fired a short burst at the offending door. He had reached the breaking point. Before the echoes had died down, Laurie cut across the spoke behind him, having hurried along one of the inner passages. She increased her pace, and ran noisily. Startled by the sound, Don turned toward the noise and again squeezed the trigger. An arching trail of pockmarks appeared along the wall, starting at about his waist level and rising above the doors into the ceiling as it stretched away down the hall.

Just inside the fourth door down the corridor, Laurie gasped and stopped. She had been hit! Her cheek! She reached up with her left hand, wiping the painful area on the left side of her face. When she pulled her hand away, there was a red streak from her palm to the tips of her fingers. The movement of her arm caused a small sharp pain in her upper arm, just above the elbow. Turning her arm, she was able to see a gash along the length of her upper arm. The cut was long and irregular, but there was very little blood. Pretty superficial, she concluded. The cut on her face bled somewhat more freely. She noticed a smudge above her left breast, the red blood producing a brown stain on the yellow blouse even before it dried. Looking around, she discovered that two large chips had been knocked out of the doorframe at just about the height of her shoulder. She reasoned, correctly, that splinters from the chips had caused the wounds. The realization of what might have been and of how close she had been to the hurtling bullets, caused her to shudder. Then, regaining control, she considered. "I wish I knew how many shells those damn guns hold. On the other hand, I have not been counting. I'll just have to keep going until he can't shoot anymore. Then I'll know it's empty."

She hurried through the rear door and back up the hall for another dash across his vision. Reaching the selected office, she decided to increase the pressure. She could hear his breathing and the shifting of his weight from foot to foot. She called out, "Give it up, Mike. I'm coming after you."

She leapt back from the door and dropped to the floor, barely ahead of the thundering sound of the automatic gunfire. Breathing deeply to recover from the shock of another close call, she hurried to the office door she had selected for her next thrust. The action continued through three more cycles. Laurie would hide and then rush noisily across a corridor, drawing fire from the increasingly panicky Mike. She had been selecting her challenging positions in such a way as to lead Mike farther and farther from the Auditorium. At last her rush failed to draw fire. A few more taunts were required to convince her that the weapon was now useless. Then calmly, almost casually, she stepped into the hallway and called out conversationally, "Well, Mike, it's over now. Why don't you just drop the empty gun and come with me quietly? You know I can take it from you if I have to. I promise you it will be easier if you just drop it."

He looked up at her. With a sigh of resignation and relief that it was actually over, he dropped the weapon and sheepishly kicked it away, over to the wall. Together, they started down the corridor to get Don.

Gun Shots And Presidential Call, All Interpreted

Terry, who had been standing silently for several minutes, staring at the Auditorium doors, turned to face Dr. Q and Kim. "Did you hear that?" he demanded.

Dr. Q had noticed and had been bewildered by this latest staccato burst of noise. "Yes, but I have no idea what it is. I've never heard a noise quite like it before, either within the Facility or outside it. I imagine a riveting hammer might sound like that, but I've never heard one. Or . . . wait a minute." Realization was dawning. "Could that have been one of those guns? Are they automatic? There were several . . . they can't possibly, not really . . . not shooting . . ." He sputtered into incredulous silence, and he gave up. The images in his mind were beyond his experience; they simply defied description. For the first time he could remember, Dr. Q was at a loss for words. Every staff member of the Facility would have found that fact as incredible as the sound of machine pistols being discharged in the corridors of the Facility itself.

Nodding, Terry looked at Skip and Brian. "You guys heard it too, right? That's an end to the Amazon. I counted four bursts, but I'm not sure I heard them all. Either of you guys hear more'n that?"

As both men shook their heads, Brian spoke up, "I knew Lefty would nail her ass. That son of a bitch can shoot. Steady as a rock." Brian was relieved. He had seen Laurie in action; as long as she was out there running around loose, he had been very worried. Now that he was sure that Lefty and the others had settled her and that bunch of weirdoes she had with her, he found it difficult to restrain his enthusiasm. He had superstitiously refrained from commenting on the success of the whole operation before they were away from the building. However, Lefty's success had already been achieved and could be talked about. "Goddamn, that Lefty nailed her ass," he said again.

Terry interrupted Brian's celebration. "Let's see how many of the bastards he brings back and in what condition." He turned again to the Executive Director. "You understand what he's saying?"

Dr. Q understood all too well. He too had concluded that Lefty and the other three armed men had managed to locate, incapacitate, and capture Laurie and the others. He silently prayed that incapacitate and capture were strong enough words. He certainly would not have expressed himself as Brian had, but his conclusion was the same.

He wondered how badly they had been hurt. He had watched Terry cycle through three complete mood swings in a matter of minutes and feared that one of these times the cycle back to more or less rational behavior might not occur. He resolved to choose his words carefully. to avoid topics that might send Terry off on another tirade.

"It would appear that your men have caught up with Ms. Bass and the others. I do hope they are not too badly hurt. Dr. Newcombe is one of the few physicians on our staff here at the Facility. It is true that she is more interested in research than the practice of medicine. However, if you will permit your men to release her, then after first treating herself, I'm sure she will be able to treat them when they return"

Looking deliberately at his watch, Terry's only comment was, "The President now has eleven hours and five minutes to deliver the money. Your release comes after that. Of course he may elect to speed up the delivery after he learns of the condition of your friends." With a flash of generosity reflecting his current mood, he added, "What the hell, when Lefty gets them back here, she can fix them up. Until then, she stays seated. Comfortably, I hope." This last comment he directed with a satisfied smile at Kim, who appeared to be regaining a measure of control. He continued, "I'm not taking any chances with you two. You got that, lady? Don't pass out; you're going to be needed soon. Remember your oath. You gotta take care of the patients."

Kim had been maintaining consciousness with difficulty, and, while improving, was not yet fully in control. She was aware of what had been said and of the implication that the Security Director and the others had been seriously wounded. She also knew that the "others" included two new members of the select Congressional Committee that controlled the Facility funding. Kim could feel control returning in proportion to the feeling that she might be needed. She did not try to hide her concern for the wounded, nor did it occur to her that the identity of the visitors should be kept secret.

"But those people could be seriously hurt," she exclaimed. Besides Laurie, there's that poor girl and the nice young man, as well as Dr. Franklin and Senator Morse. That's five people, perhaps seriously wounded. You've got to let me get some supplies together. They should be taken to the Infirmary-"

"Shut the fuck up, broad!" Terry shouted; he was away again. She stopped and gaped in open disbelief. Turning angrily on Dr. Q, Terry continued scornfully, "Well, doctor, you son of a bitch, you never cease to amaze me. Senator Morse and Dr. Franklin are just two innocent visitors? Bullshit, doctor!" Striding forward, he struck the scientist across the face with the back of his hand. Blood showed at the corner of the director's lip.

"Well, you bastard, tell me what the hell you think you're doing. Why the fuck didn't you want me to know who the old geezers are? You think it matters a shit to me?" Without waiting for an answer he continued, "It would not have mattered a tinker's damn who they were. Now it does." In frustration he struck the other side of Dr. Q's face with an open hand. "Now! Why the big cover up?"

"It is just as Dr. Newcombe said," Dr. Q replied, his steady voice belying his inner turmoil. "They are well-known men. Dr. Franklin is a scientist, and Senator Morse is from the state of Wyoming. Each has been connected in one way or another with bio-engineering, and they are both visiting this Facility for the first time. I simply wished to minimize their discomfort. I had thought you might release all the visitors, as you did the ASPGH members; obviously I was wrong. There really is no more significance to it than that. I did not wish to have you single them out; now, presumably, they've been shot. You will get Presidential attention now, all right. President Winters is more opposed to dealing with terrorists than any of his predecessors. By shooting two national figures, internationally known and respected men, you have assured his unbounded wrath. Whatever chance you had of exploiting the presence of those poor souls sealed below went up in smoke with those pistol shots."

"Don't change the subject. The fuckin' President will play ball because he has no choice. Does every visiting scientist and government official get a tour personally guided by the Director of Security at this place? I think not. So, again, what's so goddamn special about these two?" Again, he punctuated his questions with sharp backhanded slaps to the director's face.

Such actions helped him steady himself. Slapping his bound prisoner demonstrated that he was in fact in control; his perfect plan was succeeding despite these lies and surprises.

Dr. Q did not answer immediately, and Terry stepped over to Kim. "Perhaps I should ask the lady doctor and help her memory along a little," he said, raising his hand.

With a sigh of resignation, Dr. Q began. "All right, leave her alone; we need her skills. The two men with Laurie Bass are newly appointed members of the Congressional Committee that controls the funding for NAMBE and, hence, for the Facility. When new members are appointed to the Committee they are sent here to visit the Facility and receive an up-to-date briefing on our activities. Naturally, we are eager that they should receive a good impression. The normal routine is for Ms. Bass, to take them through the simple administrative routine required of new members of the Committee: registering their signatures, voice prints things like that. She then brings them here to anonymously to join one of the regular tours." His expression of defeat and exasperation gave the stamp of credibility to the explanation.

Convinced that he finally knew the truth, Terry lost all interest in the visitors. "That wasn't so bad, was it? So, you have new hands on the Facility purse strings. What's the matter; the President thinks you're dippin' into the till? Don't tell me, I can't stand any more of your sniveling lies." Again, he glanced nervously at his watch. Nearly an hour had passed since he had spoken to the Secretary of State, Herbert Aldauer. He'd expected to hear from the President by now. Screw him, he thought. The longer he waits, the tighter the schedule gets and the less time he has to try to think up surprises which wouldn't do him any good anyway; the plan is tight."

The ups and downs of the day's events and his mood swings were beginning to have take their toll, however. He glanced again at the digital watch on his wrist. The indicated time had not changed. The second look at his watch stimulated another thought. Where the hell are those guys? You'd think at least one of them would have brains enough to run ahead and report. Stupid shits! It musta been ten minutes ago that the firing stopped. With short steps he began to pace, contemplatively, back and forth. He reviewed his preparation and was satisfied that everything that should have been done, that could have been done, had been done. He had planned well. The President would soon realize that he, Terry Parker, held all the aces. Maybe there was some way to use the new knowledge just gained from Dr. Q.

"Would the President be more concerned for these two men than for all of those trapped below?" he wondered. Nah." He answered his own question. But they did represent a little added pressure, and every little bit helped. When the bastard calls, I'll let him know that I got them, and that I know they're special people." Considering how best to spring this latest tidbit on President Winters, he continued his pacing in silence for a few moments. Then, stopping suddenly, he glanced nervously at his watch yet again.

"That President of yours doesn't much give a shit about you and your goddamn Facility, does he, Dr. Q? The son of a bitch can't even bother to call."

Inside he was seething; "Where the fuck were those guys? It's been twenty minutes since the shooting. I'll have their asses!" he thought. "At least Lefty should know enough to get word back here. What if those weren't shots at all? Of course they were. What if it was the Amazon shootin' Lefty's ass off? Nah. She would certainly be here making demands. The bastards are just screwin' off, congratulating each other and takin' their own sweet time ramblin' along the corridors. Maybe, there was some "medicinal brandy" in that damned Infirmary.

The ringing of the telephone ended his speculations. "Hello, who's this?" He began speaking even before the telephone had reached his mouth. "My name is Martha," came the reply. "I'm trying to place a call for the President of the United States. He would like to speak to Mr. Terrence Parker." Terry's mind raced. He had done it! He had the President of the United States on the phone calling him! In as firm a voice as he could muster, he spoke into the mouthpiece. "I'm Terry; put him on. I ain't talking to no more secretaries." After a short pause, a deep resonant voice said, "President Winters here."

It had truly begun! The conversation took half an hour. Not that there was all that much to be arranged; the actions required on the part of the government were in fact few and simple. The counter-strategies, whatever they were to be, might be complex and involved. However, the hijacker's requirements were straightforward, and Terry's instructions were inherently simple. "Place five hundred thousand one hundred dollar bills in six three-suiter airline travel cases and load them into a station wagon that will be parked at an address in Erie, Pennsylvania. I'll give you the address later. When the station wagon is loaded just leave the rest to me."

That short speech would have been the end of Terry's comments had Terry been more of a professional and less of an egotist. However, he was compelled to explain the depth to which his analysis had reached, to demonstrate that no conceivable detail had been left unattended. To indulge his arrogance, he needed to explain in detail how fruitless would be any attempt to foil the plan. Stripped of abuse and obscenities, of boasts and swagger, the content was simple. He explained that the driver of the station wagon would first affix radio controlled bombs to the suitcases, then travel a predetermined route past an undisclosed number of checkpoints at which Terry would have men waiting, men equipped with radios capable of communicating with the driver. The route would include large stretches of road that were normally untraveled. If two or more of those sections of road contained cars when the station wagon passed through, the mission would abort: the driver would abandon the station wagon and, from a safe distance, destroy it. The price would then go up to sixty million dollars and the exercise would start again. This abort procedure would, in fact, be initiated at any sign that the government was trying to follow the money.

Once satisfied that he has not been followed by land or air, the driver will stop in a preselected place. The driver, whose army training included not only explosives but electronic bugging and tracking devices, would carefully sweep the car and the suitcases of money as he repacked them into suitcases he had purchased in advance. Needless to say, if the sweep and search disclosed a radio device or electronic signal of any kind, the mission would be aborted and the price would go up. Even though the tracking device had failed, its existence would indicate that the government had not acted in good faith. Terry liked that expression. When the money had been declared electronically clean, the driver would notify the watchers, who would call Terry to indicate that the government had kept the first part of the bargain. The station wagon would proceed to its next checkpoint. Terry did not explain that it would be a multilevel parking garage or that the cases would then be transferred to a different vehicle, which would proceed to a different checkpoint. It wasn't necessary. The President "Did not need to know all the details". The money would then be moved by Terry's men through the necessary laundry steps, arranged by the Gambler, to a suitable numbered account outside the United States. A series of phone calls, the last to Terry himself, would indicate that the transfer had taken place and phase One of the operation could be considered complete. The next and final phase was the departure of Terry and his men from the Facility and the return of the Facility and its contents to the government. Certain arrangements had been made involving the explosives presently stored in the automated warehouse next to the main ventilation ducts. He was sure that the President was well aware of the location of the explosives, but he relished the idea of causing the Chief Executive further discomfort by rubbing his nose in it.

"The same army-trained demolition specialist, who has had ten years industrial experience blowing things up since leaving the army, has set the system up in a special way. When I leave the building I will trigger the devices. That will start the timer going. If the timer is not stopped by a radio signal sent by my transmitter, the bombs will explode. Our leaving will follow a plan similar to that of the cash. We will travel a preplanned route past an undisclosed number of observers. We will, of course, be scanning the sky, and we will have swept our vehicle before departing. I'm aware, Mr. President, that you have satellites that can track a car. With one of them you may be able to see us enter a heavily wooded, heavily traveled park land. One or more of the emerging cars may be us. "I don't suppose I need to tell you that any evidence that the government has not "acted in good faith" will require that we cancel the operation. If I have to abort during this phase it will, of course, not be money that blows up. The game would be over, we all lose. You of course can decide how much you are prepared to risk.

"I am sure you have recorded this so I won't tell you again. However, before I hang up I would like to tell you that we have both Dr. Franklin and Senator Morse in here with us. You should also know that I know full well who they are and why they are here. You have thirty minutes more to get things in order. When you are ready, call me and I will give you the address to locate the station wagon. It is not necessary for you to say anything at this point. As I explained to your lackey, this ain't no negotiation. I talk, you listen." With that he slammed the phone down into its cradle to emphasis the finality of his statement. Beaming with satisfaction and riding on his most extreme emotional high of the day, Terry turned back to his local audience.

"There, guys, did you get the gist of all that? That was the President himself! I told him, didn't I?" Ignoring Skip's, "You sure did, Terry!" and "You settled his ass!" from Brian, he turned to Dr. Q.

"I hope you were listening, smart ass. I got the names of the mysterious visitors outa you as well as their goddamn connections. Bet the old Pres is burning over that. And that Amazon bitch, she's nailed too. Fat lot of good your lies did you." Terry was elated, 'over the moon' he would have said if asked. He was pulling it off. He could contain himself no longer. "I'm showing them all: Jane, the simple fool; the ASPGH, all seventy-five of them; that walkin' reference book with the quick moves, Ames; Dr. Q, with his lies and his staff of thousands; the President of the whole goddamn country with his fuckin' satellites; and those gun sniffing bugs of yours, Dr. Q." He shook his finger accusingly at his captive. "It's a damned good thing that Ames told me about them. Last fuckin' thing in the world I need is a bunch of flying, buzzing, crawling bugs. I had more'n enough fuckin' bugs in Central America to do me the rest of my life. It makes my skin crawl, just to think about them.

"Yeah, and don't forget that Kung Fu Security Director that you tried to sandbag me with. I fixed her ass too." With this last thought he pulled himself up short and looked at his watch again: Fifty-five minutes; where the hell were they? He turned away from the two scientists and walked silently to the front of the stage where he again began to pace, continuing his private thoughts and mounting fears. "For chrissake, what's goin' on?" It didn't matter how many times he asked himself that question, he kept coming up with the same unacceptable answers. "They aren't here because they're not coming. They're not coming because they've lost. Some way, somehow, that fancy cop and the walking encyclopedia have won. Impossible! But . . . . wha . . . ."

A Presidential Conference And Revelations

Tension filled the President's conference room. There was no sound except the occasional turning of a page or the scratch of a pen. The five people in the room had all listened to Terry's demands and boasts. With difficulty, they had all sat in silence as the hoodlum verbally abused the President of the United States. When the telephone connection was broken, four of them spoke at once, outraged, calling for Terry's head, proclaiming that there was no way they could possibly accede to his demands. With a raised hand and a solemn nod, the President had silenced them. Calmly, as much for his own benefit as theirs, he reviewed the facts of the present situation, explaining unnecessarily, that they had no choice but to deal with the hijacker, at least temporarily, until the matters of State were satisfied. The other members of the committee had, of course, known this. It was, in fact, that knowledge that had angered and frustrated them in the first place. The finality of hearing their President agree with their own analysis did not assuage their anger; on the contrary, it exacerbated it. However, when Prescott Winters spoke, you listened, and somehow it was not possible to rage irrationally in the face of his reasoned arguments and that soothing southern drawl. Their anger grew, but more importantly it had evolved. Volatile anger had matured to a focused determination.

This man will be brought down, not by emotional outburst but by careful planning and cold-blooded execution, they concluded.

When the President had finished his synopsis of the situation arising from the phone call, he asked Martha to replay the tape of the telephone conversation. After the tape had been played, he asked her to bring each of them a copy of the typed transcript, which he was confident she had already prepared. Now, as each member of the select completed the reading and notating of the transcript, he laid his pen down alongside the papers before him and sat silently in deference to his colleagues. Only when he noticed that the last pen had lowered did Prescott Winters call the meeting to order and invite questions and discussion. The objective was to foil Terry without jeopardizing the lives of the visiting scientists or the security of Projects Eight and Nine, while at the same time preventing the accidental or deliberate release of Beta 4. Devising a strategy to accomplish these objectives was not a simple task; but the process had begun.

A Small Conference Room nt The Facility

En route to the small conference room to which Brian, George and Herm had originally led them, Laurie Bass and the two men she had just captured stopped at the Women's Lounge to collect Jane, who was essentially recovered. Her color had returned and she had had time to wash her face and generally freshen up. As she waited alone, Jane had grown apprehensive and had worried over the fate of her benefactors.

She was frightened at the prospect of her own future now that the siege had failed. Would they be hurt by Terry's men? Would she and her members, her friends, face a protracted incarceration? Would the Movement be destroyed forever? In a sense she felt relief. Her hatred for Terry had supplanted fear as the uppermost emotion in her mind. By focusing on him she could avoid, or at least defer, facing the nagging uncertainties of her future. Always skilled at introspection, she had been conscious of the fact that she was using her hatred of Terry as an escape mechanism, avoiding other unpleasantness for which she was totally to blame. She was aware, but she didn't care.

She had been shocked by loud staccato noises, like a string of firecrackers reverberating like thunder. It's not thunder, she had realized suddenly. "It's those damned guns. What was going on?" She had listened. There was only silence. They were finished. Jane's fears of disgrace for herself and the Movement and even her hatred of Terry were suddenly displaced by fear for her life. Terror flooded her. "Will they find me in here? How long can I hide? How long will the siege last." Her thoughts were interrupted by a gentle knocking at the hall door of the lounge. She was startled by the rapping. "Who . . . who's there?" she called.

She was pleased to hear the gentle voice of the Director of Security, "It's Laurie. You can open up, Jane; the danger is past, for the moment at least."

Elated by the realization that Terry's men had lost, she jerked open the door to see Laurie standing there with congealed blood on her cheek, telltale brown stains marring her bright yellow blouse, and a smile on her face. Jane gasped at the sight. "You've been hurt. Let me help."

"I'm all right," the taller woman assured her. Only then did Jane notice the two men, bound by their own belts standing sheepishly in the corridor. She turned back to Laurie.

"Are you sure you're all right?"

"Yes, I have a few scratches from flying splinters, but I'm sure it looks much worse than it is. I'll clean up later. We still have several things to do. Let's go down the hall to the left. I want to get something in the maintenance rooms just down the hall."

Directing her attention to the two men, she commanded, "You two lead the way slowly; I'm right here behind you. I'll tell you when to stop." At the maintenance rooms, Laurie picked up a roll of brown rubber-coated, double stranded wire used to make extension cords. She also selected a large roll of black electrician's tape. Using these, she tightly bound the arms of her two captives, who would have to remain unattended for some time as the next phase of the plan unfolded. This time she did not want them to escape. As they left the maintenance rooms, he picked up an additional quantity of tape and wire. Laurie led the way to the concealed guardroom where Ames and his two captives had joined Dr. Franklin and Senator Morse. There was little time to exchange stories. No one knew how long it might be before Terry sent out another team with more violent instructions.

"Let's get this collection of trash back to the small conference room and leave them there with Herm," Laurie suggested. After answering, or deferring until later a few more questions about what had happened, Laurie let the procession down the Green Spoke toward the outer ring, Ring One. Minutes later they entered the original small conference room. Here they found George, unbound and sitting dejectedly in one of the conference chairs bent over to ease the pain of his broken ribs. Mesmerized by Herm's inert body and his own fears, George barely glanced up at their arrival, before turning away, shaking his head slowly. He had nothing to say, even when the electrical wire and black tape were applied to him and the two men Ames had captured. His breathing ragged, Herm was still unconscious.

His associates looked over at him, but their gags prevented them from commenting. Laurie Bass and the others did their best to ignore him. Ames, of course, could not avoid noticing his condition and his short, jerky breath; but no one else seemed to be aware of Herm at all. At least there was no overt acknowledgment of his existence. Ames wondered if the prostrate hulk would survive; he silently dismissed the question as being the least of several problems that still faced them. Using the remaining extension cord wire, the captives were tightly bound to conference room chairs. The others adjourned to the second small conference room, where they settled themselves around the rectangular table. Laurie was the first to speak.

"We've all just come through some pretty harrowing moments. I'm sure that we could each do with a long rest. Unfortunately, we don't have time to rest at this point: that is, Mr. Fromme-ah Ames-and I are not finished. It must be clear to all of you that this criminal cannot be allowed to succeed. However, the government is in no position to stop him from outside of this Facility, at least not under the present circumstances. For obvious reasons"-here she glanced at Dr. Franklin and Senator Morse—"the lives of the people on the lower levels are potentially at risk, should that madman set off his charges, particularly if a significant quantity of explosives has been set in place."

Jane, who had regained her composure, was again the protestor, looking to prove the basic evils of bio—engineering. "You mean that you have some kind of wild, dangerous, and untested life forms down there that might be released and infect those poor souls trapped in the basements of this Godforsaken place? Or, worse something that has already been tested and, in spite of its harmful effects has not yet been destroyed?"

She's not far from the truth, Laurie thought. Aloud, she said, "Of course not. I am referring to potential damage to the ventilation system. The seals of each level are extremely effective, the very best that could be devised. They were designed to prevent the very thing you suggest, the accidental release of an untested life form.

Remember, we are frequently requested to develop specific biological tools for combating particular pestilences. In those instances we also have quantities of the virus or insect being studied, and the release of such agents would be highly undesirable. Consequently, the seals were designed to minimize the probability of such an accidental release. We here at the Facility like to think that such a release is impossible if the seals remain intact.

"Should there be an accident of some sort with the sealing mechanism itself, the seal's fail safe mode trips in automatically. That is the seal system is in a closed and locked position. The locally stored compressed air supply is adequate for a day, perhaps longer if it is carefully husbanded. But if relief has not been provided by then, the people would all suffocate. That is the source of my concern for the scientists trapped below."

Laurie had presented this explanation of the seals, or variations of it, to numerous audiences in her years as Director of Security. She knew that her arguments were sound and the reasons given for the seals were valid. She also knew that they represented only half the truth.

She had noticed an exchange of glances between Franklin and Morse when Jane had made her assertion. She could only hope that Jane failed to notice and Ames did not guess the significance. Perhaps she was overly sensitive. She too, had been under considerable strain; she still was. Just because she was aware of the activities on the lower levels did not mean that she should fear disclosure in every comment.

Ames's Realization

"They are afraid! Ames thought, but not for their own safety. Something more important is at stake. Jane's accusation caused their reactions." He reviewed her words. "That's it, he thought. In a flash it all made sense. The large number of guards with their concealed rooms, the SWARM to protect a Facility that had nothing worth stealing: it all made sense now. There are obviously secret military programs going on, right in the middle of the most open international research laboratories imaginable." The consequences of his conclusion flooded his mind. This Facility, for all the good it did for mankind, also housed research facilities for the development of the world's worst kind of weapons, the most frightening weapons systems ever conceived by man. There was no end to the variety of diseases that could be designed with the facilities of NAMBE at your disposal. But, biological warfare agents existed decades ago. What was different now? The answer was obvious. Everything was different since the discovery of the Morris theory and the development of computers capable of evaluating the equations. There was no longer any need for trial and error mutations. One could now sit down and design a virus with the precise desired characteristics. The very genetic structure could be attacked, or worse.

"What's worse?" Even as the question occurred to him, the answer and its terrible consequences flashed into his consciousness. Man could engineer the genes of man. They could design human weapons, perhaps immune to the very diseases they was designing in a neighboring laboratory. They could develop mindless drones . . . . The list was endless. One need not wait for evolution. A suitably trained bioengineer could design his own idea of a perfect human being, for whatever activity the engineer had in mind. The necessary modifications could be made to the appropriate genes, and there you were, smack in the middle of Huxley's Brave New World with all its horrors.

"No, a program involving human beings could not be hidden, even in so complex a building as the Facility. They were not creating people . . . not adult people anyway. But would it be necessary to have them grow to adults to verify that the desired traits had been engineered in? No." He answered his own question. He was not completely at home with Wilson's theory of prenatal evaluation, having read only a single article required of all students of bio-engineering; and he had read nothing at all about the testing methods. But from his limited knowledge of Wilson's theory, he felt confident that adequate tests and evaluations could be devised and performed on very young fetuses.

"It would not be necessary to let the test tube creations mature. Theories and designs could be tested with the fetus still in the test tube stage." He continued his silent analysis. "Of course the fetus would then be destroyed. But not necessarily; what if biological and genetic warfare research were going on here? Then human tissue would be required to evaluate the developed weapons. My God! Of course! There are hidden laboratories here at the Facility in which weapons are developed; and there are others that actually experiment with human genetic structure. They are developing weapons and the material against which to test them. It's incredible but obviously true! Of course that explains why there needs to be all of the security precautions and systems?

"But if one of the test tube fetuses matured, what then? If such an error occurred, a person with strange and unusual characteristics might well emerge. He would have especially engineered traits-like enhanced memory and sensory acuity, for instance!" After the initial shock, Ames's analysis continued in his characteristically emotionless manner.

"I am, of course, such an error or, worse, a deliberate experiment. Are there more like me in the world somewhere? Laurie Bass, my mysterious Auntie Laurie, was obviously assigned the responsibility to monitor my progress, keeping a close eye on developments while maintaining a safe distance. What better way to conduct such an experiment? Find a nice steady couple, who for some reason want children but cannot have them, someone who would not ask too many questions and who could be trusted and would trust NAMBE's agent. Enter beloved Aunt Alice and Uncle Ben. No wonder they were opposed to my being sent away to school, to a place where I might be tested and understood."

Ames Describes His Plan To End The Siege

His entire thought process had taken only seconds. But for Ames it was now all clear. Confident that he could recall it all later without loss of detail, he turned his attention back to Laurie Bass, whom he now viewed in an entirely different light, as part of a deep conspiracy that stretched, no doubt, from the Oval Office to the Frommes front porch. Laurie had just concluded her explanation of the seals and stopped as if to invite questions. There were none.

She was still soeaking, "If this madman is to be stopped today, we have to do it. Rushing the Auditorium will, of course, not solve our problem; he has two armed men left and two valuable hostages. Even more importantly, he has that radio control contrivance of his. If he were to activate the explosive devices, our whole reason for attacking him would quit literally go up in smoke. We do have a potential solution, however. That is, Ames has a solution. His plan is based on his knowledge of Terry, as well as his knowledge of some of our security systems here at the Facility. I'll let Ames describe his scheme to you. The essential features seem sound; however, please feel free to make suggestions or to criticize. I doubt if we'll have more than one chance."

She nodded to Ames. Feeling slightly ill at ease at being thrust forward, Ames began. "I only know what I read about Terry in a newspaper article after his trial in Chicago and what he told me over lunch when we met here before. His army career covered three years, including the last US military action in Central America, where he was an effective leader of a small hit and run squad in the Counter Guerrilla Corps. He was discharged honorably.

"As a civilian, he led a number of criminal activities, all of which were small-time. Two and a half years ago he was caught in an armed robbery attempt, along with three other men. I don't know if they knew one another before the crime. In any case, Terry turned state's evidence and received a suspended sentence. However, the most interesting things I know about Terrence Parker came from Terry himself, three months ago. I came here on a regular tourist tour, and Terry and I happened to have lunch together. Terry likes to talk about himself. Jane, you know Terry better than anyone else. As I briefly explain what I have in mind, please comment on whether I have read him correctly and how you think he will react."

Ames described their luncheon discussion and the conclusions he had reached. Then he briefly outlined his plan for overturning the hijacking. Jane's reply was immediate. His plan centered around two conclusions he had drawn about Terry's character and behavior.

"You're right, on both counts. It's easy to think of Terry as simply an egomaniac; but you are right he is in reality a very a complicated person and often unsure of himself. He cannot accept failure, even a momentary setback. Right now he should be riding high because he is confident that he has won and the President must deal with him; or he could be in the pits wondering why his men have not returned with our heads.

"On your other point, I would say that if anything, you may have understated the effect. You will absolutely blow his mind."

"It's settled then," Laurie said, bending over to retrieve her wire and tape. "Let's go."

Terry's Concern Grows

At that very moment one of the two key Terry characteristics was in complete control of his behavior. Terry resumed his pacing and cursing. His mood was dark again. His disappointment and anger at his men for not sending back some word was spiced with fear that they were unable to do so. "Can that bitch have pulled if off?" he asked himself for perhaps the hundredth time. "Impossible!"

He turned to Skip. "Where the fuck are those bastards? Why the hell don't they report in?"

"I don't know," was the instant reply. "They should'a been here by now, even if they had'a crawl. I don't think they're coming back. I think they got nailed."

"You're fuckin' crazy, Skip. There were four of them, well armed. She couldn't stop that."

"You're hung up on that lady cop, Terry. There were four others not countin' Jane."

"Well, they gotta be found," Terry said.

"Go get them and bring their asses back here. Don't tackle the Amazon. This is a straight recon and recovery operation, not a fight. Ya got that?"

"I sure as hell don't wanna fight! You told us this was a simple hijacking. But the lady with the black hair may have somethin' different to say about. If those four couldn't take her, I'm beginning to think she can't be taken."

"Chicken shit! I'd go do it myself, but I gotta wait for the President's call. Make sure all those doors are locked." Indicating Brian, Terry added, "Take that other chicken shit with you. I have a pistol and my little black box. That's all hell I need. Go on, shag ass." Heavy-heartedly, the two men double-checked the locks and started toward the rear door. Just as Skip reached for the handle, there was a timid knock on the main door.

"What the hell is that?" asked a startled Terry. "There at the door in the center of the wall." He listened. There was another knocking, much more distinct this time.

"Who is it?" demanded Terry. "What the hell you want?"

A timid, hesitant reply sounded meekly through the door, "It's m-me, Ames. "It's all over out here. They're all finished. I need to talk to you. Let me in, please. I have this disgusting automatic pistol but it's empty. Here, I'll drop it on the floor."

Following a heavy thud from beyond the door, Terry heard, "Open the door. I'll come in slowly." Terry nodded to Skip.

Skip slowly walked over to the indicated door and unlocked it, his gun leveled at the center of the door, waist high. "Okay, come in slowly," he called out to Ames, "and kick your gun in ahead of you." Ames complied. He kicked the gun in gently. It slid slowly along the floor, leaving behind a barely discernable trail of black powder. Ames dropped the handkerchief with which he had been holding the weapon and slowly entered the auditorium with his hands raised high.

"Hand me that gun, Brian," Terry ordered. Brian obeyed and Terry, the experienced ex-soldier, expertly opened the chamber and checked the magazine.

"This gun's been fired all right. Okay, it's empty. What's this shit you got all over it?" he demanded of Ames.

Ames had no chance to answer before the room came alive. It reverberated with a rushing, roaring buzz created by tens of thousands of tiny wings furiously beating the air. Like a black cloud the SWARM justified its name as it darkened the space around the men's weapons, attacking the guns themselves in a fruitless attempt to reach the powder their flawless olfactory sensors detected. The path along which Ames's pistol had skidded was alive with them;

from the doorway, where Ames's once-white handkerchief now lay, alive with a frantic buzzing mass, a seething black snake of agitated insects flowed toward the stage. Brian had instinctively thrown his infested weapon to the floor and jumped back. A number of the bioengineered attackers followed the discarded weapon, but a host remained. Terry and Skip quickly followed suit, but while their dropped pistols were immediately covered, the frenzied hoard continued to crawl and buzz around Terry's hands and arms. Slowly, the insects left Skip's hands, which had never touched the discarded automatic pistol, but they clung relentlessly to Brian, and the number on Terry's hands and arms steadily increased. The bugs were enraged by the raw gunpowder that covered everything that had touched Ames's weapon. It was more than Terry could bear. He ran in mindless circles shouting repeatedly, "Fucking bugs!" By the time Ames had released Dr. Q and Kim, Terry was rolling on the floor, screaming and sobbing incoherently. The small black box sat untouched on the podium. The siege was over.

Questions, Some Answered, Some Not

Following the use of the SWARM, events moved quickly. At Dr. Q's suggestion a call was put through to McPherson, stating that the occupation of the Facility had ended and asking him to notify the President. That left Dr. Q and Laurie Bass free to go about releasing the imprisoned scientists and permitted Dr. Newcombe to take care of the medical needs.

The Secretary of the Interior told Lieutenant Bradley to arrange for the telephone problems of Micro City to be repaired, and all the other barriers to communication between the outside world and the environs of NAMBE were lifted. As a result, the story of the occupation of the Facility and its heroic rescue spread across land and sea with all the speed of modern communication methods. In spite of her protestations, Laurie Bass was an instant hero; her exploits grew each time Brian was permitted to tell his story. Laurie and the new members of NAMBE all knew that Ames had played the key role in the capture of the hijackers, but the media found her physical exploits more impressive than his memory. Both Laurie and Ames were happy to have attention directed away from his background as much as possible. Buzz Cochran made another round trip by military jet and conducted his own in-depth review of the events.

At the beginning of the investigations, Laurie Bass and the members of NAGMBE were the only ones fully cleared for the activities on Level Eight and Level Nine. Before the inquiries were completed, there was another. True, it was against the rules to discuss classified information with Ames Fromme prior to the governments completing his clearance formalities, but his guesses were too close to the truth. The only practical way Buzz saw to silence him was to get him to sign the forms acknowledging that he knowingly agreed to accept classified information and then to feed him his own guesses as sensitive material. The President's technical adviser was not satisfied that his action was legal, nor was he sure that Ames would feel bound by his agreements once he had had time to reconsider.

Now, a full day later, the President of the United States sat in his private study with his old friend. Buzz was finishing his summary of the previous day's events. "Those details in the reports you have are factual, Prescott. You asked me to help you untangle the multiple aspects of this siege and the events that led up to it. It will help to strip away most of the forest so that we can concentrate on a few of the trees. "The ASPGH leader was duped by the criminal, Terry Parker. The Movement was and is essentially harmless. In fact, while I obviously don't agree with their tenets, it is probably a good idea that such organizations exist and at least attempt to keep our feet on the ground.

"This Terry Parker had constructed an excellent plan. The details were, as you know, well thought out. We might have gotten to him without the help of Ms. Bass and Mr. Ames, but I would hate to bet on it. His big mistake was in his selection of staff. He chose men that would blindly follow him. That in itself is not a bad idea. He was also careful to select men who would not go off half-cocked and shoot at anything that moved. On the face of it, that was also a sound strategy. He had expected little or no need for force. Under ordinary circumstances, Herm would have been adequate for what little actual force was required. Of course Ms Bass is no ordinary circumstance. Herm is still on the critical list and I haven't yet found a physician who will give better than even money on his survival.

"On her own, even the resourceful Ms. Bass would have been unable to storm Terry's stronghold. He had all of the odds in his favor even after she neutralized Herm. She could not communicate with the outside or let anyone in. It was Ames who saved the day. He knew that Terry was strongly repulsed, psychotically so, by insects of any kind. Having read that the SWARM, while bred to detect trace amounts of explosives, went berserk when exposed directly to gunpowder and that there was a range limit on their range of their abilities, he recognized the need to move them to within fifty feet before releasing them. And, furthermore, he had read of the upcoming test of the SWARM at outside locations and reasoned that there would be a large supply on hand. You begin to get the idea, Prescott: this guy knew everything. I'll come back to that in a moment.

"Because of the black box with its detonator switches, it seemed necessary to reduce Terry's gang to a small enough that the attack of the SWARM would absorb Terry's attention. As it happened his phobia about insects was considerably more pronounced than even Ames had guessed, and dividing the gang into smaller teams may not have been necessary. Using gunpowder extracted from shells to coat the weapon that Ames surrendered was Dr. Franklin's idea. He was one of the outside consultants used when the SWARM was developed.

"Splitting the gang down into smaller units was made possible by exploiting Terry's ignorance. Ames had reasoned that Terry had no patience for studying articles and books about the Facility and would accept the need for a backup release mechanism. The plan required a safe hideout for Dr. Franklin and Senator Morse and a couple of people with detailed knowledge of the layout of the Facility. Ms. Bass, of course, had such knowledge. Ames had noticed the one-way mirrors on a previous visit, and he the internal hall structure in minute detail because he had read a map in the employee's handbook on the previous evening.

"Given all those advantages against a gang of thieves, as opposed to killers, Laurie and Ames were able to carry it off."

"Yes, I can see what you meant earlier; it was quite a stroke of luck that Ames was able to know all those details and all about the one-way glass," the President commented.

Buzz paused to loosen his dangling tie seill further. "Luck has nothing to do with Ames's memory and powers of observation. The points I just summarized are included in your reports in considerable detail. I am sure you have arrived at the same questions that I did. Simply put, this guy Ames has a fantastic memory. "Furthermore, the most sensitive eyes I ever heard of would not be able to discern detail in the low level low contrast images that are available through a one-way mirror. And if we can believe the firsthand accounts of Dr. Franklin and Senator Morse, he has ears with equally remarkable acuity. No doubt his other sensors have similar qualities. He is also incredibly cool for such a young man, almost without emotions according to the intuitive Senator Morse.

"For his role in yesterday's events he should be a national hero. If we permit this story to break, he will be. But we cannot allow this event to be fully and truthfully reported. I am sure that you have deduced the essential feature of Ames's parentage; he hasn't any. As you know, I have been worried about Dr. Peters's behavior these last few months. He has always been secretive about his work on Level Nine, but he has become even more aloof than usual. I have been planning to replace him. In fact, I had hoped I would be able to convince Dr. Franklin to take up the position in the not too distant future. I had planned to discuss it with him immediately following his visit to the Facility. I was also concerned that Nathan was being tempted to carry his experiments beyond the point we had authorized.

"You know he has been supplying fetal tissue for years now. The process was approved on the basis of its being socially and morally less repugnant to experiment with artificial tissue than with that of aborted fetuses.

"We had all consoled ourselves with the belief that not only were these fetuses artificial, but they were not capable of maturing. In short, they were in no way human despite their chemical makeup. I for one always considered that belief to be pure rationalization. I have always believed that given a chance those fetuses would become infants and the infants would become adults. I believe we all harbored such beliefs, as well as a secret fear of what might be produced by permitting one of them to mature.

"Our fears were based on two classes of questions. The purely physical ones, such as, 'How complete is his model?' and 'How precise are his formulations within that model?' What would result, a freak, a monster, or a superman?

"Then there are the moral and ethical questions. These include such things as, 'What is such a creature? Is it human? Does it have a soul? Can a creation of man rival a creation of God in this regard?' The ethical questions probably have no limit.

"Then there are the countless legal questions. 'Does such a being have civil rights? Is it a citizen? Just what the hell is it?' Those are all questions for you, not me. I believe that Ames is just such an adult and that we must now face those questions. I don't know how it happened; but one of Dr. Peters' experiments matured. From his questions to me, I believe that Ames has come to the same conclusion. That is only an inference, of course. If he hasn't already figured it out, I don't see how we can avoid his finding out; he is a very bright lad and was at the center of this fiasco. I don't even know what other characteristics Peters might have designed into him. Can he read minds? Can he leap tall buildings in a single bound? I really have no bloody idea at all. I have not approached Nathan yet; whether I do or not is your decision. In the meantime let's take it as a given that Ames does not know but soon will. In addition to the somewhat esoteric questions I already mentioned, there are several practical matters to be considered. "How will he react to that knowledge? I don't want to guess. Of course there are no psychologists on my staff either.

"How will the public react if they find out. I should think that question is more in your line than mine. However, I will make a guess that you don't want them to know. If the public learns, then our allies will. How will they react? Again, my guess is that you don't want to have to answer to that question. "We can't stop Ames from finding out. But we can probably prevent the public from knowing if we can keep Ames and Nathan silent. No one else knows; I feel confident in that. Louise has made a lot of headway keeping the media focused on the ASPGH. Terry and his bandits believe that all their problems are directly attributable to the Director of Security, Laurie Bass, or, as they choose to call her, the Amazon with the Black Belts. We can let Louise create a folk hero.

"The report you have before you was not seen in its entirety by anyone but you and me. Sure, the participants will talk among themselves, but the details will become confused and blurred-except of course for Ames. Besides they all work for us and are bound by security pledges. I issued an instant clearance to Ames as a method of controlling him. I would not put a lot of faith in the efficacy of that move unless you can intervene in some way. It's possible to keep Project Eight and Project Nine secret only if Ames can be kept silent."

Dr. Cochran stopped again and completely removed his tie, tossing it over the back of an overstuffed chair. Prescott Winters once again squared the sheets of the report on his desk. The two old friends sat in silence. Speech was not necessary for them to share their thoughts at this moment. At last the President spoke. "Buzz, he is a man. I won't pretend to have the answers to the fundamental and moral issues you so accurately summarized; but Ames is a man, a human being, whether he was constructed entirely in a test tube or not. Like you, I read the arguments of Dr. Peters and accepted them; I agree that your term, rationalization, is a better description of our actions. I can agree to accept artificial fetal tissue. I can argue that the fetus so produced is not really human; at least I was once able to accept that argument. But by no stretch of the imagination is Ames anything less than human.

"We have committed a grave error. We! We are responsible. By the word we, I mean not just you and me and the POC, but the whole country—all of civilized man. We all worship at the temple of progress. We demand more and more from nature until at last we demand even that we control nature herself. All manner of research is justified in the name of progress; when that is not quite sufficient, we add the final unanswerable argument: We require it for national defense. Anything that by any stretch of the imagination improves the lot of man is by definition good.

"Using the resources of NAMBE, we have created a twenty first century Frankenstein. This is a serious mistake. Theologians will settle the questions of whether or not Ames has a soul, and whether it is more or less than the soul of a man created by God. In fact some wily ministers may even argue that simply being the creation of man, who is the creation of God, is equivalent to being created by God. I don't know, and frankly I don't care. Ames is not less than human, and he was born in this country. Furthermore, the Constitution does not require that a citizen not be born of a test tube. He is an American citizen. I admit that I sidestepped all of the moral and ethical issues in arriving at this conclusion by the arguments I used. Think of it as merely an expression of Presidential prerogative if you like, but Ames is not an interesting scientific experiment that got out of hand. He is a human being and a citizen of the United States.

With that question out of the way, we can turn to some of the others. Of course it will be easier for us to maintain an appropriate level of secrecy if the true story of Ames never comes out; but in this country freedom of speech is not a selective right limited only to those whom I want to talk. We want his silence. We have the right to ask for it. He has the right to deny it. I'm sorry, Buzz, if that sounded like a campaign speech; but, damn it all, I believe it.

We permitted a mistake to be made at the Facility; and, while I'm responsible for the actions taken in this Office, it will not be repeated. There will be no more Level Nine fetuses. Project Nine has just concluded. It is settled, then. Louise will continue her activities with the media and Laurie Bass will become an instant hero. What our next moves are will be determined by Ames Fromme. It is time for us to ask what we can do for Ames. Some interesting options have occurred to me. I may suggest them; it all depends on what he wants to do.

Now, if Martha has done her job, and she always does, Ames is waiting in the outer office at this moment."

From Preston's point of view Ames is of course a citizen of the US, a very unusual and talented one to whom the nation is deeply indebted. As President, it is his responsibility to find a satisfying and meaningful way for Ames to belong and not feel like an exhibit. With his talents Ames could be a major contributor to his country if only Prescott and he can find the right opportunity. Who knows? If they do so perhaps they will need a chronicler again.